THE
Regency
COLLECTION

VOLUME
—12—

THE
Regency
COLLECTION

VOLUME
—12—

His Lordship's Dilemma
by
Meg Alexander

The Last Gamble
by
Mary Nichols

*MILLS & BOON and MILLS & BOON with the Rose Device
are registered trademarks of the publisher.*

*First published in Great Britain 1999 by
Harlequin Mills & Boon Limited,
Eton House, 18–24 Paradise Road,
Richmond, Surrey, TW9 1SR.*

The Regency Collection © by Harlequin Enterprises II B.V. 1999

The publisher acknowledges the copyright holders of the
individual work as follows:

His Lordship's Dilemma © Meg Alexander 1996
The Last Gamble © Mary Nichols 1996

ISBN 0 263 82425 X
106-0004

*Printed and bound in Spain
by Litografia Rosés S.A., Barcelona*

HIS LORDSHIP'S DILEMMA

by

Meg Alexander

Dear Reader

I hope you'll enjoy *His Lordship's Dilemma*. I've always been fascinated by the Regency era. It was truly the age of elegance, in costume, furniture, learning, musical appreciation and a love of English life. Women had few rights, but this did not deter the stronger-minded.

Miss Elinor Temple had to be very strong-minded when she found out about the lifestyle of Marcus, Lord Rokeby! She not only had to guard Hester, she had to guard herself against the insidious charm of a gazetted rake!

Enjoy your reading.

Meg Alexander

After living in southern Spain for many years, **Meg Alexander** now lives in Kent, although having been born in Lancashire, she feels that her roots are in the north of England. Meg's career has encompassed a wide variety of roles, from professional cook to assistant director of a conference centre. She has always been a voracious reader, and loves to write. Other loves include history, cats, gardening, cooking and travel. She has a son and two grandchildren.

Other titles by the same author:

The Last Enchantment
The Sweet Cheat
Farewell the Heart
Miranda's Masquerade
The Love Child*
The Merry Gentleman*
The Passionate Friends*

* linked

CHAPTER ONE

THEY were on the last stage of their journey, but the girl huddled in a corner of the carriage appeared to find no comfort in the thought.

'We should not have come,' she whispered in a voice little more than a croak. 'His lordship did not reply to your letter. Suppose he should turn us away?'

'At this time of night, my dear? Lord Rokeby will do no such thing. As your guardian he must know his duty.'

'I'm sure he does, Miss Temple, but he need not make us welcome. Oh, if only I did not feel so wretched. . .' She was seized with a fit of coughing.

Elinor quashed her own misgivings. It had been a blow to find his lordship's London mansion closed, with the knocker removed from the door. This told her at once that the owner was not in residence, but a servant had given her the direction of his estate in Kent.

Stiff and tired after the journey on the public coach from Bath, she had considered putting up at an hotel, but her funds were low, and Hester's chill was growing worse.

Even had she known of a respectable place to stay in the city, she could well imagine the reception which would be accorded to two females, one of them unwell, who were travelling with a minimum of luggage, and without an abigail.

By morning, if she were any judge, Hester would be

unfit to travel further. She made her decision quickly. They must go on. The public coach had brought them as far as Tunbridge Wells, and there she had used her last few guineas to hire a private carriage for the journey out to Merton Place. She prayed heaven that Lord Rokeby might be at home. If not, she would insist that they were given shelter for the night.

Now she peered into the darkness as they turned through a pair of tall iron gates. At least there was a light in the lodge-keeper's cottage. Relief swept over her as the man confirmed that his lordship had not left the house that day. She turned and put an arm about her weary charge.

'We are there, my love,' she said softly. 'You will soon be tucked up in your bed.'

As they swept along the drive, she thrust her head through the window. Ahead of her the great house was ablaze with light; as they drew up at an imposing flight of steps, the door opened and a figure hurried towards them.

Elinor stepped down from the coach with Hester close behind her. Glad to be rid of his passengers, the coachman dumped their bags beside them and set off again at speed. Elinor looked at the man who came to greet them. He was in livery, and was clearly a servant of some kind.

'Will you please inform Lord Rokeby that his ward is here?' she said pleasantly.

The man looked startled. 'Ma'am, his lordship did not say. . . I mean, he was not expecting. . .'

'I am aware of that.' Elinor began to mount the steps. 'I wrote to Lord Rokeby but my letter must have gone astray. Please do as I ask. Miss Hester Winton is not well. She should retire at once.'

'But, ma'am, his lordship has given strict instructions. He is entertaining, and may not be disturbed.'

Elinor strolled into a lofty hall. There she turned and looked at the agitated man.

'I will take the responsibility,' she announced. 'Hester, do rest upon this settle for the moment. I shall not be long. . .'

A loud burst of cheering drowned the rest of her words as a door opened at the far end of the hall. Through it appeared a half-clad maiden with a young man in hot pursuit. Shrieking with laughter, the girl fled towards the staircase. She hadn't reached it before her cavalier caught up with her and kissed her soundly, stripping the remaining draperies from her shoulders as he did so. Then he swept her off her feet and ran lightly up the stairs, still carrying his fair burden.

Elinor glanced at Hester, to find that the girl's eyes were wide with astonishment and dismay.

'Ma'am, I'm sorry. . .' The servant looked uncomfortable. 'If the young lady would care to wait in the library. . .?'

'That might be best,' Elinor agreed. 'You need not announce me. . .' Without waiting for a reply she walked towards the open door and entered the room.

A scene of chaos greeted her. On either side of a long dining-table a dozen men lounged, coatless and clearly the worse for wine. From the number of bottles on the table Elinor was unsurprised. What did astonish her was the sight of a woman standing on the table, her skirts drawn up about her waist. It was abundantly clear that this houri had no use for undergarments. All eyes were on her as she took careful aim and kicked at a row of oranges in line before her. Her expertise was undeniable. She did not miss, and grabbed eagerly at the bag of gold which was handed to her as she was lifted down.

'My turn next. . .' A red-haired woman disengaged herself from the clutches of the man who had been fondling her breasts, and attempted to climb up on the table.

For a few moments Elinor's presence went undetected. She looked quickly around the table. Surely the fat man slobbering over a voluptuous blonde at the far end of the table could not—must not—be Rokeby. If so, she would remove Hester at once. Then one of the men looked up.

'What's this?' He held up a hand for silence.   'A Puritan. . .a virgin? Marcus, you've done it again. I knew we could rely on you for something different. You haven't failed us yet. . .'

Elinor heard the scrape of a chair drawn aside. She had overlooked the man who was sitting at the head of the table with his back to her. Gently he disengaged the girl who was clinging to his neck and rose to his feet.

When he turned to face her she felt an uncomfortable churning in the pit of her stomach.

This was Rokeby, there could be no doubt of it. So dark as to be gypsy-like and swarthy in appearance, his eyes were extraordinary. In that tanned face they were of the palest blue. She had seen eyes like that in seamen, or those who had travelled to the furthest corners of the earth. She knew at once that he would make an implacable enemy.

Now they roved over her from head to toe, and she coloured, feeling naked beneath his gaze.

'You do me too much honour,' he said to the company at large. 'I do not know this lady. Bates, I had not understood you to be hard of hearing. Did I not make it clear that all visitors were to be denied?'

Elinor looked at the dejected expression of the servant who had followed her into the room and her temper rose.

'You will please not to blame your man, Lord Rokeby. I insisted upon seeing you.' Though her voice was low and musical it reached clearly into every corner of the room. The result of her words was another burst of shouts and cheering.

'Marcus, I never thought I'd live to see the day. Have your chickens come home to roost at last?' The fat man at the far end of the table rose unsteadily to his feet. It was the signal for an outburst of coarse chaffing and cries of 'Shame!'

Their meaning was unmistakable. Elinor had no intention of being taken for a wronged woman. She withdrew her gaze from Rokeby and bent it upon the unruly crowd.

That look had served to quell the spirits of many a class of undisciplined sixteen-year-olds, and it did not fail her now. An uneasy silence fell.

Elinor turned back to Rokeby to see an expression of astonishment mingled with admiration in those curious eyes.

'I have something to say to you, my lord,' she announced in a crisp voice. 'May we speak in private?'

'Certainly, madam. I am quite at your disposal.' The ironic tone did not escape her, but she suffered him to lead her from the room.

Elinor did not waste words. 'Your ward is here, Lord Rokeby. I have accompanied her from Bath.'

Rokeby's composure vanished, and when he spoke

she noted with amusement that his fashionable drawl had disappeared.

'My ward? Good God, woman, what can you be thinking of? This is no place for a child. What right had you to remove her from her school?'

'The school is closed, due to the death of the owner. And Hester is no longer a child. She is seventeen.'

'Why bring her to me?'

'You are her legal guardian, sir, and we. . . Hester had nowhere else to go.'

His lordship took a turn about the hall, running his fingers through his tousled hair.

'You can't stay here,' he said at last. 'Your coach shall take you back to Tunbridge Wells. I will call upon you in the morning.'

'Our carriage is gone, my lord.'

'I see.' His anger flared. 'Did you hope to present me with a fait accompli? It will not serve, Miss. . .?'

'My name is Elinor Temple.'

'Well then, Miss Temple, my own carriage shall convey you back to the town.'

'That will not be possible. Hester is unwell. She is not fit to travel further.'

'I don't believe you!'

'Then you had best see for yourself.' Elinor made her way to the library. 'This, my love, is Lord Rokeby.' She tried to keep her voice impersonal, but even to herself the note of contempt was apparent.

Hester was unaware of it. As she looked up at her guardian with pain-filled eyes she was seized with a fit of coughing. She tried to rise to make her curtsy. Then she fell back with a groan. Elinor laid a cool hand on her brow to find it burning with fever.

His lordship snapped his fingers for his servant.

'Bates, you will accommodate these ladies in the west wing. See to their needs.' He turned on his heel, clearly in a towering rage, and was about to leave them without another word.

'Lord Rokeby?'

'Miss Temple, I beg you will not address me again until tomorrow. For sheer irresponsibility your actions are difficult to credit. To bring a sick girl halfway across the country on what might well have been a wild-goose chase? It is unbelievable. . .'

'Hester was quite well when we started out this morning, and had you answered my letter. . .'

'I received no letter from you. Had I done so, I should have made more suitable arrangements.'

'The letter was sent to your home in London.'

'Miss Temple, I have been out of the country. I have seen no letters for many months. The lack of a reply makes your actions even less excusable. What, may I ask, would you have done if you had not found me here?'

'We should have stayed to await your return.'

'Without my permission?'

'Without your permission,' she agreed sweetly.

Rokeby muttered something beneath his breath. It sounded suspiciously like a curse. He strode away without another word.

Glad to be rid of his presence, Elinor turned to Bates.

'Will you show me to our rooms at once?' she said. 'Miss Winton has a fever. Then, perhaps, a cold drink? Some lemonade, if you would be so kind?'

Bates looked startled. Lemonade was not a beverage which was normally to be found in any of his lordship's establishments, but he nodded.

'Shall I help you with the young lady, miss?'

'No, do you lead the way. We shall manage the stairs.'

She slipped an arm about Hester's waist, and lifted the girl to her feet.

'If you will put your arm about my neck, Hester? Just a few steps, and then you will be comfortable in your bed.'

It was a vain hope. Despite the luxury of down pillows and cool linen sheets Hester coughed continually throughout the hours of darkness. As the first pale light of dawn was streaking the night sky, she fell asleep at last.

Elinor had not undressed, though she had asked for a cot to be brought into Hester's room. She lay down for a time, but could not rest. What a coil she had made of the whole business! Her cheeks flamed as she remembered Rokeby's cutting words, even though his accusations were unjust.

She could not have known that Hester would be taken ill, nor had she imagined that they would arrive at Merton Place to find his lordship indulging in an orgy. Doubtless he was annoyed to be caught at a disadvantage by his two unexpected visitors.

She heard the revellers leaving in the early hours, although the sound of their carousing had not reached the west wing. Even so, she had taken the precaution of locking the doors of their apartments against the possibility of some drunkard bursting in on them.

If this was Rokeby's usual way of life, he was no fit guardian for her charge, but where else could Hester go? Her parents were long dead, carried off seven years ago in a smallpox epidemic. And at seventeen she could not be sent back to school. Elinor herself could not offer the girl a home. The eldest of eight children, she had taken a teaching post to relieve the burden on her family, thankful that her scholarly father had insisted on a classical education for his girls. She could not return to Derbyshire, to become just one more mouth to feed.

She must find another post, but it would not be easy. Most of the girls in her care had been sent away from home to get them out of the way until they had reached marriageable age. They learned deportment, a little painting, embroidery and how to play a musical instrument.

Parents were inclined to frown on too much 'book-work' as they termed it. When Elinor remonstrated with her pupils, she had been assured on more than one occasion that mammas did not believe that gentlemen would offer for any girl regarded as 'too clever'.

Hester was different. Elinor regarded the flushed face on the pillow with affection. From their first meeting Hester had enjoyed her studies, and for Elinor it had been a joy to watch that young mind unfold.

No beauty, Hester was inclined to plumpness. Her neck was too short, and she had never had the semblance of a waist. Her fine straight hair would not stay in place, and for a time she had been the butt of the other girls. Even her academic brilliance had been greeted with contempt.

Elinor's heart went out to the shy, plain child.

'You have a good brain,' she had said. 'Remember, Hester, no one can take that away from you. There is no substitute for a keen intelligence.'

To her surprise the girl's face had crumpled. 'I hate

my face,' she had sobbed. 'If only I were pretty. . . I wish I looked like you. . .'

Elinor had stroked her hair. 'You would like to be tall and thin?' she'd teased.

'You aren't thin, Miss Temple. Emma Tarrant said that you were willowy. . .'

'That is a poetic thought.' Elinor had eyed her champion with some amusement. 'Now go and wash your face, my dear. As you get older you will grow taller and lose your puppy fat, believe me.'

But Hester had not done so, and her confidence was fragile. Her puckish sense of humour appeared only in the company of friends. With strangers she was nervous and ill at ease.

Elinor sighed. The girl would never be likely to feel at ease with the sophisticated rake who was her guardian. She found herself wondering why he had undertaken such a charge. . .a charge for which he was clearly unsuited. There had been some mention of distant kinship, but in all the years that Hester had been away at school he had not troubled to visit her. She must make it her business to find out more about him.

She began to examine the few garments which the maid had hung in the cupboard. They were sadly crumpled, but it was no matter. Hester would not rise that day. Her own grey woollen morning-dress had suffered less. She was about to change when she heard a knock at the door.

The arrival of a chambermaid with coffee, fruit and rolls was more than welcome. Elinor had not eaten since noon on the previous day, and her stomach was protesting.

She smiled at the girl as she searched for a shawl to throw about her shoulders.

'Why, miss, the fire is almost out. You'll catch your death. I'll send the footman up to you.'

'Thank you.' Elinor gave her a grateful look. She did feel cold, but she had put it down to weariness. 'I'd like some hot water, if you please.'

'Yes, Miss, at once. Bates says that you are to ask for anything you need. Must I take your gowns away for pressing?'

'That would be kind.' For some unaccountable reason Elinor was glad to realise that she would not need to face his lordship in clothing which might cause a sneer, though naturally it did not matter what he thought, either of her or her attire.

Hester was still asleep, and there was no point in wakening her, so Elinor settled down to eat her breakfast. With the arrival of hot water, a footman to mend the fire, and the return of her neatly pressed gowns she began to feel more hopeful.

By now Lord Rokeby must have had time to consider his position. Surely he would think of a solution to their problems. It could not be denied that Hester was his responsibility but, try as she might Elinor could not imagine what he would suggest. She prayed that his decision might be satisfactory.

Fond as she was of Hester her own position must be considered. The journey from Bath had made serious inroads into her few savings, and it was imperative that she find another post without delay. And, to be honest, she had no wish to remain at Merton Place. A few minutes conversation with Lord Rokeby had convinced her that he and she would quickly be at odds.

At all costs she must keep her temper during the

coming interview. No purpose could possibly be served by telling his lordship what she had thought of his behaviour on the previous evening. Whatever provocation he might offer, she must hold her tongue.

That was easier said than done. When Bates arrived at her door, he bore a message from his master. Lord Rokeby presented his compliments and would like to see Miss Temple in the library without delay.

Crushing down the flutter of anxiety in the pit of her stomach, Elinor went down to meet him. His greeting was brutal.

'You look fagged to death, Miss Temple. Haven't you slept?'

Elinor forgot her noble resolutions.

'I have not,' she told him tartly. 'Your welcome did not encourage me to spend a restful night.'

'I wonder why it should surprise you? To have some chit of a girl dumped on me in the middle of the night, together with her duenna—it would try the patience of a saint.'

'And you are no saint, my lord. That much is abundantly clear. . .'

'Shocked, my dear? A man must take his pleasures where he may. Doubtless you found the display of carnal instincts a little disturbing. Lack of experience, Miss Temple? I wonder now that I did not ask you to join us.'

It was a calculated insult, but Elinor did not rise to the bait.

'Sir, we have much to discuss. May I ask what plans you have for Hester?'

His lordship strolled over to a chair, sank into it, and stretched out his long legs.

'None whatever, Miss Temple. You appear to have

a managing disposition. Will you not give me the benefit of your advice?'

'You have not asked me how she is today,' Elinor said sharply.

'I know how she is. She is suffering from a severe chill. She will be confined to her bed for several days, and then she is like to need a period of convalescence.'

Elinor stared at him. She was surprised to find that his diagnosis matched her own.

'I was not referring to Hester's physical condition,' she said with dignity. 'I am concerned about her future.'

'Are you indeed? May I ask the reason for your interest in my ward?'

'Your ward?' Elinor did not trouble to hide her contempt. 'If I am not mistaken, sir, you had forgot that she existed. I wonder that you should have undertaken the charge since you have had so little interest in her.'

For a heart-stopping moment, she wondered if she had gone too far. A muscle in his lordship's jaw had tightened. Then he glanced at her through lowered lids.

'How well you understand me,' he said softly. 'Shall I satisfy your curiosity? You are right, of course. I was motivated by no moral arguments. My purpose was to thwart the ambitions of my late aunt's husband.'

'Your uncle?' Elinor was puzzled. 'I do not understand you.'

'Lord Dacre is my uncle by marriage only, Miss Temple. I claim him as no relative of mine. My aunt suffered much at his hands.' His face darkened.

'Might it not have been better to allow her to take charge of Hester?'

'She died in child-bed within a year of her marriage. She had no wish to live, you see.' His face was oddly twisted.

'And the child?'

'A whey-faced stripling in his twenties, so I hear. I have not met him, and have no desire to do so.'

'You would judge him unseen and unheard? Does anyone meet with your approval, sir?'

He was out of his chair in a single lithe movement. Two steps brought him to her side and he gripped her lightly by the shoulders.

'Why, yes,' he said lightly. 'I had ever a softness for a slender form and large grey eyes. This morning I fancy they are flecked with amber. May I satisfy my curiosity?'

Elinor turned her head away as she strove to free herself. He was much too close and she found that her heart was pounding, partly from the shock of his behaviour and partly from a deeper, more disturbing feeling. She could feel the warmth of his fingers through the fabric of her gown, and it caused an unaccustomed flutter in the pit of her stomach.

'Look at me,' he said softly. Lean fingers cupped her chin and he raised her face to his.

'Yes,' he murmured. 'It is as I thought. There are sparks of magical colour against the grey. . .'

Elinor stood stiff and silent within his grasp, as anger threatened to overwhelm her. How dared he insult her so? Did he hope to drive her away?

Rokeby bent closer, and she was strongly aware of a male scent of fine tobacco, soap, leather and broadcloth, mixed with a faint aroma of the outdoors. For an awful moment she suspected that he intended to kiss her. If he did so she could no longer stay beneath his roof. Squarely she held his gaze.

'Sir, we are wasting time. We were discussing Hester.'

'So we were.' He turned away with a glint of amusement in his eyes. 'May I compliment you, Miss Temple? My manners do not frighten you, I think.'

Elinor was tempted to ask if he could lay claim to any manners, but she did not. 'Why should I fear you?' she demanded coldly. 'We fear only those who are able to do us harm.'

'And you are inviolate? A charming notion, but misplaced. You will not tell me that no man has succumbed to your evident charms?'

'I shall not tell you anything of my life. I wish to know what is to become of Hester.'

'You have no suggestions, ma'am, as to what I am to do with her?'

'None, my lord. The decision must be yours. . .'

'Then naturally you will agree with whatever course of action I suggest?'

Elinor saw the glint of mischief in his eyes and knew at once that she must tread carefully if she were not to find herself embroiled in some scheme which she could not countenance.

'I can have nothing to say in the matter,' she announced in a colourless tone.

Rokeby threw back his head and laughed aloud. 'Come Miss Temple, you shall not take me for a fool. Since your arrival we have conversed for less than an hour. It has been long enough to convince me that you will fight me tooth and nail if you disapprove of my decision.'

'And that is?'

'I'll give the girl a season. It may be enough to allow her to find a suitable husband.'

'To take her off your hands? Hester is young, my lord. She is no judge of character. . .'

'I can lay claim to neither of those interesting attributes. You may rest assured that I shall choose her husband with great care. There is, however, one condition. . .'

'Which is?'

'That you stay with her for the next few months at least. If she is as green as you say. . .and I believe you . . .she will need the support of all your self-assurance. You, I am convinced, will find no difficulty in hinting away all the gazetted fortune-hunters. . .'

'Fortune-hunters?' Elinor gazed at him in astonishment.

'You did not know? Hester is a considerable heiress, ma'am, and for that we must be thankful. You will be working with unpromising material, I fear. I had not thought it possible for any girl to be so plain.'

'That is both unkind and unfair.' Elinor fired up at once in defence of her charge. 'She was feeling wretched when you saw her.'

'And looked it.' Rokeby's reply was unfeeling. 'Still, her wealth will serve to cast a veil over her shortcomings. . .'

Elinor was speechless with indignation. She was strongly tempted to strike his snuff-box from his hand. Instead, she turned away in an effort to control her rage.

'Well, Miss Temple, do you agree with my suggestion?'

'I cannot, sir.' Elinor flushed. 'I must find another post without delay.' She had no wish to discuss her poverty-stricken state with Rokeby, or to explain that each quarter she sent back to Derbyshire what little she could spare.

'I have just offered you a post,' he told her quietly. 'Your allowance would be generous. . .' He mentioned a sum which caused her eyes to widen. 'I must also reimburse you for the cost of your journey here.'

He walked over to his desk, unlocked the middle drawer, and handed her a small leather bag. The weight told her at once that it was gold.

'This is too much, my lord. I will write down the details of our travelling expenses.'

'Take it!' he commanded. 'Today I leave for London, but before I go I must have your decision.'

'Not today, Lord Rokeby. I must have time to consider.' Every instinct warned her against acceptance. True, she could watch over Hester, and her financial worries would be over, but she did not underestimate the danger.

Rokeby represented everything she disliked most in a man. Not only was he steeped in vice, but he was arrogant and unfeeling—the perfect example of one who had inherited wealth at an early age and grown to manhood with no curb upon his morals.

'You have ten days,' he announced. 'After that I shall be forced to make other plans for my ward.' His tone left her in no doubt that they would be far from pleasant.

Rokeby strode towards the door. 'Merton Place is yours until my return,' he told her. 'I beg that you will not terrorise my servants in my absence, Miss Temple. Hurling unruly servitors from the battlements is quite out of fashion.'

'I had not noticed any battlements,' Elinor replied demurely.

'Perhaps not, but the same applies to the use of boiling oil.'

Elinor was tempted. She raised her eyes to his, and again he seemed to read her mind.

'Ah, I understand,' he said with a slight smile. 'The boiling oil is to be reserved for me.'

He was gone before she could think of a suitably cutting retort, and the door had closed behind him before she realised that she had failed to discover his exact relationship to Hester.

CHAPTER TWO

As ELINOR returned to her patient, her mind was deeply troubled. Had his lordship's offer come from anyone else she might have welcomed it, though she considered Hester too young for marriage. The girl was barely out of the schoolroom, and knew nothing of the world. She doubted if her charge had ever held a conversation with a man.

Yet it might be the answer. Girls as young as Hester were betrothed and wed each season, to the satisfaction of their parents and themselves.

But Rokeby had made it clear that the choice of a suitable husband would be his alone. Elinor shuddered at the thought of the crowd of roisterers about his dining-table. Would Hester be given in marriage to some creature such as the fat man who had shared his board? That would not happen if she could prevent it.

Perhaps Rokeby intended Hester for himself? No. . . She dismissed the idea at once. It was preposterous. Rokeby was a wealthy man. He had no need of Hester's fortune. Yet, had he been penniless, she doubted if he would have offered for the girl. Even on short acquaintance she had become aware that his lordship's taste in females was that of a connoisseur. She had been well conscious of the dismay in his expression as he looked at Hester.

She had no patience with such arrogance, and she despised him for his lack of charity. As for herself. . .

he had tried hard enough to put her out of countenance.

The low murmur of his voice as he'd gazed into her eyes had been almost a promise of seduction.

And those cheap compliments had been insulting, she decided with a sudden spurt of anger. She, no more than Hester, could have no appeal for a rake. A vivid memory of the raven-haired beauty, white fingers caressing the nape of Rokeby's neck, who had been seated on his lap the night before, returned to taunt her.

Did the man feel obliged to challenge the sexuality of every woman he met? If so, she was not mistaken in her judgment of his character. She would not leave Hester in the care of such a man without as much protection as she could give.

Once her decision had been made, Elinor began to consider practicalities. The difficulties of her own situation must be set aside for the moment. She would save what money she could from the generous sum which Rokeby had suggested as her allowance. Then, if Hester did eventually marry, she would be independent.

Her thoughts returned to Hester. When she entered the bedroom she found that her patient was awake, though still feverish. As Elinor moved towards the bed she tried to struggle upright against her pillows.

'No, my dear, stay where you are. You shall not leave your bed today. Will you take a little nourishment?'

'I. . .I cannot. My throat feels as if I have swallowed thorns. . .'

'Then perhaps a cooling drink?' Elinor tugged at the bell-pull to summon the maid.

It was his lordship's housekeeper who came into the room.

'My name is Onslow, miss.' The plump little woman gave her a cheerful smile. 'Is the young lady better?'

'Her throat is painful, Mrs Onslow. She cannot eat, but if she might have some more of your excellent lemonade. . .?'

'She shall take it mixed with honey. Now, don't you go worrying, Miss Temple. As a boy his lordship never got through the winter without a putrid throat. Rest and warmth is the best cure. She'll feel more herself tomorrow.'

Elinor smiled at her. 'Have you served Lord Rokeby for long?'

'For all his life, and his father before him.' There was a note of pride in Mrs Onslow's voice. 'Now then, ma'am, shall you wish to take your nuncheon in the dining-room, or shall Robert set up a table here?'

'In here, if you please. . .and just a tray with something light. . .' The thought of eating alone in that enormous dining-room held no appeal for Elinor, and her appetite had deserted her.

She managed to eat a wing of chicken and some Italian salad, but she felt utterly weary. Hester had fallen asleep again, so she stretched out on her cot, vowing to close her eyes for no more than a few minutes.

When she awoke she found that the curtains had been drawn against the early darkness of a winter afternoon, and the fire was burning merrily in the grate.

Elinor glanced at the ornate clock upon the mantel-shelf and was surprised to find that she had slept for several hours.

'Miss Temple?'

'Yes, my dear?' Elinor was on her feet at once. 'How are you feeling now?'

'My throat is better, but I'm sorry to be a trouble to you, and to Lord Rokeby.'

'You did not fall sick on purpose,' Elinor said reasonably. 'And Mrs Onslow tells me that, as a boy, his lordship suffered often from the same complaint.'

'But what must he think of me? I did not even make my curtsy to him. In fact, I can't remember much about him, except that I thought him a black-looking man.'

'You were tired and ill,' Elinor soothed. 'As you learn to know him better, you will grow fond of him.' She kept her fingers firmly crossed behind her back.

'Shall I?' Hester put a hand up to her head. 'It all seemed so strange last night. There was so much noise . . .and a girl ran across the hall. . .and then a man. Was I dreaming?'

'Lord Rokeby was entertaining his friends,' Elinor told her smoothly. 'They are gone away, and so is he . . .to London, for a time. We have the house to ourselves.'

'Then I need not see him again just yet.' Hester gave a perceptible sigh of relief. 'I thought he seemed . . .formidable.'

'That was your imagination. Now let me help you out of bed. You shall sit by the fire and bathe your face and hands whilst the bed is made for you. Then I shall go down to the library and find a book. We'll have our supper up here, and spend a cosy evening together.'

The girl looked up at her with a sigh of gratitude. 'I

wish it could always be like this. . .with just the two of us.'

'You would soon tire of that, my dear. Now that you are a woman grown, you must take your rightful place in society.'

'Must I? I had much rather not.' Hester wore a hunted expression. 'Miss Temple, I don't know what to say to people. . .to strangers, I mean.'

'Young ladies making their come-out are not required to be brilliant conversationalists, Hester. In any case, you will find that most of the people you meet prefer to talk about themselves. It is a common human frailty.' Elinor rang for the maid. Then she made her way down to the library.

She was amazed by the range of books she found there. For a time she lingered over the beautifully bound volumes of Greek philosophy and ancient history, eyeing them with appreciation. Then she turned to more modern works.

Evelina, or a Young Lady's Entrance into the World looked promising. She had heard of the book, which was by a female author—a Miss Burney. The subject, she hoped, would interest Hester.

She returned to find her patient looking more comfortable in a clean bed-gown, and propped up against her pillows. A tantalising smell arose from the table which had been set beside the bed, but Hester would not eat.

'Now, Miss Temple, don't you fret yourself.' Mrs Onslow stood beside the steaming dishes. 'The young lady has flesh upon her bones. 'Twill do her no harm to fast for a day or two.'

Elinor managed a faint smile. 'I don't feel very hungry myself,' she confessed.

'You are tired, miss, that's all. Now do you try a little of cook's cream soup. 'Tis made with leeks and potatoes and is very nourishing. . .' She removed the lid from a great tureen and served Elinor without more ado.

Elinor refused the timbale of macaroni which followed, but she accepted a little of the fish.

'That was delicious,' she said at last. 'We seldom saw fish at Bath. . .being so far from the sea. You will give my compliments to his lordship's cook?'

'Chef will be disappointed, Miss. You ain't touched his glazed beef, or the orange jelly.'

'Perhaps tomorrow,' Elinor promised. 'Then we shall both enjoy the jelly. Hester, won't you try a little now? It will slip down easily.'

Hester shook her head. 'Just a drink,' she croaked.

When the dishes had been removed, Elinor began to read aloud, but the story which had kept Sir Joshua Reynolds awake all night failed to do the same for Hester. In a very few moments she was asleep.

Elinor laid the book aside. She had much to think about. It was a blessing that Rokeby had decided to return to London for the time being, but she would have given much to know his plans. Did he do much entertaining at Merton Place? She would try to learn more from Mrs Onslow. Hester could not stay in her room for ever, but she must not be exposed to the rackety company of his lordship's friends. An heiress would be an obvious target for such men.

Still, Rokeby had spoken of giving Hester a season, and that meant London. But how was he to launch her into society? He would need the good offices of some lady who had the entrée into the highest circles to act as chaperone to Hester.

A lady? Elinor's lips twisted in scorn. She doubted if he were acquainted with a respectable woman. And, even if he should succeed in finding such a person, what would be her own position? Most probably little more than a lady's-maid.

There was another consideration. Where were they to live? Rokeby's bachelor establishment could not be considered suitable as a home for two unmarried females. If only the wretched creature had a wife! She sighed in despair. Whatever her worries, she could could not wish that fate upon some unfortunate girl.

She undressed slowly, still searching for some solution to her problems, but exhaustion overtook her. Within minutes she was sound asleep.

By the following day Hester's throat was much improved though she still felt unwell. Her cough had given way to fits of sneezing and her eyes were streaming.

''Tis the usual course of a chill,' Mrs Onslow had announced. 'Miss Temple, you are looking pale. Will you not step out for a breath of air?'

Elinor welcomed the suggestion. She had hardly left Hester's sick room since their arrival, and she prayed that she, too, would not catch the infection. She would need all her wits about her if she were to deal with Rokeby.

The air was still as she left the house in the cold of a December morning. Frost rimed the grass and, though she was wearing pattens, she kept to the gravel paths as she walked through the parterre. Locked in their winter sleep, the gardens appeared as desolate as her mood, but when she reached the height of an elevated knoll and turned to look back her spirits lifted.

The old stone house was beautifully sited in a fold of the Kentish hills. It looked as if it had been a part of that rolling countryside for centuries. No battlements, she noted with amusement, though the frontage had been embellished with colonnades, which she guessed were of more recent origin.

It looked what it was—a comfortable country mansion eminently suitable for a gentleman of means, surrounded by parkland designed in the modern taste. Capability Brown? She thought not. There was no lake, and no sign of a river with its course altered to improve the landscape, or evidence of a hill being raised and planted with an artful arrangement of trees. This was the work of a gifted amateur.

She had wandered further than she had intended; when she consulted her watch, she was surprised to find that it was already noon. She turned and hastened back towards the house. It would not do to upset Chef.

Bates met her in the doorway.

'Miss Temple, you have a visitor. It is Mr Charlbury—one of his lordship's friends. I have put him in the library.'

Elinor's heart sank. She had no wish to meet any of the men who had so disgusted her on the night of her arrival.

'You did not tell him that Lord Rokeby was away from home?'

'I did, miss, but he said that he would wait.'

Elinor straightened her shoulders. Her unwelcome visitor should be sent about his business without delay.

Mr Charlbury's appearance came as a shock to her. Tall and thin, she guessed him to be in his early thirties, about the same age as Lord Rokeby. What disarmed her was the sweetness of his smile.

'You must forgive me, Miss Temple,' he said quietly. 'I had no notion that Marcus was to be away. We meet each week, you see, for a wrangle on questions of philosophy.' He gestured vaguely in the direction of the books.

Elinor looked her astonishment. 'You surprise me, sir. I had not thought his lordship interested. . .'

'Have you known him long?'

'We met but a day ago, Mr Charlbury. I have accompanied his ward to Merton Place.'

It was Charlbury's turn to look astonished. 'His ward? He said nothing of her to me.'

'I believe he had forgotten she existed.' Elinor's tone was dry. 'At present she is suffering from a chill, and is confined to her room.'

'I am sorry to hear it, ma'am, and trust that the young lady will soon be recovered. If there is anything I can do in Rokeby's absence. . .?'

'Perhaps you would care to stay for a light nun-cheon?' Elinor had taken a liking to this shy creature. She could not imagine him in the company of Rokeby, but clearly he was one of his lordship's closest friends, and an ally would be useful.

Charlbury took little persuasion, and they were enjoying a dish of oyster patties when Elinor broached the subject of his friend.

'You have known Lord Rokeby for long?' she asked.

'Since boyhood, ma'am. We have always been close. He is the best of men.'

Elinor looked her astonishment, and he hid a smile.

'You must not let Marcus tease you,' he said gently.

'His manner can be provoking, but you will admit that the sudden arrival of his ward must have been a shock.'

'It was indeed!' Elinor could not let this masterpiece of understatement pass. 'I fear too that we appeared at an inopportune moment. His lordship was entertaining. . .'

'The hunting fraternity? They are a high-spirited crowd.' He was careful not to elaborate. 'I do not care for the sport myself, so my acquaintance among them is slight.' He avoided Elinor's eye, and she made haste to change the subject.

There was no point in mentioning the ladies of questionable virtue who had shared the gentlemen's board that night, and later, no doubt, their beds.

'I had not thought of Lord Rokeby as a philosopher,' she said with a smile. 'Yet you tell me that you and he enjoy the subject. . .'

Charlbury waxed enthusiastic, and in the next hour Elinor learned much about her enigmatic host. Rokeby's interests were evidently wider than she had imagined.

'We are both members of the Royal Society,' he continued. 'We study matters of scientific interest.'

Elinor nodded, though she was convinced that Rokeby's scientific interest lay more in the study of the female sex.

'I see that you are surprised, Miss Temple. It is not to be wondered at. Marcus likes to give the impression that he lives for pleasure alone. Nothing could be further from the truth. You will not find a better-run estate than this in the length of England.'

'Doubtless his lordship is able to rely upon the experience of his bailiffs and his steward. . .'

'That's true, but the men who served his father are no longer young. They are inclined to be set in their ways. It has been no easy task for him to persuade them to adopt new methods of farming the land, but he has done it.'

'I don't doubt it,' Elinor said tartly. 'He does not strike me as a man who would brook opposition.'

Charlbury looked at her, his head on one side. 'He believes in persuasion. Should it surprise you to learn that the welfare of his people here is foremost in his mind? At Merton you will find no wretched hovels and starving labourers. When you drive out, you will see that each man has a patch of ground beside his home, where he may keep a pig or some chickens, and grow enough food to feed his family.'

Elinor smiled. 'I begin to see why you think so well of Lord Rokeby. Do you farm yourself?'

'In a much smaller way. Marcus allows me to borrow all his works upon the subject. I believe he has every modern treatise that is published.' He looked at the clock and jumped to his feet. 'Do forgive me. I have outstayed my welcome.'

'Not at all. I have enjoyed your company.'

'Then I may come again? You have caused me to forget the main purpose of my visit. Marcus gives a Yuletide feast for friends and tenantry each year, and my family shares it with him. There were some small matters to discuss.'

'Then you are our neighbour, Sir Charlbury?'

'I live just beyond the hill. When Marcus returns, he shall bring you and Miss Winton to visit us.'

It was not until he had ridden away that Elinor thought to question the propriety of dining alone with a total stranger. True, Rokeby had assured her that in his absence she was to be sole mistress of Merton Place, but... She frowned. In future, perhaps she should be more circumspect, but she could not regret the time spent in John Charlbury's company.

He had given her much food for thought. Perhaps she had judged Lord Rokeby too hastily. Clearly there was another side to his character, yet she distrusted him.

It was some days before Hester felt able to leave her room, and Elinor found that time hung heavily on her hands. She had explored his lordship's library and found that Charlbury had not exaggerated the breadth of her employer's interests. The man was an enigma, and he intrigued her.

She looked across at Hester as they sat together by a roaring fire in a small withdrawing-room. A week of voluntary fasting had resulted in a spectacular loss of weight, and the girl's blue eyes now looked enormous in her pale face. Yet she was smiling as she read aloud from the *Spectator*.

The smile vanished quickly as a visitor was announced and Hester jumped to her feet. Elinor stayed her with an outstretched hand.

'You shall not run away,' she said gently. 'Mr Charlbury is no ogre. I liked him very much, and so will you.'

Hester looked unconvinced. Her hunted expression had returned, and after the first conventional greetings she was silent.

Wisely, Charlbury addressed most of his words to Elinor, giving Hester time to recover her composure.

'No sign of Marcus yet?' he asked.

'We expect Lord Rokeby daily,' Elinor assured him. 'I hope that your arrangements may then go ahead.'

'There is plenty of time, Miss Temple.' Charlbury picked up the copy of the *Spectator* which Hester had laid aside. 'Are you enjoying this excellent paper, Miss Winton?'

'Very much, I thank you, sir.' Hester blushed to find herself at the centre of attention.

'You have read the essay on Sir Roger de Coverley?'

'Not yet.'

'Then you must do so.' He began to quote and soon had his listeners laughing so heartily that they did not hear the bustle in the hall.

Then the door opened and Rokeby strolled towards them, snuff-box in hand.

'I must congratulate you, John,' his lordship murmured smoothly. 'You have succeeded where I could not. You have made Miss Temple smile.'

'Marcus, behave yourself! You shall not put the ladies out of countenance, especially when we are having such a famous time. . .'

'So I see.' Rokeby looked at Hester. 'I trust you are much recovered, my dear.'

Hester jumped to her feet and sank into a clumsy curtsy, wobbling uncertainly as she did so.

Rokeby put out a hand to steady her.

'Still a little lightheaded, I see.' He assisted her to her chair, and looked across at Elinor. 'All is well here, Miss Temple?'

'You will find no broken bodies, my lord.'

Charlbury and Hester looked mystified, but Rokeby's lips twitched.

'I am glad to hear it. John, you will dine with us, I hope?'

'A pleasure!' Charlbury smiled at his companions. During their nuncheon, he set himself to put Hester at her ease, and succeeded so well that the girl was soon absorbed in his conversation.

Elinor heaved an inward sigh of relief.

'A charmer, is he not?' Rokebury murmured in her ear.

'He does not strive to be so, which makes his kindness all the more endearing.'

Rokeby smiled. 'So he has become a favourite with you? I am happy to see that at least one of my friends meets with your approval.'

Elinor ignored his reference to the night of their arrival. She changed the subject.

'Mr Charlbury called upon us last week,' she said. 'I believe that you entertain your tenants during the Christmas season. He wished to discuss the arrangements.'

'Ah, yes.' An imp of mischief lurked in his eyes as he looked at her. 'Yet another orgy, I fear, Miss Temple, but this one you will be required to attend.'

Elinor refused to be drawn. Her chin went up.

'I look forward to it, sir.'

'To an orgy? Come, come, Miss Temple, I had supposed you to be set against such frivolity. There will be feasting, dancing, kissing beneath the mistletoe. . . Are you quite sure that you approve?'

'You are pleased to joke, my lord. I can assure you that I am not—'

'Quite the strait-laced miss that I suggest? I know that well, Miss Temple. Your expression can be severe, but your mouth gives you away. Those full lips. . .the curve when you smile. . .'

'Lord Rokeby, this is nonsense! At our first meeting you described me as the duenna of your ward. That is my position, and so it shall remain. If you wish me to undertake her charge as you suggested, I trust that you will treat me—'

'With proper respect? You have my word on it.' He laid a hand over his heart.

To her fury Elinor realised that he was laughing at her.

'You have made arrangements for our stay in London?' she demanded.

'I have. We shall discuss them later. Am I to understand that we are in agreement? You will stay with Hester?'

'I will. . .for the time being—'

'Dependent upon my good behaviour? You drive a hard bargain, Miss Temple. Think what it means for a man of my unbridled appetites to be forced to tread the path of virtue.' The blue eyes sparkled in his dark face.

Elinor turned to Charlbury, who was engrossed in a discussion about the recent Treaty of Amiens.

'Will the peace with Napoleon last?' she asked. It was enough to draw the four of them into an animated discussion, and Hester so far forgot her shyness as to give a good account of herself in the general conversation.

Rokeby was surprised, but he withheld his comments until later in the day.

He had summoned Elinor to the library.

'You have done well with the girl,' he said without preamble. 'She appears to have a mind of her own.'

'She has. I wonder why it should surprise you.'

'It is not usual, Miss Temple. You will not tell me that all the girls in your charge had similar interests?'

'No, they had not,' Elinor admitted. 'Hester was outstanding, no matter what you may think of her appearance.'

'That is no matter,' Rokeby mused. 'It can be improved, and she has lost flesh since her illness.' For some moments he was silent, lost in thought. 'There will be much work to do,' he said at last. 'We shall spend Christmas here, and then we shall go to London.'

'My lord, where are we to live?'

'Well, hardly beneath my own roof.' He was laughing at her again. 'I have made some arrangements with a lady of my acquaintance, Miss Temple—' He raised a hand to forestall Elinor's objections.

'You will find the lady beyond reproach,' he assured her. 'My aunt has entrée to the highest circles. Even you may feel that she is a little. . .shall we say. . .high in the instep.'

'Sir, I should like to be quite clear. . . What is my own position to be?'

'My dear Miss Temple, you are to be the equal of my ward, of course. You will be her friend and mentor.'

'You forget my situation, your lordship.'

'Just as you forgot to mention your distinguished connections? Your maternal grandfather is General Marchington, is he not? I wonder that you did not tell me of the relationship.'

'It did not seem appropriate or necessary.' Elinor was startled. It was clear that her future employer had taken the trouble to make inquiries about her.

'Then let us have no more of this nonsense. If you will guide my ward I shall be grateful. This charge is a trouble to me. I shall be happy to be free of it.'

'I wonder that you should have undertaken it in the first place,' Elinor flung at him. The words were out before she had time to consider their effect.

Rokeby's face darkened, and when he spoke his voice was icy. 'I thought I had explained,' he gritted out.

'A disagreement with your uncle? It seems little enough reason to wish to gain control of another person's life. . .'

He gave her a sardonic smile. 'I did not wish it, ma'am. The charge was laid upon me by a distant cousin.'

'You might have refused it,' she pointed out.

'True, but I did not. Hester might have found herself in very different circumstances.'

'I don't understand you.'

'Then let me explain.' The grim smile had returned. 'This may come as a shock to you, Miss Temple, but the courts do not require kinship when determining the disposition of an orphan. Anyone may apply to be a guardian.'

'Surely not? What possible motive could there be?'

'The answer is not far to seek when the orphan in question is an heir or heiress. A guardian has full control of their fortunes at least until they reach majority, or, in the case of a girl, until she marries. There are rich pickings to be had.'

'I find it difficult to believe that anyone would abuse such a trust.'

'Do you? Then I fear I must disillusion you. Hester might easily have fallen into unscrupulous hands.'

Elinor stared at him. 'Then you do care about her?'

'I do not know the girl. How should I care about her?' His face was a mask of indifference. 'As you so rightly guessed, I had almost forgot her existence. Her fees were paid through my man of business...and I had no news of her.'

Elinor gazed at him in disbelief. 'You did not think to seek her out...to comfort her in her loss?' She turned away before he could reply and was about to leave the room.

'One moment, please. Charlbury has suggested that we visit him on Thursday. This meets with your approval?'

'It will be a pleasure,' Elinor said with feeling. At least in Charlbury's company she was spared the verbal sparring which seemed to be her lot whenever she met Lord Rokeby.

She heard what sounded suspiciously like a chuckle, but when she glanced up Rokeby's expression was bland.

'There is one other point,' he murmured smoothly. 'You will find some boxes in your room—trifles of dress and so on. I hope you will find them to your taste. I was...er...forced to guess at the sizes.'

'The sizes? Sir, I hope this does not mean that you have taken the liberty of choosing a garment for me.' Her voice was warm with indignation.

'Garments, Miss Temple...garments. Now do not fire up at me. We shall be entertaining over the festive season, and you have had no opportunity for shopping. If your virtue is outraged you may reimburse me as you think fit. Look at the gowns...you may not like them.' His eyes were veiled, and she could not see his expression, but she guessed that he was laughing at her again. She flounced out of the room.

How dared he presume to choose her clothes? She could well imagine his idea of a suitable gown for evening wear. If he hoped to present her to his friends in the type of finery worn by the half-naked strumpet she had last seen upon his lap, he was mistaken. She would not even look at the gowns.

She was too late. When she reached her room, she found that the boxes had been unpacked and Hester was in raptures.

'Miss Temple, do but look at this! It's mine...my name was on the box.' Hester held up a gown of cream silk tobine. The short puffed sleeves were trimmed with self-coloured ribbon delicately embroidered with pale blue flowers.

Even to herself, Elinor was forced to admit that it was an ideal choice for a young girl's first ball-gown. And cream was, for Hester, a more becoming shade than white. It warmed her pale skin, and made a perfect background for the small string of river pearls which she wore about her neck.

'The pearls?' Elinor questioned.

'They are a present too, and so is this, and this.' She pointed to a morning dress made up to the throat, with sleeves buttoned tightly at the wrists in a deeper blue. Beside it lay another morning gown in lavender.

Elinor hugged her, disarmed by the girl's excitement.

'You will be very fine,' she announced. 'Which shall you wear when we visit Mr Charlbury on Thursday?'

Elinor had half expected protestations of dismay at the prospect of their outing, but none were forthcoming.

'The blue, I think. Miss Temple, the gowns on the other bed are yours. Won't you look at them?'

Elinor hesitated. Would it be possible to explain to Hester that, whilst her guardian had the right to buy whatever he wished for her, there was a question of propriety where Elinor was concerned?

'Do hold them up,' Hester urged. 'The colours are so lovely. . .'

A glance at the girl's bright face decided her. It would be churlish to rob the child of so much pleasure. After all, Rokeby had promised that she could pay for the gowns, and her allowance was more than generous. It was just that she disliked the notion of wearing anything which might be his lordship's choice.

It could do no harm to look at the garments. Doubtless they would be quite unsuitable, or at best they would not fit her. Then it would be a simple matter to return them to him.

Pleasure mingled with exasperation as her eye fell upon a half-gown of amber-figured silk with a treble pleating of lace falling off the neck. It was so exactly what she would have chosen for herself, had she the means. It was beautifully cut, but she fingered the fine material with a sigh, guessing rightly that her allowance would not begin to pay for it.

A charming day-dress of dark green challis was accompanied by a small matching spencer for extra warmth, and she could see at a glance that both gowns would fit her to perfection.

Her cheeks burned. What more could one expect from a rake? Doubtless he kept half the mantua-makers in London in business.

'Miss Temple, don't you like them? You are very quiet.'

'Hester, they are quite beautiful. Lord Rokeby has excellent taste.' And his expertise was no credit to him, she thought fiercely.

'But he did not give you a necklace. . .'

'Of course not, Hester. You are his ward. He may give you whatever he wishes. With me it is a different matter.'

'You don't like him, do you?'

Elinor had forgotten Hester's quickness of intelligence. Shy and self-effacing, the girl was a shrewd observer, and Elinor had often marvelled at the way in which she picked up the smallest nuance of feeling. Poor child! That sensitive character had learned early to be aware of snubs and humiliations.

'Did you not say yourself that he was a fearsome character?' Elinor chaffed. 'He makes me quake in my boots.'

Hester threw back her head and laughed. 'You are making gammon of me, Miss Temple. I know you aren't afraid of anyone.'

'Well then, let us be in charity with Lord Rokeby, Hester. Mr Charlbury speaks so highly of him, and he has known his lordship for many years.'

It would serve no purpose to explain her own misgivings. For the next few months they must both be dependent upon the master of Merton Place. It was no pleasant prospect, but it must be endured. Elinor found herself wondering where they would be a year from now.

CHAPTER THREE

By the following Thursday the light covering of snow had melted, but the day was dank and cold. Seated in a corner of the comfortable carriage, with a fur rug about her knees and a hot brick at her feet, Elinor prepared to enjoy her first look at the Kentish countryside.

They had not far to go, but she delighted in the vista of rolling hills, and the tracery of leafless branches against the leaden sky.

'You do not know this part of England?' Rokeby lounged opposite the ladies, scorning the comfort of a rug.

'This is all new to me, my lord. My home is in Derbyshire.' Elinor had determined to be civil.

'Ah yes...a sterner countryside, is it not? I have been to Matlock and found it impressive.'

'Parts of Derbyshire are wild and beautiful,' she agreed.

'Like their inhabitants?' he said in a teasing tone.

'I doubt it, sir.' Elinor gave him a repressive look. 'The natives of Derbyshire are hard-working. Their main concern is to earn a living.'

'Very worthy! Am I permitted to hope that some of them find time for more frivolous pursuits?'

'One may always hope.' Elinor turned away from him to gaze through the carriage window.

Rokeby turned his attention to Hester. 'I must compliment you, my dear. You are in looks today.'

Hester stroked the fabric of her new blue gown. Over it she wore a matching fur-trimmed pelisse.

'This is so pretty,' she said softly. 'I have not worn such dress before.'

'It is vastly becoming.' He smiled at her, and his face was transformed. 'You shall have many more such gowns, Hester. Do you look forward to a London season?'

The question reduced Hester to confusion. She gave Elinor a pleading glance.

'Hester will enjoy it,' Elinor said firmly. 'There is so much to see and do. We intend to visit the Tower of London and St Paul's Cathedral. . .'

'Sparing some little time for a visit to the theatre, and to Almack's, with possibly a rout or two, I hope.' The blue eyes twinkled.

Elinor was strongly disposed to strike him. Why did he always bring out the worst in her? She wasn't priggish, she told herself. Nor did she despise dancing, or a visit to the theatre. Why then did she feel obliged to behave like a staid schoolmarm?

Perversity was her besetting sin, or so her mamma had proclaimed on more than one occasion. Yet this time it was justified. Lord Rokeby must be kept firmly in his place if he were not to. . . Not to what? Disturb her peace of mind? No, that was ridiculous.

She stole a glance at him. Resplendent in a perfectly fitting coat of fine blue Melton, and immaculate from his beige pantaloons to the tips of his mirror-like Hessians, he was every inch the gentleman of fashion. Yet there was something else about him. . .some quality which she could not quite define. Was it his vitality? That was certainly overwhelming. Or perhaps it was those curious eyes, so light in that dark face? They seemed to see everything with remarkable clarity.

As if aware of her scrutiny, he turned to her.

'I dine from home tonight, Miss Temple. I trust you will excuse my absence?'

Elinor felt tempted to observe that she could bear the prospect with equanimity. Instead she held her tongue, merely inclining her head in acknowledgment of his words.

Better to have him pursue his questionable interests elsewhere than to invite his rackety friends to Merton Place. Though in fairness, and much to her relief, there had been no repetition of the evening party which had so disturbed her.

She looked out of the window once more to find that they were approaching a long, low, rambling house set in grassland beside a lake. The central portion, she guessed, was Elizabethan, but successive owners had added a wing at each end of the building, each in a different style of architecture. It was not in the classical mode, but even on that damp December morning it looked both comfortable and welcoming.

Her first impressions were not mistaken. As the carriage drew to a halt, Charlbury appeared on the steps, surrounded by a number of young people. Two of the boys ran towards the carriage, flinging open the door before the coachman could alight.

Rokeby jumped down, laughing at the barrage of questions which awaited him.

'Monsters!' he announced. 'What will the ladies think of you?' He turned to assist Elinor to the ground, but Charlbury was before him, and it was Hester who took her guardian's hand.

'Miss Temple, may I present my eldest sister,

Anne?' Charlbury led her towards a slender girl who was trying vainly to hold the younger ones in check. Anne was a beauty, with a cloud of chestnut hair framing a piquant little heart-shaped face. Her eyes, so like her brother's, were smiling, and Elinor warmed to her at once.

'Then you must meet Celia and Judith, and these two obnoxious creatures are Sebastian and Crispin.'

As Charlbury's brothers and sisters surrounded her, Elinor looked across at Hester, who wore a wistful expression. She is thinking of the family she never had, Elinor thought to herself. Then Anne took Hester's arm and drew her into the house.

'Mamma will not forgive us if we keep you standing here,' she murmured. 'She is in the salon.'

Elinor was surprised to find that the mother of this attractive brood was homely in the extreme. Small and plump, she looked like some little downy bird, but her eyes were quick and bright.

'My dears, you must be frozen with the cold. Do you sit by the fire. Then you shall take some mulled wine.' She tugged at the bell-pull. 'Miss Temple, I cannot tell you what a pleasure it is to meet you. John has spoken of nothing else for the past weeks and of Miss Winton too.'

Elinor was quick to notice that Charlbury, with his customary courtesy, had taken his place by Hester's side, and was fielding the questions which his sisters asked of her. She gave him a grateful smile. He was kindness itself.

She turned to find that Mrs Charlbury was looking up at Rokeby.

'Marcus, you have given us a pleasant surprise. Two

more ladies in the neighbourhood will be a positive boon if they will agree to give us their company often.'

Rokeby dropped into a chair beside his hostess and kissed her hand.

'I can claim no credit, ma'am. We must all be grateful to Miss Temple.' The irony in his tone was not lost on Elinor, but Mrs Charlbury picked him up at once.

'Don't try to gammon me, my dear boy. The responsibility will do you the world of good. You look a different person already.'

'Are my grey hairs showing?' He grinned at her with affection. 'Ma'am, if you must know it, I am bowed down with care.'

Mrs Charlbury turned to Elinor. 'Marcus likes to tease, as I'm sure you have discovered.'

'Indeed, ma'am.' Elinor managed a faint smile, but her back had stiffened, and the tension in the air was palpable. The older woman glanced at the faces of her two companions, but she made no further comment.

'Anne,' she commanded, 'do beg your papa to join us. It is now past the hour for nuncheon.' She turned to Elinor with a rueful smile. 'When my husband is working on his book he would starve, if we did not remind him of the time.'

'It is kind of you to ask us here today,' Elinor said with feeling. 'Hester, as you must know, has not been well since we arrived. This outing will give her so much pleasure.'

'I hope it will be the first of many visits, Miss Temple. Your charge is a little shy, I think. To be thrust among so many strangers must be somewhat daunting.'

'In your family one could not be ill at ease,' Elinor

assured her. 'They seem to have such a gift for friendship.'

'You have family of your own?'

'I have three brothers and four sisters, Ma'am. I am the eldest. Our home is in Derbyshire.'

'You must miss them, my dear.'

Rokeby was fondling the ears of a fat spaniel sitting at his feet, but Elinor was aware that he was listening.

'I visit them whenever possible,' she replied. 'And at Bath there was little time for moping.'

'John tells me that you taught at the school there. My husband will be interested. He has strong views on education.'

It was at that moment that the subject of her conversation entered the room. Henry Charlbury was an older version of his eldest son, and as Elinor gave him her hand she found herself looking up into the same brown eyes.

Seated beside him at the dining-table, she found him remote, but she guessed that he was still preoccupied with the latest chapter of his book. It was when Mrs Charlbury remarked on Elinor's teaching post that he looked at her with interest.

From then on she was the sole object of her host's attention until Mrs Charlbury was forced to intervene again.

'Charlbury, pray do not monopolise Miss Temple. She is to visit us again, you know.' Her smile robbed her words of all offence. 'Now tell me, my dear, how do you celebrate the Yuletide season in Derbyshire?'

'Much as you do here, I imagine, Mrs Charlbury. We burn the great Yule log, and decorate the house with greenery.'

'And do you have presents? You must have presents.' Crispin's question was urgent.

'We do. . .and games such as bobbing for apples.'

'With prizes?' asked Sebastian.

'These two are a mercenary pair,' John Charlbury told her with a smile. 'Miss Winton is like to believe them capable of holding up the mail coach.'

'No, she won't.' The boys had been quick to seize upon Hester as an ally. 'We're going to show her our new kittens.'

They led her away as soon as the meal was over.

'Now you shall not let the boys be a trouble to you,' Mrs Charlbury told her. 'You must be firm with them.'

'They won't be a trouble,' Hester said shyly. 'And I should like to see the kittens.' It was clear that she felt more at ease with the casual cameraderie of the children.

Elinor glanced across the table. It had come as no surprise to find that Rokeby had seated himself beside the beauteous Anne. The girl gazed up at him, oblivious of the others.

It was only too clear that she was in love with him. Elinor wondered why the knowledge should depress her so. In the eyes of society it would be an ideal match. The wealthy Lord Rokeby would be allied to the daughter of one of his oldest friends. But had those friends any idea of the depths of his depravity?

Elinor tried to suppress the emotions which filled her mind. It was nothing to do with her, but Anne was a sweet girl. Would she find happiness with a heartless rake? Even on short acquaintance she had realised that Mrs Charlbury would brook no ill behaviour on the part of a prospective son-in-law but, once married, even she would be powerless to control Rokeby.

She glanced at his smiling face in profile. She was aware of the clean lines of his jaw, and the straight, classical perfection of his nose. Swarthy though he was, he was still an attractive creature.

Had she not known his character as she did, she too might have found him pleasing. Yet still there was something about him which eluded her. Hester had described him as fearsome, but what was her other term? Piratical? Yes, that was it! There was somehow an underlying sense of recklessness. . .of fierce energies held in check by the thinnest of threads. This was a man who would be capable of anything.

And was she the only person who could see it? She glanced about her, and was aware only of the casual conversation of old friends. Could she possibly be mistaken in her judgement of Rokeby's character? Mr and Mrs Charlbury were not fools, and neither was their son, yet they seemed to hold his lordship in high regard.

Elinor's lip curled. Rokeby was clever, she must give him that. Whatever his motive for wishing to be accepted in this household, he played the part of a charming neighbour to perfection.

'Until next week then?' He bowed over the hand of his hostess as they prepared to take their leave.

'Oh, Marcus, we can't wait.' The boys were racing round him as he handed the ladies into the carriage.

'Patience, my friends. It is the best of all virtues, together with perseverance.' Rokeby was laughing as he took Elinor's hand.

She pulled away as if she had been stung. The touch of that warm flesh against her own had caused an unaccustomed flutter in the pit of her stomach. If he was aware of it, he gave no sign. On the way back to

Merton Place he chatted to Hester about her new acquaintances, and chaffed her about her friendship with the boys.

'Take care or they will have you climbing trees and swimming in the lake,' he teased.

Hester looked at him uncertainly. 'Is it not too cold to swim?' she ventured.

'It is, indeed. Far better take a trip into Tunbridge Wells with Miss Temple. You will wish to purchase one or two small trifles...and you must see the Pantiles, and the church of King Charles the Martyr.' He caught Elinor's eye, and she was quick to thank him.

The mention of presents had troubled her a little. She of course, would neither give them nor receive them, but Hester should have some small gifts by her to reciprocate any unexpected offerings which might be made by Anne and her sisters.

And his lordship had thought of everything. That evening he came to them attired in formal dress. He made no mention of his proposed destination. Instead, he asked what time they would wish to order the carriage for the following day. It was only when he had gone that Elinor found a small leather bag of guineas beside her place in the dining-room. Hester too had been amply provided with funds.

Elinor laid the bag aside. If Rokeby hoped to bribe her into lowering her guard, he would find himself mistaken. Her appetite seemed to have vanished. As she toyed with a slice of glazed ham and an Italian salad, she found herself wondering what his lordship was doing at that moment. Better not to think of it. She forced herself to attend to Hester who had discovered a book on the history of Tunbridge Wells.

'I hope we shall not be disappointed, Miss Temple.' Hester's eyes were shining.

'I doubt it, my dear, though the place was in its heyday some fifty years ago, when it rivalled Bath as a watering place. I believe they still have balls in the Assembly Rooms.'

'Shall we need to attend them?' Her voice was shaking with anxiety.

'Of course not, Hester. You are not yet out. Now pray do not trouble yourself with needless worries. You did so well today. Is it not pleasant to make new friends?'

'I liked the Charlburys,' Hester said simply. 'They make me feel so easy and comfortable. . .but. . .'

'What is it then?'

The girl hesitated. 'You will think me ungrateful, but I cannot like Lord Rokeby. I don't understand why he became my guardian. I know he thinks me dull and plain. . .' Her eyes filled with tears.

'Hester dearest, will you not try to understand? Lord Rokeby undertook the charge of a young child who was away at school. He has not seen you in all these years, and thought most probably that you were still in pinafores. It was unfortunate that he had no warning of our arrival. Then he was presented with a young lady and her companion, come to live with him. He has had a shock.' Her lips twitched in spite of herself. 'I shall not soon forget his face that night. I might have had horns and a tail. . .'

'I believe he wishes us far away.' Hester could not manage an answering smile. 'He makes jokes which I do not understand and, when he looks at me with that curious smile I can find nothing to say to him.'

'I doubt if we shall see much of him when we are in

London,' Elinor soothed. 'We are not to live with him, you know, and I doubt if he would care to appear at Almack's or such places.'

'Emma told me that Almack's was a marriage mart. Does his lordship wish me to be wed? I suppose I should then be off his hands. . .' Her look of desolation wrung Elinor's heart.

'You shall do nothing which you do not like,' she promised. 'And there is plenty of time before you make your come-out. Now tell me about the chalybeate spring at Tunbridge Wells. Is not the water said to cure all ills?'

The question served to divert Hester's attention and she went to bed in a happier frame of mind. Elinor was not so fortunate. She could not be easy when she considered Rokeby's plans for Hester's future. Any other girl would have welcomed the prospect of a London season, with balls, parties and routs, and a wardrobe of new clothes to set her off to the best advantage, but she was well aware that Hester dreaded it. Yet there seemed to be no alternative.

After hours of fruitless speculation she fell asleep at last, still with no other solution in mind.

Much to Hester's disappointment, the chalybeate spring at Tunbridge Wells was closed on the following day.

'I doubt if we should have liked the taste, though,' she admitted. 'The water is full of iron and must be bitter.'

Elinor shivered in the keen wind. 'The church of King Charles the Martyr is quite close, I believe. It is just a few yards across the highway. Let us go there quickly, Hester. We have not yet done our shopping and we should strive to return to Merton Place before it grows dark.'

They hurried towards the plain red-brick building, built by subscriptions from supporters of the Stuart cause. The somewhat nondescript exterior gave no hint of the beauty within, but Hester was soon in raptures over the splendid plaster ceiling and the unusual wooden gallery.

Elinor dragged her away at last to walk back through the colonnaded Pantiles. The cold had sent the usual crowd of pedestrians to seek the comfort of their firesides, and the place was almost deserted.

Elinor turned into a draper's shop, and though she was appalled by the prices in that fashionable watering-place, she purchased ribbons and a number of lace-trimmed handkerchiefs, as well as a charming pin-cushion and some needle-cases, all with Hester's enthusiastic agreement.

'And the boys? Shall we take them some sweetmeats?'

'A good idea, Hester. Do you choose those from the shop next door whilst I am paying for these.'

She came out to find Hester laden with small packages.

'Heavens!' she cried. 'Are those all for Crispin and Sebastian? You will spoil them.'

'It is not so very much,' Hester murmured. 'But, Miss Temple, I have nothing to give Lord Rokeby...'

'Don't worry about it, Hester. His lordship will not expect a gift from you. In any case, I should be at a loss to know what would please him.'

The girl looked downcast, and Elinor had an inspiration.

'Let us go into this bookshop,' she said. 'We may find something. . .'

It was by happy chance that they came across the essays of Montaigne, translated from the original French.

'This is ideal!' Elinor turned the pages with a loving hand. Montaigne was one of her favourites. The pungent wit would appeal to Rokeby's mordant sense of humour, she hoped, as would the Frenchman's cool intellect.

Rokeby had returned to Merton Place before them, and Elinor sought him out. In her hand she carried the bag of guineas which he had left beside her plate that morning.

His lordship was looking jaded. It was not, perhaps, the ideal time to confront him, but Elinor plunged ahead.

'This belongs to you, sir.' She laid the bag on the table by his hand.

'You are mistaken, Miss Temple. It belongs to you. It is an advance upon your allowance.'

'I prefer to earn my salary before I am paid,' Elinor said stiffly.

'You will earn it, my dear. Nothing is more certain.'

Elinor eyed him with dislike. Even by candlelight she could see that the lines beneath his eyes were more pronounced.

'Do you feel quite well, my lord?' she asked sweetly.

'Self-inflicted wounds, Miss Temple. I expect no sympathy, and will get none, I imagine.'

Elinor ignored the sally. She guessed that his head was pounding after a convivial evening with his friends. She turned to go.

'Miss Temple, you will please to obey my wishes.'

He picked up the small leather bag and came towards her, holding it out.

'I cannot, sir.'

Rokeby made as if to seize her hand, but she moved away. She had no wish for a humiliating struggle which she had no hope of winning. Then a thought struck her.

'Will you hold the money against the cost of my gowns?' she said quickly. 'Until I have paid for them, at least in part, I shall feel unable to wear them.'

Rokeby sighed in exasperation, but he set the bag aside.

'Miss Temple, you are something new in my experience,' he announced. 'Obstinate...provoking...and determined to have your way.'

'I am not alone in that,' she told him sharply.

His firm mouth curved into a reluctant smile. 'No, you are not, my dear. But I wonder if you have the least notion...' He caught himself in time. He had been about to tell her that most of the women of his acquaintance would have been happy to accept whatever he chose to give them. Her fierce independence both piqued and intrigued him. She was totally without means. He knew that. Yet it did not stop her from clinging to her pride and her own notions of honour.

'You enjoyed your day at the Wells?' he asked.

'Very much, my lord. With your permission we shall visit the town again. There is so much to see...'

'I hope you spared the time to do your shopping.' He was laughing at her again, making her feel like some dowdy schoolmarm who thought only of antiquities and such. She would show him.

*　*　*

She dressed with extra care that night. The new green gown became her to perfection, and in a moment of madness she released her curls from their constricting band and allowed them to fall about her face.

'Miss Temple, you look different,' Hester murmured shyly.

'I will quote the old saw to you, my dear, "Fine feathers make fine birds." You look quite charming yourself.'

It was true. The dusky pink of Hester's modest half-dress gave her pale skin a glow. She looked almost pretty, though her hair, as always, showed a tendency to hang limp about her face. That must be altered when we reach London, Elinor vowed to herself. She took Hester's hand and led her into the salon.

Rokeby must have taken some remedy to clear his head, Elinor decided. He looked himself again, and was, as always, a credit to the attentions of his valet.

As they entered the room he walked towards them with his customary bow.

'I am dazzled,' he said lightly. 'Hester, how much that shade of pink becomes you! You shall wear it more often. And Miss Temple, what can I say?'

Elinor longed to beg him to say as little as possible, but he was determined to torment her.

'A vision!' he announced. 'May I be permitted to hope that you are pleased with my choice of gown?'

'It is delightful,' Elinor told him with a stony look.

For some reason this bald statement sent him into whoops of laughter.

'I cannot bear these transports,' he announced at last. 'Miss Temple, I beg that you will try to control your enthusiasm.'

At that precise moment dinner was announced,

much to Elinor's relief. Whenever she was in his lordship's company, her self-control was sorely tested. How she longed to give him a crushing set-down, but it would not do. No matter how provoking he might be, she would not abandon Hester to his tender mercies.

As the soup was served Rokeby began to discuss the forthcoming festivities, and Elinor felt obliged to offer her assistance, if it should be needed.

'No, no!' He brushed the suggestion aside. 'I thank you, but all is well in hand. I advise you to get plenty of rest beforehand. My tenants invariably make the most of this annual feast.'

He did not exaggerate. For the next week Merton Place hummed with activity as green boughs were brought indoors, together with gaily berried holly. The Great Hall was transformed, but it was not until the eve of Christmas when the long trestle tables were set out that Elinor realised just how large a celebration it would be.

'Surprised, Miss Temple?' Rokeby stood by her side. 'We shall not be dull this Yuletide, I can promise you.'

'Do you plan to roast an ox, my lord? I cannot think how else you might feed such numbers.' She smiled, feeling more in charity with him for his generosity to his dependants.

He laughed as he shook his head. 'I believe you will find that no one will suffer from lack of either food or drink,' he assured her. Then he tilted his head. 'Listen!'

Elinor could hear the sound of singing from outdoors, and she looked at him in surprise.

'We are being serenaded. Let me send for your cloak. The night air is cold, but you shall not venture beyond the open doorway.'

As Bates threw wide the great oak door, Elinor gasped with pleasure. By the light of lanterns held aloft she could see a circle of men, women and children with their voices raised in song. As the old hymns followed one another she felt a sense of peace.

'Later they will go in procession to the church,' Rokeby told her. 'It is an old tradition here, though I believe the custom originated on the continent of Europe.'

As the music died away Rokeby stepped forward and she heard the clink of coins. Then, as she turned to move back into the hall, he laid a hand upon her arm.

'Are you cold?' he asked.

Elinor shook her head. The music had lulled her into a dreamlike state. 'Thank you,' she said impulsively. 'I enjoyed that so very much.'

'You are fond of music?'

'I love it. It is one of my greatest pleasures.'

'Then you will enjoy yourself in London. There are many concerts, or perhaps you prefer the opera.' He drew her arm through his. 'Shall we take a turn about the terrace? The night is so fine that it seems a pity to retire just yet.'

Unresisting, Elinor allowed him to lead her out of doors. Still in a trance, she seemed to have no will of her own. Overhead the moon shone full, bathing lawns, trees and shrubberies in its silver light. The stars in their vast canopy seemed low enough to touch. She caught her breath at the sheer beauty of the scene before her.

'You sense the magic, too?' Rokeby's lips were close to her ear.

'There is something mysterious about the eve of Christmas, above all nights in the year for me,' she murmured in reply. 'I cannot quite say why.'

'Tonight I think I have the answer, for myself at least.' Rokeby turned to face her. 'Have you any idea how beautiful you are, Miss Temple? Here, with the moonlight on your face you might be Aphrodite, the Greek goddess of love.'

Elinor moved away from him at once. There was a low caressing note in his deep voice which she found disturbing. They had moved some distance from the doorway leading to the Great Hall, but she forced herself to resist the temptation to flee indoors as fast as she could run.

'I fear your imagination rivals Hester's, sir,' she told him stiffly. 'I do not care to listen to such nonsensical ideas. May we return to the house? I find it colder than I thought.'

She heard a cynical laugh.

'I suspected that we should have a frost before morning,' he chuckled. 'Allow me to lead you back to safety.' He took her hand and tucked it into his pocket, keeping her fingers entwined in his. 'Better?' he asked smoothly. 'It distresses me to find you cold.'

Elinor was furious, both with him and with herself. She had been lured into dropping her guard for the briefest of moments, only to find herself the object of his lordship's unwelcome attentions.

She could think of no set-down crushing enough to express her feelings. As they reached the hallway she tore her fingers from his grasp and hurried to her room.

CHAPTER FOUR

By the following morning Elinor had come to a decision. If she and Lord Rokeby were to continue to deal together she must take good care never to be left alone with him.

His attitude towards her was impossible to understand, though she suspected that it amused him to attempt to put her out of countenance with his advances.

Such behaviour was unworthy of a gentleman, she thought bitterly. Her affection for Hester had made it impossible for her to leave the girl, and well he knew it. It was cruel of him to use that knowledge to pay her out for her evident dislike of him. She clenched her fists. It would take a stronger man than Rokeby to break her.

Feeling as she did, it went much against the grain to wear the amber gown that he had chosen, but the feast that day was clearly the occasion of the year for the staff and tenants of Merton Place and the Charlbury estate. Some effort would be expected of her, and of Hester too. She was being well paid for her services, though Rokeby had assured her that she would earn every penny of her allowance. She was beginning to believe him.

And the gown itself was beautiful, she could not deny it. Caught high beneath her bosom with a self-coloured satin ribbon, it fitted her to perfection, and the glowing colour emphasised the whiteness of her skin. She glanced at herself in the long dressing mirror, fearing that she might be over-dressed for what was, after all, a country gathering.

She could not think it so. Though the fabric was rich, the style was simple and she gave a wry smile. Such classic elegance came at a high price. She turned to Hester.

'Ready, my dear?'

'Miss Temple, do I look. . .?'

'Hester, you look charmingly.'

It was not quite true, though Hester's gown became her as nothing she had yet worn. Sadly it could not disguise the look of terror in her eyes. Her hunted expression had returned.

'I. . .I don't know. . . There will be so many people and I do not know them. . .'

'You know some of them,' Elinor encouraged. 'The Charlburys are to bring Sebastian and Crispin, and the girls were kind to you. . . You will not tell me that you are afraid of their mamma, or of John Charlbury?'

'No. . .' It was a reluctant admission. 'But, Miss Temple, did you see the tables? There will be hundreds come to dine.'

'All you need do is to smile and bid them welcome. Some may be shy and ill at ease. We should think of them. Now let us go down before the guests arrive.'

Hester was thoughtful as she moved towards the door. It had not occurred to her that others might feel as timid as she did herself. As she stepped on to the landing her foot caught a small package.

'Oh, look!' she cried. 'This is for me and there is another for you.'

Hester tore at the wrapping and drew out a small pearl bracelet, clearly chosen to match her necklace.

It came with his lordship's good wishes at the festive season.

Elinor opened her own gift with misgiving. She had not expected it and would prefer to have returned it unopened, but with Hester's eager gaze upon her she could not ignore it.

'Oh, Miss Temple!' Hester caught her breath. 'That is exquisite. . .'

Elinor looked down at the fine Kashmir shawl which nestled in its wrapping. Hester had not exaggerated. It was the loveliest thing she had ever seen. Fine and warm, the rich colours were an excellent choice to complement her gown.

'See, there is a note for you.' Chester handed her a card.

As Elinor read it she felt her colour rising. 'I would not have you cold' was the message. It was unsigned.

She laid both card and shawl upon her bed and turned away.

'Will you not wear it?' Hester questioned in surprise.

'I have no need of it at present.' Elinor tried to keep her tone impersonal. It would not do to give vent to her true feelings. 'In a large gathering I am like to feel overheated.'

That was no lie. She felt ready to explode with rage. How like Rokeby to accompany his gift with a clear reference to their conversation on the terrace. He was a master of innuendo, but she would ignore it.

'I must not forget my present for his lordship.' Hester picked up the neatly wrapped book. 'I think I had best give it to him now.'

Elinor felt incapable of further speech as she followed her charge downstairs. She longed to run away, to hide, anything to avoid all further contact with her lascivious employer. Instead, she accompanied Hester to the library.

Rokeby gave her a quizzing look as Hester handed him the package. Then, as he opened it, his expression changed.

'Montaigne?' he said. 'How clever of you, Hester! I have searched for a copy of this book.'

'Miss Temple chose it,' Hester told him shyly.

'Did she, indeed? Then it is a joint gift, though I see that she scorns to wear my own. . .'

'I am not cold,' Elinor said shortly, then bit her tongue.

'Really?' His eyes were dancing. 'I am delighted to hear it. In the meantime, I must thank both of you for this kind thought.'

Elinor felt anything but kind. She had not thanked him for the shawl, which she had every intention of returning to him, but she could not express her displeasure in front of Hester.

At that moment the Charlburys were announced, followed by a long procession of tenants, and Elinor took her place in the receiving line, with Rokeby by her side.

To her surprise he had dropped his provoking manner. He welcomed each family with enthusiasm, remembering the names of all their children without apparent effort, and urging them all to eat and drink their fill. As forelocks were tugged and curtsies dropped Elinor felt that the line would never end, but finally all were seated.

The tables were a splendid sight. Great glazed hams lay side by side with roasted geese and turkeys. Pies and pasties in abundance filled the gaps between, whilst creams and syllabubs and jellies stood in waiting on the side. Barrels of ale had been broached and were in readiness, but the bowls of punch were universal favourites.

Elinor watched in awe as the food began to disappear. She had not thought it possible that the tables could be cleared so fast, but as the hams were reduced to a single bone, and the poultry to a few fragments, the dishes were replaced with joints of beef and mutton.

Beside her Henry Charlbury chuckled. 'The English were ever the best of trenchermen, Miss Temple. Their meat consumption is the envy of Europe.'

'They look well on it,' she smiled.

'It gives them stamina, that is certain. We shall be longing for our beds before the night is ended, I assure you.'

He was right. Toasts to their employers followed the end of the meal, and both Rokeby and Henry Charlbury responded with grace and humour. Then the tables were cleared away and the musicians struck up in the gallery.

'Shall you care to join in the country dance, Miss Temple?' John Charlbury was by her side.

'I think not, thank you. Perhaps Hester?' Elinor looked across the room, but Hester, regardless of her finery, was bobbing for apples, cheered on by Sebastian and Crispin.

'Oh, dear!' Elinor gave him a rueful look. 'Her gown will be ruined, I fear.'

'Is that so important?' He took her arm. 'Miss Winton is at her ease with children. It is pleasant to see her enjoyment.'

'You like her, don't you?' Elinor asked impulsively.

'I do indeed, Miss Temple. When she comes out of her shell she is a joy.'

'Hester is underrated, but you, at least, seem to understand. Now as to your offer to join in with the dancing...?'

'A pleasure!' He gave her his arm and led her into the centre of the floor.

It was long since Elinor had enjoyed herself so much, and her delight increased at the sight of the smiling faces round her. Then, as she went through the figures of the dance, she glanced across the room. Rokeby was watching her intently. As she caught his eye he raised his glass to her in an ironic toast.

Elinor did not acknowledge it. When the music ended she pleaded lack of breath, and went to sit by Mrs Charlbury.

Rokeby, she noted, was now deep in conversation with Anne. The girl was looking up at him with what could only be described as adoration. Elinor looked at Mrs Charlbury, wondering if she too had seen the expression on her daughter's face. She was not left long in doubt. The older woman shook her head as she patted Elinor's hand.

'Don't trouble yourself, Miss Temple. Anne is suffering from hero-worship.'

Elinor blushed as she made a hasty disclaimer.

'Ma'am, I hope you do not think... I meant no... criticism.'

'Of course not. You are much too kind for that, but I believe you are a little disturbed. Marcus is a charming creature, isn't he? Yet Anne is not the wife for him.'

Elinor was overcome with embarrassment. She had

been indiscreet. In future, she must keep a closer guard upon her expression.

'First love can be an agony,' the older woman continued. 'Poor Anne is in the throes, but she will recover.' She surprised a question in Elinor's eyes. 'You are wondering, perhaps, why her father and I would never countenance such a match?'

'Ma'am, I beg of you... There is no need to explain.' Elinor felt acutely uncomfortable. On the surface, Rokeby appeared to be a welcome visitor in the Charlburys' home, but perhaps his neighbours were well aware of the darker side of his character.

'Miss Temple, I hope that you do not mistake me. Marcus is like another son to Charlbury and myself. His weaknesses are far outweighed by his virtues, but Anne is too young for such a man as he. Nor has she the strength of character to match him. We are thinking of his happiness as well as Anne's.'

'He is lucky in his friends,' Elinor said with feeling. 'You are very good to him.'

'And he to us. He is a sensible man. To give him credit, he does not encourage Anne above the common ties of friendship.'

Elinor's expression grew wooden, and her companion smiled.

'I see that you are not in charity with him, my dear. That is unfortunate, but you will grow to know him better. He can be the most provoking creature in the world, and he has a love of mischief.'

'I had noticed,' Elinor said bitterly.

'But you will handle him. It is a blessing that you are here with Hester.'

'I could not leave her, ma'am.'

'Of course not. Marcus would be lost without your

help, yet I believe that this business of his ward will be the making of him.'

'Ma'am?'

Mrs Charlbury chuckled. She seemed about to speak and then she changed her mind.

'You think the responsibility. . .?'

'Yes, my dear. Now let us rescue Hester before she is quite drowned in the apple barrel.'

As the ale flowed and the punch bowls emptied, the noise in the room increased. Rokeby, Elinor noted without surprise, was in the middle of a kissing ring, holding a sprig of mistletoe above his head. She skirted carefully past the group, hoping that he had not seen her. The prettiest of the village girls was in his arms, and he was saluting her with relish.

Elinor made her way to Hester's side.

'Are you quite soaked?' She asked the kneeling girl.

Hester raised a glowing face. 'It is only water, Miss Temple. It won't stain.'

'But it is cold water, Hester. You must not catch another chill.' Her smile belied her anxious look.

'Oh, don't take her away, Miss Temple. Hester is the winner.' Sebastian, as always, was ready to champion his ally.

'She shall return directly,' Elinor promised. 'But, Hester, I believe you should change your gown. I will go with you.'

Obediently, Hester rose to her feet. It was the work of a few moments to help her strip off the sodden garment, and once attired in lavender muslin Hester was anxious to be off again.

'May I go now?' she pleaded.

'Very well, my dear, but I believe you should suggesr

hunting the slipper, or some game which will keep you dry.'

Hester nodded and ran out of the room.

There was no need to ask if she were enjoying herself, Elinor thought with relief. She had never seen Hester look so animated. Children's games were not, perhaps, an ideal preparation for her London season, but at least she had forgotten her shyness among strangers.

Elinor turned to the pier-glass. The energetic country dancing had loosened her piled-up hair. As she pinned it back into place, she noticed that it seemed almost chestnut in the candle-light. She pulled a face at her reflection. It was the effect of the amber gown again. She shrugged, and gathered up her reticule.

In the corridor outside her room the candles burned low in their sconces and the light was dim. In the distance she could hear continuing sounds of revelry, but the west wing was far from the Great Hall.

She caught up her skirt preparatory to descending the staircase. Then she jumped as a figure stepped from one of the embrasures.

'Did you think to escape me?' Rokeby had one hand beneath his back. 'I am come to claim my due.' He raised his hand above her head, and looking up she saw the pearly berries glistening.

Elinor stepped back in dismay. Her heart had begun to pound. There was no way she could escape him in the empty corridor.

'My lord, this is childish. Allow me to pass if you please.' To her relief her voice was steady, and even cool.

'But this is the festive season,' he protested in feigned indignation.

'I believe that you find all seasons festive, sir.' Elinor moved as if to pass him, but he caught her by the waist.

'There is much to be said for festivity, or do you not find it so? I thought you enjoyed the dancing.'

'I did, sir, because I was treated with courtesy by all.'

'None would challenge the ice-maiden?'

'Lord Rokeby, you have a mistaken idea of my character. Is it too much to ask that you treat me with respect? That much, surely, is due to a woman in my position.'

'But, my dear, I am your slave. . .'

Elinor lost her temper. 'That is exactly what I mean,' she cried hotly. 'You persist in talking non-sense. I do not like it, sir.'

'You find me repellent, Miss Temple?'

'I can have no opinion on that subject.' Elinor stood rigid within his grasp.

'What a bouncer! And you a model of rectitude! Come now, admit it! You think me a loose fish?'

'I do not understand that expression.'

'Then allow me to explain. It refers to one who has no moral principles.'

Elinor was silent, though it cost her much to bite back her reply. She longed to tell him exactly what she thought of his behaviour from the moment of her arrival.

'Careful!' he advised. 'I fear you will explode! Have you no urge to reform me?'

'None whatever, sir. In my opinion you are beyond reform. . .'

'Unkind!' he reproved. 'Must I remind you that this is the season of good will to all men, including me?' There was no mistaking the glitter in his eyes.

'You will please to let me go,' she said stiffly.

'Certainly, my dear, when we have observed this charming tradition. . .' He twirled the sprig of mistletoe between his fingers. 'It is but once a year, you know. I may have long to wait before you grant me another kiss.'

'You should save your kisses for those who may want them, Lord Rokeby. I'm sure there is no shortage of willing candidates.' Her voice was icy.

'And you do not care to be one of many? That is understandable. . .' The amusement in his voice made her long to strike him.

'Miss Temple, delightful though I find this tryst, may I remind you that we should join the others. Our absence may give rise to comment.' He was laughing at her again. She saw the gleam of white teeth against the tanned skin.

'The remedy is in your hands,' she snapped.

Incautiously she lifted her chin, and he bent his face to hers. Elinor turned her head, and his lips merely grazed her cheek.

'Ungenerous!' he murmured. One hand came up to cup her face and his mouth came down on hers.

In that moment the world was forgotten. The touch of his warm flesh against her own caused a tide of fire to course through Elinor's blood. Unconsciously she clung to him. Her head was spinning and her legs refused to support her. She was suffocating. . .drowning in delight, and she seemed to have no will of her own.

He released her at last, and held her away from him.

Elinor opened her eyes to see a strange expression on his face. It was a mixture of shame and vulnerability.

'I'm sorry!' he said abruptly. 'That was ill done of me. I should not have used you so.' He turned on his heel and left her.

Elinor ran back to her room. She closed the door and stood with her back to it, trembling in every limb. Rokeby's kiss had shaken her to the very core of her being. For the first time she had beome aware of the true nature of passion. At last she could begin to understand his lordship's obsession with the opposite sex. Flesh against flesh, she thought in awe. She had not suspected that it could lead to such delight.

Her face burned at the direction her thoughts were taking. Could Rokeby possibly be right? He had accused her once of latent sensuality...something about her mouth, she recalled. She had proved him right, she realised to her own disgust. Her surrender to his lips had been that of a wanton.

The memory of her own behaviour made her squirm. She must have disgusted him, else he would not have apologised so quickly. How could she ever face him again? Yet she must do so, and the others too.

Slowly she bathed her face and hands. The cold water served to bring her to her senses, and some of her judgment returned. Was she not making a great piece of work about nothing? One kiss beneath the mistletoe at Christmastide? It was not so very wonderful to find herself enjoying it. And Rokeby was experienced with women...none more so. He had known how to give her pleasure, as he had done with countless others. He had spent much of the evening saluting every female in the room.

But had they felt as she did, or returned his kiss with such abandon? She could not think so. Some spark had flashed between herself and Rokeby in that tender moment, and she was too honest to deny it, though it was difficult to define. Was it simple lust? Her mind recoiled from the idea. Whatever that strange emotion was that disturbed her so must be crushed out of existence.

Her expression was wooden as she made her way downstairs. At that late hour the crowd of revellers was thinning fast.

At the far end of the hall she could see Rokeby's tall figure standing by the open doorway as he bade his guests farewell.

Elinor looked round for Hester. If she could find the girl they might retire before Rokeby came to join them.

'Over here, Miss Temple.' John Charlbury's voice drew her towards a small knot of people who were chatting by the dying embers of the fire. Hester stood among them smiling, but clearly ready for her bed. Beside her Crispin and Sebastian were asleep on an oaken settle.

'A successful day, I think, my dear.' Mrs Charlbury's bright eyes searched Elinor's face. 'You have found it tiring?'

'I must confess that I envy Crispin and Sebastian.' Elinor looked down at the sleeping boys. 'But I believe that everyone has enjoyed the celebration.'

'Indeed they have, and so have I. It is pleasant to see so many old friends. . .and our new ones. . .'

Elinor was quick to thank her.

'We shall be away as soon as my husband has bidden everyone goodbye. Meantime, my dear, will you sit with me for a moment? My spirit is willing to continue standing, but my feet are not.'

Mrs Charlbury perched on the settle beside her boys and made a place for Elinor.

'I hope we shall see you soon,' she said.

'I cannot promise, ma'am, much as it would please me. I believe Lord Rokeby intends us to move to London shortly. There is much to do before Hester makes her début.'

'But you will not go before the start of the new year?'

'I cannot say. We are quite at his lordship's disposal.'

Something in her voice caused the older woman to give her a sharp look, and Elinor was aware of it. She made an effort to retrieve her composure. 'Shall we see you in London for the Season, ma'am?' she asked.

Mrs Charlbury chuckled. 'I see you do not know my husband yet, Miss Temple. To suffer the rigours of a London season is his idea of purgatory. He finds that he cannot work upon his book, and he will not be parted from his library.'

'You do not mind, I think. You and he seem always to be in such accord. . .'

'Mind? I welcome his decision. Apart from the expense, I would not have my girls exposed to flattery and temptation.'

'I could wish that Lord Rokeby felt the same,' Elinor mused. 'I cannot believe that Hester if ready for a season.'

'This case is different, Miss Temple. Hester is an heiress, and Marcus wishes to do his best by her.'

Elinor was silent. She could not bring herself to agree. Rokeby, she was certain, wished only to rid himself of all responsibility for his ward.

'And a season would not serve for Anne,' Mrs Charlbury continued. 'She has not expressed the least desire for such a thing, which is a relief to her papa and myself.'

Anne had already found her love, Elinor thought in dismay. She had eyes for no one but Rokeby.

'Yet we are not to be quite unrepresented in the great world, so I hear.' Mrs Charlbury did not trouble to hide her amusement. 'This is the first time that John has expressed a wish to visit London for the Season.'

'Oh, I am so pleased! At least we shall have one friend. . .'

'You will find another in Lady Hartfield, I believe. Are you not to stay with her?

'Do you know her, Mrs Charlbury? Lord Rokeby warned me. He described her as. . .er. . .top-lofty.'

'Letitia brooks no nonsense from him. He has had the rough edge of her tongue. She believes him lacking in his duty to the family. He has no nursery yet, you see.'

'Does she not find it strange to think of him as Hester's guardian?'

Mrs Charlbury crowed with laughter. 'She insisted on it. Perhaps I should not mention it, but he did his best to persuade her to relieve him of the charge. She would have none of it.'

'She sounds formidable,' Elinor murmured.

'I doubt if you will find her so. You and she will deal together extremely, I imagine.'

Elinor twinkled at the older woman. 'Two managing creatures together, ma'am?'

'I believe you will always do what you feel to be right, my dear, and so does Letitia.'

'Let us hope that our judgment of what is right happens to coincide...' Elinor rose to her feet as Henry Charlbury came towards his wife.

'Shall I ask Robert and Jem to carry the boys out to your coach, sir?' Elinor raised a hand to signal to the waiting footmen.

'No need, my dear. John and I will manage these sleeping beauties.' Henry Charlbury lifted Crispin from the settle and smiled across at Hester. 'My sons are in your debt, Miss Winton. They won't forget your kindness to them on this night.'

Hester blushed and nodded. She was disconcerted to be singled out for praise, but she thanked him with more assurance than Elinor had thought possible.

Elinor herself felt as shy as any school-miss as Rokeby came to join the group. She could not look at him, and was thankful when he addressed his words to Hester.

'Say your farewells, my dear. There is no necessity for you to wait up longer. Mrs Charlbury will excuse you.'

It was a clear dismissal, and Elinor could only feel relieved. She needed time to think, and to recover her composure in his lordship's presence. She hurried her charge away.

Hester was too tired to talk. She was asleep almost before her head touched the pillow, leaving Elinor a prey to her own turbulent thoughts. Rokeby's kiss meant nothing, she decided. He was simply following the old Yuletide tradition. It was her own reaction to it which had disturbed her so. She, who had always been so sure that she knew herself well, knew now that she was mistaken, but those hitherto unsuspected yearnings must be crushed.

And Rokeby did not know of her dismay. She would take care to hide it from him, pretending that she had accepted his embrace in the spirit in which it was given.

It would not be easy to convince him of her indifference. Too distant a manner would suggest the matter of too much importance. Neither should she be too friendly, else he might imagine that she had mistaken his intentions.

Her face grew fiery. Now she regretted her decision to stay with Hester. The child would doubtless have done quite well in the care of Lady Hartfield. A moment's reflection convinced her that she was being selfish. Bonds of affection tied her to Hester, and they could not be broken for her own convenience. She had given her word, and she must abide by it.

She would stay, but who knew at what cost?

CHAPTER FIVE

THE baying of hounds aroused her on the following day. Throwing aside her coverlet, she hurried to the window to find the meet assembled on the gravel drive before the house.

Rokeby, resplendent in hunting pink, was prominent among them. Glass in hand, he was laughing with his friends, some of whom she recognised. As the last of the stragglers joined them, the hunt moved off.

Elinor sighed with relief, guessing that his lordship would be away for most of the day. After a disturbed night she was glad to return to her bed for another hour or so.

It was not until almost noon that she was roused again by the arrival of her breakfast tray. Absently she nibbled at a roll, only half attending to Hester's chatter.

'Miss Temple, was my guardian cross with me last night, do you suppose?'

'I doubt it, Hester. Why do you ask?'

'When he came to say goodnight, I thought he seemed a little strange. . .I mean, he sent me off to bed so sharply. . .'

'He saw that you were tired, that is all.'

'I thought he might be angry because I played games with the children instead of joining in the dancing.'

'I don't believe he noticed. There were many people with claims upon his attention.'

'Then that's all right.' Hester's face cleared. 'I

should not care to make him angry, but I don't know how to dance.'

'Hester, what a bouncer! Did you not take part with the others in the dancing classes at school?'

'No, I hid. No one wished to be my partner, you see.'

'You will soon learn, my dear. You have such a love of music. That will set your toes tapping once you are shown the steps. Now let us dress. We are slug-a-beds today.'

'May we go out for a walk?' Hester asked eagerly. 'Sebastian says there is a grotto at the entrance to the wood. The inside is full of shining crystals and some-times it is lit by candles when there is an evening party.'

'It sounds delightful.' Elinor glanced through the window at the lowering sky. 'You must wear a warm pelisse and take your muff. I fear we shall have snow before the day is out.'

The grotto was all that Sebastian had promised, but it was too cold to linger. Elinor drew her cloak about her as they began to walk back to the house. Then she heard the sound of a horseman at full gallop. At the sight of his strained face she broke into a run.

'Stop!' she cried. 'What is it?'

'It's Rokeby, ma'am. He's injured.'

'Go ahead and warn Bates. How bad is it?'

'His leg is broke, but that's not the worst of it. He is unconscious.'

'Then will you ride on for the surgeon?'

The man nodded. He was away before Elinor and Hester reached the house. They found a scene of confusion, with the servants milling about.

Elinor dismissed the servants about their business except for Bates and Mrs Onslow.

'How will they bring Lord Rokeby home? she asked.

'The grooms have taken a gate. Oh, ma'am, it does sound very bad. . .' Mrs Onslow's face crumpled.

'Let us not imagine the worst until we know the extent of Lord Rokeby's injuries,' Elinor comforted. 'The surgeon will need hot water and clean cloths. Will you see to it?'

Wiping her eyes, the woman hurried away.

Bates looked very white. 'His lordship's father was killed on the hunting field, Miss Temple. He, too, was brought home in the same way. . .'

'Lord Rokeby is still alive,' Elinor said firmly, as she took a decanter from a side table. 'Drink this, Bates, and remember that his lordship will have need of all your help.' She forced the glass into his hand.

He downed the spirit quickly, and some of his colour returned. 'I hear them coming, ma'am.'

Elinor followed him to the door to see a small procession of men moving towards the house. At each end of the gate the grooms were sweating under their burden.

As they passed into the hall and she caught sight of Rokeby, Elinor's heart sank. Above the torn and muddied coat his face was ashen and there was no sign of life.

'Upstairs!' she ordered. 'Lay him on his bed as gently as you can. Bates, when you and his lordship's man remove his clothing you must try not to move him more than is absolutely necessary. The surgeon will soon be here. . .'

She looked again at the inert figure. There was a

huge lump on Rokeby's forehead, which was already turning blue. He must have fallen forward, she surmised. At least his neck did not appear to be broken.

'Ma'am?'

Elinor turned to stare into the eyes of a very young man. She had last seen him in the hall on the night of her arrival. Now he looked very different from the gay cavalier who had been intent on chasing his quarry up the stairs.

'Ma'am, if there is anything I can do to help. . .?'

'You might begin by telling me exactly what has happened, sir.'

'I don't know.' His face was miserable. 'The hedge was high, and there is a ditch on the other side, but Rokeby knows it well. He could not have been attending. . . We heard a thud, and he was down with the horse on top of him.'

Elinor laid a hand upon his arm. 'If you care to wait the surgeon will tell us more. . .'

'Thank you. I confess I cannot understand it. Marcus is such a bruising rider. . .'

'Then you shall not tease him when you see him, else he will be badly mortified.' Elinor forced a smile which belied her own misgivings.

She seized upon the arrival of the surgeon with relief, but it was a sombre crowd which gathered in the hall.

'I could tear up cloths for bandages,' Hester whispered at her side.

'Will you do that, dearest? Mrs Onslow will be glad of your help.' Elinor sensed that the girl was badly shaken by the accident. It would do her good to find some occupation.

'Bates, will you see to the gentlemen? You may fetch out more of the brandy.'

Elinor walked slowly up the stairs and sank on to a seat outside his lordship's bedroom. All her antagonism towards him had vanished. She could think only of that broken body, lying helpless on the makeshift hurdle.

The next hour was the longest of her life. Then the door opened and the surgeon came towards her.

'I have set the leg,' he said. 'But I cannot like his lordship's condition. He has not regained his senses.'

'His neck. . .his backbone. . .?'

'Nothing else is broken, ma'am, but he has taken a nasty blow to the head. I have made him as comfortable as possible. . .but only time will tell if he will make a full recovery.'

'Shall you return today?'

'I cannot do more, I fear. I will see him in the morning. You will stay with him? If there is any change you may send for me at once. No visitors, mind! He must have rest and quiet.'

Elinor nodded, stricken by his grave face.

When Elinor entered the room she found Bates bending over his master's unconscious form. The mud had been washed from Rokeby's face, but his pallor was intense, and the huge lump on his brow had swollen even further.

Bates looked at her with anguish in his eyes.

'He's uttered never a sound, ma'am. Not a murmur or a groan. . .'

'We must be thankful that he wasn't conscious when the surgeon set his leg,' Elinor murmured gently. 'Bates, do you go about your duties. . .I will stay with Lord Rokeby.'

'Did the surgeon say...?' It was a plea for reassurance.

'He will return tomorrow. We are to send for him if there is any change... Meantime, his lordship is not to be disturbed.'

Bates wiped his eyes. Then he turned to Rokeby's valet, who was gathering up a pair of bloodstained buckskins, a shirt which had clearly been cut from his master's person, and a pair of boots which had suffered the same fate.

'You heard Miss Temple, Jervis. Get you gone!' He pushed the man out of the room.

Elinor knelt down beside the bed, praying for some sign of returning consciousness. She took Rokeby's hand in hers and stroked it gently, murmuring to him as she did so, but there was no response. She kept on with her self-appointed task as the leaden hours crawled by. Then Hester crept into the room.

'Mrs Charlbury is here,' she whispered. 'Will you see her? I will stay here.'

'You will call me if you see a change?'

Hester nodded, but she could not hide her agitation.

'Don't worry so, my dear.' Elinor managed a faint smile. 'Had there been any immediate danger the surgeon would have stayed. We can do naught but wait until his lordship recovers his senses.'

Her comments to Mrs Charlbury were less sanguine.

'How is Marcus now?' the older woman asked.

'He looks ghastly, ma'am. The leg is set successfully, but it is his head...' Elinor sat down suddenly, and buried her face in her hands.

'Do not give way, Miss Temple. We are all relying upon you, my dear, but you are tired and shocked. Have you eaten?'

Elinor shook her head.

'Then you shall do so.' Mrs Charlbury removed her cloak. 'My family will spare me for tonight. John may bring my things. . .'

'Ma'am, you are very good, but I have promised to stay with his lordship.'

'And so you shall, but first you must rest. When Marcus comes to himself, you are the person he will wish to see.'

'I doubt it, ma'am.' Slow tears rolled down Elinor's cheeks. 'We do naught but quarrel. It may be that I am to blame for this accident. Last night, you see. . .' She could not go on.

'Such nonsense! You are overwrought, my dear. You shall take a little broth and go to bed.'

It was useless to argue against such determination.

'You will tell Hester?' Elinor murmured in a low voice.

'Yes, yes. . .I am on my way.' Without more ado Mrs Charlbury bustled towards the staircase, leaving Elinor a prey to a myriad of conflicting thoughts.

Of course, it was foolish to imagine that she could have caused Lord Rokeby's thoughts to wander. Hunting accidents happened all too often, even to the best of riders. . .but last night he had looked so strange. Even Hester had noticed it. There must be some other cause. Wearily she pushed her hair back from her brow and sought her room, leaving the tray of food untouched.

There was a hollow feeling in the pit of her stomach, and as she lay in her bed she was consumed by dread. Suppose the worst should happen, and Rokeby did not recover? No, she would not think of that. She pressed her hands against her brow as if by so doing she could dispel such a horrifying idea.

It was true that she had longed to get away from him, but she had never wished his death.

The full difficulty of her situation burst upon her then. With his lordship gone, what would become of Hester? Her tears were very near the surface. She bit her knuckle to force them back, and buried her face in her pillow.

The sound of her name roused her from an uneasy slumber. At first she thought that she was dreaming. Then a hand on her shoulder shook her awake. It was Mrs Charlbury.

'I think you should come at once,' she said. 'Marcus is in high fever.'

Elinor threw a shawl about her shoulders and followed the older woman along the corridor.

Rokeby was no longer lying still and his face was flushed. Groaning, he tossed and turned about the bed, muttering unintelligibly. His dark curls were damp with sweat and when Elinor touched his skin she found it burning hot.

'Bates has sent Robert for the surgeon,' Mrs Charlbury said. 'Meantime, we must do what we can for him. Will you wipe his face whilst I soak more cloths?'

Elinor sponged away the sweat as best she could. 'I wish we could keep him still,' she cried. 'If he thrashes about, the leg must needs be set again.'

It took the combined strength of both women to prevent their patient from rolling on to the injured leg as his restlessness increased.

Elinor looked up with relief as the door opened.

She was expecting to see the surgeon, but Robert brought bad news.

'I could not find him, ma'am. He's attending a confinement. I left a message. . .'

Elinor's heart sank. It might be many hours before the surgeon arrived.

'Do you get dressed, Miss Temple. Robert will help me hold his lordship. We can but keep him as cool as we may.'

Elinor flew back to her room. It took but a few moments to bathe her hands and face. Then she threw on the first gown to hand, and dragged a comb through her hair, scarcely knowing what she was about.

When she returned to Rokeby's room, his struggles had abated. She threw a fearful look at Mrs Charlbury.

'No, he is no worse. In fact, I think his pulse is steadier. Take heart, my dear, we may be over the worst. . .'

Elinor bent her head to hide the tears which would not be denied. She sat beside the bed and again took his lordship's hand in hers.

'He is still unconscious,' she choked out. 'Oh, how I wish the surgeon would arrive. . .'

It was afternoon before her wish was granted, and still her patient seemed unaware of his surroundings.

'The only remedy is to bleed him, ma'am.' The surgeon's face was grave.

'But he has lost so much blood already,' Elinor protested.

A gesture of dismissal sent her out of the room. Perhaps the man was right, she thought in despair. Something must be done to rouse Rokeby from his coma.

She made her way downstairs to find John Charlbury sitting with Hester and his mother.

'Admirable woman!' Charlbury's eyes glowed with approval. 'Thorne told us how you had taken charge when you heard news of the accident.'

'Thorne?' Elinor was mystified.

'The young man who told you what had happened. From now on, ma'am, he is your devoted servant, as are we all.'

'I didn't feel very brave,' Elinor confessed. 'But Hester has been of the greatest help.'

'Miss Temple! All I did was to roll the bandages and sit with my guardian for a little while...' Hester had flushed at the words of praise.

'You kept your head,' Elinor told her gravely. 'No one can ask more.' She turned to Mrs Charlbury. 'Ma'am, I feel we cannot impose upon you further. Your husband and your family...'

'My dear Miss Temple, let us see what the surgeon has to say before I think of leaving you.'

Four pairs of eyes looked up as the door to the salon opened.

'I have taken a pint of blood and I think his lordship is a little easier,' the surgeon announced. 'Keep him quiet—'

'He will live?' Elinor's voice was raw with emotion.

'He is holding his own at present. More I cannot say. Only time will tell.' The man was clearly unwilling to commit himself.

'John shall stay with you for the present,' Mrs Charlbury announced when the surgeon had gone. 'I will return this evening.' She took Elinor in her arms and kissed her cheek. 'Be of good heart, my dear.

Marcus is young and strong. He will come through this.'

Elinor pressed her hand. Then she hurried away before her face betrayed her. The awful suspicion that Rokeby meant more to her than she dared to admit was uppermost in her mind. It was foolish in the extreme to feel as she did, just because her employer had been injured.

What had happened to the self-assured Miss Temple? In the aftermath of a single kiss she had been reduced to a quivering mass of nerves. She, who prided herself upon her common-sense and her ability to handle any situation? She was behaving like an idiot.

Her distress was due solely to the shock of the accident and its possibly appalling consequences, she told herself. Mrs Charlbury was right. Someone must keep up the spirits of the household at this anxious time. She would not fail.

Her resolution was sorely tested when she returned to the sickroom. Rokeby lay still and silent, and his face had taken on a greyish hue. Elinor's heart sank. In profile, the aquiline nose looked sharp and the contusion on his brow seemed more prominent than before.

Elinor laid a hand upon his forehead. It was still hot to her touch, but he did not seem to be sweating quite so much. She sat down by his side and took his hand in hers.

She had heard somewhere that hearing was the last of the senses to fail, and the first to return. She began to speak to Rokebury in a low voice, telling him of her family, her work at the school in Bath, and the visit which she and Hester had paid to Tunbridge Wells.

The wry thought crossed her mind that had Rokeby been himself his eyes might have glazed with boredom at her chatter, but what she said was unimportant. A phrase or even a single word might penetrate his consciousness.

At length she fell silent. It was hopeless. She did not know how long she had been sitting by his lordship's bedside, but her efforts had been in vain.

She gazed in anguish at his face. If only he would speak or give some sign that he was aware of her presence, she would forgive him everything.

The door opened softly and Bates came into the room.

'Ma'am, will you not rest? His lordship must be washed and changed.'

Elinor nodded and attempted to withdraw her hand. A convulsive shudder ran through her patient as he gripped her fingers with surprising strength.

'My lord?' She was on her feet in a second to bend over him.

Rokeby's lips were moving, but she could not distinguish the words. She put her ear to his mouth.

'Don't go!' The blue eyes flickered open. 'I want you here. I don't know why. . .'

'I won't leave you.' Elinor found that she was shaking with relief. She looked across at Bates to find the tears coursing down his cheeks.

'He's come to his senses, ma'am?'

'I believe so.' Elinor's smile was radiant. 'Bates, will you tell the others? And a message should be sent to Mrs Charlbury. . .'

Rokeby's fingers squeezed her hand, and she turned

back to him. His eyes were filled with pain, but a faint smile hovered about his lips.

'Still managing everyone?' he murmured. Then he fell into a deep sleep.

Elinor sat with him for the rest of that long night, but he did not wake again until the early hours.

Elinor was dozing by the light of a shaded candle, her hand still held in Rokeby's grasp when a small sound aroused her. She opened her eyes to find them held in Rokeby's blue gaze.

'Oh, thank God! You are awake! My lord, you should have told me. . .'

'I liked to look at you. . .so peaceful and defenceless.'

'I am not in the least defenceless,' Elinor began hotly. Then she heard a chuckle.

'I see that you are feeling better, sir,' she said in a dry tone. 'I will send for Bates.'

The grip on her hand had tightened. 'Wait! How long have you been sitting here, Miss Temple?'

'I can't recall. . .since some time yesterday, my lord.'

He nodded. 'I thought I sensed you near. What day is this?'

'It is the twenty-eighth day of December. Now, sir, you shall not talk. The surgeon insisted that you must have rest.'

'Damned sawbones! He's naught but a blood-letting leech. No wonder that I feel like something the cat would not give her kittens. . .'

'He set your leg, sir.' Elinor frowned at him. It was clear that his lordship was unlikely to be the best of patients.

Rokeby raised a hand to finger the lump upon his brow. Then he winced.

'Fool!' he cried impatiently.

'Sir?'

'Myself, not you. What of Beau, my horse?'

'He had to be put down, Lord Rokeby. I'm sorry.'

'So am I...for my own folly.' He reached out for the bell-rope.

'What are you doing?' Elinor cried in alarm.

'I want Jervis.'

'For what purpose?' Elinor cried in alarm. She would not put it past him to insist on his valet dressing him and helping him out of bed.

'My dear Miss Temple!' Rokeby raised a quizzical eyebrow.

'Oh, I beg your pardon.' Elinor blushed and fled as Jervis entered the room. There were the calls of nature to be considered. She should have thought of it before and sent for Jervis.

The great house was silent at that early hour as she crept back to her room. The fierce energy which had sustained her for so long had drained away and she felt utterly weary, but her mind was at rest.

She stripped off her clothing, lay down on her bed, and was asleep in seconds.

It was afternoon when she awoke to find Hester by her side.

'The surgeon is here again, Miss Temple. Shall you wish to see him?'

'I think so, Hester. He may tell us what treatment he recommends.'

Hester giggled. 'Lord Rokeby swore at him. He says that he will do exactly as he wishes.'

'Did he indeed? I may have something to say about that. His lordship shall not give us another fright!'

She found the surgeon by his patient's bedside, engaged in fierce argument. Rokeby was refusing to be bled again. At length the man threw up his hands and turned to Elinor.

'I can do nothing more,' he announced stiffly. 'His lordship will not heed my advice.'

'May I have a word in private?' Elinor led him from the room. 'Let us see how he goes on,' she pleaded. 'His lordship is growing agitated. Did you not tell me that he must be quiet?'

'He was ever the worst of patients, I'm sorry to say.' The surgeon would not be mollified. 'I have changed his dressings and examined the leg, but other than that he will not allow of further treatment.'

'At least he is conscious again, and for that we must be thankful—'

'Ma'am, it was due entirely to the blood-letting.'

'I am sure that you are right.' Elinor's tone was conciliatory. 'He looks so much better, sir. Will you not tell me how we should go on? I will see that he follows your instructions.'

The man shot her a sharp look. 'He will heed your advice no more than mine, I fear. When I arrived, he was attempting to persuade his man to help him into a chair.'

'He shall do no such thing,' Elinor said with decision. 'I shall warn him that he may suffer a relapse.'

'I wish you luck, ma'am. If he does so, you may send for me again. Otherwise there is no point in my returning.' With a last angry look he stalked away.

'But, sir, you have not told me—?'

'Rest and quiet, ma'am,' he barked the words over his shoulder. 'That is all you can do.'

When Elinor returned to the sick-room, her patient was unrepentant.

He grinned at her. 'Did you get rid of him?'

'I did, my lord, but he is not best pleased. You were not over-civil. . .'

'Come now, you shall not scold me. I am a sick man. . .'

Elinor saw the gleam of mischief in the blue eyes.

'You will be much sicker if you persist in behaving foolishly,' she retorted. 'I hear that you were planning to leave your bed.'

'Oh, I have no wish to do so if you will stay with me.'

Elinor looked at him straightly. His splendid constitution had served him well. Newly shaven and in a clean night-shirt, he looked a different man from the broken creature of three days ago. His complexion was no longer grey, and the blue eyes were very bright.

Bates came into the room and busied himself in mixing something in a glass. Then he walked towards the bed.

'What's this?' Rokeby said suspiciously.

'You are to take this dose three times a day, my lord.'

'Nonsense! Take it away!' He waved a hand in dismissal.

Elinor reached out for the glass. 'Will you worry us all again?' she asked gently. 'These last few days have not been easy. . .' She held the glass to his lips.

Rokeby swallowed the contents with ill grace. Then he leaned back against his pillows and closed his eyes.

Elinor signalled to Bates to leave them.

It was some moments before Rokeby spoke. 'You must believe there is a curse on Merton Place,' he murmured.

'How so, my lord?'

'Since your arrival you have spent all your time in sick-rooms. . . You must be tired of it.'

'No, sir.' Elinor sought for words. 'I am content.'

'You are easily contented, ma'am. I think you do not ask for much from life.'

Elinor chuckled. 'You are mistaken. I ask a lot.'

'In what way? I have seen no evidence of it.'

'Sir, you must not talk. You are to rest—'

'For God's sake, woman, what else have I been doing? You do not answer my question.'

Elinor considered carefully before she spoke. 'I value friendship and affection,' she said quietly. 'Those, to me, are all important.'

'You do not seek the wilder shores of love?' The self-mockery in his voice surprised her.

'I. . .I do not understand you.'

'Oh, I think you do, Miss Temple.' The blue eyes opened and raked her face. 'I am speaking of an overwhelming passion. . .'

'I know nothing of such things. Sir, shall I ring for Bates? I am sure you have not eaten—'

'Don't change the subject. How old are you, Miss Temple?'

'Sir?'

'I asked how old you were.'

'I am twenty-three. . .though what that has to say to anything. . .?'

'What a waste! How long have you been teaching?'

'I went to Bath four years ago, through the good offices of a friend.'

'You were not begged to stay in Derbyshire?'

'No, my lord. My father agreed that I should go to Bath.'

'I was not speaking of your father, ma'am. You did not leave behind a lovesick swain or two? I can't believe it!'

Elinor smiled. 'I had an offer, sir, but it would not serve.'

'Why not?'

'My affections were not engaged.'

'He was old and fat, and without means?'

Elinor bridled. 'He was my own age, sir, and not ill looking. As to means, he was heir to his father's properties.'

'Then I wonder that your parents did not insist upon your being safely settled.'

'They would not force me,' Elinor cried indignantly. 'Their standards are not yours, my lord.' She was about to say more, but caught herself in time. She must not irritate her patient.

Rokeby seemed untroubled. A mocking smile played about his lips. 'At nineteen you could have been no judge of what was best for you.'

'Perhaps not, but my father is not wanting in judgment. He was happy to allow me to do as I wished.'

'And you have been doing so ever since?' Rokeby gave her a sly look. 'You are young to have such self-command.'

'I am able to look after myself.'

'Indeed you are! It is a source of some disappointment to me, I confess.' His mouth curved.

'Sir, you are making gammon of me, and tiring yourself at the same time. I will leave you now. Jervis will sit with you, but do not, I beg of you, persuade him into folly.'

'I have not the least wish to persuade Jervis into folly, I assure you. Now, as to persuading you. . .?'

Elinor rose to her feet. 'You are quite comfortable?' she asked.

'My pillows. . .they need re-arranging.'

As Elinor bent over him a strong arm slid about her neck, and Rokeby drew her face to his.

As his mouth found hers, the same dizzying sensation assailed her as it had done on Christmas Eve. She struggled to free herself, but he would not release her. Then a tide of love swept over her as the pent-up emotion of the last few days found release. She gave herself up to the pleasure of that kiss with an abandon which shook her to the very core of her being.

Rokeby was murmuring endearments as he rained kisses on her eyelids, her brow, and the tip of her nose. At last she pulled away from him.

'I see that you are much recovered, sir,' she gasped. 'That was unfair! You tricked me!'

'I must be delirious,' Rokeby murmured wickedly. He raised a hand to his head. 'Yes, it is as I thought. I am on the verge of a relapse.'

'Oh, you. . .you. . .you are impossible! Sir, you shall find another nurse—'

'How can you be so cruel? The agony!' Rokeby let out a counterfeit groan. 'Send for the surgeon, I beg of you!' He opened one eye and looked at her.

'He will not come,' Elinor said briskly. 'Nor do I blame him. He is up to all your tricks, and I am learning them to my cost.'

'My dear Miss Temple, how can you rail at a sick man? Please go! These strictures are too much for me.

There is no need to summon Jervis. I shall rest now
. . .alone in my bed of pain. . .'

Elinor began to laugh. She could not help herself.

'Heartless!' Rokeby murmured. 'I knew it from the
first moment I looked at you.'

'And you may believe it, my lord!' Elinor fled.

CHAPTER SIX

THE Charlburys, she knew, were waiting in the salon. Since Rokeby's accident they had paid a daily visit, but she felt unable to face anyone in her present state of confusion.

She slipped along the corridor to the Long Gallery. There she began to pace the floor, striving to come to terms with her own emotions.

Lord Rokeby was becoming a serious threat to her peace of mind. Since Christmas Eve, she had managed to convince herself that she was making far too much of a single kiss, stolen beneath the mistletoe. Since the day of her arrival she had been so stiff and prim with him. For a man of his temperament it was only to be expected that he would try to tease her into losing her composure. And he had succeeded. The knowledge had angered and disturbed her.

Yet as she sat beside his bed, looking at his still unconscious form, she had vowed to forgive him anything if only he would speak. By now she knew every detail of that swarthy face, from the strong line of his jaw to the curving, mobile mouth. She had brushed away the damp curls which clustered on his brow as he lay in fever, and held his hand until her own had ached from the fierceness of his grip as he writhed in pain.

A wry smile played about her lips. She had prayed for his recovery, and today he had given her proof that he was on the mend.

She should have been furious, but she couldn't find it in her heart to censure him! It was a joy to see the twinkle once again in those blue eyes, but she was honest enough to admit that her own reaction to his kiss had not been one of unmixed relief at his recovery.

She had enjoyed it, and therein lay the danger. Bored and confined to his bed, Rokeby was merely amusing himself, but her own reaction had been far from casual. He now occupied her mind to the exclusion of all else, and the sensation was new to her.

She turned at the end of the gallery and glanced up at the portraits which lined the walls. Those same blue eyes had been in the Rokeby family for generations. Now they seemed to follow her as she moved past, some indifferent to her predicament, some disapproving, some amused, and some filled with the light of mischief which she had grown to know so well.

She stopped before a portrait of Rokeby's father and looked up at him.

'You have much to answer for, my lord,' she scolded aloud. 'The sooner your son is wed and settled down, the better for his family.'

It was strange that the thought gave her no pleasure when it was clearly the sensible answer to her own problems. With Rokeby safely married to some charming girl, his suitability as guardian to his ward could no longer be in doubt. Rather than marrying off Hester, she might become a part of his household. Then she herself would be free to pick up the threads of her own life.

It was an oddly depressing idea. Elinor frowned. It was what she wanted; indeed, she had longed for the chance to do so, and the day must come when she would be forced to face her future alone. Better sooner rather than later, she thought to herself. She was becoming too involved with the inhabitants of Merton Place.

'Oh, here you are!' Hester walked towards her. 'Are you not cold in here, Miss Temple?'

'No, I have been walking. I was stiff after sitting by his lordship's bedside for so long.' Her excuse sounded reasonable enough. Apart from its function as a portrait gallery, the long chamber had been intended as a place for taking exercise in inclement weather.

'Mrs Charlbury would like to see you,' Hester said shyly. 'She is here with Mr John.'

Elinor gathered her scattered thoughts. For the moment there was nothing she could do about the problems which faced her. Rokeby, as far as she knew, had, as yet, no thoughts of marriage. He would be incapacitated for some time, and might even be forced to put off Hester's début until the following year.

She was soon disillusioned. As she entered the salon Mrs Charlbury's quick eyes noted her heightened colour and her glowing looks but she made no comment.

'I have seen Marcus,' she began. 'He has written to Lady Hartfield explaining that your arrival in London is like to be delayed. Meantime, he suggests that Hester takes dancing lessons from Monsieur Gaston in Tunbridge Wells.'

Elinor nodded her assent.

'I hope you don't think I was interfering,' Mrs Charlbury added. 'Marcus asked me for the name of the man who taught my girls—'

'Not at all, ma'am,' Elinor disclaimed quickly. 'I do not know the town. I could be of no help in such matters.'

'The town bronze must wait for Lady Hartfield's expert guidance, but Hester is a pretty-behaved girl. There will be no difficulty. . .'

'Then his lordship is determined?' Hester looked alarmed.

'Come, Miss Winton, you will not deprive me of the pleasure of your company in London? Had we not decided to sail upon the river and visit the Tower?' John Charlbury pleaded.

Hester nodded, but she was not altogether reassured.

'And, with Monsieur Gaston's permission, John shall come and partner you,' Mrs Charlbury promised.

'Always providing that you do not mind a partner with two left feet.' A chuckle accompanied John Charlbury's words.

'Marcus seems to be in spirits today.' Mrs Charlbury looked at Elinor with affection. 'It is all due to your devoted nursing, my dear.'

Elinor blushed. 'His lordship has a splendid constitution. . . We are all so thankful that the worst is over.'

John Charlbury gave a shout of laughter.

'Optimist!' he cried. 'Your troubles are just beginning, Miss Temple. He has just assured my mother that he is ready to come downstairs. . .'

'Oh, no!' Elinor rose to her feet in dismay. 'Ma'am, I hope you advised him that it was out of the question?'

She moved to the door, intending to return to the sick-room. Then she remembered. She had made up her mind that she would not be left alone with Rokeby again.

'Will you not speak to him?' she asked John Charlbury.

'I will do my best, Miss Temple, but I fear that we shall lose this battle, at least within a day or two.' Still laughing, he left the room.

'Now do not upset yourself, my dear.' Mrs Charlbury patted her hand. 'Marcus is impatient with his own weakness, but if we threaten him with a setback. . .'

'Doubtless he will announce that we are talking nonsense,' Elinor said ruefully. 'Ma'am, he really is—!'

'Yes, he is, isn't he? But that is Marcus. Do your best with him, Miss Temple. He will not wish to distress you or add to your worries, I believe.'

Elinor was not so sure.

By dint of summoning the younger Charlburys to play cards with his lordship, by persuading Hester to read to him, and allowing John to chat to him by the hour together she managed to confine her patient to his bed for the next few days.

Anne and her mother were with him, together with the younger Charlbury girls and Hester, as Elinor walked past his door. Gales of laughter sounded from the room, but Elinor did not enter. She felt oddly excluded from that merry crowd, but it was of her own doing.

Since the day he had slipped an arm about her neck and kissed her, Elinor had taken care never to be alone with Rokeby. That he was well aware of her decision she had no doubt.

She had seen the glint in his eyes as he looked at her, but he had not referred to the fact that when she entered his room she was not alone.

As the days passed and he grew stronger, she had

cut down upon her visits to the sick-room, restricting them to a brief daily greeting, and an enquiry as to his health. Forestalling any remonstrations, she had pleaded the need to supervise Hester's dancing lessons and her deportment classes. Rokeby had nodded and made no comment.

Elinor felt guilty. After his daily visitors had left she had abandoned him to hours of boredom, but it must be for the best, though it wasn't easy. She had learned to look for the way his eyes lit up as she walked into the room, and she missed the banter which was common currency between them.

A week later she was in the salon, playing for the dancers, when the door opened and Rokeby was assisted into the room on the arm of a large footman.

Elinor rose to her feet with a gasp of dismay.

'No, no, don't get up, Miss Temple!' His lordship gave her a smile of charming innocence. 'I heard the music and felt that it was time I bestirred myself to join you. Do please go on.' He settled himself in a chair with the injured leg stretched out before him, and bent a benevolent look upon the startled dancers.

Elinor could have hit him. For one thing he should not be out of bed, and for another his presence was sure to undermine Hester's growing confidence in her ability to learn the complicated steps.

She was right. It was not many moments before Monsieur Gaston threw up his hands in despair.

'Mademoiselle Winton, I beg of you! Please to remember that here you must turn towards your partner. . .'

Hester made several more attempts to follow him, but all to no avail.

The little Frenchman had an inspiration. 'Perhaps if Miss Temple would demonstrate. . .?'

It was the last thing Elinor wished. With Rokeby's cynical gaze upon her she would feel like some houri of the east, performing especially for his benefit.

'Miss Temple?' Monsieur Gaston looked anxious.

'Of course!' Elinor rose from the instrument and held out her hand to the dancing master. A coy refusal would give the matter far too much importance. She went through the dance as Hester watched. Then she returned to her seat, aware that Rokeby had enjoyed her discomfiture.

'Will you assist me, Miss Temple? If I might sit beside you, I could turn the pages of your music. . .?'

Elinor eyed him coldly. 'I fear you might sustain a fall, my lord.'

'I see. You feel perhaps that you are not strong enough to bear with me? Then John shall help me.'

Unaware of the tension between Elinor and her tormentor, John Charlbury set a chair beside the music stool and lifted Rokeby to his feet. Ignoring his lordship's close proximity, Elinor began to play. At least with his attention diverted from herself Hester might recover her composure.

It did not serve, and at length, aware of Monsieur Gaston's increasing agitation, Elinor dismissed him until the following day.

'Miss Winton is a little tired, I fear,' she told him with a smile. 'She will be more herself tomorrow.'

'You do look pale, my dear.' Rokeby raised his quizzing glass to inspect his ward. 'Fresh air is what you need. John shall take you for a turn about the grounds, if he will be so kind.'

'I will go with you.' Elinor stood up. It was a blatant

attempt on his lordship's part to be left alone with her, and she would have none of it.

A strong hand closed about her wrist. 'Will you not spare me a few moments of your time, Miss Temple? We must talk. . .I have some news for you.'

Elinor threw a despairing glance at her companions, but they seemed unaware of the pleading in her eyes. She had no choice but to resume her place on the music stool.

'You should not be here, my lord,' she announced stiffly. 'You will give yourself a set-back.'

'I thought I had already been given one.' Rokeby grinned at her. He was not referring to his broken leg. 'You have been avoiding me, Miss Temple. If Mahomet won't go to the mountain, you know. . .then the mountain must come to Mahomet.'

'Your news, my lord?'

'Ah, yes. I have heard from Lady Hartfield. She suggests that you bring Hester to London without delay.'

Elinor's heart sank. 'Surely there can be no immediate hurry?' she protested.

'I fear there is. You have heard the old saw about "February fill-dyke"? It is only too true. When the spring rains come the roads in these parts will be among the worst in England. It is the Wealden clay, you see. It turns into a greasy mass which clogs the carriage wheels.'

'I see.' Elinor was silent for a time. Then she decided on a last plea to Rokeby's better nature. 'Sir, won't you re-consider your decision? Hester, as you see, is not ready for a season. Perhaps next year. . .?'

'Impossible!' His face was implacable. 'You know my reasons for a wish to see her wed.'

'I do indeed!' she cried bitterly. 'They are for your own convenience!'

'Must you always think so hardly of me?' He lifted her hand and raised it to his lips. At the touch of his warm mouth against her skin, Elinor began to tremble. It took a great effort of self-control not to snatch her hand away. Instead, she allowed it to lie limp within his grasp.

'You give me no reason to think otherwise,' she told him steadily. 'You make every effort to put me out of countenance—'

'You!' He threw back his head and laughed aloud. 'I doubt if I, or any other man, would succeed in doing that. Come, my dear, you do not object to a little chaffing?'

'Sir, you are a trifler!' she burst out in a rage. Disappointment was mixed with anger. She had made a perfectly reasonable request on Hester's behalf, and he had refused it. Now he was back to his old tricks, treating her as if she had been put on earth merely to amuse him.

'A trifler? Surely not with your affections?' He looked at her with half-closed eyes. 'You cannot be at risk from me, the invulnerable Miss Temple? No, it is too much to hope.'

With what dignity she could command, Elinor disengaged herself from his grasp. 'When does Lady Hartfield expect us?' she asked coldly.

'I believe the weather will hold until next week. Shall we say Monday? You will need an escort, but John assures me that he will be happy to oblige. It is strange...this sudden desire of his to visit London for the Season... I can't recall it happening before.'

Elinor could not mistake the mockery in his eyes

and she blushed a fiery red. Surely he did not suspect that John Charlbury hoped to capture her affections? The idea was ridiculous.

'You think highly of him, do you not?' Rokeby's question was apparently casual, but Elinor sensed the tension in him as he waited for her answer. Doubtless he thought her an unsuitable match for his friend. Some imp of mischief prevented her from telling him the truth.

'He is charming, sir. No one could fail to warm to his delightful character.'

She had the satisfaction of seeing Rokeby's expression change. A crease appeared between his brows and his mouth set in a hard line.

'Shall I ring for Robert, my lord?' she asked sweetly. 'You will not wish to sit here alone.'

'Your round, I think, Miss Temple.' Rokeby made a swift recovery, but a spasm of pain crossed his face as he shifted in his chair.

Elinor was beside him at once. 'You will be more comfortable in your bed,' she said more gently. 'My lord, may I not persuade you to take more care, just for a little longer?'

A smile lit his eyes once more. 'You could persuade me of anything, I believe. Well, I suppose it is bed again, but alone, alas!'

Elinor hid a smile. He was incorrigible. 'Bear up, sir,' she said with mock asperity. 'It will not be many weeks before you are able to resume your normal way of life.'

'I doubt it. I have suffered a severe blow to my self-esteem. I shall not be the same again. When you look at me so, I feel like some curious type of insect.'

'What nonsense!' Elinor said robustly. 'If you go on like this, I shall think you suffering from delirium.'

'I have thought so myself, especially when the sun catches your hair as it is doing at this moment. You appear to have a halo, ma'am.'

'That is an illusion, sir. Must you always have the last word?'

'It is some comfort to me,' Rokeby admitted weakly. 'For the moment it is all I have, but I promise you that when I am recovered. . .'

Elinor laughed and pulled the bell-rope. 'Threats will not weigh with me, my lord. Nuncheon shall be sent up to your room. Then, I hope, you will rest.'

'I am like to die of boredom,' he told her with a grim smile. 'I am tired of looking at those four walls.'

'It is trying for you,' Elinor admitted. Then she had an inspiration. 'Sir, it cannot stop you making plans . . .for the estate, I mean. Your time need not be wasted. Only this morning there was some treatise arrived upon the latest seed-drills, and the use of seaweed for manuring land. I could make notes for you as you study it.'

'You would find it a boring task, Miss Temple.'

'Not at all, my lord.' Elinor had noticed the change in his expression. 'You forget that I was brought up in the country, and you are keen to improve the yield of all your crops, are you not?'

His face grew sombre. 'It may be vital to our survival. This peace with Napoleon cannot hold. He intends to make himself master of Europe, including this country. The French will blockade our ports, to starve us into submission.'

'Then there is no time to lose,' Elinor told him

briskly. 'I will fetch the books, and my writing materials.'

At that moment Mrs Charlbury came in through the garden door. 'Marcus, what are you about?' she cried.

'Disobeying orders, ma'am.' His lordship looked so guilty that Elinor was tempted to laugh.

'So I see!' Overriding all his protestations, Mrs Charlbury insisted that he returned to his room at once. Elinor gathered up a pile of books and pamphlets, found a notebook, and followed them.

'There, my lord!' She laid the pile of books beside his bed. 'I shall return directly after nuncheon.'

'I am glad to see that you intend to insist that Marcus does not overtax his strength,' the older woman told her when they were alone. 'I have told my girls that they may not visit him today.'

Anne's reddened eyes told Elinor of her disappointment, and she was moved to pity. 'Perhaps tomorrow?' she suggested.

As the girls departed, Elinor blushed. 'Ma'am, I hope that I did not go against your wishes in suggesting that the girls might come tomorrow?'

'You are thinking of Anne, I believe? Miss Temple, I am much too old a hand to make the mistake of keeping Anne away from Marcus. Nothing is more likely to confirm her notion that she loves him than parental opposition.'

Elinor was silent.

'You do not agree? My dear, Anne would become so obsessed with fighting us that she might forget to consider that she and Marcus are not suited to each other.'

'How wise you are!' Elinor gave her a warm smile. 'We shall miss you, ma'am. We are to leave for

London on Monday. I confess, I cannot be easy about Hester's coming season. She is so shy, you see. It is a torment for her to mix in company and try to be what she is not.'

'Then she should not do so,' Mrs Charlbury said with conviction. 'It is always a mistake to dissemble. Hester is quiet, but she is a charming girl with a loving heart.'

'I know it, but Lord Rokeby is determined that she shall wed as soon as possible. I cannot think it right.'

'Trust him!' her companion advised quietly. 'Marcus is no ogre, my dear. Behind that teasing manner lies a cool head, and much kindness.'

'I hope you may be right.' Elinor felt a little happier. Mrs Charlbury had known Rokeby since he was a child, and she was shrewd. It was unlikely that she could be mistaken in him. Even so, she could not repress a twinge of doubt.

'Now, Miss Temple, you must be strong. Do not allow Marcus to repeat his folly of this morning, however much he tries to browbeat you.'

'I think I have the solution, ma'am. I have offered to become his secretary. He is to give instructions, and I am to write them down.' Elinor smiled in spite of her misgivings. Had she not vowed to avoid his lordship's company unless others were present? Hopefully, he would be too absorbed in his plans for the estate to persist in teasing her.

She was not mistaken. When she returned to his room that afternoon, he was lost in thought. A map of the estate and the open treatise on the new seed-drill lay across his knees.

'There you are!' he said impatiently. 'I thought you were never coming.' He began to dictate at speed.

Elinor was astonished by his quick grasp of the way in which the new methods could be used on his own land, and the clear way in which he defined his plans. Soon she found herself infected by his own enthusiasm, and she forgot the passage of time until it became too dark to see her paper.

'How thoughtless of me! You will ruin your eyes,' Rokeby said suddenly. 'Will you not ring for candles?'

Unthinking, she reached out for the rope which lay beside his bed-head, and was startled when his fingers closed about her wrist.

'No, don't pull away from me,' he murmured in a low tone. 'I wish only to thank you for your kindness. You have borne this dull discourse with a good grace.'

'My lord, I have enjoyed it,' she told him truthfully.

He gave her a smile of indefinable charm. 'You are a woman of many parts, my dear. I confess that today I am more content than at any time since that stupid accident. Why did we not think of this before? It has been a productive afternoon, and I am grateful to you.'

As always, she had found his touch disturbing. 'That is because your mind was occupied with matters which are of use to you, sir.'

'That as much as anything. May we do the same thing tomorrow?'

'Only if you promise to stay where you are, Lord Rokeby.'

'Your wish is my command.' He gave her a mock salute as she left him.

She went downstairs to find Hester in reflective mood.

'Is something wrong'?' she asked.

'No, but I was wondering what Lady Hartfield will be like. She is my guardian's aunt, is she not?'

'She is, but that is no reason for you to be afraid of her. Lord Rokeby is a young man. His aunt's ideas are likely to be very different from his own.'

'A young man?' Hester sounded astonished. 'He seems old to me.'

'As does anyone over the age of twenty, I make no doubt.' Elinor's eyes began to twinkle.

'Oh no, you are not old,' Hester disclaimed hastily. 'Nor is Mr Charlbury.'

'He is the same age as Lord Rokeby,' Elinor teased. 'He must be all of thirty-two, or so.'

'No, he isn't. He's twenty-eight. He told me so himself. . .'

It was becoming clear that Hester's discussions with John Charlbury had progressed from learned matters to others of a more personal nature. A warning bell sounded in Elinor's mind. How stupid she had been in thinking of Hester as a child, not much older than Sebastian or Crispin. It was only to be expected that the girl would develop an affection for their gentle neighbour.

And what a solution that would be, Elinor thought wistfully. Hester would be welcomed into a loving family where she already felt at ease. She wondered that Rokeby had not thought of it. Perhaps he had, only to dismiss the idea out of hand.

For all she knew, he might have suggested the match to John Charlbury already. It seemed unlikely. His friend was no dissembler, and his manner towards Hester was that of an elder brother.

Her main concern was that Hester should not be hurt. The child had suffered enough rebuffs in her

short life. She glanced across at her charge. Hester
met her gaze with such a candid look that Elinor was
satisfied. There was no harm done as yet, but she must
be on her guard.

Mrs Charlbury might be right in supposing that
Anne's passion for Lord Rokeby would fade with
time, but Hester was of a very different temperament.
Once she formed an attachment, she would not
change.

Elinor sighed. She would feel the same herself,
should she ever give her heart to another, but how
was it possible to be sure of one's judgment?

On this very day, for example, she had seen another
side of a man whose character she despised. They had
sat together in pleasant amity for the whole of the
afternoon, and she had liked him better than at any
time since their first meeting. His quick mind had
delighted her, and she had been as absorbed as he in
his plans for the estate.

It did not alter the fact that she found him both
exciting and disturbing. Even so, she found that she
was looking forward to the following day, when she
would be taken into his confidence again.

It was all so confusing, but their time together would
be short. The knowledge should have cheered her, but
she found it strangely depressing.

'We should make a start on our packing,' she murmured. 'The maid will wish to know what we are to
take.'

Hester was startled. 'Shall we return to Merton
Place?'

'I do not know. . .so much depends. . .' The look on
Hester's face caused her to amend her words. 'I mean

that it will depend on Lady Hartfield's wishes,' she said quickly.

'Or if I marry.' Hester's face crumpled. 'Oh, it is all so hateful. I wish that I were dead.'

Elinor hugged her close. 'Don't worry, my dearest. Let us pin our faith on Lady Hartfield. Mrs Charlbury thinks well of her. . .'

Hester would not be comforted. 'She will be exactly like Lord Rokeby,' she wept. 'And I shall hate her.'

CHAPTER SEVEN

IN THAT she was mistaken. Lady Hartfield was a surprise to both Elinor and her charge. Tall and thin, she could never have been a beauty, but her elegance was unmistakable.

A pair of sharp black eyes inspected both ladies and their escort as they walked towards her. Then she smiled and Elinor saw something of her charm.

Her ladyship rose to greet them with an easy grace remarkable in one no longer young, and held out her hands to Hester.

'So you are Rokeby's ward? Welcome, my dear. Miss Temple, I have heard much about you. It is a pleasure to meet you.' She looked enquiringly at the man beside them.

'Lady Hartfield, this is Mr Charlbury, a neighbour of Lord Rokeby. He was kind enough to accompany us.'

'A friend of Marcus? You, sir, appear to have more sense than my great-nephew. At least you are in one piece... How is Rokeby? I trust you left him in better health?'

Charlbury chuckled. 'You need have no worries about him, ma'am. His health is improving, but not, I fear, his temper.'

'Fretting, is he? Serve him right! I take it he was riding *ventre à terre*?'

'It was unfortunate, ma'am—'

'So it was! Well, let us forget him for the moment.'

Her ladyship rang for refreshment, but Charlbury would not stay. He left with a promise to call upon them later in the week.

'A pleasant young man!' Lady Hartfield's gaze rested upon the faces of her companions. Then, apparently satisfied, she began to pour the tea.

'Well, my dears, what are your plans?'

'Your ladyship, we are entirely in your hands.' Elinor smiled at her. Beneath the brisk manner she sensed a kind heart, and she had warmed at once to this ugly woman who exuded such an air of self-confidence.

'What a responsibility!' The older woman made a little moue of mock dismay, and even Hester smiled.

'Rokeby has explained his wishes to you, Hester?'

'Yes, ma'am.'

Lady Hartfield laughed. 'My dear, I promise not to throw you to the lions. A season is not such a very dreadful thing, you know, and you will have Miss Temple with you, as well as myself, to frighten off anyone you may not care to meet.'

'You are very kind, your ladyship.' Hester's voice was colourless and she kept her eyes upon the carpet.

Lady Hartfield shot a speaking glance at Elinor.

'You will have a full two months before you need make your come-out,' she went on. 'We must buy some gowns for you, of course, but you will wish to see something of the London scene. Would Mr Charlbury consent to be our escort? I confess I should like to see more of him. . .'

'Oh, ma'am, would you? He is so kind. I am sure that you will like him.' Hester brightened up at once. 'I thought, you see, that you might not think it right for him to visit us.'

'Great heavens, child! Whyever not? With that handsome creature by our side we shall be the envy of every woman in London.'

Hester smiled her gratitude, but the strain of being thrust into a strange household had taken its toll. She looked very pale.

'Here I am chattering on,' her ladyship announced. 'You must both be tired after your journey. Royston shall show you to your rooms. Now you must forgive me. This evening I have an engagement which I cannot break. Shall you mind if I leave you to your own devices? Dinner will be served at eight, and you will be quite alone.'

Silently Elinor blessed her for her thoughtfulness, guessing rightly that her ladyship's engagement was the result of some deliberation. She realised in surprise that Rokeby must have mentioned Hester's nervousness with strangers to this formidable woman. Whatever his reasons, it had resulted in an act of kindness.

'There now,' she teased when she and Hester were alone. 'Do you still plan to hate her ladyship?'

Hester blushed and shook her head. 'I like her,' she announced. 'She is not in the least what I expected.'

'Nor I,' Elinor admitted. 'I think we shall be happy here, don't you?'

'Oh, yes. . .' Hester considered for a moment. 'She thinks Mr Charlbury handsome, doesn't she? I had not thought of it before.'

'Well, Hester, he is not exactly ill looking. I mean he has neither horns, nor an extra eye in the middle of his forehead.'

Hester began to laugh. 'Miss Temple, you are making game of me,' she reproached. 'I mean. . .well. . .he is just our friend.'

'And a good one. Hester, think of the fun we shall have. We shall drive in the park, and see the sights.'

'And he says that there are balloon ascents.' Hester sighed in ecstasy. 'Of course they depend upon the weather, and it may be summer before we see them. . .'

Hester lay upon her bed. Her eyelids were drooping, and in minutes she was sound asleep.

Elinor heard a gentle tap upon the door, and opened it to find her ladyship standing in the corridor.

'She is asleep?'

Elinor nodded.

'I thought as much, poor child. Will you spare me a few moments of your time?'

Elinor followed her into a pretty boudoir at the end of the corridor.

'We have a task upon our hands, I think, Miss Temple.' Her ladyship closed the door.

Elinor looked at her in some trepidation, but ready with a fierce defence of her charge.

'No, there will be no need to fire up at me,' Lady Hartfield gave her a faint smile. 'I mean to do my best for Hester, but I should be glad of your advice.'

Elinor was disarmed at once. 'Hester is not at her best with strangers,' she admitted slowly. 'She had a bad time at school. She is reserved, you see. . .and then. . .she was never a pretty girl.'

Her ladyship leaned back in her chair, her fingers toying with her fan. 'That is what decided me to take her.'

'Ma'am?' Elinor was startled.

'Ah, looking as you do you will never understand. Beauty is fleeting, so they say, but every woman longs for such a gift. Look at me, Miss Temple. As a child my nickname was "The Maypole".'

'But, ma'am that cannot be. . . You are so—'

'Elegant, my dear? That is my answer to the world. The French term is *une jolie laide*, which is almost untranslatable, but I believe it to mean an ugly beauty.'

Elinor was silent. There was nothing she could say.

'Rokeby was worried about Hester,' the older woman continued. 'He begged me to take over all responsibility for her, but that was not possible. I should have refused in any case. It will do my nephew no harm to have someone else to think of.'

'His lordship is very good to his tenants, Lady Hartfield.' To her own surprise Elinor found herself defending her employer.

'So I should hope. It is his duty. I hear too that his estate is something of a model, but it is not the same thing, you will agree? Marcus knows my views. It is high time he settled down and found himself a wife.'

'Oh, ma'am, you do not think of Hester for him?' It was a tactless remark, but Lady Hartfield did not take it amiss.

'Of course not! Two people more ill suited would be difficult to find. Now you shall not worry about Hester, my dear. I know how fond you are of her, and she shall not be pressed against her will, but it can do her no harm to acquire a little self-confidence and acquire her own style during these next few months.'

'Of course not. But, ma'am, with all respect, you cannot hope to transform her into a woman of fashion. . .I mean. . .she will never look as you do.'

'I should hope not. The art is in being an original. A copy can be nothing but false coin. Now, Miss Temple, will you trust me?'

Elinor gave her a smile of purest gratitude. 'I could wish that you were her guardian, Lady Hartfield.'

'As a woman that would not be possible, my dear. For some reason best known to themselves, the courts believe that females are inferior creatures, incapable of handling either their own affairs or those of anyone else. It is only when one is widowed that one has a little freedom.'

She looked so cheerful about her loss that the words of sympathy died upon Elinor's lips.

'You think me unfeeling? I was married against my will to a man much older than myself. I cannot grieve that that particular trial did not last for many years. . . Now, Miss Temple, you must excuse me. I shall see you in the morning.'

As Elinor returned to her room her mind felt more at ease. Perhaps she had found an ally. Lady Hartfield's experience of marriage might make her more sympathetic to Hester's cause. And at least she was not the dragon that she and Hester had expected.

She found herself wondering if Rokeby knew his aunt as well as he thought he did. Lady Hartfield's idea of a suitable match might not be his own. The ensuing contest was likely to be a battle of the Titans. She was smiling as she entered Hester's room.

Her ladyship was not an early riser and it was not until noon on the following day that they were summoned to her presence. She was sitting up in bed with a most becoming boudoir cap perched upon her head.

'You slept well?' she enquired. 'You both look rested. . . Now Hester, let me look at you in daylight. Walk over to the window, my dear, then turn and come towards me.'

In silence, Hester did as she was bidden.

'Yes, your carriage is good,' the older woman mused. 'It makes you look taller than you are. Your complexion, too, is excellent. Thank heavens that you are not covered in spots. I suffered from them mightily when I was a girl.'

Hester managed a reluctant smile.

'Today I thought we might go shopping,' Lady Hartfield continued. 'We shall not wish to be abroad in the town when Mr Charlbury comes to call, but I believe he mentioned Thursday, did he not?'

'Yes, ma'am.' Hester was all attention. 'I should like to go shopping today, if you please.'

'And tomorrow is Wednesday. Perhaps the hairdresser?'

Hester made no demur. She would have agreed to anything if she might be free to greet their visitor on Thursday.

Elinor felt a twinge of alarm, but her ladyship's expression was bland, so she crushed her own misgivings. Hester was merely looking forward to seeing their friend again.

It was all too easy to grow accustomed to companionship when one was in daily contact with another person. Already she herself was missing Rokeby's easy banter and the rakish look which was a constant challenge.

Her thoughts were taking her in a dangerous direction and her face grew rosy. Glancing up, she found Lady Hartfield's eyes upon her and her blush deepened.

She must pull herself together, or her hostess might imagine that John Charlbury's proposed visit was of more than common interest to her. She stiffened, expecting a little gentle chaffing, but Lady Hartfield did not pursue the subject.

Later that day Elinor brought it up herself. She and Lady Hartfield were seated side by side, enjoying the refreshments which were offered only to Madame Germaine's most favoured customers. Madame herself was deeply sensible of the fact that she owed much of her success to her ladyship's patronage, and she welcomed her distinguished client accordingly.

Now they were surrounded by fabrics of every hue in fine wool, silks and muslins, together with the latest pattern books. Her ladyship wasted no time. She knew exactly what she wanted, having already discussed her requirements with the little Frenchwoman.

'Simplicity must be our choice for Miss Winton,' she announced. 'You have seen her, *madame*. Do you agree?'

'I cannot fault your taste, your ladyship. It is a mistake, I find, to gown the very young in too many frills and flounces.'

Elinor felt relieved. Before meeting Lady Hartfield, she had been concerned lest Hester be dressed for the Season in garments chosen to proclaim her wealth. Her ladyship, she realised, would not be guilty of such vulgarity.

'Not white, I think,' her ladyship mused. 'Hester needs something to warm her skin. . . This shade of apricot bloom would be ideal, and also the coral. Hester, my dear, will you go with *madame*? She will take your measurements.'

Hester's eyes were sparkling as she followed the mantua-maker, and she threw a look of gratitude at her two companions.

'Hester is in spirits today,' her ladyship observed. 'I think we may put it down to the prospect of some new gowns, as well as to the thought of seeing Mr Charlbury again. . .'

She had given Elinor the opening she needed.

'Ma'am, I hope you do not think that Hester regards John Charlbury as more than a friend. . .any more than I do myself. . .'

The black eyes rested on her face. Then Lady Hartfield smiled. 'I have no worries about Hester. . .as to you, Miss Temple, whatever Rokeby may believe, I cannot think Charlbury the man for you.'

Elinor blushed to the roots of her hair. 'Lord Rokeby said. . .? Oh, ma'am, I cannot imagine how he came to think. . .Mr Charlbury has been kind to Hester and myself, but that is all.'

Her ladyship turned to finger a bolt of pale green silk. 'Rokeby is not always the wisest of men. . .at least, where emotions are concerned. Miss Temple, this shade of green would become you well. Do you like it?'

Elinor was too confused to do more than murmur her assent, and anger mingled with embarrassment. How dared Rokeby discuss her prospects with his aunt? It was the outside of enough.

At that moment Hester returned to them dressed in a classical gown which was the height of fashion for that season. The pale blue gauze was caught high beneath a fitted bodice with a velvet ribbon of deeper blue, and the short puffed sleeves were trimmed with the same fabric.

Lady Hartfield regarded her critically. 'Yes, that is the style for you for evening wear,' she said.

'You do not find it too low at the front, ma'am?' Hester tugged anxiously at the neckline.

'Not at all, my dear. Your skin is good, and you are without those ugly hollows at the neck. When one is too thin this style can be a disaster.'

Elinor blessed her silently. Hester had always hated her chubby figure, and even though she had lost weight she was still well rounded. To be told that this was an asset made her flush with pleasure.

With the preliminaries over, Lady Hartfield gave her order with dispatch. High-collared spencers with long sleeves to be worn over matching spring gowns were bespoken, together with several pelisses in wool.

'Those will serve for the present season,' her ladyship announced. 'Miss Temple, will you not choose something for yourself whilst *madame* and I decide upon a summer wardrobe for Hester?'

Elinor hesitated. She had guessed at once that anything ordered from Madame Germaine's establishment would be far beyond her means, and she had not yet paid in full for the gowns which Rokeby had brought back to Merton Place.

Yet her travelling cloak was shabby, and none of the garments she had worn in Bath would do for London. It would be impossible to wear her one good gown on a daily basis.

Lady Hartfield drew her to one side. 'Miss Temple, pray do not worry about the cost,' she murmured. 'I have an arrangement with *madame*. . .'

Elinor's colour was high. 'Ma'am, you will think me foolish, but I have not yet paid Lord Rokeby for the gowns he chose. . .not in full, I mean.'

Lady Hartfield laughed. 'You give Rokeby too

much credit, my dear. He did not choose them. They came from here, and the same arrangement applied.'

'You chose them?' Elinor stared at her. 'But how did you know? They were just exactly right for me.'

'I had a most excellent description of your height and your colouring, Miss Temple,' her companion answered drily. 'Now please, I beg of you, do make your choice.' She turned her attention to the pile of muslins, lawns, cambrics and gauzes, both plain and patterned.

Elinor obeyed her in silence. She kept her order modest, though she could not resist a new pelisse with a fitted bodice, long sleeves and a full-length skirt which was buttoned to the waist. Two round robes with fitted sleeves would serve her for day wear, and her amber gown must suffice for evening functions. Her ladyship would have none of it, insisting that Elinor chose another, to be made up in either tiffany or sarsenet. To argue before *madame* was out of the question, so Elinor did as she was bidden.

Her ladyship's determination was evident also on the following day, when confronted by the hairdresser. She made her wishes clear.

'No curls,' she announced. 'Miss Winton's hair is fine and straight. With a short curled style, she will spend her life in hair papers or with heated tongs.'

Monsieur René muttered to himself. A fashionable crop was quite his favourite, especially as it could be bound with either a fillet or a length of gauze for evening, but he was forced to agree.

'And high off the neck, I believe,' her ladyship continued. 'Such a style will enable Miss Winton to wear neat earrings to the best advantage.'

Hester sat patiently as the hairdresser continued his ministrations, but when he had finished she could not hide her pleasure. It was a transformation. Parted in the middle, the gleaming wings of hair were caught high at the back, lengthening her neck and adding to her height.

'I look so different,' she murmured in amazement. 'Miss Temple, do you like it?'

'Hester, it is charming!' Elinor said truthfully.

She was not the only person to think so. On the following day, John Charlbury's look of admiration brought a flush to Hester's cheeks, though he was careful not to comment upon her changed appearance.

His visit was brief, and intended mainly to enquire if he could be of service to the ladies in their expeditions.

Hester was given first choice of the places she would like to visit, and settled upon a trip to see the menagerie in the Tower.

'Then, my dears, you will not mind if I do not accompany you,' Lady Hartfield laughed. 'The smell of those beasts is more than I can bear, even if I carry a nosegay.'

'Ma'am, we may well choose somewhere else if you should wish it?' Hester's look was anxious.

'No, no, you shall leave me to my own devices. I have much to do.'

The visit was planned for the following week and Charlbury took his leave of them.

The intervening days were filled with yet more shopping expeditions, until even her ladyship professed herself satisfied with the number of small hats trimmed with flowers or plumes, lace shawls, scarves and gloves which they had ordered.

'Best to get it done with now,' she announced to Elinor. 'As the weather improves, Hester will not wish to be concerned with such mundane considerations. I suspect that we shall all become well acquainted with the sights of London.'

'Ma'am, you are very patient with her.' Elinor gave the older woman a look of affection. She was beginning to grow fond of this forthright *grande dame* who brooked no nonsense.

'But this is such a pleasure for me, my dear Miss Temple. I had no children of my own, you know.' For a moment her ladyship looked wistful. Then she straightened her shoulders. 'Hester is improving, I believe. She is more at her ease with me now that we are better acquainted, and she will enjoy herself tomorrow.'

She was not mistaken. Happy in the company of Elinor and John Charlbury, Hester made the most of their outing.

In her new pelisse of dark red wool, with a small fur hat and matching muff, she was warmly clad against the chill February wind, and her face glowed with pleasure as they wandered about the Tower. Even the rank smell of the beasts in the menagerie did not detract from her enjoyment, though Elinor wrinkled her nose.

The day was far advanced by the time they returned to Berkeley Square, and the street-lamps were already lit against the darkness of a winter evening. The wind was chill as they hurried indoors, with Hester still chattering about the wonders she had seen that day.

She hurried her companions through into the salon

without stopping to put off her outdoor clothing. Then she stopped upon the threshold with a small gasp of surprise.

'My lord?'

'Yes, Hester. . .I am not a ghost.' Rokeby was seated in a wing-chair with his injured leg stretched out upon a footstool. He reached out for the walking-cane beside him, and was about to struggle to his feet when Lady Hartfield stopped him.

'Marcus, kindly do not add to your folly. Hester and Miss Temple will excuse you.'

Elinor could only stare at him. Her heart was pounding in a most unreasonable way as she looked at that familiar face. Now the firm mouth was curved in amusement as his eyes met hers.

'Lord Rokeby. . .what are you doing here? I had not imagined that you would be fit to travel so soon?'

'I was forced to escape my nurses,' he said blandly.

'But, sir—'

'Now, Miss Temple, you shall not give me a roasting. My aunt has lectured me non-stop since my arrival. I confess it is hard to be taken to task when naught but the knowledge of my duties called me to your side.' The blue eyes danced with laughter.

'Nonsense, Marcus!' her ladyship said briskly. 'Doubtless you were bored at Merton Place.'

'Quite true.' Rokeby smiled up at John Charlbury. 'John, this is no reflection upon your mamma, but I fear she intended to keep me bedridden for a twelve-month.'

'And now you are in her black books?'

'I admit it, but I shall beg her to forgive me.'

'So I should hope. What could you have been

thinking of?' His aunt's forgiveness was not to be given so easily.

'Well, ma'am, it was the roads, you see. As it was, the horses almost foundered in the mire. Another week of rain and they would have been impassable. I might have been unable to join you for another month.'

'We should have borne the prospect with fortitude,' her ladyship announced.

'But sadly I could not.' There was no mistaking the glint in his eyes as he looked at Elinor.

Suddenly she felt breathless as her feelings threatened to overcome her. Rokeby was up to his old tricks again. Now the peace of the last two weeks was likely to be shattered into fragments. His behaviour was sheer folly, and she should have been displeased, but her heart was filled with joy. It was irrational to be delighted that she was wearing her new walking-dress and was looking at her best.

Rokeby's eyelids drooped and he lay back in his chair. 'Most probably you are right,' he murmured. 'I feel a little fatigued. Ma'am, if you will order my carriage, I will go at once to Grosvenor Square...'

'To that great house, with no one to care for you? You shall not think of it.' Her ladyship rang the bell. 'Heaven knows what other folly you may commit. You will stay here until you are quite well again.'

'If you think it best,' Rokeby agreed meekly. He turned his head in Elinor's direction and the heavy eyelids lifted. Behind them she saw a lurking smile.

She realised with exasperation that it was what he had intended all along. She turned to John Charlbury and gave him her hand as she thanked him for their outing. He was about to leave them when her ladyship stopped him with an invitation to dine with them that evening.

He demurred at first. 'Marcus will wish to rest,' he said quietly.

'Just give me an hour and I shall be myself again. I look forward to sitting at a table and eating something other than gruel and broth.' Rokeby gave him a cheerful grin.

'You may put that idea out of your mind at once, Marcus. You will go to bed and stay there, for this evening at least,' Lady Hartfield said with resolution.

Elinor was tempted to laugh. It appeared that Rokeby had merely exchanged one strong-minded nurse for another and, as he had claimed to feel fatigued, he could not argue.

'I should be glad of a little company after you have dined,' he murmured. His eyes were intent upon Elinor's face.

'I shall call in to bid you goodnight,' Lady Hartfield promised.

Elinor's shoulders began to shake. From the look on Rokeby's face, that was *not* what he had in mind at all. Stifling her amusement she bore Hester away to change her gown.

The girl's high spirits had completely vanished, and her eyes were troubled.

'I wish Lord Rokeby had not come here,' she announced when she and Elinor were alone. 'It will not be the same. . .'

'You will see little of him,' Elinor promised. 'Her ladyship will insist that he takes care, and she will not expect us to change our plans.'

'I did not expect him quite so soon. I was hoping that he might go to France again when he was well.'

'My dear, you must not dread him quite so much. You have a staunch ally in Lady Hartfield.'

'I know it, but Lord Rokeby is my guardian. He has come to make quite sure that I find a husband.'

'He will find that a difficult task if he cannot get about,' Elinor said drily. 'His lordship has, I fear, jumped from the frying pan into the fire.'

Yet in one way Hester was right. With Rokeby's arrival, the atmosphere in the house had changed. Her ladyship did not succeed in keeping him in bed beyond the following day, as he advised her with conviction that the surgeon had advocated a little exercise.

'Very well, my dear boy, on the understanding that you will not overdo it. Perhaps you will make use of the library. We cannot spare much time for you, as Hester must go for fittings. . .'

'Pray do not change your plans for me. Shall you need Miss Temple with you? If she would but spare me an hour or two, it would help the days to pass. . .'

Thus appealed to, Elinor could do nothing but agree, though she did not trust Rokeby in the least. He appeared to have some machiavellian plan of his own, but what it was she could not imagine. He could hardly hope to seduce her in his aunt's home, with the servants always at his beck and call. The injured leg she dismissed as irrelevant. Such a trifling thing would be unlikely to stop him.

She was careful always to stay out of reach of those long arms, until at length he began to tease her.

'Your caution is commendable,' he said one day. 'I might almost imagine that you were afraid of me, Miss Temple.'

'My lord?' Elinor's expression was as blank as she could make it.

His look was full of mischief. 'I was referring to the fact that you keep the library table between us.'

'Sir, we have our books upon it. That is its purpose, surely?'

'Fencing with me, my dear?'

'I am at a loss to understand you.'

'I think not. You understand me very well, and have done so ever since we met.'

'I do not care to be reminded of that evening,' Elinor told him stiffly.

'Ah, yes. . .how shocked you were! You have not yet recovered? I wonder why the thought of human passions should disturb you so? It is a natural process after all.'

'I do not think it in the least natural to have to pay for. . . .for affection.'

'You mistake the matter. We were not paying for affection.'

'No, you were not,' she cried bitterly. 'You were paying to slake. . .' She could not go on.

'Our lusts? Well, that is natural, too.'

'You are satisfied with very little, sir. There are other things to be considered in the connection between a man and a woman.'

'And they are. . .?'

Elinor was silent.

'Go on!' he urged. 'You interest me.'

'I think you have not. . .well. . .what of respect and love?'

'Love, my dear? What is that? I have seen symptoms of infatuation in others. They led inevitably to disaster. I determined never to commit the folly of falling in love myself.'

'That must be your choice, my lord. I will say only that infatuation is not love, in my own opinion.'

'And you are something of an expert in these matters?'

The taunt brought a flush of colour to Elinor's cheeks, but she held his gaze steadily.

'I am not, sir, but should my affections ever be engaged, I should want something more than paltry coin.'

'Your demands are high, my dear. You ask for a man's soul.'

'No, I do not,' she retorted hotly. 'But I would wish to be treated as an equal in entrusting my life to that of another. Lord Rokeby, I cannot imagine how we came to discuss this subject. We shall never understand each other. You speak of one thing, and I of another.'

'Bear with me,' he suggested lightly. 'Invalids have curious fancies—'

'And that is another thing,' Elinor snapped. 'Whenever you are routed, sir, you plead ill-health. I may tell you that it does not wear with me.'

'Great heavens! I must be careful. Next thing you will kick my stick away and leave me prone upon the ground.'

Elinor's lips twitched. 'Sometimes you tempt me, sir.'

'I only wish I did. Consider my position, ma'am. Here I am, an incapacitated rake, robbed of all opportunity to indulge my usual vices. Life is hard indeed. I had supposed you to be more understanding.'

'Sir, you are quite impossible.'

'I know it, and, ma'am, I am deeply sensible of your goodness in spending so much time with a reprobate.' The firm, full-lipped mouth curved upwards at the corners. Under their heavy lids, the penetrating eyes were fixed upon her own.

'Lord Rokeby, I wish you will stop behaving in this odious way. You have no propriety of taste—'

'None whatever,' he agreed promptly. 'Propriety is dull you will agree?'

'And what is more, you are *utterly* without conduct. . .'

'You are right, of course.' Rokeby hung his head in mock humility. 'I am much in need of reform, as I believe I mentioned to you once before.'

'The task is beyond me, sir.' Elinor gathered up her reticule and left him. She was still smiling as she welcomed Hester and Lady Hartfield from their shopping expedition.

'You look more than commonly glad to see us, Miss Temple.' Her ladyship drew off her gloves. 'Marcus, I take it, has been at his most provoking. . .?'

'I believe Lord Rokeby is feeling more himself today, ma'am.' Elinor's reply was carefully non-committal.

'That, my dear, speaks volumes! Well, it will not do. You have spent far too much time indoors. A drive through the park will do you the world of good. We shall leave Marcus to reflect upon his misdemeanours.'

Elinor hesitated. Rokeby was becoming restive with his enforced confinement. She thought of suggesting that he, too, was in need of a change of scene, but she could scarcely contradict her hostess. And she must not give her ladyship cause to think that she desired Rokeby's company.

It was not true, of course, except that she had grown accustomed to the way his face lit up as she walked into the room. Even his chaffing she found entertaining, though she disagreed with his more outrageous statements. It was a challenge to be forced to defend her own ideas. Somehow, in his presence, there was always an underlying current of excitement.

She could not understand it. Was it his vitality, she wondered, or that impression of power barely under control? There was something unpredictable about him, and she found it impossible to guess what he would say or do next. He could always manage to surprise her.

It occurred to her that she was playing with fire, and she was unusually silent for the rest of the evening.

CHAPTER EIGHT

THE weather on the following day was fine, with the promise of an early spring in the air. Somewhat to Elinor's relief, John Charlbury was an early caller, announcing himself happy to bear his lordship company as the ladies took their drive.

The air was chill, and Elinor had taken the precaution of wearing her warmest clothing, though they were amply provided with warm bricks for their feet, and fur rugs for their laps.

The green pelisse was becoming, as was her jaunty little hat with its curving feather, but she could not help thinking that she was wearing borrowed plumage. Not all her ladyship's assurances could convince her that it was right to accept more gowns from Madame Germaine's establishment.

'Ma'am, I have been thinking,' she said shyly. 'I am quite handy with my needle and the classical style of fashion is so simple. If I might buy some fabric, I might contrive something which would not disgrace you.'

'Elinor, are you sure?' Her ladyship looked doubtful. 'I do not mean to be unkind, but an aunt of mine was fond of remarking that many a girl had ruined her social position by attempting to make her own hats.'

She saw the humour of that startling statement as soon as she had made it, and joined in Elinor's peal of laughter.

'I promise that I shall not venture into the millinery

trade,' Elinor assured her. 'But I have been accustomed to make my own gowns.'

'Really? Well, my dear, I confess that I admire the way your garments seem to fit you to perfection.' She reached up to tap the carriage roof, and directed her coachman to Bond Street.

It was as they were about to enter the portals of a well-known emporium that Elinor heard a voice behind her.

'Letitia, my dear?'

All three ladies turned to face the man who stood beside them. Of commanding presence, he was tall and burly, and his impeccable clothing proclaimed him a gentleman of fashion. He was smiling as he bent to kiss Lady Hartfield upon the cheek, but the grey eyes in the fleshy face were as cold as the winter sea.

'Dacre, I had not thought to see you here in town so early in the Season.' Lady Hartfield was ramrod-stiff in his embrace.

'I needed some new guns, and Tobias wished to see his tailor. Ah, here he comes. . .' He bent a fond glance upon his son. 'Will you not present us to your friends?'

Lady Hartfield's manner was so unlike herself that Elinor was startled. Normally pleasant and easy with her acquaintances, she made the introductions with obvious reluctance. For the first time Elinor saw something of the iron beneath the velvet glove.

'Miss Temple, this is my brother-in-law, Lord Dacre, and his son, Tobias. Hester, my dear, I think you have not met before. Dacre, this is Miss Winton. Miss Temple is a friend of hers.'

Dacre did not spare Elinor a second glance. His eyes were upon the girl who was at that moment making her curtsy to him.

'Miss Hester Winton? What a pleasure it is to make your acquaintance, my dear. Such a tragedy about your parents! You may not know it, but I have always taken an interest in your welfare. I had hoped to offer you a home, but Rokeby would not hear of it.'

Hester was too stunned to answer him. Her ladyship stepped into the breach.

'You will forgive us, Dacre. We are a little pressed for time today.' She gave him her hand and turned away.

'Shopping for the Season? Quite right. . .quite right! We shall hope to see much more of you in the coming months.' He bowed and bore his son away.

'That was unfortunate,' Lady Hartfield muttered. She was breathing hard. 'In a busy street I could not give him the cut direct, or the tale would have been all over London, but how I longed to do so.'

'Ma'am, I fear you are distressed. Should you prefer to return at once to Berkeley Square?'

'No, not at all. Let us not disrupt our day.' She directed Elinor's attention to the bolts of fabric, but it was clear that her mind was elsewhere.

Elinor made her purchases quickly, more disturbed than she cared to admit. Dacre, she remembered, was the man whom Rokeby held in such contempt. It was hardly surprising that Lady Hartfield should feel the same in view of his brutality towards her sister.

And this was the man who had hoped to become Hester's guardian? Elinor shuddered. She had taken him in dislike on sight, before she knew his name. There was something about his manner which spoke of violence barely hidden, and his eyes were stony.

As for the boy, Tobias, she had noted only that he was exceptionally handsome. Rokeby had described him as whey-faced, but that was an injustice. True, the boy was fair-skinned, but his classic features reminded her of a Greek sculpture. He had said nothing, other than to offer conventional greetings, and she guessed that he lived in his father's shadow.

It was not until they were alone that Hester questioned her.

'Lady Hartfield seemed so cross,' she said in wonder. 'She does not like Lord Dacre, does she?'

'It is an old story, Hester, and a family matter.'

'I did not like him either, and. . .and he said that he might have been my guardian. . .' Her face grew pale.

'Well, now you will understand how lucky you have been. I'm sure you prefer Lord Rokeby.'

'Lord Rokeby is alarming. . .but I do not think him a wicked man.'

Elinor judged it time to change the subject, but once again she marvelled at Hester's quickness of perception.

'How did you like my purchases?' she asked. 'I thought the worked muslin particularly elegant.'

'They were very pretty. Miss Temple, do you think we shall meet that man again?'

'Not if Lady Hartfield can prevent it.' Elinor smiled. 'Hester, there is something I have meant to say to you before. Will you call me by my given name? If we are to be introduced as friends, rather than teacher and pupil, it will seem a little strange if you address me as Miss Temple.'

'Oh, may I?' Hester flushed with pleasure. 'We are most truly friends, are we not?'

'Of course we are.' Elinor dropped a kiss upon her brow. 'Now we should go down to join the others. They will wonder where we are.'

'Do you go on ahead. . .I must re-tie my sandal.'

The door to the salon was ajar, and as she walked towards it she heard Rokeby's deep tones. There was an urgency in his voice which was unfamiliar to her.

'Unfortunate is a masterpiece of understatement, my dear aunt. I had hoped to keep the knowledge of Hester's Season from him. . .'

'You must know that it would have been impossible.' Lady Hartfield's voice was equally decisive. 'Dacre is looking for an heiress for his boy. Where better to find one than the Season?'

'That is what worries me,' Rokeby confessed. 'He has always had an eye to Hester's wealth.'

'But, Marcus, you are her guardian. You may accept or refuse any offers as you will. And pray do not imagine that I shall invite Dacre to this house. Nothing is further from my mind.'

'I shall accompany you in future,' Rokeby announced with resolution.

'My dear boy, is that wise? Your leg. . .?'

'Is much improved.' His tone invited no argument, and, as Elinor entered the room, he rose to his feet.

'Miss Temple, I have been malingering,' he told her with a smile. 'I have just been explaining to my aunt that when one is cherished as I have been there is a great temptation to wish that it could last.' He took a step towards her and appeared to stagger.

Elinor was beside him in a second to throw her arm about his waist. He chuckled as he looked down at her.

'You understand my meaning, aunt?' A smile of purest mischief lingered in his eyes.

'Only too well, Marcus. I am only surprised that

Miss Temple has the patience to tolerate your nonsense.'

'She doesn't find it easy, I assure you.'

Elinor disengaged herself from his grasp. 'I am glad to find you better in health, my lord. I imagine that you are now able to walk without your stick?'

Rokeby gave his aunt a look of mock despair. 'You see how it is, ma'am. As far as this lady is concerned, I might be made of glass.'

'I am delighted to hear that she is so well able to see through you.' Lady Hartfield looked from one face to the other and gave an odd little nod of satisfaction. 'Elinor...I may call you Elinor, may I not? I have been telling Marcus that I intend to start the Season by giving a ball.'

'And I have promised to limp about, looking quite as distinguished as Lord Byron,' Rokeby assured her.

'You will, of course, recite your poems, sir?' Elinor said demurely.

'No, I will spare you those. They are intended solely for the ears of my own true love...'

As always, he had had the last word, but the tense atmosphere had lightened, and when Hester joined them she joined in the conversation with more vivacity than Elinor had imagined possible. Even the proposed ball appeared to hold no terrors for her, and Rokeby was constrained to compliment both Elinor and his aunt when Hester went upstairs to find a handkerchief.

'You have done wonders,' he told them with a smile. 'Hester will never be a beauty, but now she has a certain something.'

'It is all down to perfect grooming, Marcus. Hester has a quiet charm, and not all men, you know, prefer a chatterbox.'

'You are right. The thought of endless conversation at the breakfast table is enough to daunt the strongest heart.' He grinned at Elinor, who ignored him.

'Well then, my dears, let us make our plans. I think possibly the beginning of April will be a suitable date. It is a little early, to be sure, but I'm sure we shall assemble sufficient company to make it a success.'

'You are too modest, my dear aunt. Your invitations are prized like gold dust. I don't doubt but what we shall have a frightful crush.'

His predictions were correct. In the intervening weeks Elinor had been too preoccupied with addressing cards and making herself useful wherever she could to note that most of the fashionable world intended to be present.

Her ladyship appeared untroubled by the need to oversee the preparations. Her servants were well trained, and her household continued to run with its customary efficiency as she made arrangements with caterers, florists and musicians.

'What will you wear, my dear? Have you a favourite gown?' Her question was meant kindly, but it succeeded in reducing Hester to a worried silence.

'Hester?'

'Yes, ma'am?'

'What is the matter, child?'

'I. . .I shall not know what to say to the guests, Lady Hartfield. . .'

'Then I will let you into a secret.' Her ladyship twinkled. 'Ask people about themselves. That fascinating topic is guaranteed to persuade them to talk so much that you need do nothing more than put in an odd word here and there. You may find this hard to believe, but it will gain you the reputation of being a brilliant conversationalist.'

'Do you think so?' Hester looked doubtful, but she managed a faint smile.

'Nothing is more certain. Now, my dear, what do you say to these arrangements for the ballroom?' With a sheaf of drawings in her hand, she succeeded in diverting Hester's attention from the terrors to come.

'Aunt, will you tear yourself away from your labours for an hour or two?' Rokeby's limp was barely noticeable as he walked into the room. 'I thought you might like to visit the Botanical Gardens today.'

'What a splendid idea! The spring flowers will be at their best.'

'Where is Miss Temple? She will like to join us, I expect.'

'I believe she planned to busy herself with her sewing.'

'Nonsense! The day is much too fine to be cooped up indoors. Hester, I shall rely upon you to persuade her.'

'Oh, yes. I know she will wish to come.' Hester gave him a shy smile as she hurried out of the room.

Elinor demurred at first. She was cutting out a plain white satin slip which would serve as an under-dress beneath a number of open robes in different colours.

'But Lord Rokeby wishes you to make up the party,' Hester pleaded. 'He said so most particularly.'

Elinor's heart gave a little jump. For the past few weeks, she had made an effort to keep his lordship at a distance. It had not been easy but she had countered all his pleas for companionship with murmured excuses. She was too busy...his lordship was almost recovered and well able to visit his friends...and should he wish to stay indoors, Mr Charlbury would bear him company.

'Losing your nerve, my dear Miss Temple?' There was dancing mockery in his eyes.

Elinor coloured. 'Sir, I cannot imagine what you mean. . .I have explained. . .'

'So you have. . .and I don't believe a word of it. One might almost suppose that you felt yourself at risk from me.'

Elinor's temper had risen. It was too close to the truth.

'You flatter yourself, Lord Rokeby,' she had said coldly. 'Why should I be at risk from you?'

'It was just a notion of mine. Perhaps the fancy of a sick man? You must forgive me. For a libertine such as myself enforced withdrawal from the Polite World has been something of a strain, as I'm sure you'll understand.'

'From the Polite World, sir?' The sarcasm in Elinor's voice had been evident. All her old distrust of him had returned in full measure. 'I would not describe your favoured company so.'

'I had not expected that you would. But then, your standards are so high, Miss Temple. Nothing but perfection will do for you. Could any man live up to that?'

'That is not true,' Elinor had cried hotly. 'We all have our faults. . .myself as much as anyone. . .but. . . there are limits, sir.'

'Are there? Perhaps I have not found them.' He had bowed and left her.

Since then she had avoided him, and he had appeared to have accepted her decision. For the most part he had not dined with them, and had been absent in an evening.

It had not taken long to revert to his old habits, Elinor reflected bitterly. For the past week they had merely exchanged civilities in passing. On occasion she had been aware of his return to the house in the early hours of the morning, and had remarked his absence at the breakfast table, but Lady Hartfield had not referred to it.

I wonder that she does not invite him to return to his own home now that he is well again, Elinor had thought to herself. For the time he spent in it, her ladyship's establishment might have been an hotel. Now, apparently, he intended to make amends.

Rokeby was all attention as he settled the ladies in the carriage.

'Aunt, do you care to drive through Hyde park first? You will see many of your acquaintances.'

Lady Hartfield nodded. She was pleased to find that the town was filling up, as hopeful mammas came in from the country to present their daughters to the marriage market. Those with sons were more than civil to her, and the coach was pulled up again and again as she greeted old acquaintances.

Elinor was amused to find that she herself might have been invisible as far as the older women were concerned, though she attracted admiring glances from their sons. It was Hester who received an abundance of kind words and distinguishing condescension. The news that Miss Winton was an heiress must have spread through the town like wildfire for invitations rained upon her head, but though she smiled pleasantly enough she shot a pleading look at Lady Hartfield.

Her ladyship took pity on her. 'Would you care to walk a little, Hester?' she enquired. 'Elinor will accompany you, I'm sure. I must speak to the Princess Esterhazy for a moment. You may rejoin me at the far gate.'

'A splendid idea!' Rokeby jumped down from the carriage. He offered an arm to each of the ladies and began to stroll through the busy throng.

'Why, here is Mr Charlbury!' Hester looked up with a happy smile as a horseman made his way towards them. Charlbury dismounted and began to lead his horse.

'This is Brutus.' He gestured towards the splendid animal. 'What do you think of him?'

He drew them a little apart to allow a party of fashionably dressed pedestrians to pass them.

Elinor had imagined that Rokeby was behind them, but he had been accosted by another horseman. Elinor recognised the man at once. She had last seen his flabby features at Rokeby's dining-table on the night of their arrival at Merton Place.

'Bad luck, Rokeby! I hear that your *chère amie* has found consolation elsewhere...' He must have imagined that his lordship was alone, for he made no attempt to lower his voice.

Elinor glanced at her companions, but they had moved a little way ahead of her, and were absorbed in conversation.

'Can't expect anything else, I suppose,' the fat man continued. 'That particular bird of paradise has expensive tastes, I'm told.'

'Are you, indeed?' Rokeby's voice was icy. 'I wonder that you should care to enquire.'

'Oh, Lord, have I set you into a miff? A sore point, is it? Don't worry...plenty more fish in the sea...I hear there is a little opera dancer new in town. She might suit you. . .'

Rokeby bowed. 'Kind of you to think of me, Talworth, but I'm not in need of a pander.'

Elinor began to tremble. It was an insult which could only invite a challenge. She looked at the two men to find that Talworth had flushed an ugly red. Without another word he dug his spurs into his horse and rode away.

Rokeby's expression frightened her. He was breathing hard, and his lips were set in a tight line.

She turned quickly, hoping to convince him that she had heard nothing of his conversation, but he caught her arm.

'Don't pretend!' he said roughly. 'You could not fail to hear the whole.'

'Sir, you are hurting me!' It was true. His fingers were digging deep into her wrist. 'Let me go! How you wish to conduct your own affairs is no concern of mine.'

'Ah, I had forgot! It would come as no surprise to you to hear that I kept a woman.'

Elinor was scarlet with embarrassment. She did not reply.

'Merely confirms your opinion of me, does it?'

'Sir, please lower your voice. Do you wish Hester to hear you?' She almost ran towards John Charlbury.

All her pleasure in the day was ruined. As an eavesdropper she had got her just deserts, though it was through no fault of her own. Those few idle words had served to remind her of Rokeby's true nature, if she needed such a reminder. What had she expected . . .that Rokeby would spend his evenings in philosophical discussions? That he had been converted to a blameless life, indulging merely in card parties with his friends? Her lips curved in a bitter smile.

She had suspected...she had wondered how he spent his evenings, but it was appalling that the confirmation of her worst fears should hurt so much. She felt that someone had stabbed her through the heart.

She could not look at him, and turned away, thankful that the brim of her poke bonnet served to hide her face. To avoid any further conversation with him, she placed herself between Hester and John Charlbury as they strolled towards the far gate of the park.

Her troubles were not yet over. As they reached the waiting carriage, she saw a figure she knew standing by the door.

'Good morning, ladies.' Lord Dacre bowed and smiled. 'Rokeby, I hope I see you well?'

'Do you?' Rokeby's answer was so abrupt as to be insulting.

'Why yes, of course! I have just been chatting to Talworth. He told me of your accident. Hard luck, my boy. I hear that it came at an inconvenient time.' The smile on Dacre's face did not reach his eyes.

Elinor was startled by something in his tone. It was almost a warning. Certainly she felt a sense of menace.

'A broken leg is always inconvenient,' Lady Hartfield murmured. 'Dacre, we seem always to be rushing away from you, but we have promised ourselves a trip to the Botanical Gardens...'

'Then I must hope that, when we meet again we shall have more time for an interesting chat.' He did not attempt to detain them further.

'A hateful creature,' Lady Hartfield announced. 'But, Marcus, really! Need you look like thunder? I thought you were about to strike him.'

'He tries my temper, aunt.'

'Well, kindly control it, sir. A fit of the sullens does not suit you. Neither does it please me.'

Rokeby had the grace to apologise, but his light-hearted mood had vanished. Elinor too was silent until they reached the Gardens. There she roused herself to admire the blooms, until her ladyship was satisfied that whatever disagreement had occurred between Elinor and her nephew was on the way to being resolved.

In that she was mistaken. In the course of the day Elinor had made a discovery which shocked her to the core of her being. She was in love with Rokeby. Libertine he might be, but she could no longer pretend, even to herself, that she did not care for him. He filled her mind to the exclusion of all else. When he smiled at her, her heart leapt in her breast, and when he touched her hand she felt herself begin to tremble.

The knowledge filled her with dismay. It was little short of disastrous, and panic filled her soul. She had known the danger and closed her eyes to it. Why had she been such a fool? Had she imagined that her disapproval of his way of life would protect her? It had not done so.

If only she could get away before she betrayed her feelings. Rokeby would despise them, believing, as he did, that love was an illusion. She could plead the need to visit her family, she thought wildly, but Lady Hartfield would find it strange to be presented with such a decision at this time. Then there was Hester to consider, and she had given her word that she would stay.

But where was it all to end? The answer was not far to seek. Hester would marry and she herself would be forced to find another position.

This was ridiculous. She was growing maudlin merely because she had been fool enough to allow herself to fall in love with a man so far beyond her reach that she could have no hope of happiness.

It must be a lesson to her. It would take all her strength of character to control her feelings until the Season ended, but she must do so. The punishment for her folly would be to see him every day, knowing that her love was not reciprocated.

On the day of the ball she was standing in her under-garments when Lady Hartfield tapped upon her door.

'The hairdresser is here,' she announced. 'If you put on your dressing-robe, my dear, I will send him to you.'

'Really, m'am, there is no need. It is kind of you, but—'

'Nonsense, Elinor! I wish you to look your best.' Her eye fell upon the evening gown laid out upon the bed. 'Shall you wear this? It is quite charming, but the spangled net becomes you even better.' With an unerr-ing eye she had decided upon the most expensive garment in Elinor's wardrobe.

'Silly child!' she said fondly. 'I shall not allow you to stay in the background, which, I believe, was your intention. Weekes has already dressed Hester. She will come to you shortly.'

Faced with such determination, Elinor could only submit to the ministrations of the hairdresser and her ladyship's personal maid.

The results surprised her. The silver thread of her gauzy overdress gleamed softly in the candlelight over a slip of jonquil yellow crepe. Cut low at the bosom it revealed her milky skin to perfection.

I look much too fine, she thought doubtfully as she studied her new hairstyle. Drawn high into a chignon at the back, she had been persuaded to allow a couple of ringlets to fall softly on each side of her face.

Still, at least she was not bedecked with jewellery. Fresh flowers were her only ornament. Satisfied that she would not disgrace her hostess, she drew on her long white gloves as Hester came to find her.

Clad in a delicate shade of apricot, Hester, too, had benefited from the hairdresser's attentions. The smooth fair hair shone like satin, and Hester could not resist a little preening in front of the dressing-glass.

She reached up a cautious hand to touch her new coiffure. 'It does make a difference, doesn't it?' she asked anxiously.

'It does indeed. Did I not tell you that, "Fine feathers make fine birds"? I can hear the music, Hester. We should go down to Lady Hartfield.'

From Hester's expression, it was clear that she might have been condemned to enter the lions' den. Elinor tucked an arm through hers as they descended the great staircase.

Rokeby and his aunt were already stationed by the entrance to the ballroom. He was deep in conversation with Lady Hartfield, but as Elinor greeted them he turned to look at her. She heard a small intake of breath. Then he recovered and bent to kiss her hand.

'My dears, I must compliment you. You look quite lovely.' Lady Hartfield smiled upon her protegées. 'Marcus, as you see, is speechless.'

'On the contrary, my dear aunt, I see that I must put in a bid for dances without delay. Hester, may I have your card?'

Hester blushed, but she did as she was bidden.

'And Miss Temple?' Rokeby's eyes were glowing as he looked at her. Scanning her card, he continued to mark dances until she took it from him.

'My lord, what are you about?' she murmured. 'To dance with a partner more than twice must give rise to comment.'

'Do you care? he whispered in her ear. 'You look ravishing, my dear, though still, alas, unravished. . .'

'Kindly remember where you are,' Elinor hissed at him. She had flushed to the roots of her hair.

'Marcus, pray give me your attention,' her ladyship reproved. She looked towards the door. 'Here is Mrs Templewood and her daughters.'

'Both of them? Oh, Lord!' He raised a quizzical eyebrow as he took his place beside her in the receiving line.

'Hush! You wicked creature!' Lady Hartfield gave the first of her guests a gracious smile and directed them towards a room where they might leave their cloaks.

They were followed at once by Lord Bertram and his sharp-featured wife, who was engaged in shepherding a covey of young hopefuls.

'Lord preserve us!' Rokeby spoke with feeling as the guests moved on, but was silenced by a quick glance from his aunt.

Stationed at the end of the receiving line, Elinor was beginning to enjoy herself.

From the languishing glances cast at Rokeby by a number of young maidens and the arch remarks of their mammas, she gathered that his lordship was a prize much to be desired.

She could only admire his *savoir-faire* as he brushed aside both leading questions and innuendo with a

bland expression and every profession of his deep
regard. He must have used those skills to good effect
to avoid being inveigled into matrimony, she decided.

Looking up, she caught his eye and he grinned at
her. He had read her mind, and they were in accord.
Oh dear, it would not do. She forced herself to attend
to the woman who was at that moment addressing
Hester.

'Charming, my dear girl! Charming! I have so
longed to meet you. As to Henry! Well, he has spoken
of nothing else these past three weeks. . .' She gestured
towards a pale young man who looked as if he never
spoke at all.

Hester smiled and nodded.

'Henry!' His mother nudged him in the ribs.

'Oh, yes!' Henry recalled the purpose for which he
had been dragged here, much against his will. 'Miss
Winton, will you honour me with a dance?'

His speech was so clearly rehearsed that Elinor's
lips began to twitch.

'He'll sweep her off her feet!' Rokeby had manoeuvred himself to stand beside her. 'Such passion! What
woman would be proof against it?'

Elinor's shoulders began to shake. 'Sir, you are
behaving very badly. Do, I beg of you, control
yourself.'

'You make it very difficult, Miss Temple.' There
was no mistaking the glint in his eyes.

CHAPTER NINE

MARCUS had no opportunity to speak to Elinor again for some time as the press of guests converged upon them. It was a full hour before her ladyship felt able to leave her post. Few members of the *ton* had refused her invitations, which were not given lightly, and the crush was a clear indication that the evening would be a success.

The room was growing warm, and body odours mingled with the scent of French perfumes, some of them stale, which drifted towards her as she shook hands endlessly at the end of the receiving line.

As the crowd began to thin, Lady Hartfield gave the signal for the dancing to begin.

'Now, Hester, shall we start the proceedings?' Rokeby drew his ward's hand through his arm and led her on to the floor. 'The quadrille is quite your favourite, I believe?'

'I hope I shall remember the steps,' Hester murmured nervously.

'Of course you will. . .and if not, I shall prompt you . . .very quietly, of course.'

As he smiled down at the girl, Elinor's heart turned over. Her eyes were fixed with great intentness upon his face. The firm, well-defined mouth curved up at the corners, and against the swarthy skin his teeth showed very white. Tonight he was in full evening dress and in deference to his aunt's wishes, he wore knee-breeches and silk stockings. A starched neckcloth, meticulously arranged, rose in splendour above a waistcoat of watered silk.

He was quite the most distinguished-looking man in the room, Elinor decided. The black swallow-tailed coat fitted his athletic figure to perfection, and he moved with a grace surprising in such a large man.

An urgent voice beside her broke into her musings.

'Miss Temple, they are making up the numbers, and you promised me this dance, if you recall. . .?'

Elinor turned to face a young sprig of fashion, who had dared to brave the dagger-looks of his mamma in order to claim her hand.

Shaking off her preoccupation, she accompanied him towards a group of dancers, only to find, to her dismay, that she was in Rokeby's set. Knowing him as she did, she felt quite sure that he would attempt to enliven the evening by an effort to shake her composure.

Well, he would not succeed. She turned to her partner and exerted all her charm to put him at his ease. He was very young, and clearly dazzled by her beauty to a degree which made him tongue-tied.

Elinor persevered, and soon she had him laughing gaily as he told her of his visit to Astley's Amphitheatre.

'I am not quite in the way of things just yet,' he admitted. 'Mamma was not best pleased that I should go there, but I had a famous time. She thought, you see, that I should take more dancing lessons.' At that moment he missed a step, and gave her a rueful look. 'It seems that she was right.'

'You dance very well,' Elinor encouraged. 'It may be that I am a little clumsy myself. This is my first large ball. . .'

'Is it?' His face cleared. 'I should not have thought it, ma'am. You look. . .well, you look so perfectly at your ease.' The effort of making the compliment, artless though it was, caused him to blush to the roots of his ginger hair.

At that moment, Rokeby took his partner past her in the figure of the dance. His brows went up at the sight of her companion's face, and his eyes were filled with laughter.

This time it was Elinor who missed a step.

'There, you see, sir. Now you must believe that I am a novice in this art. . .'

'Is it over?' The boy gave an almost audible sigh of relief as the musicians struck the final chords, and Elinor was tempted to chuckle. Instead, she nodded gravely.

He realised at once that he had shown a remarkable lack of tact. 'Oh, pray do not think that I did not enjoy it,' he said quickly. 'I meant only. . .well, I hope I did not disgrace myself. . .'

'It was kind of you to partner me,' Elinor said gently. 'Now, I believe that you should find your partner for the next dance. It is a waltz. . .'

He looked alarmed. 'Ma'am, I have not yet learned to waltz. My mother disapproves. . .but if I might bring you a glass of lemonade, or fruit cup if you should prefer it? It is very warm, is it not?'

'It is indeed!' Rokeby was beside them, and his deep voice made Elinor jump. 'How thoughtful of you to offer refreshment, sir. Your mother will be glad of your attention. . .she is looking fatigued.'

'But I have just offered to fetch something for Miss Temple. . .' Uncertain, the boy looked at the faces of his companions.

'Miss Temple will excuse you. She is promised to me for the waltz, you see.' Rokeby's face was bland, but his expression brooked of no argument.

'That was not well done of you, my lord.' Elinor looked at the boy's retreating back and frowned. 'To send him back to his mamma as if he were a child. . .?'

'He is little more.' Rokeby was unrepentant. 'I imagined I was coming to the rescue.'

'Of whom?'

'Of your young admirer, naturally. The boy appears to be besotted. Was it wise, I wonder, to exert upon him the full weight of your charm? From his mamma's expression she does not seem to have missed a word or a look. At present, I imagine, she is wishing you elsewhere.'

'How dare you criticise my conduct, sir? Your own leaves much to be desired. Are you telling me that I have stepped beyond the bounds of propriety?' In her anger, Elinor had forgotten that she was addressing her employer.

'Alas, no, Miss Temple. I live in hopes, but it would appear that I am always to be disappointed.' He grinned at her in such a provoking manner that Elinor was robbed of speech for an instant. 'Even should such a moment arrive, I should not dare to mention it.'

'One day, sir, you will go too far,' she forecast darkly.

'I am waiting for that happy moment to arrive. Will you not tell me how I may go about it?'

'I was not referring to your light manner towards myself, which serves, apparently, to amuse you. Take care, my lord. The duennas in this room may take your banter for serious intent. Then where will you be?'

'I shall be fleeing for my very life.' His laughing face was very close to hers. 'The waltz, Miss Temple?' He took her hand preparatory to leading her out.

Elinor pulled away from him. 'I do not care to waltz with you,' she said stiffly.

'You promised.' He took her hand again. 'To refuse me now really would be a breach of propriety.' He led her on to the floor and slid an arm about her waist.

Elinor tried to hold herself away from him.

'No, no!' he urged. 'You must enter into the spirit of the dance. . .just trust yourself in my arms. . .'

Elinor gave him a withering look and he chuckled.

'An unfortunate remark on my part,' he admitted. 'You will never do that.'

He was holding her closer than propriety dictated and she felt unaccountably breathless. In an effort to change the subject, she glanced about her.

'I do not see Mr Charlbury here tonight. Is he otherwise engaged?'

His mouth seemed to harden. 'He is. Shall you miss him?'

'Hester will most certainly do so. She looks to him for support on these occasions. . .'

'I did not ask you about Hester.' Beneath their heavy lids, the blue eyes were studying her face.

Suddenly Elinor was exasperated beyond belief. 'You cannot imagine, sir, that I have the least interest in Mr Charlbury, or he in me. He is a friend, and has shown us much kindness but that is all.'

'I am glad to hear it,' he said smoothly.

'And you believe me?' It seemed important that he should do so.

'Yes, I do. I have never known you lie.' He was silent for a few moments. 'Miss Temple, I think you should prepare Hester for the fact that she may not see John Charlbury for some time. I believe he intends to return to Kent.'

'But why? The Season is only just beginning. . .?'

'That is part of the reason. He has been aware for some time that, by acting as her constant escort, he may be considered as Hester's accredited suitor.'

'And would that be so very dreadful?' Elinor cried without thinking. 'She is already more than half in love with him, though she does not know it.'

'He is aware of his position,' Rokeby told her shortly. 'He will not dangle after an heiress.'

'And you agree with him?' Elinor did not wait for his reply. 'I might have known it. What did you tell him? That Hester is destined for someone far above his touch?' She looked at him straightly and was surprised by his look of anger.

'What an opinion you have of me,' he gritted out. 'Must I remind you that Charlbury is a friend of mine?'

'Yet you do not encourage his suit?'

'Miss Temple, I cannot force him to offer for Hester. He believes, as you do, that she is too young for marriage.'

'But you do not, my lord?'

'You know my opinion on the subject. It least you will agree that she should be given these next few months to look about her before she makes her choice.'

'I thought you intended to make it for her,' Elinor retorted. 'Lord Rokeby, you do not know her as I do. Once having given her affection, she will not change.'

'You taught her that?' There was a curious expression in his eyes.

Elinor shook her head impatiently. 'That is not something one can teach...it is a question of character.'

'I see.'

A silence fell between them as they pursued their own thoughts. Elinor had been considerably surprised to hear that Rokeby had discussed Hester's future with John Charlbury. And how like the latter it was to refuse to stand in the way of a splendid match for her. His sudden decision to return to Kent was understandable in the circumstances, but Rokeby's announcement that his friend would not dangle after an heiress spoke of something more.

'My lord...' She faltered. 'Am I to understand that Mr Charlbury is growing attached to Hester?'

'I cannot speak for him.' There was an underlying note of anger in Rokeby's voice. 'I advise you to put the matter out of your mind, Miss Temple.'

But Elinor could not. Preocuppied with her musings, she was unaware that Rokeby had signalled to the musicians to continue with the waltz. It was indiscreet of him to depart from custom in such a way and it resulted in a number of indignant looks from the elderly ladies who were seated by the side of the ballroom.

Rokeby ignored the buzz of gossip. He was an excellent dancer, moving with grace and dignity as he held her lightly in his arms, and Elinor matched her steps to his. As he whirled her about the floor, she gave herself up to the music almost insensibly, revelling in the pleasure of the dance.

'That's better!' He looked down at her with a smile. 'I knew that we should partner each other to perfection. Now, Miss Temple, I cannot ask for yet another reprise or I shall be in serious trouble with my aunt. May I offer you the refreshment which you missed?'

Recalled to the present, Elinor looked about her as the music stopped. She and her partner were the cynosure of all eyes, and many of the glances thrown in their direction were hostile.

'Sir, we are giving rise to comment,' she murmured in a low voice. 'Please take me back to Lady Hartfield. You must seek your partner for the next dance.'

'Not just yet. My leg is paining me, you see.' It was said with a chuckle, and Elinor gave him a suspicious look.

'It is the unaccustomed exercise, I assure you,' he continued blandly. His limp was pronounced as he led her from the floor.

'I am not surprised, my lord,' she hissed, aware for the first time that he had prolonged the dance deliberately. 'That was thoughtless of you. . .'

'On the contrary, I gave it some considerable thought. The opportunity to hold you in my arms is all too rare. I felt that I should make the most of it.'

'You deserve to be in pain,' she ground out. 'You are impossible!'

'Pray do not glare at me, Miss Temple. That will give rise to further gossip. You will be glad to hear that I am in severe pain, and have been for some time, from a wounded heart, as much as from an injured leg. . .'

Elinor gave him a fulminating glance and walked to where Lady Hartfield stood in a group of friends.

'How well you and Marcus dance together, my dear! It is a pleasure to watch you, but the waltz is so exhausting, even for young people. Marcus, where are your manners? Miss Temple will be glad to rest for a time, perhaps with a little refreshment. . .?'

'Ma'am, I have just suggested it.' Rokeby smiled down at her.

'Will you not join us, Lady Hartfield?' Elinor said in despair.

'No, no, my dear. . .off you go.' Her ladyship dismissed them with an airy wave of her fan. 'I will join you later.'

'Foiled again, my dear?' Rokeby took Elinor's arm and led her away. 'Everything conspires against you, and in my favour.'

Elinor had reached a decision. It was time to put an end to Rokeby's folly. If she did not do so without delay, she would acquire an unenviable reputation as his lordship's latest flirt, if not worse.

Unresisting, she allowed him to lead her to a secluded embrasure, and sat quietly as he went away to procure her a glass of lemonade. As she waited, she cast about in her mind for some way to discourage his casual attentions. She was still lost in thought when he returned.

'So grave, Miss Temple?' He handed her the glass. 'Let me assure you that I have not added some mysterious potion to this liquid which will rob you of your senses.'

She gave him a long look and set the glass aside.

'I am here because I wish to talk to you, my lord.'

'At last! I am delighted to hear it. Can it be that my patience has been rewarded?' He grinned as he took a seat beside her.

'Mine has been sorely tried, Lord Rokeby. It is not kind in you to attempt to destroy my reputation.'

'I shall never do that.' His smile vanished. 'I would not seek to harm you, as you know.'

'But I do not know it. I cannot think you a fool, sir, and you must realise that I am in a difficult position in this household?'

'Beloved by all? Come, ma'am, is that such a very dreadful fate?'

Exasperated, she raised her face to his. 'That is exactly what I mean. Must you say such things? They are quite meaningless, and serve only to distress me.'

He took her hand in his and began to stroke her fingers in an absent way. She could feel the warmth of his flesh even through the fabric of her gloves and it disturbed her. She tried to draw her hand away, but his fingers closed about hers.

'And if it were not meaningless? Would it distress you still?'

Elinor froze for a moment. Then the colour rose to her face.

'I shall not pretend to misunderstand you, sir. I am astonished that you should offer me such insult under your aunt's roof.' She stood up swiftly and removed her hand from Rokeby's grasp.

He was too startled to do more than stare at her. Then, in a single lithe movement, he was beside her, reaching out to take her in his arms.

'Elinor...' His words died on his lips as Talworth moved towards them, smirking.

The fat man did no more than bow as he walked by, but his face wore a look of secret satisfaction.

Elinor wished that the ground might open at her feet. Talworth, she guessed from his expression, had heard the whole of her conversation with his lordship, and would judge the pair of them accordingly.

'Damnation!' Rokeby swore beneath his breath. 'What is he doing here? Does my aunt not know that he is the worst rattle in London?'

The tears sprang unbidden to Elinor's eyes. She could have wept with mortification. Now she longed only to run up to her room.

'I hope you are satisfied,' she choked out. 'I shall be a laughing-stock. . .'

'Stay here! I'll go after him and explain.'

'Explain what? That you offered me a *carte blanche*? He knows it already. . .' Without waiting for his reply she ran from the room.

Her hopes of escaping before the end of the ball were dashed as she was claimed by first one partner and then another. Later she could recall nothing of the rest of the evening other than Hester's wistful face as they bade their guests farewell.

'Mr Charlbury did not come. I wonder why?' she appealed to Lady Hartfield.

'Oh, Hester, I forgot to tell you in the bustle. He sent a message to explain why he must fail us for this evening.' Her ladyship patted Hester's cheek. 'You did not want for partners, my dear. In fact, you were a great success and we were proud of you. . . Is that not so, Elinor?'

Elinor nodded, but her heart was moved to pity by Hester's disconsolate expression.

'He. . .he is not ill?' the girl asked, and there was no hiding the anxiety in her voice.

'Nothing like that, my love. Some little difficulty, I understand, which may force him to return to Kent.'

Hester looked stricken. 'You mean that we shall not see him for some time?'

'It may not be for long.' Her ladyship dismissed

John Charlbury from her mind. 'Now tell me, Hester, which of your partners did you find the most agreeable?'

Hester murmured something in reply, but her mind was not upon the conversation and suddenly she looked weary.

'My dear ma'am, Hester is ready for her bed.' Elinor pleaded. 'Will you excuse us now that the last of the guests have gone?'

'Yes, yes, my dears. . .I hope you enjoyed it. . .it was a success, I believe.'

Her two companions murmured all that was proper, adding their thanks to all their compliments, and her ladyship was pleased.

'Now, where is Marcus?' she said suddenly. 'I have not seen him this age. Ah, there he is, by the door. I might have guessed that he would not fail in his observance of civilities.' She moved across to stand beside her nephew.

Elinor seized the opportunity to take Hester by the arm and hurry her away. Another confrontation with Lord Rokeby at that hour of night would be beyond bearing. After the events of that evening she doubted if she could face him again with any degree of equanimity.

Talworth would talk, she was convinced of it. He would not miss such an opportunity to be revenged on Rokeby for the insult offered to him in the park. The news that his lordship desired to take Elinor in his keeping would be discussed in every drawing-room in London before the following day was out. She felt that she must die of shame.

The cynical eyes of the Polite World would be upon her from now on, and she felt that she could not bear the sly remarks and the innuendos which were sure to be her lot.

How could Rokeby have behaved so ill? Apart from all else, he might have considered his aunt. The ensuing scandal could not fail to affect both Lady Hartfield and Hester.

Misery gave way to anger in Elinor's mind. She would not, could not, love a man who thought only of self-gratification, destroying those about him as he pursued his lusts. She would speak to her ladyship and explain that she must leave Berkeley Square at once. It was the only course open to her.

She knew, of course, that for a wealthy man to keep a mistress gave no cause for comment among the *ton*. The lack of such an arrangement might be more surprising, but the gorgeous birds of paradise who gave their favours in return for charming little houses, dashing curricles, and a profusion of jewellery and clothing were not of her world. Some of the fair Cyprians made it their profession, whilst others, such as actresses and opera dancers, used such arrangements to augment their slender incomes.

And she was thought willing to be added to their number? Her face grew hot. When had she given Rokeby any indication that he might suggest it to her? She was tempted to ask him, but she dared not. She could not be sure that she had not betrayed her love with an unguarded look or a word, and it could not be denied that she had responded to his kisses with a passion which had shaken her beyond belief.

She had always thought that she knew herself so well, she thought sadly. Now it was clear that there were hidden depths within her soul which were unknown to her.

Was she truly a wanton at heart? With his experience of women, Rokeby must have sensed it and thought himself justified in appealing to her sensual desires. Perhaps it was she herself who was to blame?

Consumed by a miserable feeling of guilt, she found it hard to sleep. It was not much consolation to think that, if it were she who was at fault, she would most certainly be punished for it, either by leaving those she loved, or being forced to face the censure of the world.

In the event, neither of those dreaded fates awaited her. She came down next day to find that Rokeby had decided to accompany John Charlbury to Kent. That was some respite, she thought with relief.

She had viewed her first appearance at Almack's with trepidation, fearing that she could not avoid the open disapproval of the powerful patronesses, but it came as a surprise to find that she was greeted with the same civility proffered to Hester and Lady Hartfield. Perhaps Talworth had gone out of London? She hoped so with all her heart. It was becoming clear that he had not yet spread his evil gossip. She had no way of knowing what Rokeby might have said to him, but whether his lordship had resorted to threats or persuasion, his efforts appeared to have been successful.

It was as she was chatting quietly with Hester that Lord Dacre approached them, accompanied by his son. He greeted them effusively, but Elinor noticed once again that his grey eyes were as cold as the winter sea.

'Not dancing, my dear Miss Winton?' he said in a

jovial tone. 'That will not do. Tobias would enjoy nothing more than to partner you.'

Hester had no alternative but to take the young man's arm and allow him to lead her away.

'I do not see Rokeby here tonight.' Lord Dacre scanned the room. 'A pity! I wished to speak to him on a matter of some importance.'

Elinor felt a small twinge of anxiety. She was well aware of the antipathy between the two men, and she sensed at once that, whatever her present companion had in mind, it could bode no good.

'His lordship is gone into Kent,' she told him quickly. 'We do not know when he will return.'

'Very wise of him...under the circumstances.' His look was almost a leer and Elinor grew cold. It said more clearly than words that he had learned of her conversation with Rokeby on the night of the ball. She did not answer him.

'Lady Hartfield's ball was a great success, so I understand,' he continued. 'Doubtless my own invitation must have gone astray...'

Elinor could not look at him. She would not lie, but he knew as well as she did that no invitation had been sent to him. She cast about wildly for something to say, but she could think of nothing. If only someone would rescue her. She looked around, but Lady Hartfield was speaking to a friend at the far end of the room, and did not seem to have noticed that Hester was dancing with Tobias.

'I heard reports of your own success,' Lord Dacre went on smoothly. 'Your beauty won more than one heart...'

'I am not aware of it,' Elinor said stiffly.

'No?' His smile was one of disbelief. 'Come now,

you will not expect me think that you did not receive at least one offer?'

Elinor stared at him. She felt like some helpless animal mesmerised by a snake. She longed to escape, but her limbs refused to obey her.

'Elinor, my dear, why is Hester dancing—? Oh, I beg your pardon, Dacre...I did not know that you would be here tonight.' Lady Hartfield did not trouble to hide her annoyance.

'Else you would not have come, Letitia?' The big man's expression did not change from its customary benevolence. He wagged his head and turned to Elinor. 'These family feuds, Miss Temple! With your own background, I'm sure that you cannot approve of them.'

'I was not aware that you knew anything of my background, sir.' The words were out before Elinor had time to think of their possible consequences.

'Surely you have no secrets, my dear, especially from Lady Hartfield?' There was a note of warning in his voice.

It was at this point that her ladyship's patience snapped. 'Dacre, I do not know what game you may be playing, but if you are thinking of Hester for Tobias you may forget the idea. Rokeby, I assure you, will have none of it.'

Lord Dacre bowed. 'I hope to persuade him to change his mind, my dear Letitia. Will you let me know when he returns to London?'

'You will be wasting your time...' The older woman took Elinor's arm and turned away.

'That man! He puts me out of all patience, Elinor. I am tempted to scream at him like a common fishwife!'

'I know the feeling, ma'am.' Elinor made an attempt

to recover her composure, but she found that she was trembling. Her conversation with Lord Dacre had been short, but in those few moments he had convinced her that not only did he know of Rokeby's offer to her, but that he would not hesitate to tell Lady Hartfield of it. And he had mentioned her own background. Was he referring to her parents? She would not put it past him to have made enquiries in Derbyshire. She realised that it was yet another threat.

But why should he threaten her? She was not a danger to him. Perhaps it was her imagination, but she could not shake off an underlying sense of menace.

'Elinor, do not look so troubled,' Lady Hartfield urged. 'The man is unpleasant beyond belief, but he is a fool if he imagines that Marcus would consent to a match between Hester and his son.'

Elinor shuddered. 'I should hope so, ma'am. I could not bear to think of Hester in his power.'

'Now you are letting your imagination run away with you. One dance with Tobias can do no harm. Even so, I could wish that it had not happened, and I find myself wishing even more that Marcus had not taken it into his head to go back to Kent at this particular time.'

Silently, Elinor agreed with her. Rokeby, however trying his attitude to herself, was more than a match for his formidable enemy. It came to her suddenly that beyond the excitement which she found always in his company there was a feeling of security.

The knowledge puzzled her. How could she feel secure with a man who had but recently made her a dishonourable proposal and wished for nothing more than to persuade her to become his mistress?

Her feelings were irrational, but at that moment she

longed to see him walk into the room with that teasing smile and nonsensical banter upon his lips. He would know how to counter Lord Dacre's threats, she was sure of it.

It was two days later that her prayers were answered. She was standing in the hall with Lady Hartfield and Hester, when Rokeby ran lightly up the steps.

'You are lucky to have caught us in, my dear Marcus.' Her ladyship allowed him to kiss her on the cheek. 'We were about to drive out to the park.'

'I will go with you. Have you missed me?' His question was directed to his aunt, but his eyes were upon Elinor. Something in her expression caught his attention. Under their heavy lids the penetrating eyes asked another question, but it was not until later that day that she found herself alone with him.

'Something is worrying you. . .what is it?' he asked without preamble.

In a very few words she told him of their meeting with Lord Dacre at Almack's. 'My lord, I am sorry that Hester was persuaded to dance with Lord Dacre's son,' she said.

Rokeby looked at her. 'That is not it. Why are you so frightened?'

It was all too much for Elinor. The tears welled up and she found herself in his arms.

CHAPTER TEN

'MY LITTLE love! I should not have left you.' Rokeby rained kisses upon her brow, her cheeks, and the tip of her nose.

'Sir, you must not.' Elinor struggled to free herself. 'I am sorry to be so foolish...but...but please listen... I must warn you—'

'Warn me of what?' His eyes were tender as he looked down at her.

'Lord Dacre is aware...I mean...he knows of our conversation at the ball.'

'I see. Then Talworth must have told him. I could not find him on that night, else he would not have spoken.' There was a grimness about his mouth which startled Elinor. 'You fear the gossip, is that it?'

'No...that is not all. I cannot think how it came about, but I felt that he was warning me. He spoke of having secrets from Lady Hartfield...and...and he mentioned my background...'

'What the devil has that to do with him?'

'I do not know, my lord,' Elinor told him truthfully. 'He may intend to write to my parents...'

'Warning them of your life of dissipation?' Rokeby leaned against the mantelpiece. His tone was light, but his eyes were wary. 'Have you told me everything?'

'No, sir. When Lady Hartfield told him that you would not countenance a marriage between Hester and Tobias, he seemed to believe that he could persuade you to change your mind.'

'A forlorn hope, you will admit, my dear one?'

Elinor did not return his loving look. 'Lord Rokeby, I beg that you will be serious. I cannot trust Lord Dacre. If you had but heard him...I cannot say exactly...but I would swear that he has some scheme in his mind.'

'You have told my aunt of this?'

'No, I did not wish to worry her with my fancies.'

'I am flattered that you have no such scruples about worrying me.' His lordship walked towards her and slipped an arm about her waist. 'That is as it should be, my little love.'

Elinor summoned her few remaining shreds of dignity. 'I wish you will not address me so, my lord. It does not please me, and in any case, I am not little. For a woman, I am tall.'

Rokeby gave a shout of laughter. 'Of all the inconsequential remarks! You are adorable!'

'Sir, you go too far!'

'No, I do not. I do not go nearly far enough, but my time will come. Now, my dear, what do you suggest? Shall I beard Dacre in his den? Will that set your mind at rest?'

There was doubt in Elinor's eyes as she raised her face to his. 'It might be as well to find out what he has in mind. That is, if you think it best...?'

'Deferring to my judgment, my dear Miss Temple? Wonders will never cease! I must be grateful to Lord Dacre if he has brought about this change of heart.' A lean finger slipped beneath her chin and he bent towards her.

'No, you must not!' Elinor turned her face away.

'Why not? You will admit that we have both enjoyed our kisses up to now. Must I suppose that your heart is given to another? Alas, it was a mistake to leave you unattended and at the mercy of the marriage market.'

'Marriage has not been mentioned to me,' Elinor said in glacial tones. 'And a market in flesh can only be disgusting.'

He did not release her. A strong hand cupped her chin and he forced her to look at him. 'How you despise us!' he said softly. 'I do not care to see that look upon your face.'

'You are mistaken. I have met with much kindness from your aunt, and from the Charlburys. I am no ascetic, sir, and I appreciate the elegance of all I see about me. . .' Elinor had no idea why she was protesting, but it did not change the bleak look upon his lordship's face.

'So all we lack is heart?' he murmured. 'I wish I could persuade you otherwise.'

'Sir, I do not mean to sound censorious. I am not fool enough to despise the advantages of wealth and position which are so important to your world. It is just that. . .'

'Yes?' he prompted.

'I have not been brought up to believe that an advantageous match should be the main aim of a woman's life. . .or a man's either.' Her voice was so low that he could barely catch her words.

'That has been clear to me from the moment that we met!' There was a harshness in his tone which surprised her.

'I do not expect you to understand,' she added quietly.

'I should do, ma'am. Our mutual friend, John Charlbury, has been expressing similar sentiments to

me for these past few days. You and he should deal
famously together. . .'

'No, sir, we should not,' Elinor cried indignantly.
The words came out with more vehemence than she
had intended, and she knew at once that she was on
dangerous ground. In protesting a lack of interest in
John Charlbury, she must not give Lord Rokeby cause
to believe that his own advances might be welcome to
her, even though she had repudiated them up to the
present time.

'We have both missed his companionship, especially
Hester,' she murmured. 'Does he plan to return to
London?'

Rokeby gave her a sharp look. 'I am not privy to his
plans, Miss Temple. And for the present I believe that
we have much else to occupy our minds. I will see
Dacre in the morning.'

His lordship was unable to carry out this plan, as Lord
Dacre, so he was informed, had left the city for an
unspecified length of time.

Rokeby had not much time to speculate on his
enemy's reasons for such a sudden departure. Within
the next few days, he received three offers for Hester's
hand.

When he summoned her to his study, he had
expected that Elinor would accompany her, but in that
he was disappointed. Elinor had decided to accompany
Lady Hartfield to the Florida Gardens, believing that
no words of hers should influence the girl.

'Do you know why I have sent for you, Hester?' He
motioned his ward to a chair.

'No, sir.' Hester sat bolt upright, tension apparent
in every line of her body.

'There is no need to be nervous,' he told her gently. 'I must tell you that three gentlemen have offered for your hand. I wish to know your opinions. . .'

Hester's eyes grew huge with fright, but she did not speak.

'I think we need not consider Mr Thorne, unless you have a particular *tendre* for him? He is very young, and not yet in control of his fortune. . .'

Hester swallowed convulsively, and shook her head.

'I am glad that you agree with me,' Rokeby continued smoothly. 'Barrington is a much more suitable match, although he is a widower. . .'

Hester could contain herself no longer. 'No, no, I cannot marry him. Oh, sir, you will not make me do so? He is old, and when he looks at me I feel. . .' She stopped as a deep flush of colour rose from beneath the neckline of her gown and suffused her face.

'You were saying?'

Hester was driven beyond endurance. 'I feel that I am not wearing any clothes. . . I cannot bear it. . .'

'There will be no need for you to do so. I had already decided against him,' Rokeby continued in an imperturbable tone.

'Then why did you mention him?' Hester choked back a sob.

'My dear, it is only right that I should tell you of all offers. Now, as to the third. . .'

'Yes?' Hester lifted her head, and her eyes were filled with hope.

'Pangbourne, my dear. His suit, I hope, will meet with your approval. He is a young man, and his father's heir.'

'Sir, he is a fribble.' Hester's disappointment had made her bold. 'I cannot spend the rest of my life with a man whose main concern is the height of his shirt-points.' She looked at Rokeby, expecting an explosion of wrath but, to her surprise, he smiled at her.

'Very wise, my dear Hester. We shall do better than that for you.' It was an effort to restore her spirits, but Hester did not respond. She had hoped against hope that the third offer might have come from John Charlbury, and her disappointment was obvious.

Rokeby strolled over to her, and cupped her face in his hand.

'Chin up!' he advised. 'All is not lost. You may yet gain your heart's desire, as I hope to do myself.'

'You, sir?' Hester stared at him.

'Why yes, my dear. I am not made of stone, you know.'

'Sir? I. . .I do not understand you?'

'Sometimes, Hester, I fail to understand myself.' He gave her a rueful look. 'There, do not trouble yourself with my problems. . .you have many more interesting matters with which to occupy yourself.' His voice was more gentle than she had heard it.

'I may go, my lord?'

Rokeby nodded his assent, and was surprised when she sought to thank him.

'For what, my dear?'

'For not forcing me to accept one of the. . .the offers, sir.'

'You must make your own choice, my dear Hester.'

'But I thought that you were to decide?'

Under their heavy lids, his blue eyes were filled with amusement. 'My function is, I believe, to check the gentlemens' credentials. After all, we cannot have you carried off by some fortune-hunting villain who would lock you in a dungeon until you agreed to his demands. Miss Temple would never forgive me. . .'

'You are making game of me, my lord.' Hester had caught a little of his gaiety. 'I promise that you would hear my screams.'

She left him then to sit by the window in the salon. Bursting with news, she was impatient for the return of Elinor and Lady Hartfield. And, as she waited, she thought of her interview with his lordship.

His attitude had come as a surprise to her. Perhaps, after all, he was not so lost to all human feeling as she had believed. In the end, she had felt more at ease with him than she had done since their first meeting. She was still wondering at her discovery when Elinor walked into the room.

'Well, my dear?' From the expression on Elinor's face she guessed that both her friend and Lady Hartfield knew of the offers. It was only to be expected that Rokeby would have mentioned them before he spoke to her, but she found that she was blushing.

In halting words she told Elinor of her conversation with her guardian.

'But it will be all right,' she murmured. 'Lord Rokeby is not angry with me.'

'Of course not, my love! How could he be? He could scarce expect you to take any of the three. . .'

Privately, Elinor had been appalled at the idea that Hester's hand might be given to any of them, but Rokeby had warned her not to attempt to influence the girl.

'You think highly of Hester's intelligence, do you not?' he had demanded. 'Pray allow her to use it, madam.'

'Then you will not insist?'

'No, I will not.' It was clear that he was annoyed, but he made a quick recovery. 'It is early in the Season,' he told her lightly. 'Doubtless there will be other offers.'

With that she had to be satisfied, though his easy acceptance of the fact that Hester would refuse all three of her prospective suitors had surprised her.

From the beginning, Rokeby had claimed that he wished to see Hester married as soon as possible. Now, it appeared, he intended to give her at least some choice in the matter. But how long would his patience last?

Hester had given no sign of being attracted to any of the men who were quick to claim her hand to partner them at the many balls and routs which they attended. Her confidence had grown, and her modest, pleasant manner had won her several friends among the younger ladies.

Effusive compliments still caused her to withdraw into her shell, whether they came from her partners, or from their predatory mammas.

Elinor sighed. She had long suspected that Hester's heart was already given to John Charlbury. The girl might not yet have recognised her affection for what it was, but Elinor knew without being told that Hester compared her present companions with the man she missed so much, and found them wanting.

She was alone in the salon, still lost in thought, when Rokeby came to find her.

'Frowning, my dear? I had thought to find you overcome with joy?' The penetrating eyes were intent upon her face, though his tone was teasing.

'I must thank you, sir.' Elinor looked up at him.

'For allowing Hester to show us that she is no fool? That should not surprise you.' His lordship sat down beside her and took her hand. Before she realised his intention he had raised it to his lips, and Elinor began to tremble as his warm mouth caressed her palm.

'What are you doing?' she cried quickly. 'Please, I beg that you will not. . .'

'I am claiming my reward, my love. Confess it, Hester is in charity with me. Surely that must please you?'

Elinor removed her hand from his grasp and rose to her feet.

'No, do not run away from me!' he begged, and she heard the laughter in his voice. 'I wished merely to know if you would care for an expedition to the Vauxhall Gardens? There is to be a concert there this evening, and we might order supper. I will take a box. . .'

'That is thoughtful of you, sir.' Elinor took a seat as far away from him as possible. 'Hester will enjoy it. She has longed to see the fireworks.'

'And you? Perhaps you feel that there are enough fireworks here in Berkeley Square?'

Elinor refused to rise to the bait. 'I too, should enjoy it, sir. . .that is, if Lady Hartfield agrees.'

Rokeby chuckled. 'Don't worry! I had not intended to lure you there alone, delightful though the prospect seems. You will be well protected from my importunate advances.'

'I am glad to hear it,' she said stiffly. 'I wonder that you should not grow tired of all this nonsense, my lord.'

'I am an optimist,' he told her with a wicked grin. 'I have not abandoned hope of capturing your heart.'

'You will not do so by continuing in your present manner.' Elinor had not reflected before she spoke and paid the penalty at once.

Rokeby walked towards her and raised her to her feet. With his hands resting gently on her shoulders, he looked down at her.

'But if I should change? What then?' There was no mistaking the glitter in his eyes.

She had no answer for him. Her feelings threatened to overcome her as he gazed into her eyes. She tore away from him before she betrayed herself and fled from the room.

She was in sombre mood as she took her seat in the carriage that evening. It was becoming increasingly difficult to keep his lordship at arm's length.

This very morning her resolution had been sorely tried. When he had held her close and had looked at her in just that tender way, she had longed to throw caution to the winds and respond to his embrace. She stifled a little moan of anguish. Such heartache was difficult to bear.

The evening was unseasonably warm, and all three ladies felt that lace shawls would be sufficient for their comfort in the open air. Elinor's was of a deeper tone than her straw-coloured gown of Berlin silk, high-waisted and cut low at the neck as fashion dictated. She could not doubt that her toilette met with Rokeby's full approval. He did not take his eyes off her on their journey across the river.

There her attention was diverted by Hester's pleasure in the Gardens. They entered the brightly lit enclosure by the water-gate and made their way through the tastefully planted groves of trees to the main arena which was lined with private boxes.

'It is like a fairyland.' Hester pointed to the coloured lamps which were strung between the trees. 'How wonderful! I had not thought that anything could be so fine. . .'

'You will see more wonders later,' Rokeby promised as he led them to his box. 'Supper first, I think. . .then the Rotunda. . .We must not miss the start of the concert.'

Even Lady Hartfield could not fault the supper, though she had expressed doubts that it could match the efforts of her own chef. Elinor was unmoved by the excellence of the various dishes. She could not have said what she was eating.

All her attention was focused upon the tall, athletic figure beside her. Tonight he was clad in a well-fitting coat of corbeau-coloured cloth and tight-fitting pantaloons with gleaming Hessian boots drawn over them.

As he pressed her to take a little of the trifle, the creams or the jellies which ended the meal she could not look at him. The urge to take his hand and press it to her lips was overwhelming.

'We should go to the Rotunda.' Rokeby consulted his time-piece. 'In the interval between the two halves of the concert, I shall show you the Cascade. . .'

He was as good as his word, as Hester exclaimed with delight at the spectacle before her. The scene drew visitors from far and near to marvel at the lifelike replica of the country vista, with its water-mill, its bridge, and its rushing waters. She could not be drawn away.

Lady Hartfield smiled at her enthusiasm. 'Marcus, do you accompany Miss Temple back to your box. We shall be more comfortable if we watch the fireworks from there. I will bring Hester to you.'

'Aunt, they do not begin until after the concert is ended.'

'Oh yes, I had forgot! Come, Hester, we must take our seats again.' She took Hester's arm and smiled at Elinor. 'Shall you wish to hear the rest of the concert, my dear?'

'I would not miss it for the world,' Elinor told her truthfully. A passionate lover of music, she had found long ago that the soaring cadences of sound transported her to another world where she could forget her present cares.

She had another reason for not wishing to leave her companions to stroll back to the private box with Rokeby. All evening she had been aware of the sly looks and malicious smiles on the faces of those who greeted them. She wondered that Lady Hartfield had not noticed it.

She was too much in Rokeby's company, and to walk back alone with him could only give rise to further comment among the *ton*.

It was unlike Lady Hartfield to be oblivious of such gossip. Her ladyship was ever quick to detect the least breath of scandal, especially when it concerned her family, or anyone close to her.

Elinor resolved to speak to her when the opportunity arose. She had wondered for some time at Lady Hartfield's attitude towards herself and Rokeby. On occasion it had seemed to her that her hostess had been eager to leave them together. She could not disguise that fact, even from herself, but she could not understand it.

She trusts us, Elinor thought sadly. It had not

occurred to her that her beloved nephew might be ailing at seduction, or that Elinor herself might be in any danger from him. It would not be easy to mention her own worries so tactfully that she did not give offence.

As the concert began again, she tried to give her full attention to the music, but she found that she could not. There was something wrong...something in the atmosphere of the Rotunda that night which she found disturbing.

She looked about her at the circle of rapt faces. All eyes were upon the musicians, or so she thought. Then a movement caught her eye. There was someone standing in the shadow of one of the colonnades to the side of them.

A slight breeze had sprung up, and the coloured lights strung between the trees began to sway, throwing beams where there had been none before. As Elinor looked towards the darkened colonnade, the shadows lifted and she recognised Talworth. He moved back at once, but not before she had seen the expression on his face.

His eyes were fixed upon Lord Rokeby and in them was a look of hatred.

Elinor gasped and turned to her companion, but a strong hand grasped her arm and held her still.

'I have seen him,' Rokeby murmured. 'You must pretend that you have not done so.'

'But, my lord, he looks as if he might plunge a dagger in your back.' Drowned by the music, her words did not reach the others. 'You will take care?'

'I will take care,' he promised. 'Don't worry! Talworth has not the courage for such a violent course of action. His revenge is likely to be of a more subtle kind.'

'I could wish that you had not quarrelled with him in the park that day. . .'

For an instant his mouth seemed to harden. 'You would have had me ignore his remarks? That was not possible, my dear.'

Elinor was silent. It had been an ugly scene, and Talworth, however much he deserved it, would not forgive his lordship's words. To be called a 'pander' was the worst of insults, and must result in a challenge.

Yet Talworth had not issued that challenge, and must, therefore, be regarded as a coward. Elinor realised that this, as much as the insult, was the cause of Talworth's hatred.

She began to tremble.

'Steady!' Rokeby murmured. 'You will not wish to worry my aunt. I assure you, there is no need for concern.'

Elinor longed to believe him, but she could not rid herself of the impression that some threat hung over him.

Common sense told her that behind the laughing, teasing manner was a man well able to take care of himself, but was he proof against treachery?

Later, as they strolled back through the crowds towards their box, she found herself starting at every shadow which moved beside the long avenues of trees. Her eyes searched faces in the press of people, but she saw nothing to alarm her.

Rokeby appeared to be untroubled. With his customary courtesy he settled the ladies at the front of the box and took a seat behind Elinor.

Hester was on her feet as the first rockets soared into the sky, and she found it impossible to sit down as the various set-pieces were set alight.

Lady Hartfield had seen the spectacle several times before and soon found more diversion in chatting to an acquaintance in the neighbouring box.

'Tonight you look lovelier than ever.' Rokeby leaned forward until his lips were close to Elinor's ear. 'In those tawny shades, with the candlelight upon your hair, there is a certain glow about you.'

Elinor tried to hush him.

'No! Listen to me!' he insisted. 'Won't you allow me to tell you—?'

'Lord Rokeby, I know that you are trying to divert me from all thought of Talworth. It is kind of you, but there is no need. I am quite myself again.'

'I think not, but you must believe that I shall take care of my own—'

Elinor seized upon a gap in Lady Hartfield's conversation to comment upon the fireworks. She took care to give Rokeby no further opportunity to speak to her alone that night.

In recent weeks she sensed that his attitude towards her had changed. Sometimes she fancied that his words were almost a declaration of love, but that could not be. It was more likely that as one method of seduction had failed he would try another.

On the following day she sought out her hostess as her ladyship was writing letters.

'Ma'am, may I have a private word with you?' she said.

'Of course, my dear. What can I do for you?'

Elinor found herself at a loss for words although she had rehearsed what she wished to say. Somehow the expression in those keen black eyes made her worries seem trivial.

In desperation, she plunged ahead. 'Ma'am, I have been thinking. It is so long since I visited my family. Would you think it wrong of me to leave you now? Hester, I know, will be quite safe in your care...and ...and...'

'And there are other reasons?' Lady Hartfield turned from her writing desk to give Elinor her full attention.

Elinor felt the colour rising to her cheeks. 'Yes, ma'am, but, if you please, I would rather not discuss them.'

'I see. Well, Elinor, I shall not press you to give me your confidence, but to leave now...in the middle of the Season? Hester has suffered one disappointment, as you know. You are her dearest friend. Is it right, do you suppose, to ask her to suffer another?'

Elinor felt her resolution waning, but she made a last attempt to press her case. 'Hester has had offers, ma'am. It cannot be so long before she is safely settled. Then, as you know, I must seek employment elsewhere.'

'That is in the future, my dear. Knowing Hester as we do, I cannot think that she will make her choice in London.'

Startled, Elinor grazed at her. 'Then...then you know?'

'Of course I know. Did you think me blind, my dear? In her quiet way, Hester has set her mind upon John Charlbury.'

'But, ma'am, he will not offer for her, or so Lord Rokeby gave me to understand...'

Her ladyship made a gesture of impatience. 'Men are such fools, my dear Elinor, but we shall not give up hope. A clever woman will often find a way to circumvent their preposterous notions.'

Elinor felt oddly comforted. It seemed that Lady Hartfield did, in fact, favour Hester's choice.

'I could wish that Hester were not an heiress,' she admitted. 'That will seem strange to you, perhaps, but it does seem to be a stumbling-block.'

'It will be overcome.' Her ladyship, who was not demonstrative, leaned forward to drop a kiss upon Elinor's brow. 'Now, my dear, let me beg you to forget your present worries. Why not write to your family? You might promise to visit them in the autumn. Meantime, none of us can spare you. . .indeed, we are not willing to do so.'

Elinor did not argue further. Her good intentions had been defeated but, rather than being saddened by her failure, she felt a sudden surge of joy. The thought of leaving Rokeby had struck like a dagger to her heart. She could only wonder at her own folly. Heartache beckoned, there could be no doubt of it, but she felt powerless to resist. Fiercely she castigated herself for her want of character. She should stand firm against him, but she could not.

She descended the great staircase, still absorbed in her thoughts, as the outer door opened to admit Lord Dacre.

Rooted to the spot, she stood in silence as Rokeby came towards him. Then the two men disappeared into Lady Hartfield's library.

Elinor could not imagine that Lady Hartfield knew of the sudden appearance of her brother-in-law. Her ladyship had not mentioned it, and Dacre was not a welcome visitor. She waited in the salon until he left, and Rokeby came to find her.

CHAPTER ELEVEN

ELINOR looked at him with a question in her eyes.

'Tobias,' he said briefly. 'He has offered for Hester
. . .at least, his father has.'

'But you refused?'

'Of course. Could you doubt it?' He began to pace
the room, looking so unlike himself that Elinor was
troubled.

'My lord, is there something more?'

Rokeby hesitated. 'There is,' he said at last. 'He
threatens to apply to the courts to remove Hester from
my care.'

Elinor's blood ran cold. 'But. . .you are her guardian,' she faltered. 'How can that be possible?'

'Anyone may challenge my suitability,' he told her.
'In this case there are witnesses to confirm that my
way of life is so depraved as to put my ward in danger.'

'Talworth?' Suddenly Elinor felt breathless.

Rokeby nodded. 'As you say.'

'But that is nonsense!' Elinor rushed to his defence.
'Suppose you do consort with. . .er. . .with lightskirts.
Does not every man in London do the same?'

'Every man in London does not admit his ward and
her companion to his home when he is entertaining
ladies of the town.'

'But that was not your fault,' Elinor cried hotly. 'I
shall swear to it. We came to Merton Place without
your knowledge. . .'

When he looked at her his face was grave. 'There is

yet more,' he said. 'I am thought to be in the act of seducing my ward's companion...a respectable woman who should, in the normal way of things, be assured of my protection.'

He looked so disturbed that Elinor lost her temper.

'That worm, Talworth!' she cried in fury. 'He shall be made to eat his words! How dare he malign you so?'

Rokeby leaned forward and touched her hand. 'Elinor, you are generous,' he said quietly. 'I have given you no reason to think well of me.'

Elinor was too angry to think before she spoke. 'I will see Lord Dacre. When I assure him that you had no such thought in mind, he must believe me!'

'He has a witness. Don't forget Talworth.'

'Talworth was mistaken. He misunderstood your words, as I did myself.'

'Did you, Elinor?' His eyes held hers for a long moment. 'You did not allow me to explain, but sadly it is too late. My way of life has not been such that anyone would believe me.'

'You cannot mean it?' She looked at him in horror. 'Do not say that you will allow Lord Dacre to take Hester from us?'

'I shall fight the case, naturally, but I cannot offer much hope that Dacre will not succeed.'

'He must not and he shall not. Oh, there must be a way to stop him... If Lady Hartfield were to speak on your behalf?'

'It would not serve. As a woman, my aunt has no rights in this matter...'

At his words Elinor's anger increased, and a faint smile touched his lips as he saw her wrathful expression.

'I know your views, my dear, and I must agree. When it comes to good sense, both you and my aunt are the equal of any man. In fact, you have more than most of my acquaintance, but the law does not recognise it.'

'Then the law is wrong,' she told him with a kindling eye. 'Is Hester to be handed over to a brute merely because he is a member of the male sex?'

'I cannot say.' Rokeby began to pace the room, lost in thought.

'There must be something we can do,' Elinor pleaded. 'If we returned to Kent...? Or perhaps we might take her to some other part of England?'

'It may be too late for that. I do not know what steps Dacre may have taken before he came here. He must have known that I would not consent to the match.'

'What steps could he take? He cannot force his way into this house to take her by force.'

Rokeby looked at her and she grew cold with apprehension. 'Oh, no!' she cried. 'That *must* be against the law.'

'It has been done before. I do not say that he would take her from this house, but I suspect that he has set men to watch the place. At the first suggestion that we planned to leave, he would make his move.'

'Abduction?' she cried in horror. 'No magistrate would allow it!'

He came to her then and took her hands in his.

'Don't look like that!' he begged. 'I cannot bear that you should suffer so. It is all my fault. Had I not been such a fool, this could not have happened.'

Slow tears rolled down Elinor's cheeks. 'Do not say

so, my lord. I believe that you intended from the first to do your best by Hester.'

'You will give me credit for good intentions, my dearest?' He lifted her tear-stained face to his. 'Ah, if only I could tell you. . .' His mouth came down on hers and the world was lost to both of them.

Elinor clung to him as if her very life depended on it. She could fight him no longer, whatever his reputation. With her arms about his neck, she held him to her. Then the full implications of that embrace came home to her.

'Sir, this is wrong,' she whispered. 'How can we hope to keep Hester with us if I allow. . .?'

'There is one way, my love.

Elinor pulled away from him to gaze into his eyes.

'You have thought of a solution?'

'I have.' His arms were still about her and the firm, full-lipped mouth curved into a smile. 'Elinor, will you marry me?'

For a moment she could not believe her ears. She looked at him in stupefaction. 'My lord?'

'I asked you to marry me. Is it such a dreadful suggestion?'

Elinor's head was spinning. It was the last thing she had expected.

Her legs seemed unwilling to support her, and she reached out an arm to grasp the back of a chair.

'But why?'

Rokeby helped her to a sofa and sat beside her with an arm about her waist. Then he began to stroke her hands.

'Elinor, please consider,' he said softly. 'I know that you do not care for me in the way that I should wish. I am no plaster saint, God knows, but with me you

would have security. And I give you my word that you
would have no further cause to think ill of me. I
should not humiliate you by...by...seeking other
company.'

'You have not answered my question,' she
whispered.

Rokeby looked ill at ease. He rose and began to
pace the room.

'I can think of no other solution,' he said at last. 'If
we wed it will put an end to all the gossip.'

Elinor was beginning to understand, and her heart
felt like a stone within her breast.

'I see! As a married man your suitability as a
guardian would be beyond question? How clever of
you, my lord! I had not supposed you capable of such
a sacrifice.'

Rokeby paled as if she had struck him a mortal
blow.

'You misunderstand. Elinor, have I not shown you
how much I want you?'

'You have, sir. Your intentions were all too plain,
though I did not imagine that they included marriage.'
In her anger she longed to hurt him. 'Your offer is an
insult, my lord.'

'I regret that you should find it so.' He was as white
as Elinor, and his anger matched her own. 'I offer you
my name and my protection, only to have it thrown
back in my face...? Well, madam, I shall not insult
you further. You must prepare yourself for Hester's
imminent departure from this house.' He made as if
to leave the room, but Elinor stopped him.

'Wait, I beg of you!' Her thoughts were in chaos,
but one fact alone stood out in her mind. Hester must
not be handed over to Lord Dacre.

'Lord Rokeby, I spoke in haste,' she told him frankly. 'Will you give me time to consider your. . .er . . .proposal? That is, if you are still of the same mind?'

He bowed. 'The offer holds, Miss Temple, though I should warn you that there *is* no time.'

'One hour is all I ask?' Her eyes were pleading, and he gave her a brief nod. His set expression told her that she had pushed him beond the limits of endurance. She was on the verge of tears as she hurried to her room.

There she sobbed as if her heart would break. Rokeby's offer had been little short of blackmail. He wanted her, and if he could have her no other way then it must be marriage. And there had been no word of love. His object was to gratify his lust, and to achieve it he had used Hester as a pawn.

Wildly, she cursed her own beauty. Had she been plain everything might have been so different. Rokeby would not have given her a second glance.

Such thoughts were useless, she reflected as she grew a little calmer. At least she, too, had a bargaining tool; she would use it.

To save Hester she would marry Rokeby, but upon her own conditions. His lordship should not learn of them until after they were wed. Then he would discover that a match arranged simply to foil his enemies could have no place in it for love and passion.

She would be cheating him, she knew, but he had cheated her of the love for which she longed. She stifled the small voice which told her that she was also cheating herself.

It would not do to examine her own motives too closely. A guilty conscience was an uncomfortable thing with which to live, and so was self-delusion. Had she not admitted that she loved Rokeby to distraction? She brushed the disturbing thought aside. In time the pain would lessen.

She bathed her face in cold water, washing away all traces of her tears. Then she returned to the salon.

Rokeby stood by the window, still and silent. He turned as she came into the room.

'Well, Miss Temple? What is your decision?'

Elinor hesitated for only a moment. 'Sir, you feel that this is the only course of action open to us?'

'I do.' His eyes betrayed no emotion, and he did not move towards her.

'Very well then. I. . .I will accept your offer, sir.

'You have made me the happiest man alive.' He gave her an ironic look. 'Shall we ask my aunt to share our joy?'

The swarthy face was so austere that Elinor was seized with panic as she nodded her agreement.

'Come, then, I believe we shall find her in the study.'

Elinor swept past him as he opened the door for her. His sneering manner was hateful. She had been playing with fire, and now, it seemed, she was about to get her fingers burned. And she had promised to marry him?

Outside the study door she checked. There was still time to change her mind.

'Afraid of me?' he jeered.

'Certainly not!' With her head held high she walked into the room.

To Elinor's astonishment, Lady Hartfield showed no surprise at their announcement.

'I have been longing this age to wish you both happy.' She enveloped Elinor in a hug.

'Ma'am?' Elinor's face was warm with colour, and her ladyship laughed.

'You have been slow about your wooing, Marcus.' She tapped his face affectionately. 'I had begun to think that I must make the offer for you.'

Rokeby kissed her. 'There was no need, my dear. I knew it was your dearest wish.'

Her ladyship looked at him in mock reproach. 'You will not tell me that *my* wishes weighed with you, wretch! Do you believe me to be blind?'

'I do not think it for a moment.' He took Elinor's hand and raised it to his lips. 'Aunt, shall you be disappointed if we have a quiet wedding? We wish to be married without delay.'

'You must do as you think best, my dears, but Elinor will wish for her parents' permission.'

'A letter shall be sent today. I will see to it.' He sat down at the writing desk, and applied himself to the task. At length, he turned to Elinor. 'Do you wish to add to it,' he asked, 'or perhaps you will desire to write at length?'

In silence, Elinor took the pen from him and scribbled a few sentences. Her parents would think it strange, but she could not think it wise to undertake a long explanation of her sudden decision to marry Lord Rokeby. Her father knew his daughter well, and he would not sanction any match which had resulted from coercion. Unwittingly, she might betray her reasons for agreeing to the marriage.

Rokeby took the letter and left the room as Lady Hartfield turned to Elinor.

'Marcus was right, my dear child. I consider him the luckiest man in the world. How I prayed that he would

win you in the end, though in recent weeks I have had
no doubt of it. You love him dearly, do you not?'

To her ladyship's consternation Elinor burst into
tears.

'There, there,' the older woman comforted. 'It is the
strangest thing, but tears of happiness are just as real
as those of grief.'

Elinor dabbed at her eyes, and blew her nose upon
the scrap of lace proffered by her companion. How
could she explain that there was no cause for celebration in her forthcoming marriage? She had
accepted Rokeby for all the wrong reasons, and misery
awaited her. He would never forgive her. She had seen
it in his eyes.

She turned away as Hester came to join them.

'Elinor has a surprise for you,' her ladyship cried
gaily. 'I will leave her to tell you of it. I must find
Marcus. I have a thousand things to say to him.'
Beaming, she bustled away.

'Elinor, what is it?' Hester's eyes were intent upon
her friend's face. 'Why, you have been crying! Is
something wrong?'

'Nothing at all, my love!' Elinor managed a watery
smile. 'It is just that...well...I am to marry Lord
Rokeby—'

'No! You can't! I won't believe it!'

'It is true.' Elinor took Hester's hand in hers.

'No, no! You don't even like him.' Hester snatched
her hand away. 'What has he said to you? How has he
forced you to agree? There must be some reason.'

'I love him,' Elinor said with perfect truth. 'Is it so
strange that we should wish to make each other
happy?'

'You don't look happy to me.' Hester ran from the room.

Elinor followed, but it was only with the greatest difficulty that his ward could be persuaded to offer Rokeby her congratulations later that day.

He accepted them with grave courtesy, affecting not to notice that her eyes were red with weeping. His aunt threw Elinor a significant glance and kept the conversation going at the dinner table with various items of inconsequential gossip. Even so, the air of tension in the room could not be denied.

To Elinor, the meal seemed interminable. She looked about her sadly. This should have been an occasion for celebrations but it was not.

At length, Lady Hartfield rose from the table, leaving Rokeby to his wine. She had hoped to offer Hester a few words of consolation for the loss of her friend, but Hester would not wait for the arrival of the tea-tray. Pleading a headache, she begged to be excused.

'Pray do not worry about her, Elinor.' Lady Hartfield comforted. 'Your news has come as a shock. In a day or so she will grow accustomed to the idea that you are to wed.'

'Ma'am, I am sorry that she has taken it so badly. It is disrespectful to both Lord Rokeby and yourself.'

'We shall both make allowances, my dear. She is very young, and then, you know, for the past few years you have been her only friend.'

As Elinor sipped her tea, she prayed that her ladyship was right. Rokeby had sat through the meal in a silence unusual for him. Hopefully Lady Hartfield would put this down to his disapproval of Hester's conduct.

'Now here is Marcus come to claim you.' The older

woman twinkled at her nephew. 'I do not propose to
sit here like a gooseberry, sir. You may have your
bride to yourself, though I hope that you will not keep
her from her bed for long. She looks a little tired this
evening.'

'It is the excitement, ma'am.' As Rokeby opened
the door for her he bowed, but his smile did not reach
his eyes.

Alone with him at last, Elinor was lost for words.
Then he broke the silence.

'I believe it may be best that I go into Derbyshire
myself to see your father,' he announced.

'Oh, pray do not!' Elinor's involuntary exclamation
brought an expression of quelling severity to Rokeby's
face.

'You have changed your mind?'

'No, it is not that. . .but perhaps. . .'

'You think he may take against me?' The sensitive
mouth curved in a sneer.

Privately, Elinor believed that in his present mood
it would be impossible for his lordship to convince her
parents of his regard for her. Her father would sense
at once that there was something strange about this
sudden betrothal, and Rokeby's insistence upon an
early marriage.

'Of course not!' she disclaimed. 'I thought merely
that it might be better if I went myself.

'You cannot go alone, and it would be unwise of us
to leave Hester without protection at this time. That
is, unless we take my aunt into our confidence?'

'Oh, no! It would hurt her so to learn the true
reason for our marriage. Let us leave matters as they
are. You have sent the letter?'

'I have not. It is impossible to offer your father such

discourtesy. I don't flatter myself with the notion that you will miss me, but I shall travel fast. The journey should take no more than a few days.'

He would not be dissuaded, and Elinor realised that further argument was useless.

'You have messages for your family?' he asked briefly.

'Will you give them my love?' Elinor struggled for composure as she swallowed the lump in her throat. 'When do you plan to leave, my lord?'

'At first light. Elinor?' He stretched out a hand towards her, but she had turned away and did not see it. Rokeby's arm fell to his side. 'If you wish to write to them you may leave the letter in the hall. I shall not forget it.'

'Thank you.' Her voice was colourless and her eyes were fixed upon the carpet. Absently, she smoothed at the skirt of her gown with trembling fingers. If only he would lose his temper and rail at her, instead of treating her with his present distant courtesy. He might have been speaking to a stranger.

'You wish to continue with this farce?' she asked quietly.

'I told you. I have no choice.'

'There is always a choice,' she said. 'You might walk away from your responsibilities—'

'As you intend to do? Your opinion of me is so low that you would deny me a sense of honour? No, ma'am, we shall go on. You shall not find me wanting in that respect.'

'Then, if you will excuse me, I shall write my letter.' As she walked towards the door he spoke again.

'You know the danger? You will keep Hester close?'

Elinor nodded her assent and left him.

As she had expected, the letter to her parents caused her much soul-searching. She tore up her efforts again and again, and it was well into the early hours of the morning before she had completed it to her own satisfaction.

She sealed the envelope and, taking a candle, stole down into the darkened hall. A gleam of light shone beneath the door of the study, and she guessed that Rokeby had not yet retired.

She had no wish to see him. She was too exhausted to indulge in any conversation, but as she laid the letter upon a small brass tray a drop of burning candle wax fell upon her hand. The pain made her jump and her fingers caught the tray, sending it crashing to the marble floor.

The door of the study opened, and Rokeby looked at her. Then he held out his hand for the letter. She gave it to him without a word.

'I have written to Charlbury to ask if he will support me at our marriage. You agree?'

'Of course. . .whatever you wish. . .'

For a second a faint smile of mockery played about his lips. 'I fear it will take all your powers of persuasion to induce Hester to attend you.'

'I am quite sure that she will do so.' Elinor told him stiffly.

'Perhaps! But only if she were convinced that I should make you happy. A vain hope, I imagine. . .'

'Goodnight, my lord.' Elinor did not trust herself to say more. She picked up her candle and turned towards the stairs.

'Not so fast, my promised bride!' He moved so

quickly that she had no opportunity to evade him. 'Shall we not seal our bargain with a kiss?'

His arm was about her waist, and Elinor was acutely aware that she was clad only in a diaphanous night-robe beneath her filmy dressing-gown. Her maid had taken down her hair from its fashionable chignon and brushed it until it shone. Now the tawny mane hung in a cloud about her shoulders.

'Charming!' His lordship observed in a silky tone. 'What pleasures I have in store...' There was no tenderness in his voice, and the note of cynicism roused her to fury. Bitterness and despair made her throw caution to the winds.

'You will not be the loser by our bargain,' she cried angrily. 'Doubtless you will make sure of that.'

'Indeed I shall.' He was stroking her shoulders. 'Kiss me, Elinor!'

'Let me go!' She struggled furiously. He did not love her. Nothing but expediency had forced him to offer for her, and had it not been for Dacre's threats he would never have done so. 'You will wake the servants.'

'They will not think it strange that I should wish to salute my betrothed.'

'In the early hours of the morning, and when I am clad only in...in...?'

'In gauze, my dear? It is vastly becoming, and leaves little to the imagination.'

Elinor threw back her head and looked at him. There was a dangerous glitter in his eyes, and in that moment he looked capable of anything.

There was an air of reckless abandon in his manner, and it frightened her. She sensed that it was born off frustration, but surely he would not attempt to seduce her here, in his aunt's home?

'Pray allow me to return to my room, my lord,' she said more quietly. 'If you wish to talk, we may do so in the morning. At present you are not yourself.'

'You are mistaken. I am very much myself, and I have no wish to talk. That is not my object at this moment.'

His mouth came down on hers, and it was only with a supreme effort of will that she managed to offer no response. With every muscle tensed she stood statue-like in his embrace.

After a moment he released her, looking at her strangely.

'You wish to talk?' he muttered. 'Well then, let me offer you a glass of wine.' Seizing her hand, he thrust her ahead of him into the study.

Elinor began to tremble.

'You are cold, my dear? Allow me to make you more comfortable.' He slipped out of his coat and placed it about her shoulders. 'Here, drink this! It might help to thaw the ice.'

Elinor did not answer him.

'I hope you do not intend to cheat me, Elinor.' He was standing with his shoulders propped against the mantelpiece. 'If you have any thought of banishing me from your room when we are wed, you may forget it now.'

Elinor felt the hot colour rising to her cheeks. Some such idea had occurred to her, it was true. It would serve him right for his callous approach to their marriage, but she had dismissed it as unworthy of her. He might not love her, but she would keep her part of the bargain.

'I shall not cheat you,' she whispered. In her own heart, if she were honest, she knew that she could not bear to do so. When he kissed her, it had taken all her self-control not to throw her arms about his neck and melt against his lips.

'I am glad to hear it. Who knows, in time you may grow to think of me more kindly.'

There was an odd note in his voice, almost of pleading, but she knew that she must be mistaken. She turned away and did not answer him.

'No? I see that you do not agree with me. Ah well, it is not a condition of marriage after all. We must make the best of it. Others do so every day.'

Elinor was close to tears. Her heart felt like lead within her breast. He had succeeded in crushing all her dreams of happiness, and the future looked bleak indeed. She choked back a sob.

'No tears, I beg of you! I would not have you distress yourself unnecessarily. You will not find me a demanding husband. You may go your own way if you should wish it, though, of course, I shall expect the same understanding.'

Elinor rose to her feet, feeling that her heart must break, and he did not attempt to detain her.

As she stumbled blindly to her room, she came to a decision. She could not go on like this. Tonight had been the final insult.

Rokeby had left her in no doubt of his meaning. He had offered her an arrangement which was not unknown among the *ton*. Once she had given him an heir, she would be free to take a lover more to her taste.

How could he? she thought wildly. It was an offence to every finer feeling.

From the hall below she heard the front door open, and then close. She guessed that he was gone to seek more congenial company. The thought of him in another woman's arms struck like a dagger to her breast.

Was this what she must suffer in the years to come? She would not do it, not even to save Hester. Tomorrow she would put an end to her betrothal.

CHAPTER TWELVE

ELINOR did not close her eyes that night, and she rose at first light. Rokeby had planned to leave for Derbyshire at dawn, but now his journey was unnecessary. He must return her letter.

She was unsurprised to find that his lordship had not spent the night at hone. He too must have had second thoughts. It was only to be expected after the away she had repulsed him. His change of heart was for the best—it would save much argument.

She would speak to him before she broke the news to Lady Hartfield. After all, a broken engagement was not uncommon when the parties found that they had been mistaken in their feelings for each other.

She should have felt happier now that the decision was made to free herself from an intolerable situation. Instead, she was convinced that she had never been so miserable in her life.

Only Hester would be pleased, and she, poor child, had no idea of the probable fate in store for her.

She stared at her face in the mirror. It did not seem possible that such pain would not have left its mark but, apart from a certain heaviness about the eyes, she looked just the same. She buried her head in her hands. If others could but look into her mind, it would be a different story.

What a coil it was! And how could she, the cool and sensible Miss Temple, have become embroiled in such a situation?

As she grew calmer she began to reflect upon a possible course of action. There was no time to lose. After one last unpleasant interview with Rokeby, she would take her leave of Hester and Lady Hartfield and return to Derbyshire. She had no intention of spending another night beneath the same roof as his lordship.

Lady Hartfield would be upset and Hester would be distraught at the thought of losing her. Her heart misgave her as she wondered what on earth she was to say to them. Only that she had been mistaken in her affections, perhaps? But would that be considered sufficient reason for her sudden departure?

She could not explain to either of them that Rokeby had tried to molest her.

And what of Hester? If Lady Hartfield knew the truth about Lord Dacre and his threats, she might find some solution to the problem. Rokeby had assured her that it was impossible for her ladyship to intervene, but was there not a chance?

In her distress, Elinor knew that she was clutching at straws, but she felt trapped. Whatever happened, she must get away from Rokeby. She felt that she was fighting for her very life, and her decision to leave must be irrevocable.

It was noon before she joined the others at the nuncheon table. Rokeby had not returned, but Lady Hartfield saw nothing strange in this.

'Dear Marcus!' she said fondly. 'Is it not like him to rush away to Derbyshire so soon? He cannot wait to claim you, my dear Elinor.'

Elinor's response was non-committal, and Hester gave her a sharp glance. Her ladyship did not appear to notice it.

'He had no sleep, you must know, which was foolish of him, but we cannot blame a young man in love.' Lady Hartfield helped herself to a wing of cold chicken and some salad, and then exclaimed at the lack of appetite shown by the others.

'This will not do, Elinor. You will be worn to a shade before your wedding day. Marcus will not be away for long, and he will not care that you should pine for him.'

Obediently Elinor filled her plate, but she took no more than a mouthful of the food. Preoccupied with the thought that this might be the last meal which she would eat with her companions, she took no part in the conversation.

'Elinor, you are dreaming!' Lady Hartfield challenged. 'It is natural, though I hope you have not forgot. Tonight we are promised to the Morcotts for their evening party.'

'I have not forgotten, ma'am.' Elinor gave her hostess a mechanical smile. For all she knew, Rokeby might have decided upon some days of debauchery. She could only wait for his return.

As the long hours dragged, by it took all her self-control to behave as if nothing was amiss. She had no choice but to dress for the party, and to join the others in the carriage.

In the crush of the Morcotts' overheated rooms she bowed and nodded to her acquaintance, but later she could not recall a word of their conversation.

Thankfully there was to be a musical recital after supper, though Lady Hartfield had announced her intention of making up a table at cards. Hester had been borne away by some hopeful scion of a noble house with a promise of a glass of cooling lemonade.

Elinor sank into a chair beside a window, half-hidden by the heavy draperies, as she waited for the recital to begin. The music, at least, would relieve her of the need to exchange inanities with those about her. She closed her eyes as the first chords sounded, and was lost to all sense of time until the piece had ended.

When she opened them it was to see an unwelcome sight. Lord Dacre was standing in the doorway, with Hester by his side.

Elinor rose to her feet with the intention of joining them, but the rows of small gilt chairs, each occupied, barred her path. The music had begun again and angry looks were thrown at her as she tried to pass.

Panic seized her. In desperation she turned towards the long window behind her chair. It was unlocked, and led on to a terrace. She slipped out, praying that she might gain access to the house again by another window further along. This too was unlocked and led into another, smaller salon. She pushed through the crowd of chattering guests, but she could see no sign of Hester.

Dear God! Would Dacre abduct the girl in full view of the Polite World? She could not think it, but her terror grew as she moved among the diners, and those who were playing cards. Hester was nowhere to be found.

She appealed to her hostess, striving to keep her voice as calm as possible. 'I am looking for Miss Winton, ma'am. Have you seen her?'

'She is gone into the garden, I believe. She found it warm indoors. . .' Mrs Morcott was only half attending. She turned back to her guests.

Elinor was terrified. In the darkness anything might

happen. She brushed past the people in her way, ignoring their startled looks, and ran on to the terrace.

At first she could see no one. The Morcotts' garden was not large, but it was long and narrow. As she picked her way along the path, the shrubs on either side threw dark shadows in the moonlight.

She had reached the far wall which separated the house from the road which ran behind it when she saw Hester. The girl was sitting on a low bench in the gazebo. Thankfully, she was alone.

'My dearest, what are you doing here? You will take a chill without your shawl.' Elinor's voice was shaking with relief.

'It does not matter. Nothing matters. . .' Hester did not raise her head.

'Is something wrong? What has happened? I saw you speaking to Lord Dacre. . .' A nameless dread filled Elinor's heart.

'You lied to me,' Hester said dully.

'Hester! How can you say such things? I have never lied to you.'

'But you did not tell me the truth, did you? It is much the same. . .'

'I cannot imagine what Lord Dacre has been saying to you, but will you not tell me? I cannot bear to see you so distressed. Dacre is not to be trusted, you must know that?'

'I do.' Hester gave a convulsive swallow. 'I did not believe him at first. He asked if I knew of Lord Rokeby's evil reputation and then. . .'

'Yes?'

'Then he said that Lord Rokeby planned to ruin you.' She would not meet Elinor's eyes.

'But you knew that was not so,' Elinor cried warmly.

'Have I not just accepted his lordship's offer of marriage?'

Hester raised her head and gave Elinor a level look.

'Why did you do so, Elinor?'

'Because I loved him. Did I not tell you so?'

'I didn't believe you then, and I don't believe you now. Was it not to give my guardian some semblance of respectability? Lord Dacre told me that he had planned to apply to the courts for permission to take me into his own care.'

'Hester, you are overwrought...'

'I am not blind. You are not happy, are you, whatever Lady Hartfield may say?'

'My dear—'

Hester rose from her seat and bent to kiss Elinor's cheek. 'You shall not sacrifice yourself for me,' she said quietly. 'Shall we go indoors? The wind, I find, is cold.'

It was true that she was shivering, but Elinor suspected that it was as much from shock as from the chill night air. She took Hester's arm and hurried her towards the house.

'Let us speak of these matters later,' she urged. 'I'll explain... I must make you understand.'

Hester stopped at the entrance to the salon.

'I do understand. I have been both foolish and selfish. I should not have refused all the offers made to me.'

'Oh, do not say so,' Elinor pleaded. 'That is not true. Hester...?' She sighed as the girl brushed past her and entered the crowded room.

This was a very different Hester from the girl who had always taken her advice. There was something

about the set expression upon that small face which
gave her cause for deep anxiety.

She would make it right, she vowed to herself. If
she could but talk to Hester for an hour...but what
was she to say? How could she convince his ward that
she was in love with Rokeby when she had decided on
that very day to break off her engagement?

The problem seemed insuperable, but she would
think of something... She could not leave matters as
they were. In Hester's present mood the child might
do something irrational.

Later that evening she was unable to carry out her
plan to speak to Hester. On their return to Berkeley
Square the girl was quick to plead exhaustion and beg
to be excused.

And Rokeby had not yet returned from the illicit
pleasures which were doubtless still detaining him.

Despair filled Elinor's heart. She hated him, but if
only he would come back. She *must* tell him what had
happened at the Morcotts'. Without him, she had the
odd sensation of being on shifting sands, not knowing
when she might be sucked down into unimaginable
horror.

On the following morning she was surprised to find
Hester at the breakfast table before her. The girl was
polite and pleasant, and totally unapproachable. The
presence of the servants made it impossible for Elinor
to do more than make casual conversation.

Elinor cast a covert glance at her as they made their
morning visits later in the morning. Lady Hartfield
was punctilious in her observance of the social niceties
and she nodded her approval of Hester's calm
civilities.

'We shall make something of her yet,' she whispered happily to Elinor. 'She is growing more mature.'

Elinor fought the urge to tell her ladyship all. Her anxiety was increasing. This cool, composed creature was a Hester she did not know. Pray heaven the child had not decided upon some wild plan of her own. If so, she must discover it before any harm was done.

She was given no opportunity to do so. For the rest of that day Hester took care not to be left alone with her, and retired at once after their evening visit to the opera.

Elinor followed as soon as it was practicable to make her own excuses, and hurried along to Hester's room.

'Miss does not wish to be disturbed.' The maid who opened the door to her announced.

'I shan't keep her a moment.' Elinor brushed past her and walked over to the bed. To all appearances Hester was already asleep, but Elinor was undeceived. It was clear that Hester did not wish to speak to her. With a shrug of resignation, she turned away. She would try again in the morning.

But on the following morning, Hester sent a message to her hostess. She had the headache, and believed that she should stay in bed.

'Do you believe her, Elinor?' Lady Hartfield's face was stern. 'I had imagined yesterday that she was becoming resigned to your marriage. I do not care to think that she has given way to another fit of the sullens.'

'Ma'am, I am sure that it is not so. I will go to see her.' Elinor half rose from her chair.

'No, you will not! Sit down, my dear! You are much

too careful of Hester's whims and fancies. I will see
her myself. Sometimes, I confess, she puts me out of
all patience with her.'

'But, ma'am, she may indeed have the headache.'
Elinor thought it more than likely, after the events of
the past few days.

'Then she shall stay in bed, but we shall not change
our own plans, my dear Elinor.' She summoned a
footman and ordered her carriage.

When she came downstairs her expression of severity had softened.

'Hester does look pale,' she admitted. 'She tells me
that it is a certain time of the month. I have advised
her to rest. The pain will ease in a few hours time if
she takes the dose I recommended.'

Elinor did a few calculations, well knowing that
there was something wrong. It was not time. . .though
the shock might have upset Hester's normal functions.

A little niggling doubt stayed with her throughout
their drive through the park. She was impatient to get
back to Berkeley Square, but their carriage was
stopped again and again as Lady Hartfield's friends
approached them. To her the hours seemed endless,
as greetings were exchanged and invitations offered.

She could not repress a sigh of relief when the
coachman was free at last to whip up his horses. Her
hand was on the carriage door almost before he had
drawn to a halt.

Then, as she followed Lady Hartfield up the steps,
the door flew open and an agitated butler hurried
towards them.

'Ma'am, it's Miss Winton,' he gasped. 'We can't find
her anywhere.'

'Nonsense, man! She is in her room.'

'No, your ladyship, she isn't. What's more, her outdoor things are gone, and so is her bandbox!'

Elinor ran through the hall and up to Hester's room. It was all quite true. Very little of Hester's clothing had disappeared, but enough had gone to fit into a bandbox, and of the girl herself there was no trace.

'Elinor, the maid found this. It is addressed to you...' Lady Hartfield sat down suddenly, looking much older than her years. 'What can have possessed the child? Has she eloped? She gave no sign of a preference for any particular man...'

With shaking fingers, Elinor ripped at the envelope. The note was brief, and it begged her forgiveness. Hester had decided to marry Dacre's son.

Elinor went scarlet and then white. Her world seemed to reel about her and she put out a hand to steady herself. Lady Hartfield gripped it tightly and took the note from her nerveless fingers.

'What does this mean?' the older woman asked. 'Hester gives no explanation. Were you aware of her affection for Tobias?'

Elinor shook her head. She could not trust herself to speak.

'Then I cannot understand it. She has not met Tobias above three times, and she always confides in you. This is Dacre's doing, I make no doubt, but how did he persuade her? I thought she held him in dislike.'

'She does,' Elinor replied briefly. 'Ma'am, I should have told you, but I did not wish to worry you. Lord Dacre spoke to Hester at the Morcotts' ball. He...he told her something which distressed her very much.'

'And what was that?'

'He...he tried to blacken Lord Rokeby's character...'

'I see.' The sharp black eyes were intent upon Elinor's face. 'There is something more, I think. Won't you be honest with me?'

Elinor flushed painfully, and turned her head away.

'Come, my dear, out with it! Hester may despise my nephew, but it would take more than a recital of his shortcomings to cause her to leave her friends. What is behind her decision?'

'Lord Dacre convinced her that his lordship offered for me merely to lend himself respectability. Otherwise Hester would be removed from his care.' Elinor's eyes filled. 'Worst of all, she now believes that I accepted him in order to save her.'

Her ladyship gave a snort of disbelief. 'Is the child blind? Does she not see what is beneath her nose? Elinor, you must have told her of your love for Marcus. . .'

'I did.' The slow tears were rolling down Elinor's cheeks and she made no effort to wipe them away. 'She did not believe me. I disliked him so, you see, and I made no effort to hide it. She said that she could not allow me to. . .to sacrifice myself for her.'

Lady Hartfield shook her head. 'Sometimes you young people make me wonder. Hester does not understand you very well, I fear. If your affections were not engaged, you would never have agreed to marry Marcus, whatever pressure might be brought to bear upon you. I am sure of it.'

Elinor dried her eyes. Now was not the time to explain that she had decided to end her betrothal.

'I will go to Lord Dacre,' she announced. 'If I can but see Hester, I know I can persuade her to return with me.'

'Is that wise? Do but consider, my dear. We have

not heard from Dacre. Hester may not yet have reached him. If he learns that she is missing from her home, that is yet another reason for him to claim a lack of care for her well-being. And then, you know, we may have misjudged her reasons. . .'

Elinor stared at her companion and was disturbed by her ladyship's expression.

'Ma'am?'

'You will not like what I have to say, but Hester may not have been perfectly open with you, Elinor. I confess that I thought she had an affection for John Charlbury, but Tobias is a handsome boy. Young girls are not always true to their first love, my dear.'

'Your ladyship, I think you are mistaken.' Elinor told her steadily.

'Perhaps so, but it is not impossible, and you will admit that Hester has a secretive side to her nature.'

'She is reserved and shy, but I have never known her to lie, and she is incapable of deception.'

'Very well, I shall not quarrel with you, but if I am right and she had but told us of her feelings, Marcus might have reconsidered—'

'What might I have reconsidered?' Tall and straight, Marcus stood in the doorway, looking from one face to the other.

Elinor's heart began to pound. She longed for nothing so much as to run to him and throw herself into his arms, but the memory of their quarrel stopped her. His behaviour and his cruel words could not be forgiven. She stared at him, her lips almost as pale as her face.

'Thank heavens you have come back to us.' Lady Hartfield reached out a hand to him. 'Oh, Marcus, what is to be done?'

Rokeby dropped a kiss upon her brow and then he turned to Elinor. 'What has happened?' he asked quietly. 'The servants are running about like headless chickens. At the very least, I imagined a death in the family.'

'Hester is missing,' Elinor told him stiffly. 'We were out this morning, Lady Hartfield and myself. When we returned, Hester had gone—'

'And she is gone to Dacre,' her ladyship broke in. 'She wishes to marry Tobias.'

'Rubbish.' Rokeby's reply was pithy, to say the least. 'Did she give you a reason for this sudden decision?' There was silence, but a glance at Elinor's face told him all he wished to know. A smile of utter contempt curved his lips. 'I'll go to Dacre at once,' he said.

There was something in his face which frightened Elinor. His jaw was set, and the mobile mouth had hardened into a thin line. The expression in his eyes was murderous.

'Take care!' she cried involuntarily. 'He is a dangerous man.'

'And so am I, as he will soon discover. I will bring Hester back with me,' he promised. 'You have not long to wait.'

Elinor's heart turned to lead within her breast, as terror consumed her. 'You will take no chances?' she pleaded.

Rokeby bowed. His face was enigmatic. 'I thought I had taken those already.' Without more ado he strode from the room.

Elinor sat in silence, picking aimlessly at the lace trimming on her gown, and unaware of her companion's bemused expression.

'You disappoint me, Elinor,' her ladyship said at

last. 'I thought that we were friends. There is so much about this situation which I do not understand. Won't you trust me?'

Elinor cast about wildly in her mind for some words which might express what she wished to say, but she could find none.

'Very well,' her ladyship said at last. 'I won't press you, but, my dear, you will remember, will you not, that I shall always stand your friend?' She rose to her feet as if to leave the room, but Elinor caught her hand.

'Lady Hartfield, forgive me! I have no wish to deceive you, but I can say naught at present. It is only fair that I speak to Marcus...to Lord Rokeby, before ...before I can take you into my confidence.'

'You have quarrelled, have you not?'

Elinor nodded. Her lips were trembling and her heart was too full for speech.

'I thought so.' Her ladyship patted Elinor's hand. 'My dear, we can't always be in agreement with those we love, and lovers' quarrels are soon mended. Take heart! Both you and Marcus are under a strain at present, and this business with Hester cannot help.'

'It is more than that,' Elinor told her sadly. 'We may have been mistaken in our feelings for each other.'

Lady Hartfield shook her head. 'My dear Elinor, for two intelligent women, both you and Hester have been singularly blind. How can you doubt my nephew's love for you? Do you not see the way he looks at you, and the way his voice changes when he speaks your name?'

Elinor looked at her with brimming eyes. 'That may have been so before...before... But, ma'am, he had no word for me just now. You must have been aware of it.'

'He will come back to you, my love, no matter what your present differences.'

'I don't know.' Elinor felt unutterably weary. 'I am confused. . . I don't know what to think.'

It was true. She had been determined to end her betrothal, but at the sight of Marcus a wild surge of love had shaken her to the core. She could not deny her passion for him, try as she might.

And now she was filled with dread. Lord Dacre hated him, and she shuddered to think of the outcome of their meeting. A duel in which Dacre was the victor would resolve Hester's future without recourse to the courts.

Dacre would see it as an answer to his problems, especially if, as she suspected, it would not be a fair fight.

She pictured Rokeby's lifeless body stretched upon some lonely field of turf. The thought was unbearable and she swayed in horror.

Please God, anything but that. Let Rokeby leave her for his lights-o'-love. She could bear it, if only he were safe. She put a hand up to her eyes as if to shut out the spectres which tormented her. Then she found herself in Lady Hartfield's arms.

'Don't, my love. Please don't look like that. You shall not be so frightened. Marcus will come back to us and then you will be happy again.'

'I wish I could believe it,' Elinor cried in bitter despair. 'Did you not see his face? There was murder in it.'

Lady Hartfield shook her gently. 'You know his

temper, Elinor, but it will not lead him into folly. He has you to think of now, as well as Hester.'

'He no longer loves me. I know it.'

'Then you are more foolish than I had imagined possible. He was yours from the first moment of your meeting. I never doubted it from the day he asked me to choose a gown for you. It is not quite usual, you know, for a gentleman to be so exact as to the colour of a lady's eyes, her height, her build, and the way the candlelight reflected the tawny beauty of her hair.' There was a chuckle in her voice. 'You were always with him, Elinor, in his mind's eye. A love like that is not easily destroyed.'

Elinor dried her eyes. 'Ma'am, you are very good to me,' she murmured. 'I am ashamed to have worried you at a time like this.'

'Then you shall not continue to do so,' her ladyship said briskly. 'As for Hester, when Marcus brings her back, that young lady will learn what I think of her behaviour.'

Her promise was not destined to be soon fulfilled. Marcus returned within the hour, but he was alone. As both women looked at him, he shook his head.

'She is not there. Dacre has not seen her.'

'He is lying,' Elinor cried wildly. 'Surely you don't believe him?'

'Perhaps not his words, but certainly his actions. His men are scouring London for her.'

'No, it is a trick! He would tell you anything to get his way. He *must* be hiding her.'

'I think not.' Rokeby's face was grim. 'You did not see his face. It is a picture of baffled rage. Hester was to arrive at his house by noon. That he did not deny.

When she did not, he thought she'd changed her mind. Now he is as anxious as we are ourselves.'

'Though not from any care for Hester's safety, you may be sure.' The lines on Lady Hartfield's face had deepened. To Elinor she seemed to be ageing by the minute.

'Quite so! He sees his prize eluding him, my dear aunt.'

'I don't believe him, whatever you may think.' Elinor sprang to her feet and began to pace the room. 'He is deceiving you.'

'Will you not sit down?' Rokeby was alarmed by her pallor. 'Whatever else, I think we may believe Tobias. The boy is distraught. Hester has been kind to him and he holds her in affection.'

'Then it is true? Hester has agreed to marry him?' Lady Hartfield looked more hopeful.

'She has agreed. . .and without my permission. That I shall never give.' Rokeby's face might have been carved in stone, his jaw was set, and his mouth a tight line.

'My dear boy! Are you not being unreasonable? Hester must marry, you said as much yourself. This match may not be what we would wish, but if the two young people hold each other in such high esteem, why then should you stand in their way?'

'And leave them at the mercy of Dacre? No, ma'am, I cannot do it. You know something of him, but I know more. Once married, Hester might not live out the year.' He looked at their horrified faces and turned away.

'Oh, Marcus, you cannot mean. . .murder?' Lady Hartfield's voice was little more than a whisper.

'Why not? He is capable of it, and he is deep in

debt. An accident might be arranged...it would not look like murder.'

'Then he would be in control of Hester's fortune? Oh, my dear, I cannot believe it...'

'But I believe it, ma'am.' Elinor rose and faced them. Her face was as set as Rokeby's own. 'What I will not believe is that Hester loves Tobias. Now we are wasting time. Hester must be found without delay.'

'Agreed, but where are we to look? Do you recall if she had any money by her?'

'She had not used up her allowance—'

'Then I'll send men to the coaching depots. Someone may remember her.' Rokeby pulled at the bell-rope.

'But where would she go?' Elinor cried in anguish. 'She can't return to Bath...the school is closed...and she would not go back to Kent...to Merton Place.'

'To Kent?' Rokeby stood lost in thought for a few moments. 'What of the Charlburys? She is fond of them, and they of her.'

'I don't know...they are friends of yours... She might not think it wise...'

'Where then? Can you think of anyone else?' He stood at the far end of the room, cool and unapproachable.

'No, I can't.' Elinor's look was pitiful. 'She has never ventured out alone before, and she knows no one in the city.'

'She has one or two friends among the younger girls,' Lady Hartfield pointed out. 'Though, of course, their mammas would not encourage her to leave the protection of her guardian.'

'That's true, aunt. She would have been returned to us at once.' Rokeby was quick to issue his instructions to the men who came in answer to his ring. Then he turned back to his companions. 'Try to think,' he urged. 'Has she ever mentioned anything which might tell us of her present whereabouts?'

'I have racked my brains these last few hours,' Elinor said in a low voice. 'I believe she intended to go to Dacre as he told you. Something must have happened on the way.'

Thoughts of the nearby river rose unbidden to her mind and she sat down suddenly as her legs gave way beneath her. Then Rokeby was on his knees beside her.

'What is it?' he said gently.

She choked out her reply so quietly that he had to bring his lips close to her ear to catch her words.

'Do you think she might have decided to...to do away with herself?' she whispered. 'Rather than go to Dacre?'

'No I do not. One does not pack a bandbox with suicide in mind.' He slipped a lean finger beneath her chin and forced her to look at him. 'Let us not fear the worst, Elinor. Hester, as you know, is unaccustomed to travel alone. She may simply have given a wrong direction to whichever hack took her up.'

'I wish I could believe it.' She would not be comforted, and she could not hide her agony of mind. 'Even now she may be in danger of abduction, or, at best, being accosted in the street by some unscrupulous creature. We must look for her...I will fetch my cloak.'

'You will stay here,' Rokeby told her firmly. 'Hester may yet return, having thought better of her foolish plans. Besides, my aunt has need of you.'

'Oh, ma'am, I am so sorry!' Elinor turned to Lady Hartfield in quick contrition. 'How selfish of me to be thinking only of myself! Will you not let me help you to your room?' She was as alarmed as Rokeby by the ashen pallor of the older woman's face. 'If you were to rest for an hour? I will come to you at once if there is any news. . .'

'Thank you, my dear.' Her ladyship struggled to her feet, but the spring had gone from her step as she allowed herself to be supported from the room.

Beyond the door, she paused to allow a stalwart footman to take each arm. 'My dresser and the maid will look to my needs,' she told Elinor in a thread-like voice. 'Do you go back to Marcus. You may yet think of a way to bring Hester back to us.'

'No, I shall not leave you,' Elinor protested. 'Ma'am, you don't look at all the thing. . .'

'Neither do you, my love, but I know that you will not rest. You may leave me now. I know that you will both do all you can.'

Elinor knew that further argument would be useless. With a sinking heart she returned to the salon. Marcus raised his head as she approached him, and she shrank back at the expression in his eyes. His face was dark with anger, and she was reminded of their first meeting when she had believed that she would hate him for the rest of her life.

'Well, madam, it seems that the fates conspire against me. Now I am to be repaid in full for my transgressions.'

'You are tired, and worried about your aunt as well as Hester,' she said quietly. 'Pray do not blame yourself. . .the fault is mine.'

'How can that be?' His lips curved in a cynical smile. 'Hester believes that I am the devil incarnate . . .she would go to any lengths to prevent our marriage!'

'She did not understand. She thought it was a sacrifice on my part.'

He came towards her then and took her hands.

'I thought so myself, Elinor. I would not believe that you could care for me, and it almost drove me into madness. It was only when your father told me that you would never marry without love that I—'

'My father? You have seen him?'

'Of course!' As he looked at her his face changed. 'You knew that I was going into Derbyshire. . .?'

Elinor could not meet his eyes, but she flushed to the roots of her hair.

'I had supposed that after. . .after that night. . .you would not care to go. . .'

'I see.' His voice was that of a stranger. 'I wondered why you had not asked about your family. Do you care to tell me how you imagine I have spent my time these last few days?'

She did not answer him. In the silence which followed, the ticking of the clock on the mantelshelf was clearly audible, and when it struck the quarter-hour she jumped. She moistened her lips and tried to speak.

'No!' he said sharply. 'There is no need to explain. Your expression tells me all I wish to know, and it has convinced me of one thing. There will never be trust between us, will there, Elinor? You couldn't believe that I should keep my word to you.'

She put out a hand as if to ward off his accusations. The bitterness in his voice had wounded her to the heart. She had misjudged him yet again, and now she knew that she had lost him. He would not forgive her lack of trust. She told herself that it was for the best.

'Please. . .' she murmured faintly. He would never know what she had been about to say, for at that moment there came the sound of a commotion in the hall.

Rokeby strode over to the door and flung it open as Elinor raised her head.

There, in the doorway, stood Hester. Behind her was the tall figure of John Charlbury.

Elinor heard a rushing in her ears and the world seemed to spin about her before she slipped into darkness.

CHAPTER THIRTEEN

ELINOR returned to consciousness to find herself supported by Rokeby's arm. He was holding a glass to her lips but her first sip of the strong spirit made her cough. She struggled to sit up unaided.

'Don't move!' his lordship ordered. 'In a few moments you will feel better. . .then you shall go to your room.'

'No. . .no, I won't. I must know. . . Oh, Hester, where have you been?' She looked down at the girl who knelt beside her, chafing her hand as the tears rained down upon her fingers. 'Are you unhurt?'

'Hester has not been harmed, though why you should care I can't imagine.' Rokeby's face was dark with anger. 'She has forfeited any claim to consideration.'

Hester's sobs increased.

'Don't be angry with her,' Elinor pleaded. 'I'm sure she believed that her actions were for the best.'

'Then she is even more of a fool than I had supposed. Get up, you stupid child! It is too late for tears.'

'Marcus, you will not address Hester in that tone.' John Charlbury spoke for the first time. His normally gentle manner had vanished, and there was anger in his eyes.

'I shall address her in any tone I please. Must I remind you that I am her guardian?'

'You have not exactly shone in that capacity, have you?'

233

Within the circle of his arm, Elinor felt Marcus stiffen. Gently, he laid her back against a pile of cushions and rose to his feet. Oblivious of her pleading looks, he walked over to his friend.

'Would you care to explain what you mean by that remark?' he said very quietly.

Elinor could not bear the tension in the room. She began to speak, but Rokeby hushed her with a look.

'I am waiting,' he continued.

'Then you need wait no longer, Marcus.' Charlbury's look was long and deliberate. 'I had thought better of you. Imagine my feelings when I found Hester wandering alone in Berkeley Square. She was attempting to hire a hackney carriage. . .and at the mercy of any passer-by who cared to accost her.'

'*Your* feelings? What of the rest of us? My aunt is overcome with worry, and Elinor has been near-demented. . .'

'I am sorry for it, but the fault is yours.'

'You think so?' Rokeby's eyes narrowed. 'You came upon Hester quite by chance, I suppose? Or had you planned to help her leave this house?'

Charlbury took a step towards him. His fists were clenched. 'Do not try our friendship further,' he warned. Then he checked and his voice grew calmer. 'I make allowances for your natural anxiety, Marcus. You will not believe that of me if you consider. Why should I bring her back to you?'

'Why indeed?' his lordship jeered. 'Would you have me think that you met her by coincidence?'

'Is it so strange?' Charlbury had regained his self-command. Now he turned to help Hester to her feet, and handed her his handkerchief. 'Sit down, my dear, and wipe your eyes,' he said gently. 'There is no need to be afraid.'

'No?' His tenderness towards the girl had served only to incense his lordship further. 'Take care, my friend, you presume too much. . .'

To Elinor's astonishment Charlbury began to smile.

'In your high ropes, Marcus? Come down, I beg of you, and listen to what I have to say. I was coming to you anyway. Did you not invite me to attend your marriage?'

Rokeby would not be mollified. 'How fortunate that you were just in time to succour a maiden in distress.' The sarcasm brought a tinge of colour to Charlbury's cheeks.

'Yes, she *was* in distress,' he replied. 'To save Miss Temple from an unfortunate marriage, she had planned to agree to Lord Dacre's suggestion that she betroth herself to his son, Tobias.'

'Remarkable.' Rokeby sneered. 'I had no idea that she was besotted with the boy. Must I give you my permission to wed him, Hester?'

'Oh, please don't!' Hester cried in falling tones. 'I don't wish to marry Tobias in the least—'

'It is out of the question,' Charlbury intervened.

Rokeby stared at him, and when he spoke some of the anger had left his voice.

'I suppose we must be thankful that you have talked her out of that piece of nonsense,' he said grudgingly. 'But did it take all day? You might have brought her back before. Is that the action of a friend?'

'Hester is also my friend. She had no wish to return.'

'And her wishes are paramount?'

'They are with me.'

'Then I wonder why you brought her back.'

'I came for a purpose,' Charlbury said deliberately. 'I wish to marry Hester.'

'To save her from the cruelty of her wicked guardian?'

'Marcus, don't be such a noddle-cock. I want to marry Hester because I love her.'

'Indeed!' Rokeby turned away, but not before Elinor had seen the sparkle in his eyes. . .it was the old familiar glint of mischief. 'You surprise me! Here is Hester, on the verge of betrothal to Tobias? She will find it hard to make her choice. The boy is devoted to her. He told me so himself.'

Charlbury chose to ignore such baiting. 'You may not like the idea,' he said steadily, 'but Hester has promised to be my wife.'

'I have not said that you may pay your addresses to her.' Rokeby took a leisurely pinch of snuff. 'Upon consideration, I do not think I can allow it.'

'You must! We are betrothed.'

'Dear me! I fear I shall be forced to call you out for your importunate behaviour. Shall we say at dawn tomorrow? You may name your friends.'

Hester gasped. Her face was as white as her gown. It was Elinor who broke the silence.

'Marcus, the joke has gone far enough,' she reproved. 'Hester thinks you mean it.'

'But I do!' When he turned, Rokeby was laughing. 'I should like nothing better than to challenge this idiot.' He gave Charlbury a friendly blow upon the shoulder. 'A noddle-cock, did you call me? What of yourself? If you hadn't been so damned stiff-necked, none of this need have happened. You have known from the first that this is what I wished for you.'

He shook Charlbury warmly by the hand, and then he turned to Hester.

'You deserve a beating, miss, but I shall leave that to your husband. You had best go to my aunt, and take John with you. It may take some time to persuade her to forgive you.'

'Pray do not be too hard on her,' Elinor faltered when they were alone. 'She meant it for the best.'

'Your forgiveness comes readily,' he replied. 'I could wish that it applied to me.' Once again he might have been a stranger. 'Your father believes that you must have some regard for me. Can it be true?'

'I think you did not tell him all, my lord.'

'No, I did not.' His face was sombre. 'I am not proud of my behaviour on the night I left.'

Elinor was silent, and he turned away.

'It is over between us, then?' he asked. 'Well, it is no more than I deserve.'

'There is no trust between us,' Elinor cried brokenly. 'You told me so yourself.'

'That's true!' There was a quality of stillness about him which filled her with despair. 'You were quick to believe that I had left your arms to return to the women of the town. I suppose I cannot blame you. My life has not been such that you could doubt it.'

Elinor was silent. His words were true, and she could not deny them.

Rokeby straightened his shoulders. 'Do you wish to tell my aunt at once that we no longer plan to marry?'

'I don't know.' Elinor plucked at the trimming on her gown. 'Lady Hartfield has had a shock. Another may be too much for her.'

'As you wish. We shall keep up the charade for

another day or two.' He bowed and made as if to leave her.

'My family?' she pleaded. 'Will you not give me news of them?'

He paused, looking down at her, and then his expression softened.

'I beg your pardon. That was remiss of me.' He took a seat beside her. 'They are well, and I have a letter for you.' He reached inside his coat.

Elinor sat in silence, turning the envelope in her hands.

'I should tell you that your parents received me with great kindness. They were sorry only that you could not accompany me.' His air of formality was forbidding. 'They hope to see you soon.'

'Yes...yes, of course. I will go to them,' she said mechanically. She thought that she had never been so miserable in her life. She could not bear to open the letter. It must contain such loving wishes for her future happiness that each word would turn the knife in her wounded heart.

'You will stay for Hester's wedding?' Rokeby enquired in a cool tone. 'I imagine it will not be long delayed.'

Elinor nodded, but it was only with an effort that she managed to speak calmly of the coming nuptials.

'I am glad that you are pleased with Hester's choice,' she murmured. 'She and Charlbury are ideally suited to each other.'

'Indeed. Their betrothal is all that reconciles me to Hester's folly. Had Charlbury not convinced himself of my neglect, he might never have offered for her. Her fortune was the stumbling-block.'

'Hester will be happy with him. He is a man of honour.'

'Unlike myself?' His smile was bitter as he looked at her. 'Well, what's done is done, and we cannot change it. There is no point in going over it again.'

'None whatever,' Elinor agreed. She was close to breaking-point. 'If you will excuse me, my lord.'

She had reached the door before he spoke again.

'Elinor!' There was anguish in his voice, but she did not turn her head. She must be strong in her resolve to leave him, but the urge to run to his arms was overwhelming. She thrust it aside. There could be no future for them.

She walked slowly through the hall in a daze of misery, only half aware of a knock at the outer door. Her hand was on the newelpost of the staircase when she heard the sound of an altercation with the footman who had opened it. The voice was familiar, and she paused.

All visitors were to be denied, but beyond the servant's brawny figure she caught a glimpse of Tobias.

'But I must see Lord Rokeby,' he was saying. 'At least send in my card. . .'

Elinor walked towards him, dismissing the footman as she did so. 'I'm sure his lordship will see you, sir. I'll take you to him.'

'Oh, ma'am, have you any news of Hester. . .Miss Winton, I mean?' His anxiety was piteous and Elinor took his hand.

'She has returned and is quite safe,' she reassured. 'Lord Rokeby will tell you what has happened.' She led him into the salon.

Rokeby favoured him with the briefest of nods, but

Elinor's pleading glance persuaded him to mend his manners.

'You had best sit down,' he muttered. 'This may take some time. . .'

'Is something wrong?' Tobias looked from one face to the other. 'Miss Temple said that no harm has been done.'

'None to Hester,' Rokeby told him briefly. 'But you will not care for what I have to tell you.'

'I. . .I don't understand. . .'

'Hester is betrothed.'

The news came as a brutal shock to Tobias. He flushed scarlet and then his face grew pale.

'She. . .she eloped?' He sounded as if he could not believe his ears.

Elinor felt a pang of pity. 'No. . .no. . .she is not married, but she has accepted the offer of an old friend. She has loved him for some time.'

'I can't believe it.' Tobias was bewildered. 'Father was so sure that she would marry me. I did not care for the idea at first, but then I found that she was not so. . .so frightening as the other girls. She has been very kind to me.'

'She is a gentle soul,' Elinor agreed quietly. 'And she is lucky to have you as her friend, but if you are fond of her you must wish only for her happiness.'

'I do.' Tobias was the picture of dejection. 'But. . . well. . .Father said she wished above anything to be my wife .'

'Your father was mistaken,' Rokeby told him grimly. 'Pray give Lord Dacre my compliments when you tell him that his hopes are dashed.'

'Thank you, my lord.' Tobias was unconscious of

the irony in Rokeby's words. 'He is sure to be disappointed.'

'I don't doubt it,' came the brief reply.

'Do you think...well...may I see Miss Winton? I should like to wish her well.'

'At present she is resting, but I will give her your good wishes.' Elinor knew what he was feeling and her heart went out to him as he took his leave. She could only imagine that Tobias had inherited his gentle nature from his mother. There was nothing of his father in him.

She said as much to Rokeby when they were alone.

'The lad is well enough,' he replied with a gesture of impatience. 'Doubtless he fancies himself ill used, but he won't be allowed to pine for long. Dacre will wed him to the next heiress to appear in the marriage market. That is, if he can find some reason for such a girl to take him.'

'Tobias was not thinking of the money,' Elinor said quietly. 'I believe he has a genuine regard for Hester.'

'And your heart bleeds for him?'

Elinor flushed at the sarcasm in his voice.

'Bear up, my dear,' he continued in the same tone. 'Tobias will not die of unrequited love. It is a condition which is soon mended.'

Elinor's temper rose. 'Naturally you would think so,' she accused. 'What is your remedy, my lord?'

'Why, Elinor, I thought you knew it.' His eyes held hers and his meaning was unmistakable. 'Have I not given you evidence enough?'

'Indeed you have! To you, one woman is as good as another.' She flounced out of the room.

She was breathing hard as she climbed the stairs to Lady Hartfield's boudoir. Rokeby was impossible. He had no finer feelings. Who could look upon the young man's misery and remain unmoved? Only someone with a heart of stone. Let him go to his birds of paradise. She was well rid of him.

She was still clutching her father's letter in her hand, but she would not read it yet. She needed all her composure to face Lady Hartfield.

Pushing the letter into the pocket of her skirt, she stood quietly for a moment before she tapped at her ladyship's door. Then she took a deep breath before she entered the room.

Her fears were not unfounded. It was an uncomfortable trio which faced her. There was a reserve in Lady Hartfield's manner which Elinor had not seen before, and John Charlbury's calm appeared to have deserted him. It was clear that he was very angry.

Elinor went at once to Hester, saddened to see her swollen face and reddened eyes.

'This is no time to be weeping, my love.' She slipped an arm about the girl's shoulders. 'I had thought you must be very happy.'

'Hester deserves no happiness,' her ladyship snapped at once. 'When I think of the trouble she has caused... She is a selfish, stupid girl.'

John Charlbury stepped forward, but Elinor intervened before he could reply.

'I believe Lord Rokeby would like to see both you and Hester,' she said quickly. 'Will you go down to him? There are arrangements to be made...'

Charlbury read the message in her eyes. She wished to be alone with Lady Hartfield. His sigh of relief was almost audible. He reached out a hand to Hester and drew her to her feet.

'Do bathe your face, my dear,' Elinor suggested. 'John will wait for you.'

Hester was quick to hurry from the room, with John behind her. She neither spoke nor raised her head.

'The girl is a fool,' her ladyship announced with snapping eyes. 'She deserves a beating, and were she not betrothed I should see to it.'

Elinor sat down beside the chaise-longue and took Lady Hartfield's hand. For all the tension apparent in the older woman, Elinor could not repress a smile.

'I see nothing in the least amusing, Elinor. Perhaps you had best leave me.'

'Forgive me, ma'am, I do not mean to be uncivil. It is just that...well...sometimes you are very like his lordship. You echoed his words to Hester.'

The black eyes stared at her. 'And you persuaded him to forgive her for her folly? You will not get round me so easily. I cannot abide a fool!'

'Ma'am, will you not consider? Hester was wrong to run away, and to cause you so much worry. I know how you must feel. I could have shaken her myself, but it is a natural reaction, rather like the urge to whip a child who has just escaped some dreadful danger.'

Lady Hartfield tossed her head and looked away.

'Please don't destroy her present happiness,' Elinor pleaded. 'Hester has had so little in her life...'

'She had one piece of good fortune.'

'Ma'am?'

'She has you to stand her friend. She doesn't deserve you, Elinor, nor that charming man who has been weak enough to offer for her. I fear she is one of those wishy-washy creatures who will always lean on others.'

'You are wrong.' Elinor stood up. 'It took courage

to do what she has done today. She fears Lord Dacre, yet she went to him for my sake.'

'Now, Elinor, don't go into alt! Sit down. . .sit down. We shall not quarrel, you and I. Hester will wed, and there's an end to it. I can't say that I shall be sorry to see her settled, as much for your sake as for her own.'

'Then I may tell her. . .'

'You may tell her and her bridegroom that I wish them well. It is the truth.' A faint smile curved the corners of her lips. 'Marcus is delighted, I suppose. It is what he has wished from the beginning.'

'He has given them his blessing,' Elinor told her in a neutral tone.

Lady Hartfield cast a sharp glance at her face. Then she lay back and closed her eyes. 'I suppose we must be thankful that some good has come from Hester's folly, however well intentioned it may have been. Elinor, you may leave me now. I think that I shall rest before I dress for dinner.'

'Must you come down this evening, Lady Hartfield? If you wish it, I should be happy to bear you company in your room,' Elinor coaxed in the hope that her ladyship would consent. Beneath the fashionable paint, her skin was the colour of ancient parchment, but she shook her head.

'I am just a little tired. It has been a trying day, but I shall join you later.'

She would not be dissuaded, so Elinor left her to the ministrations of her maid. As she walked back to her own room the rustle of paper in her pocket reminded her that she had not yet read her father's letter. The sight of his familiar writing brought a lump to her throat, and her vision blurred as tears rose to her eyes.

She dashed them away with an impatient hand and began to read, though she was forced to lay the letter aside on more than one occasion as her feelings threatened to overcome her.

As she had expected, her family's love reached out to her across the miles which separated them. Their affection flowed towards her from those few sheets of paper. How they rejoiced in her good fortune! Lord Rokeby had convinced them, even on short acquaintance, that he was worthy of her, and who, they asked, could be more deserving of his love?

Elinor smiled through her tears. No one would ever convince them that they were not biased in her favour. A tide of homesickness swept over her. Suddenly she longed to lay her present cares aside. In Derbyshire there were no luxuries, except for kindness, good-will and the warmth of tenderness. If she were asked to choose, it would be no hardship to give up all the gaieties of the London season in return for a home such as her own.

Yet it was but a dream. She might return to her family for a short time, but poverty would drive her away again to make her own way in the world. She would not be a charge on them. In their present circumstances, one more mouth to feed would mean disaster.

She lifted a hand to her eyes as if to shut out a dreadful vision. Her future must be bleak indeed. Her lips trembled as she thought of the letter she must write. It would end all their hopes for her. As yet she could not bring herself to set pen to paper. Perhaps it was deceitful, but she would give them another day or two of happiness.

What a coward she was, she thought wretchedly. A

sterner character would have grasped the nettle at once, and set about the painful task. But how was she to explain her change of heart? She was still wrestling with the problem when she heard a tapping at her door. Dear God! Was she never to be left in peace?

Hester came towards her with a contrite look. She sensed at once that her company was unwelcome.

'I. . .I expect that you do not care to see me, Elinor,' she faltered. 'But won't you say that you forgive me? I cannot bear to think that we are no longer to be friends.'

Elinor held out her arms. 'There is nothing to forgive, my love. You must excuse me. It is just that I had a letter from my father. . .and. . .well. . .perhaps I feel a little homesick.'

'It must be hard to be away from them.' Hester sat by her feet. 'How stupid I have been. I never think of you as being lonely. You always seem so. . .so. . .'

'Self-sufficient? Perhaps I have been too much so.' Elinor shook her head as if to free it from unpleasant thoughts. 'Enough of me. Now tell me, are you truly, truly happy?'

'I can't believe it!' Hester told her simply. 'Am I really to be John's wife? It all seems like a dream. If I pinch myself, I shall wake up.'

'Then you must take care not to pinch yourself,' Elinor teased. 'You will believe it when you are ordering your household and looking to your children.'

Hester's eyes were filled with rapture. 'I've loved him for so long, you know, but I never thought he'd look at me.'

'Oh, I don't know about that. . . Some men have a curious longing to wed a monster of depravity.' Elinor began to twinkle.

'Have I been depraved? Oh dear, I had not thought to be so. . .'

'Of course not, goose! John loves you because you are kind and gentle, and your interests are his own. My dear, I wish you all the happiness in the world. No two people could be better suited to each other.'

'I wish that Lady Hartfield thought so,' Hester told her wistfully. 'She was very cross with me.'

'Her ladyship was worried about you, Hester. Her anger stemmed partly from relief to find that you were safe. She sent her good wishes to both you and John, and she meant them sincerely.'

'I will go to thank her—'

'No! At present she is resting. It may be best to speak to her this evening. Have you made your arrangements with Lord Rokeby?'

Hester brightened. 'There is such a lot to do. . . before a marriage, I mean. Did you know that banns must be called. . .that is. . .if John does not get a special licence?'

'I had heard of both banns and a licence,' Elinor said drily. 'My dear, there is much to consider when you are deciding where to marry. John will wish, perhaps, to have his family to support him?'

'Oh, yes! Lord Rokeby has left it to us to decide whether we shall marry from here or from Merton Place. Either way, his parents must be there. . . Elinor, now I have a family like yours.'

'So you have, my dearest, and they will love you as mine loves me.' Her smile was tinged with sadness. Had things been different between herself and Rokeby, she too might have worn that inner glow which gave the girl beside her a radiance of her own.

Hester reached out to slide a confiding hand into hers.

'It is strange,' she whispered softly. 'Already the world looks different. I can't explain it, but even ordinary objects look beautiful. I feel as though I've just been born, and am seeing everything about me for the first time.'

Elinor bent and kissed her. 'Hold on to that special feeling, Hester. Not everyone is lucky enough to know it, even in a lifetime.'

'You sound sad. Oh, Elinor, I didn't mean to hurt you. It will happen to you, you'll see.' She hesitated.

'What is it, Hester?'

The girl buried her face in Elinor's skirt, and muttered a few words, but they were inaudible.

'What is troubling you?'

'I was just thinking…now that I am to be John's wife there will be no need for you—'

'To stay with you? Of course not!'

'I did not mean that,' Hester muttered. Then her words came out in a rush. 'You need not marry Lord Rokeby, need you?' She lifted a pleading face, and was startled by Elinor's sharp intake of breath.

When it came, the reply was uttered in a toneless voice.

'No, I need not,' said Elinor.

'I'm so glad,' Hester told her earnestly. 'I know you said you loved him, but I knew that you could not. He's such a harsh, unfeeling man, and he would not be kind to you.'

'Your beloved John thinks well of him.' Irrationally, Elinor was spurred into a protest.

'John thinks well of everyone. He is the best of men—'

'Spare me a list of his perfections,' Elinor cried sharply. 'My dear, I am sorry, but I have the headache. Will you excuse me if I rest before we dine? I crave your pardon. I did not mean to snap at you.'

As a subdued Hester stole away, Elinor threw herself upon her bed. Her nerves were at breaking-point. What was happening to her? She had been on the verge of snarling like a madwoman. Surely she could not be jealous of Hester's happiness? That would be unthinkable.

If it were true, it showed a want of character, a lack of generosity. It revealed an aspect of her nature which she did not care to examine too closely.

She lay on her bed dry-eyed, staring at the ceiling. She *did* wish happiness for Hester, but she prayed heaven that John Charlbury would be impatient to claim his bride. Then, her promise to Hester fulfilled, she would go away and put all thoughts of Rokeby from her mind.

CHAPTER FOURTEEN

LATER that evening Elinor joined the others to find them deep in a discussion of the forthcoming nuptials. They broke off at her entrance, and John Charlbury came towards her.

'I have much to thank you for, Miss Temple.' He raised her hand to his lips. 'How beautiful you look tonight! You remind me of some sea-nymph, newly risen from the foam.'

'A poetic thought, my dear John! Love has made you lyrical...' Rokeby's voice was soft, but Elinor detected an undertone of sarcasm. He, too, kissed her hand, and it took all her self-command not to drag it from his grasp. Even through the fabric of her glove she felt that his lips must burn her skin.

'But it is true.' Hester gave her a fond look. 'Lady Hartfield, don't you agree?'

'I do!' Her ladyship patted the seat beside her. 'Elinor, come and sit by me.' She subjected Elinor's gown to a critical look. 'That misty gauze is exactly right for you, but I cannot decide if it is blue or green...'

'It is a turquoise shade, I believe. Ma'am, are you feeling better?'

'I am quite recovered. Did I not say that I was just a little tired? Enough of that, we have need of your counsel, my dear. Here is Marcus, insisting on a London wedding...'

'It will not do, old friend.' Charlbury took the hand

of his bride-to-be. 'A quiet country service will suit us better. We have few friends in London, and my family must be there.'

Hester glanced at him with gratitude. The thought of a crowded ceremony, in a fashionable London church, filled her with dread.

'Well, that is better than to wed by special licence,' said her ladyship with a flash of her old spirit. 'That would be a havey-cavey thing to do. I am surprised to hear that you considered it.'

'Ma'am, it was to be a last resort.' Charlbury gave her his enchanting smile. 'I feared that in the end I must abduct my bride. Marcus offered to call me out, you know.'

'Marcus has an unfortunate tendency to levity,' her ladyship said severely. 'It is high time that he controlled it.'

Elinor stole a glance at Rokeby. He was smiling, but there was no amusement in his eyes. As if aware of her regard he looked at her, but she turned away.

'Well then, that is settled. Mr Charlbury, you may take me in to dinner.' Lady Hartfield laid her hand upon his arm.

Escorted by Lord Rokeby, Elinor and Hester followed them in silence. As they took their places at the table Elinor resolved to exert herself. It was ridiculous to allow what should have been a celebration into a funeral wake.

She turned to John Charlbury. 'When do you return to Kent?' she asked. 'I expect you will have much to do.'

'I don't quite know, Miss Temple. That must rest with you and Marcus, as you will wed before us, and I have promised to stand up with him.'

Elinor thought she must be turned to stone. She heard a gasp of surprise from Hester.

'But, Elinor,' the girl began. 'Did you not tell me. . .?' She subsided at a warning look.

'We have changed our plans since we received your news,' Rokeby announced smoothly. 'I believe we shall now wait until the end of the season. We cannot cope with two such ceremonies in the course of the next few weeks.'

'We could make it a double wedding,' Charlbury suggested happily. He was puzzled by the ensuing silence. 'Oh, I see! I beg your pardon, Marcus. I was not thinking. A quiet wedding will not do for you. The world and his wife will come to wish you joy.'

Lady Hartfield jumped into the breach. 'You young men have no idea—' she sounded a little breathless '—announcements must be made, and bride clothes chosen. . .'

'I quite understand,' Charlbury's brow cleared. 'I hope that we have not put you about.'

'Not at all.' Elinor forced out the words through stiff lips. She could not go on.

'We are disposed to wait,' Lord Rokeby assured him. 'Elinor wishes to see her parents.'

That much at least was true, but it was an ambiguous remark which failed to satisfy John Charlbury.

'I thought you had but just come from them,' he said.

'I went alone to ask for Elinor's hand. Her family longs to see her.' His words did not invite further comment, and Charlbury did not pursue the subject. He had begun to wonder if Marcus had not received the welcome for which he'd hoped.

'My place in Yorkshire is yours for the asking,'

Rokeby continued in a softer tone. 'You will wish to take Hester away after you are married. It is kept fully staffed. You will be comfortable.'

Charlbury looked at Hester's sparkling eyes. Then he turned to Rokeby in gratitude. 'Thank you,' he said simply. 'It is a generous offer, and we'll be happy to accept. From there we might go on to Northumberland. I have an old aunt. She is too frail to make the journey into Kent, but she will want to wish us happy.'

Elinor's eyes were fixed upon her plate. She felt as if she were upon the rack. The talk of her own marriage had been torture to her, now that all her hopes of happiness had vanished. Later, she could not have described the rest of the conversation at the dinner-table, and it was with a sigh of relief that she followed Lady Hartfield and Hester into the salon, leaving the men to their wine.

Her ladyship rang for the tea-tray.

'Elinor, will you pour?' she said.

Elinor was only too thankful to busy herself with the task. The evening had been a trial, but such trying situations promised to be her lot for the next few weeks. She glanced at her companions, but they were engaged in planning Hester's wardrobe. At least her ladyship appeared to be more in charity with the girl, and for that she must be grateful.

Hester's mind was only half on the discussion. Her eyes strayed constantly towards the door, and. when Charlbury appeared, accompanied by his lordship, she gave them a radiant smile.

'Hester, the night is fine. Mr Charlbury will wish to see the gardens.' Lady Hartfield dismissed the lovers to a welcome tryst.

Rokeby sat down, but he was restless. At length he began to pace the room.

'Marcus, for heaven's sake! Pray take yourself off if you cannot be still. It makes me tired just to look at you.'

'I beg your pardon, aunt. Pray excuse me if you will. I should send off the announcements to the papers.' He bowed to both of them and left the room.

'Now then, my dear, this will not do, you know.' Her ladyship's sharp eyes were intent upon Elinor's face. 'Am I to understand that all is at an end between you?'

'We had hoped to keep it from you, ma'am.'

'Then you must think me a fool. When Charlbury spoke of your coming marriage, I feared that you would faint.'

Elinor did not reply.

'And you must not forget that I know my nephew very well,' the older woman continued. 'He is not the same man. Has your father refused his permission for Marcus to address you?'

'No, it is not that.' Elinor's expression was bleak. 'My family thought him charming.'

'Clearly his charm has been wasted upon yourself. Oh, my dear, whatever he has done or said to you, will you not find it in your heart to forgive him? He loves you so.'

'You are mistaken, ma'am. Things have been said which cannot be forgotten. Forgiveness is not enough. There is no trust between us.'

'I see. My love, I am so sorry. I had such hopes for both of you.' She was silent for some time, seeming almost to shrink within herself. 'Elinor, what will you do?' she asked.

'I have promised to stay with Hester until she weds. Then I must find another post.'

'Will you not make your home with me? I have felt for some time that I shall not wish to live alone again. You would be my friend, as well as my companion.'

'How kind you are!' The tears sprang unbidden to Elinor's eyes. 'But, Lady Hartfield, it would not do. I could not bear—'

'To see him constantly? Before you came, his visits were infrequent. We might arrange it so that you were not in his company.'

Elinor shook her head.

'Well, promise me at least that you will think about it? You are overwrought, my dear. Perhaps if you paid a visit to your family?'

'They will be so sad for me.' Elinor was weeping openly. 'This news will hurt them so.'

'Need you tell them yet? Why not go to bed and sleep on it? You are so tired, but you will feel better in the morning. Now give me a kiss before you go.'

Elinor hurried away before the others could return. John and Hester would wonder at her reddened eyes, and above all, Rokeby must not see her weeping.

She would not sleep. . .she was convinced of it, but nature was too strong for her.

It was morning before she opened her eyes. A glance at the clock on the mantelshelf showed her that it was early, but the sun was already peeping through a gap in her drawn curtains.

Her sleep had not refreshed her, and the leaden feeling in her limbs persisted. She longed for a breath of air, and rising, she dressed quickly in her thinnest

muslin gown. She met no one as she made her way
down to the garden door.

How cool it was out of doors! She pressed her hands
to her burning face. Within an hour or two the sticky
heat of a summer's day would return, but meantime
she was free to wander along the flagged path towards
the fountain at the far end of the garden.

There she sat down upon the raised stone wall that
surrounded the pool and dabbled her fingers in the
water. A green frog stared at her from a lily pad, and
in the depths she could see the flash of golden carp.

Then a shadow fell across the pool and she turned
quickly to find Rokeby by her side. She was on her
feet at once.

'No, don't run away!' He said curtly. 'I wish to
speak to you.'

'We...we can have nothing to say to each other,'
she faltered. She would not look at him.

'On the contrary...I have much to say. My aunt
tells me that you have refused the offer of a home
with her.'

'I am sorry that she found out...I mean...'

'She could scarce miss it, could she, Elinor? We
have no gift for dissembling, you and I. John's remarks
last night were less than fortunate, though he could
not know it at the time.'

Elinor said nothing.

'That is not the point I wished to make.' Abstractedly
his lordship tossed a pebble into the pool, watching the
widening ripples as it broke the surface and sank into
the depths. 'What is your objection to this plan? You
are fond of my aunt, as she is of you... It would seem
to be a solution.'

'Would it?' She turned to him then, her eyes ablaze.

'My lord, you may not order my life for me. My future can be no concern of yours. I am sensible of her ladyship's generosity, but nothing would persuade me—'

'To risk yourself in my company? You need have no fear of that. When Hester is wed I intend to go abroad again to Europe. That is. . .if this peace with Napoleon should hold.'

'And if not?'

'Why, then I shall offer my services to a grateful country.'

'You would fight if the war should break out again?' Elinor's face grew pale.

'Other men will do so. Would you have me hide behind their valour?'

'But. . .but you might be killed!'

'Very possibly. That is not unknown in time of war, my dear Elinor.' A cynical smile curved his lips. 'It would be no great matter, I assure you, and then you would be rid of me for good.'

'That is foolish talk,' she cried sharply. 'I have no wish. . .I mean. . .a broken engagement is no reason for you to throw your life away.'

'How true!' His eyes flickered reflectively across her face. 'Let us forget these morbid thoughts. The Treaty may hold and possibly it will not come to war, though I must doubt it. Napoleon, so I understand, is using these months of peace to good effect.'

'He is preparing?'

'I believe so.' He tossed another pebble into the pool. 'Elinor, what will you do when you leave us?'

'I shall go home to Derbyshire for a while. It will give me time to look about me. . .'

'And then…another teaching post?' His voice sounded oddly harsh.

'If such is to be had,' she told him lightly. 'I enjoyed my work at Bath…' He could have no notion of the despair which filled her heart.

'I don't doubt it. You have qualities of courage and endurance which are rare. I could wish…' He stopped and rose to his feet. 'The sun grows warm and your head is unprotected. Will you not come indoors?'

Elinor looked up at him, willing him to go on with what he had been about to say. What did he wish? His eyes were sad, and his expression tore at her heart. If only the events of that dreadful night had not occurred, or if the cruel words which had passed between them might be unsaid…

She bit her lip. Wishing would not change matters now. It was better that she knew him for what he was …a man capable of brutality. He could have no idea of how badly he had frightened her, else he would not have gone into Derbyshire to ask her father for her hand.

She walked ahead of him in silence and went up to her room. She had no wish to eat, but she made a dutiful appearance at the breakfast-table, to find herself alone with Hester.

'Lord Rokeby is gone out,' Hester told her cheerfully. 'Elinor, I think I like him better now. He has been very good…I mean about my marriage.'

Elinor looked at her. Does she not know that she is treading on my heart? she thought in anguish. Nothing of that must show upon her face.

'Lord Rokeby is happy for both of you.' Even to herself her voice sounded unnaturally calm, but Hester did not notice.

The shy little creature who had been so sensitive to the feelings of others was now oblivious to everything but her love. She chattered on until John Charlbury was announced. Then her face lit up, and she flew into his arms.

Charlbury kissed her gently. Then he disengaged himself, though he kept her hand in his.

'I am come to take my leave of you, Miss Temple. Today I go to Kent.'

'We shall miss you quite dreadfully, shan't we, Elinor?' Hester gave him an adoring look and raised his hand to her cheek. 'I shall be miserable.'

'No, puss, you will not. You will have much to do, and the time will fly. It is but four short weeks, and then we shall not part again.'

'Must you go so soon?' Hester pleaded. 'Lady Hartfield will wish to see you. . . Shall I tell her you are here?'

He smiled his assent and Hester hurried away.

Charlbury was silent for a moment. Then he sat by Elinor's side.

'I am sorry if I caused you pain last night,' he said. 'I did not know, you see, but Marcus has explained. This is distressing news and must have been the cause of much unhappiness.'

'We did not intend to deceive you,' Elinor murmured. 'We kept up the pretence for Lady Hartfield's sake. She was not well. . .'

'And I gave the game away? She did not take it amiss, you know. I spoke to her last evening, when you had retired. The old can be surprisingly resilient. They see much in the course of a lifetime, and they learn to endure. . .and also to hope.'

'She must not hope,' Elinor told him quietly.

'As you do not?' A large hand covered her own. 'Miss Temple, love is not so easily crushed. Who should know better than I? I might have sacrificed both Hester's happiness and my own for the sake of pride. I could not bear that the world should see me as a fortune-hunter.'

'Who could think that of you?' Elinor managed a faint smile.

'Myself for one. She is so very young, and all the advantage is on my side.'

'What nonsense! You are all that I could wish for her. Hester needs protection. . .and, above all, love. You will transform her life, and I wish you joy with all my heart.'

Charlbury raised her hand to his lips. 'What a friend you are!' he said unsteadily. 'I see why Hester is devoted to you, but so is Marcus, believe me.'

'Please. . .I wish you would not speak of him.' Her voice was not quite under her control.

'I must, my dear. He too is my friend. Won't you reconsider? Marcus is not perfect. He would be the first to admit it. He has a hasty temper, and sometimes it leads him beyond what is acceptable, but then it is over like a summer storm.'

'Leaving wreckage in its wake? Oh, I know that you mean well, but. . .'

She was spared the need for further argument, and fell silent as Hester came to join them.

'Her ladyship is still abed. She sends her compliments, John. You are to give her love to your mother, and—'

'I will leave you to your farewells.' Elinor gave him her hand. 'May I too send my regards to your family?'

'Thank you. There is one more thing, Miss Temple.

Should you think of visiting your family...after the wedding, I mean, we should be happy to have your company on our way into Yorkshire. Is that not so, Hester?'

'I should like it above anything,' Hester agreed earnestly. 'Do say that you'll come with us.'

'Would you have me play gooseberry?' Elinor smiled in spite of herself. 'I should be *de trop*. To quote the old saw there are occasions when "Two is company but three is none".'

She shook her head at their protestations, but they would not let her go until she had promised to consider travelling with them.

Hester returned to the subject later that day.

'I shall miss you after I am wed,' she said wistfully. 'And Derbyshire, you know, is on our way to Yorkshire...at least, it would be only a little out of the way, and I should like to meet your family. You've told me so much about them.'

'You might call on your way home. And John, you know, will wish for your undivided attention.'

'He shall have it...for the rest of our lives...but I do wish...'

'Well, there is time enough to decide,' Elinor told her briskly. 'At present we are neglecting Lady Hartfield, and I know she wishes to speak to you.'

They found her ladyship at her desk, absorbed in making lists. She looked up as they entered.

'There you are, my dears. Hester, we must consider your bride-clothes without delay.'

'Ma'am, shall I need more? We seem to have bought so much...'

'Foolish child! Your present wardrobe can form but

a small part of your trousseau. And what of the
ceremony itself? The choice of a bridal-gown is not to
be lightly undertaken.'

Hester was quick to agree. 'Though, ma'am, other
than that. . .well. . .we are to live in the country, you
know. John says that we are to have the Dower House
on his father's estate.'

'You will not lead a hermit-like existence, Hester.'
There was a note of exasperation in her ladyship's
voice. 'A bride is asked everywhere, and there is your
honeymoon to be considered. Your gowns are well
enough for the summer season, but autumn will soon
be upon us.'

Hester subsided, though she threw a despairing
glance at Elinor, knowing well enough that the next
few weeks were likely to be hectic.

She was not mistaken. The announcement of her
coming nuptials brought a flood of invitations from
milliners, mantua-makers and purveyors of boots and
shoes, begging her to inspect their stock.

Two days later Elinor found her gazing at an enormous pile of cards and letters.

'I'd like to throw them all away,' she told Elinor
ruefully. 'But some are letters from her ladyship's
acquaintance, inviting us to various functions.' She
picked up a gilt-edged card, and placed it on the
mantelshelf. 'This one is from Lord Dacre.'

Elinor felt a spurt of anger. 'That, at least, is
unlikely to be accepted. Have you shown it to your
guardian?'

'I have not seen Lord Rokeby. I expect that he is
busy. He has returned to his own house, you know.'

Elinor nodded. Rokeby had kept his word, but
whether or not it was to persuade her to make her

home with Lady Hartfield she could not guess. It was strange, but without him life had lost all its savour. She no longer looked for his tall figure whenever she entered a room, but how she missed the way his eyes lit up at her appearance. That swarthy face had a curious way of softening when he looked at her, even as his eyes devoured her.

In his company life had an edge to it...a sense of excitement. Without him it was bleak indeed.

'Elinor, look at this!' Hester held up another card. 'It is from a tradesman, but it is so interesting.'

'I wonder why it has been sent to you? These goods are bespoke for gentlemen...'

'I know, but I must have a wedding gift for John, and I don't know any other shops.' She looked at the address. 'Could we find it, do you think?'

Elinor examined the card. 'It is somewhere between St James's street and Piccadilly, I believe. The finest shops for men are in that area, but, Hester, no lady may walk along St James's street. It isn't done. You will not persuade her ladyship to agree to such an expedition.'

'Must we tell her? We need not walk, you know. If the carriage were to drop us at the door and wait for us, the purchase would not take long...'

Elinor frowned. 'I think not. I don't like it, Hester. We had best forget it. Lady Hartfield will know of somewhere else.'

Hester's face fell, but she accepted the decision with good grace, though it was not possible to ask her ladyship's advice that morning. Their hostess was much preoccupied with answering letters and adding to her list of things which must be done before the wedding. She sent word that they were to drive in the park without her.

Time and again their carriage was stopped as members of the *ton* came up to offer their good wishes. Elinor was aware of a few dark looks from fond mammas whose hopes of a wealthy heiress for their sons had just been dashed, but these were balanced by the obvious relief of those whose daughters had not yet received an offer. Hester was to marry an unknown, which left more glittering prizes still within their grasp.

As they left the park and drove down Piccadilly, Hester clutched at Elinor's arm.

'There is the street,' she cried excitedly. 'I recognise the name. May we not stop just for a moment?' She called to the coachman.

'Hester, please!' Elinor made a vain attempt to catch at her sleeve, but she was too late. Hester was out of the carriage, and was already disappearing down the narrow street.

'Stay here! We shall not be above a moment.' Elinor ignored the startled look upon the coachman's face, and hurried in pursuit.

Hester was well ahead of her, gazing intently at the names above the shops. Then she vanished round a corner.

Elinor began to run. The street was dark and noisome, and in the summer heat the foul smell from the gutters was overpowering.

As she turned the corner she saw Hester standing irresolute on the pavement.

'We must go back,' she cried. 'We have come far from Piccadilly. Hester, this is folly. Let us return at once.'

'I can't find it,' Hester said. 'It must be here. . .we are almost at the end of this lane.'

'Can I help you, miss?'

Both girls turned to face a rough-looking man in a muffler. He seemed to have materialised from nowhere. His smile did nothing to reassure them as it revealed a mouthful of broken teeth. From his flattened nose and mighty thews Elinor guessed him to be an ex-pugilist.

'No, thank you!' she said sharply.

'He might know,' Hester protested. 'We are looking for Cleggs.'

'Bless you, miss, you're almost on the doorstep. There it is. . .across the street.'

Hester darted away, leaving Elinor with no choice but to follow her. She gave no further thought to the man who had accosted them, and then was startled to find that he was behind her as she entered the shop.

A warning bell rang in her head. There was something wrong. She turned to find the pugilist leaning against the door. He was no longer smiling.

Hester looked perplexed. 'This can't be the place,' she murmured. 'There is nothing here. . .'

The interior was very dark, but as Elinor looked about her she realised that the room was empty. It was also thick with dust, and showed no signs of occupation.

'Let us go at once.' She turned towards the door, but found her way barred. Arms folded across his breast the man stared down at her.

'Get out of my way,' she cried. 'Hester, this is a trap.'

Then a cloth was thrown about her head, muffling her screams. She fought and kicked, but all to no avail.

She was picked up without ceremony and carried into an inner room. Almost immediately she heard a bolt drawn back.

'All clear?' her captor asked.

'Aye! Let's get these hellcats into the coach.'

She heard the sound of nailed boots on cobbles, and then she was flung on to a leather seat. Elinor fought to free her head from the folds of cloth, but her captor held her close.

'You won't see nothing, miss. Nor will folks see you. The blinds is drawn. Be still now, or you'll do yourself an injury.'

Elinor stopped struggling. The man was right. Her puny efforts were no match for his strength, and she would need all her own to face what lay ahead.

She was still dazed by the speed of the attack. To be abducted in broad daylight? It did not seem possible. She could not have imagined it in her wildest dreams.

Her mind was racing. What had these men in mind? She was certain that they were not the principals. She had seen only one of them, and briefly, but it was enough to tell her that he could not have been the instigator of such a careful plan.

And careful it had been. She and Hester had been lured into that narrow side-street in the cleverest way. Someone had taken pains with that apparently innocent advertisement, couching it in terms which could not fail to appeal to an inexperienced girl.

Suddenly Elinor was aware that the coach had stopped. Their journey had not taken more than a few moments. It was clear that they were still in central London. She lay inert as she was lifted from the coach and carried across a cobbled courtyard. Her captor then mounted a staircase, opened a door, and laid her upon a couch. Then the enveloping cloth was whisked from about her head.

'Welcome, Miss Temple!' The voice was only too familiar. She raised her head to find Lord Dacre standing by the door.

CHAPTER FIFTEEN

'WHAT is the meaning of this outrage?' Elinor asked in icy tones. 'How dare you treat us so?'

'Spare me your display of temper. You had best see to the girl. . .' His face was impassive as he gestured towards Hester, who lay huddled in a chair. Her eyes were closed, and Elinor guessed that she had fainted.

'Get me some water,' she snapped out. 'Have you no pity for her?'

'Not much. She is a fool, Miss Temple, but then, I was able to rely upon that. You, I believe, are made of sterner stuff, but we shall see.'

Elinor ignored him as she sprinkled a few drops of water on Hester's face. After a few moments the blue eyes opened, and Hester struggled to sit upright.

'What has happened?' she whispered. 'Those awful men. . .are they gone?' Her glance rested upon Lord Dacre. 'Did you save us, sir? I can't think how you found us. . .'

'Save your thanks, my dear Hester. We were brought here on Lord Dacre's orders. Is that not so, my lord?'

Dacre bowed. 'My apologies, Hester. You were roughly handled, but there was no help for it. I doubted that you would accept a formal invitation to my home.'

'I don't understand.' Bewildered, Hester looked from one face to the other. 'Why are we here?'

'There is a simple explanation, my dear. I fear you

have been misled into an unfortunate betrothal. Did you not assure me that you wished to marry Tobias?'

'My lord, I was mistaken. . . I agreed only when you threatened to harm Elinor and Lord Rokeby. I am sorry. I have no wish to hurt Tobias, but my heart is given elsewhere.'

'May I be allowed to hope that you may change your mind?' Dacre's eyes had almost disappeared in the folds of flesh surrounding them.

'Never!' Hester cried stoutly. 'I love John Charlbury and I intend to marry him.'

'Really? You are fond of your friend, I think.' With a speed surprising in so large a man, his hand flashed out to grasp Elinor's hair. He twisted her curls around his fingers and pulled hard. The pain brought tears to Elinor's eyes, but she did not speak.

'Please don't!' Hester cried in anguish. 'If it is the money I will give you all I have.'

'I doubt if your guardian will agree to that.' Dacre dragged Elinor to her feet. 'I'm afraid that it must be marriage to Tobias.' He stroked Elinor's hair, then his hand caressed her neck, and swept down to her bosom. The red face was very close to hers, and Elinor could smell the wine upon his breath. He bent his head to find her lips, and she began to struggle.

'I am not surprised that Rokeby finds you irresistible,' he murmured thickly. 'Will he want damaged goods, I wonder?'

'Let her go!' Suddenly Hester was on her feet, beating vainly at his shoulders. He swept her aside as if she were a fly.

The force of his blow sent Hester spinning. She landed heavily in one corner of the room, twisting her ankle as she did so.

Dacre forced Elinor back against the cushions on the couch. The powerful hands reached out to unfasten the ribbons of her gown. Then he slid it from her shoulders, feasting his eyes upon her milky skin.

'No! Please stop!' Hester took a painful step towards him.

'It is up to you, my dear. A word of consent, and your friend will remain unravished. Otherwise, you may watch as I deflower her. You are a virgin, are you not, Miss Temple?'

Elinor spat full in his face. It was a mistake. He tore the last shreds of her gown away and threw himself upon her. She was suffocating, helpless beneath his bulk. Then she heard a thread-like voice.

'I will marry Tobias,' Hester said.

Dacre was not listening. His face was suffused with passion and he was breathing hard. A large vein beat hard in his temple, and for a heart-stopping moment Elinor believed that nothing could deter him from his purpose.

Hester plucked wildly at his shoulder. 'Stop!' she cried again. 'Do you not hear me? I've agreed to marry Tobias.'

His eyes blinded with lust, the great bull-like head turned at last in her direction.

'Let Elinor go,' she shouted. 'That is my condition.'

With a grunt Dacre heaved himself to his feet, and began to rearrange his clothing.

'You shall tell Tobias,' he ground out. 'And no tricks, mind. The boy must believe you. I want no trouble with his delicate ideas of honour.'

Elinor lay as he had left her. Her eyes were closed, but she was thinking fast. They must play for time. By now the coachman must have given the alarm, unless he imagined that they had been so distracted by their shopping that they had forgot their promise to return at once.

Dacre pulled at the bell-rope, but he did not admit his servant to the room.

'Send my son to me,' he ordered through the half-opened door. Then he walked over to where Elinor lay dishevelled on the couch. 'Cover yourself,' he snapped. 'If you are wise, you'll keep a still tongue in your head. Remember that I can hold you here as long as I care to do so.'

'But you promised to let her go.' Hester raised a tear-stained face to his.

'That must depend on your behaviour, my dear Hester. Now I think I hear Tobias. . .it is up to you.'

As the door opened he moved to stand in front of Elinor, blocking her from his son's view.

'Good news, my boy!' he announced in a jovial tone. 'Here is Hester come back to us. She has been over-persuaded by her so-called friends, I fear, but now she has something to say to you.'

Tobias hesitated, looking at Hester's wan face. 'You look strangely, Miss Winton. Is something wrong?'

'I. . .I have been stupid enough to turn my ankle. . .' Hester whispered. 'It is very painful.'

'I will get help. It should be bound up.'

'Stay where you are, Tobias, and listen to what Hester has to say to you. She is now quite sure that she wishes to become your wife.'

'Can it be true?' The boy's face lit up. 'Oh, Hester, tell me that it is what you wish—'

'Of course she does not wish it.' Elinor struggled painfully to her feet. 'Hester has agreed because your father threatened to harm me. Look at my gown!'

'I warned you!' With cat-like ferocity, Lord Dacre turned and struck her a fearful blow across the face. Elinor fell unconscious at his feet.

She returned to consciousness to find herself in semi-darkness. Her head was pounding, and she could taste the saltiness of blood upon her lips. Gingerly she lifted a hand to discover the source of the wound, and found that she had a deep cut on her brow. She must have struck something when she fell.

Beside her Hester was sobbing quietly, and Elinor reached out towards her.

'Where are we?' she murmured.

'He has locked us in a cellar. Oh, Elinor, I thought that he had killed you.'

'Where is Lord Dacre now?'

'I don't know. Tobias ran from the house and his father followed him.'

'Then we are saved. Tobias will go to Rokeby. . .'

'He may not. He is terrified of his father.'

'You misjudge him, Hester. Tobias is a man of honour.' Elinor spoke with a confidence she was far from feeling.

Tobias had good reason to fear Lord Dacre yet, even had he resolved upon defiance, would he have the courage to seek out Rokeby and tell him the full story? If so, he would most certainly sign his father's death warrant.

'We shall not have long to wait,' she comforted. 'Marcus will find us. . .'

'It is all my fault,' Hester said dully. 'I should have listened to you.'

'Don't blame yourself. Lord Dacre is a ruthless man. If one plan had failed, he would have found another.'

'We shall never be safe from him,' Hester wailed.

'Of course we shall. You will marry your John and go to live in Kent. Then you will forget all this.'

'I wish that John were here in London. . .' It was a pitiful whisper. 'Perhaps I shall not see him again.'

'You will. I promise you.' Elinor squeezed her hand. 'Have you looked about you, Hester? There may be some way of escape. . .?'

Hester shook her head.

'Then let us do so now.' Still dizzy from the blow to her head Elinor struggled to her feet. 'There may be a chute for coal, or even a window. These cellars must extend below the house.'

They found the window in the adjoining passage-way. It was high on the wall and very small.

'Could you squeeze through there?' Elinor asked.

'Perhaps, but how are we to reach it?'

'There may be some bricks, or boxes. . .even old furniture. . .anything which will bear our weight.'

In the third of the cellars they found a wooden packing-case.

'Help me to drag it under the window,' Elinor urged. 'Quickly. . .we do not know when Dacre will return.'

The box was large and heavy, but they tugged it into place at last. Elinor helped Hester up, but she could not reach the window.

'Let me try.' Elinor took her place and found herself on a level with the glass. She pushed at the dusty frame with all her strength, but she could not move it.

'It's stuck,' she cried in despair. 'I doubt if it's been opened since the house was built. Find something heavy, Hester. . .some tool. . .a piece of wood. . .I'll try to force it open.'

'Get down,' Hester cried in terror. 'Someone is coming!'

The creak of the cellar door was loud as the bolts were drawn back. Both girls saw the flicker of a lantern.

'Pretend to be unconscious,' Hester whispered urgently. 'If it is Lord Dacre he may not hurt you further.'

It must be Dacre, Elinor thought in despair. It was too soon for Rokeby to have found them. She closed her eyes as she heard the sound of feet upon the steps. Then a large hand closed about her chin, moving her head from side to side.

'I must have hit her harder than I thought. A pity I did not break her neck.' Dacre brought his ear to Elinor's mouth. 'She's still breathing... Make haste there...we must get them away. That son of mine is fool enough to fetch the Bow Street Runners.'

Once again Elinor found herself enveloped in a blanket. Through the muffling folds she heard Hester's voice rising to a shriek.

'Let her go,' she screamed. 'I gave you my word. Is that not enough?'

'Not now, my dear. Tobias does not believe you. His finer feelings are offended.'

'Whose fault is that?' Had you not struck Elinor in that brutal way, I might have persuaded him.'

'I doubt it. What could you have said? That your friend had torn her own gown to give me the lie? What an innocent you are! Enough of this. Will you walk to the coach or must we carry you?'

'You shall not touch me,' Hester said with dignity. 'What do you intend to do with us?'

'Well now, I haven't quite decided. Tobias, alas, is

lost to you, but there are other possibilities. Rokeby may be persuaded to pay a handsome price for your return...that is, if you are still in your virgin state.'

'And Elinor?'

'That is another matter. I have an old score to settle with your guardian. He may keep his paramour... when I have done with her. Will soiled goods hold the same appeal, I wonder?'

The blood in Elinor's veins turned to ice. The man was a monster. She heard a cry as Hester flew at him, but it was quickly followed by a whimper of pain.

'Take care, my girl,' Dacre warned. 'Try that again and you will get the beating of your life.'

Elinor was lifted to her feet and thrown like a sack across a pair of brawny shoulders. As the man ascended the cellar steps, she gave way to despair.

Dacre, she guessed, intended to spirit them away from London to some quiet hideaway and, once he did so, Marcus could have no hope of finding them.

Then her captor stopped, and she felt him stiffen.

'Stay exactly where you are,' a familiar voice advised. 'You will place that lady, very gently, in the chair beside you. Then you will remove the blanket from her head.'

With her heart in her eyes, Elinor looked up into Rokeby's face. His quick glance took in her blood-stained appearance, and his fingers tightened upon the pistol in his hand. His expression terrified her. At that moment he looked capable of murder.

'Tobias, you may call in the Runners.' His voice was not his own and he did not look round as the Bow Street men led Dacre's bully-boys away. His eyes were fixed upon Lord Dacre's face, and there was no mistaking his intent.

'Marcus, please don't!' Elinor spoke in little more than a whisper. 'Let him be tried in a court of law.'

He did not seem to have heard her.

'Elinor, can you walk?' he asked quietly.

'I. . .I think so. . .but I beg of you. . .'

'Take Hester into another room. Tobias will go with you.'

The boy started towards him with a plea for his father's life upon his lips, but he stopped at Rokeby's quick command.

'Back! I have no wish to harm you, but a single shot will break your leg. Elinor, you will do as I say.'

Elinor stood up, knowing that further argument was useless. She reached out a hand to Hester, and then she was seized from behind.

'Fire away!' Dacre was holding her as a shield before him. 'At this range you cannot miss.' He began to sidle across the hall to the outer courtyard, dragging Elinor with him. She began to struggle wildly, but he held her fast. She bent her head and bit down into his wrist. She heard a curse, but he did not release her.

Then his grip seemed to slacken, and she heard a choking sound. She spun round to find that he was clutching at his upper arm. Then his hand moved to his breast, and his eyes began to roll. She could not understand it. Marcus could not have fired. There had been no sound of a shot.

She gazed in horror at Lord Dacre. A little foam was coming from his lips and his purple face was hideously contorted.

Marcus seized her arm and pulled her away. Then he was on his knees beside the stricken man.

'A seizure,' he said briefly. He turned to Tobias. 'You had best fetch the surgeon.'

Even as he spoke the stertorous breathing stopped.

'Too late, I fear. He is gone. . . Tobias, I am sorry. . .'

The boy blinked away a tear. 'It is for the best, my lord. I could not have watched you kill him, nor could I have borne to see him standing trial. . .'

Elinor found that her legs would not support her. She sank into a chair, but Hester had walked towards Tobias.

'Try not to think ill of him,' she said. 'He was your father, after all, and circumstances were against him.'

'You have forgiven him?' Tobias looked at her in disbelief.

'I believe I shall do so in time, and so will Elinor.'

'You are generous.' Tobias raised her hand to his lips. 'This is no sight for you. Allow me to take you to the salon. Miss Temple?'

Elinor was stiff with shock. To be swept from the face of the earth in a few moments? It was a solemn thought. She stumbled towards Rokeby.

'Go with them.' he said gently. 'I will see to matters here.'

She could only obey. Averting her eyes from the still figure on the ground, she followed the others out of the room.

Tobias seemed to have grown in stature. He was quick to summon the servants to bring wine, and was solicitous for their comfort.

'You will wish to return to Berkeley Square as soon as possible, I imagine,' he told them. 'But first the housekeeper shall show you to a room where you may wash.'

Bor the first time Elinor became aware of the spectacle she must present. Her gown was rent in several places, and not only was it soiled from her sojourn in the cellar, but it bore the traces of blood-stains. The wound above her eye had closed, but even so, she could not show herself in public in her present condition.

Sadly, it was impossible to hide all traces of her ordeal. She had hoped to avoid Lady Hartfield at least until she had changed her gown, but at the sound of their carriage her ladyship had rushed into the hall.

'My dears!' The tears were rolling down the older woman's face. 'Marcus promised that he would bring you back to me.'

'We are quite safe.' Elinor managed a crooked smile. 'Ma'am, no harm has come to us.'

'And Dacre?'

'He is dead.' The curt reply brought horror to lady Hartfield's eyes.

'Oh, Marcus, you did not. . .?'

'No, I did not kill him, though I meant to. Dacre suffered a seizure.'

'Divine retribution?'

'Possibly! Aunt, will you excuse me? I must go back to Tobias. The lad has borne up well, but he is much in need of support.'

'Then go to him. Elinor and Hester are exhausted. You may see them in the morning.'

Marcus took Elinor's hand. Then he looked deep into her eyes. 'Until tomorrow?' It was at once a question and a promise, but she did not look away. Suddenly she felt breathless as the darkness of that swarthy countenance was lit by an inner glow. His lips rested lightly on her fingers, and then he bowed and left them.

Elinor looked at Lady Hartfield. She had expected to find the older woman prostrate with anxiety, but her ladyship's face was unaccountably serene. She had neither questioned Elinor and Hester, nor heaped reproaches upon their heads. There was even the trace of a smile about her mouth. It was a mystery which Elinor felt much too tired to solve.

Summoning the last of her strength, she made her way to her room. There, still swaying with exhaustion, she allowed herself to be stripped of her soiled and tattered garments, bathed in scented water, and helped into a clean bedrobe. As her head touched her pillow she fell into a deep sleep.

It was after noon on the following day when she awoke, and with returning consciousness came an overwhelming surge of joy. Hester was safe, but there was something more. She could remember little of the journey back to Berkeley Square after their ordeal. She had a vague recollection of being carried to Rokeby's coach. His arms had closed about her as if he would never let her go, but no words of love had passed between them. None were needed. Now she was sure of her love for him, and his for her.

She longed to see his beloved face, but it was Lady Hartfield who came to her.

'Are you feeling better, Elinor?' she asked. 'Your head? We thought at first that the wound must needs be sewn together, but after the blood was washed away it did not seem so deep.'

'My flesh heals quickly, ma'am.' Elinor reached up a hand to explore the tender place. 'I fear it will leave a scar.'

'Your hair will hide it, my love, but I believe that you should rest today. . .'

'And Hester? How is she?'

'Still sleeping. . . She was badly shocked, you know. I don't think it wise to wake her yet.'

Elinor's eyes met hers. 'Ma'am, you must wonder at the events of yesterday. I should explain. . .'

'There is no need. Marcus has told me the whole. He questioned the men who took you and learned how Dacre planned to spirit you away.'

'His wickedness was repaid in full,' Elinor told her in a low voice. 'I shall never forget his face as he fell to the ground.'

'You must try to put it from your mind. The memory will fade in time, and, my dear, you will admit that his sudden death was for the best.'

'I suppose so. Marcus was about to kill him. . . Lady Hartfield, if you please, I should like to see his lordship.' A delicate flush of colour rose to her cheeks. 'I feel quite well. With your permission I shall dress and come downstairs.'

'There is no immediate hurry,' her ladyship observed calmly. 'Marcus was here at first light to enquire about you, but I sent him about his business. He will return in time to dine with us.'

'Oh, I see!' Elinor's eyes were upon the coverlet. 'I wished to thank him, and. . .and. . .'

Lady Hartfield began to smile, but she did not pursue the subject. 'Let me send a tray to you,' she said. 'You may dress later, at your leisure.'

For the first time in weeks, Elinor found that she was ravenously hungry. Eagerly she devoured a dish of asparagus tips accompanied by a sauce which was known only to Lady Hartfield's chef. It was followed by an omelette filled with mushrooms. Chicken breasts were to follow, but by this time her appetite was flagging. She refused them in favour of a compôte of summer fruits, the whole accompanied by a glass of chilled white wine.

As the tray was removed, Elinor stretched luxuriously. Now all that need concern her was a choice of gown. How frivolous she had become. Must it be the sea-green gauze or the pale blue embroidered muslin? She settled at last upon a bergère gown in white, which fitted her to perfection. The design was charming, and it became her well.

As the maid brushed her hair she studied her own face in the mirror. She was still pale, but the straying curls upon her brow had served to conceal the ugly wound. She had to admit, even to herself, that her recent ordeal had left few traces. She threw a lacy shawl about her shoulders and gathered up her reticule, striving to ignore the odd little sensation of excitement in the pit of her stomach.

Rather to her surprise there were no signs of life within the household as she made her way downstairs. Even the servants seemed to have disappeared. She wandered from the salon to the study, but all the rooms were empty. The day was warm. Her ladyship must be resting, she decided. It was disappointing. She felt invigorated, longing to share her feeling of exultation with another. Her heart told her who that must be.

She made her way into the garden. As she walked along the path to the fountain her skirts brushed against the low hedge of lavender which formed an edging. The scent was mingled with that of the white lilies which stood in regal beauty in their pots. Beneath it all she detected the perfume of mignonette.

She sank down upon the wall beside the fountain. The stone was still warm from the heat of the summer sun. Elinor dipped her fingers in the pool as she dreamt of her love. They had wasted so much time in misunderstandings. If only that time might be restored to them.

'Elinor!'

Startled, she looked up to find Marcus standing by her side. She had been too lost in thought to notice his approach. Now his tender smile lured her heart from her breast, and blindly she reached out to him.

Suddenly he was on his knees before her, showering kisses upon her hands.

'Is it true?' he murmured. 'I had scarce dared to hope, but yesterday, when all was over and I brought you home, I sensed the bonds of love between us. Tell me I was not mistaken. . .'

For answer she bent forward and rested her cheek against his dark head. 'Could you doubt it?' she asked in a whisper.

Then she was in his arms, and his lips found hers. She yielded to his kiss without reserve, unfolding like a flower beneath the sun. Her very soul went out to him, powerless to resist his passionate embrace. When he released her, she was breathless.

Marcus looked deep into her eyes, and his expression was one of wonder.

'My dearest love! My heart! I have been a fool. I don't deserve that you should care for me.'

'But I do!' Elinor found her voice at last. 'I tried to hide my feelings even from myself. I would not trust my heart.'

'Nor mine,' he told her ruefully. 'Confess it. You believed me when I said that our marriage was to be for Hester's sake alone.'

'You did not say you loved me,' she said in a small voice. Her eyes were fixed upon the ground.

'Look at me!' he commanded. 'Must I convince you further?' He made as if to seek her lips again, but, laughing, she protested.

'Marcus. . .we are in full view of the house. Someone will see us.'

'Let them! May I not salute my promised bride? Oh, my dear, I have loved you from the moment of our first meeting, but you gave me no encouragement. I was desperate, knowing how you despised me. . .'

'I. . .I changed my mind quite soon, my lord.'

'You did not tell me so, and I should not have guessed. With Dacre's threats, I saw the chance to offer you a bargain. I must have been mad, but it seemed to be my only chance of winning you. I knew you did not love me, but I could not bear to lose you.'

Elinor assumed a stern expression. 'And how were you to go on, sir, with a wife who hated you so much?'

'I don't know.' Marcus ran his fingers through his hair. 'But you had refused me once. I could not take the risk again. I hoped that in time, perhaps, you might come to think more kindly of me when you were my wife.'

'Marcus! When did I refuse to marry you?'

'Have you forgotten so soon? It was the night when Talworth overheard our conversation.'

'I. . .I misunderstood you.' Elinor felt her face grow warm. 'I thought you intended. . .something other than marriage.'

'Indeed!' His eyes began to twinkle. 'So you were to be a victim of my ravening lust? It is a tempting thought, my darling, but there is more to my love than a wish to have you in my bed. You must believe me.'

'I do.' She hid her face against his coat. 'Oh, Marcus, I had not believed such happiness could exist.'

There was but one answer to that. He kissed her so fiercely that her head began to spin. She clung to him with a passion that matched his own until at last he released her.

'Will you tempt me into folly?' he said unsteadily. 'Come, my lovely witch, let us share our joy with my aunt and Hester. I am becoming importunate.'

He reached out gently to brush the hair back from her brow, revealing the unhealed scar.

'I would that I could have spared you that,' he murmured. 'Does it trouble you still?'

Elinor shook her head. 'I fear I shall always bear the mark though,' she admitted. 'It is a disfigurement.'

'Not in my eyes.' He rested his lips close to the injury. 'It will remind us of the day we found each other at last. Elinor, how soon shall we be wed? I am not a patient man. . .'

'Do I not know it?' she teased. 'You must consider your high state, my lord. The ceremony must befit your rank. I doubt that it can be arranged before next year.'

He stared at her in horror. 'You cannot mean it? Is that what you wish?'

She was laughing as she hurried away from him, but he caught her before she had taken more than a few paces.

'Elinor, tell me the truth. Do you wish to celebrate our marriage here in London? I cannot rob you of your heart's desire, but I had hoped. . .'

'You have other plans, my lord?' Her expression was demure as she stood before him with lowered eyelids.

Marcus hesitated. 'John mentioned a double wedding down at Merton...'

'Yes? Shall you prefer that, sir?'

He gave her a suspicious look. Then he slipped a hand beneath her chin and raised her head. 'Cruel creature. You are laughing at me.' He reached into his pocket and brought out a piece of paper, which he handed to her with a grin.

'A special licence? Marcus, when did you...?'

'This morning, my dear love. If you wish it, we may be wed today.' He took her in his arms again, and made as if to seek her lips. 'Will you agree?' he murmured.

'But it is too soon. Your aunt—?' The rest of her protest was lost as he gathered her to his breast. His mouth came down on hers, and she was lost to the world about them.

Then he took her hand and led her into the house. A look at their glowing faces told Lady Hartfield all that she had hoped to hear. Her eyes sparkled with unshed tears as she held out her arms to Elinor.

'You have all my good wishes for your future happiness, my dears.' She felt about her for a handkerchief, and then she blew her nose. 'Marcus, I congratulate you. You are a lucky man to have won Elinor for your bride.'

'I know it, my dear.' Marcus bent down and kissed her. 'Aunt, we are to be wed today. I have the licence...'

A shriek of protest drowned his words. 'Are you quite mad? Elinor, you have not allowed my nephew to persuade you into such a havey-cavey thing? Your parents will wish to see you wed—I cannot countenance such folly. There can be no reason for this unseemly haste.'

Her ladyship might have offered a challenge. Beside her Elinor felt her lover tense. She glanced up at him to see that the firm, full-lipped mouth had hardened.

'We cannot marry today,' she said quickly. 'Marcus, you have forgot the time. It is evening. We should be too late.'

There was a long silence. Then he smiled, and it was like sunlight breaking through the clouds.

'You are right, my darling. Aunt, you must forgive me. Am I quite sunk beneath reproach? I cannot yet believe in my good fortune. Suppose that Elinor should change her mind?'

The two women exchanged a look. Then Lady Hartfield spoke.

'Let us go into dinner,' she said, half in amusement and half in exasperation. 'Otherwise, Marcus, you will provoke me into banishing you from my table. Have you no eyes, man? Look at Elinor! Does she seem about to cast you off?'

Obediently her erring nephew gazed at his love. Her heart was in her tender expression, and he could not doubt her further.

'Let us have no more of such nonsense,' her ladyship said briskly. 'Here is Hester. You shall tell her your good news.'

'Hester, you will be surprised with what I have to say,' Elinor began hesitantly. 'Marcus and I intend to marry.'

Hester beamed upon her. 'I am not in the least surprised,' she said. 'It is I who have been blind. Oh, Elinor, I am so happy for you, and you too, my lord.'

'But, Hester. . .?' Elinor looked at her friend in

wonder. 'You would not believe me when I told you of my love.'

'John made me see that I was wrong...and her ladyship too. Are we to have a double wedding after all?'

Elinor looked at Marcus, and then at Lady Hartfield.

'I should like that above anything,' she said at last.

'But, my dear, it is a bare three weeks away,' her ladyship protested. 'How can we possibly make the arrangements? Elinor must buy her bride-clothes, and...'

'She looks like a bride already,' Marcus announced to the company at large. 'Whatever she wore, she could not look lovelier than at this moment... My love, three weeks will seem like an eternity. Will you keep me waiting longer?'

Elinor blushed. 'Let us agree to the double wedding down at Merton,' she said firmly. 'Your ladyship, I do not wish to disappoint you, but Marcus and I...well, we have no wish for an elaborate ceremony. Three weeks will be long enough to enable my parents to attend...and it must please the tenantry...'

'That is thoughtful of you, Elinor. I suppose I must agree. Marcus?'

'It shall be as you wish.' His eyes were hungry as he looked at Elinor, but he made no further demur.

'Give us but a week or so. Then we shall go to Merton. You will write to Elinor's parents?' Her ladyship was clearly abstracted at she nibbled at an oyster patty. Her mind was elsewhere as she considered the serious matter of Elinor's trousseau.

*   *   *

Elinor herself was lost in a daze of happiness as she was borne to mantua-makers and milliners. Lace-trimmed underclothes were ordered by the dozen, until she was moved to protest.

'We shall visit London again, I make no doubt,' she told Lady Hartfield shyly. 'Ma'am, there is sufficient. . .'

'Nonsense, Elinor! You can have no idea! From now on you will have a place in society to consider. . . that is. . .unless my nephew intends to keep you hidden in the country.'

'He has not said so, ma'am.'

'I should not put it past him. Now, my dear, what do you think of this lilac silk? It has a demi-train, and the violet ribbons are a charming contrast.' She looked at Elinor's face and sighed. 'The Lord preserve me from young lovers! You have not understood a word.'

Recalled to herself, Elinor tried to apply attention, but her heart was with her love. What did it matter what she wore? Marcus did not care. He longed, as she did, for the day when they were one.

It came at last, though later her memories were but a blur. As she walked towards him on her father's arm, she heard the voices raised in reverent song within the village church, but her recollection was only of his beloved face as he stood still and straight, waiting to claim her for his own.

Later, well-wishers came and went, and the feasting continued long into the evening. Beside her, Hester's face was radiant, her hand clasped tightly in that of her new husband. Elinor thought only of Marcus.

At last the revellers departed, and she felt a twinge

of fear. Would she disappoint him? She was so inexperienced.

She made her way to their room, and there she suffered herself to be undressed and bathed. Her bedrobe was but a wisp of gauze, and her attendants smiled as they drew it over her head. Then they left her.

Lost in the downy comfort of the massive bed, Elinor looked about her. The last time she had seen this room was when Marcus had been in danger of his life.

That time seemed long ago, as did the first day of their meeting. How she had hated him...his arrogance...his lack of feeling! Now it seemed that she had never known him for the man he was. Yet today she had become his wife. She pinched herself to make sure that she was not dreaming.

As the door opened, her heart began to pound. As Marcus came towards her, his eyes alight with love, she held out her arms to him.

'My dearest love.' He took her hands and kissed them. 'This is the happiest day of my life, and yet I can't believe that you are mine at last...here at Merton as my bride...I must be the luckiest man alive.'

Shyly, she reached out and touched his cheek. 'I have loved you for so long,' she whispered. 'Oh, Marcus, we have been so foolish...there were so many misunderstandings.'

'I know.' He gave her a rueful smile. 'I had begun to despair of winning you. You gave me no encouragement, you know.'

She coloured a little. 'I dared not, lest I betray

myself. I. . .well. . .I believed that there could be no question of our marriage.'

'Do I not know it'?' he said with feeling. 'In the end I had to resort to underhand methods to persuade you.'

'Oh, no!' She blushed prettily. 'It was not underhand to think of Hester's happiness.'

Marcus dropped a kiss upon her nose. 'I was thinking also of my own. I hoped in time that you would learn to care for me, that is, if I behaved myself.' He was smiling as he looked into her eyes.

'And shall you do so, sir?' she teased. 'You made your conditions clear. You were to enjoy a certain freedom to lead your own way of life, and I was to be allowed a circle of admirers. . .'

He threw off his robe and slipped into bed beside her. 'Come here, my lady Rokeby. Let me assure you now that I will kill any man who looks at you.'

'And what of yourself, my lord? Have you changed your mind already?'

'There was no need to change it, Elinor. I spoke in anger and frustration. What other woman could compare with you? You are my only love.'

He turned her face to his and kissed her tenderly. 'I shall guard you with my life,' he murmured as the world was lost to them.

Elinor held him close as his hands caressed her.

'You are not afraid of me?' he whispered.

Elinor pressed her lips into the hollow of his neck.

'I shall never be afraid of anything again, my love. I cannot live without you. I knew it on that dreadful day when Hester disappeared. As you walked into the room I wanted to run to you, to hold you in my arms, and to beg you to forget the past, but I thought it was too late for a new beginning.'

'This is our beginning, Elinor.' His caresses grew more urgent. 'I worship you, my beloved wife, and to know that you love me in return is a constant wonder to me.'

'Believe it, my darling.' Suddenly Elinor lost her shyness. With a cry of passion she threw her arms about his neck, and held his head against her breast.

Her body was aflame as he led her gently through the rituals of love, and she was amazed by her own response to his passion.

When she lay at last content within the shelter of his arm, she prayed that he had not been disappointed in her. She was inexperienced, after all. Yet for her own part she had not thought such happiness existed.

His cheek was against her hair. Then he lifted his head to look down at her, and her misgivings vanished. His face was radiant, and she could not mistake the ardour in his eyes.

'Now we are one,' he told her simply. 'Long ago we spoke of the bonds of friendship, but now we are held together by a stronger tie. . .the bonds of love.'

THE LAST
GAMBLE

by

Mary Nichols

Dear Reader

It was after I had written two or three 'ordinary' historical romances that I thought it might be fun to try my hand at a Regency. The period has always fascinated me and many of my novels have been set in the early nineteenth century, so the background research was not too difficult. But the Regency romance is different. It is such a light, 'bubbly' genre, a little outrageous, highly improbable, full of mannerisms and conventions which the hero and heroine often scandalously flout, it is a joy to write. I am almost sorry when the ramifications of the plot bring it to an end. I enjoy creating the characters for you, making them come to life and setting them on the road to true love. If, along the way, I make you smile, or even shed a tear on their behalf, then I will have achieved my aim. I hope you enjoy re-reading *The Last Gamble*.

Mary Nichols

Born in Singapore, **Mary Nichols** came to England when she was three, and has spent most of her life in different parts of East Anglia. She has been a radiographer, school secretary, information officer and industrial editor, as well as a writer. She has three grown up children, and four grandchildren.

Other titles by the same author:

CHAPTER ONE

OUTSIDE a watery sun shone in a pale sky and swallows twittered in the eaves, gathering for their autumn migration. Inside it was gloomy because the library curtains had been drawn almost fully across the windows. The only sound was the rhythmic ticking of the clock, even though there were two people in the room, an elderly man and a young lady dressed from head to toe in black crepe.

She was tiny, though perfectly proportioned. Her straight raven-dark hair, topped by a wisp of black lace, was drawn up into a Grecian knot, with one or two tendrils of curl left to frame an oval face which, in the last two weeks, had lost every vestige of colour. The silence seemed to stretch interminably.

'Miss Sanghurst,' he said, at last. 'You do understand what I have been saying?'

'Yes.' She looked up at him, green eyes wide with shock; otherwise, there was no indication of how she felt. Her hands were perfectly still in her lap. 'I think I do. Is there nothing left?'

He hated having to tell her that the father whose death she mourned had gambled away her inheritance and left debts of such magnitude his passing had changed her almost overnight from a pampered, wealthy young lady into nothing short of a pauper. But there had been no point in trying to soften the blow with half-truths and platitudes, she would know the extent of it when his lordship's creditors, hearing of his demise, started knocking on the door. 'Nothing, I am afraid, except the money you inherited from your mother. She made sure he couldn't touch that.'

'She knew then?'

'What he was like? Yes, I am sure she did.'

'And yet she still loved him.' It was a statement, not a question; she knew her mother had adored her father.

'I believe she did, and that he loved her. You know how much her death affected him.'

'Yes.' Papa had shut himself away for days when her mother had died four years before. When he finally emerged, red-eyed and grey-faced, he had been a changed man, broody and curt instead of cheerful and considerate as he had hitherto been. And he started staying out at night, all night sometimes, as if he couldn't bear to be in the house without his wife. Until today Helen had no idea he had spent those nights gambling. How could she have been kept in such ignorance?

She had tried to understand how he felt about losing his wife, tried to make it up to him, and occasionally he would pull himself together and they would laugh and chat together and make plans. Last year they had been planning a European Tour. She had been unusually well-educated for a young lady and had been looking forward to learning more. It was meant to recompense her for her disappointment in not finding a husband.

Her come-out the year before her mother's last illness had been lavish and he could never understand why none of the young eligibles of that year had offered. Several had shown an early interest, but there had been no proposal because Helen herself had not encouraged them to think they would be looked on favourably.

She did not know why she was so particular, except that she had a clear idea of the man she would like to marry and would not accept anything less, and in this she had had the support of her mother. Her father failed to understand that she did not subscribe to the premise that any husband was better than none at all. Now, at four-and-twenty, she was almost an old maid.

In the event, their journey had been postponed because one of Papa's investments had failed. It was something to do with a ship carrying his merchandise which had sunk on its way from the Orient. He had assured her it was only a temporary setback and they would go the following year. Now she never would.

'I wish he had told me the extent of it,' she said. 'I could have made economies.' Her father had never stinted her, never complained when she asked him to buy her a new gown or a bonnet. In truth, he positively encouraged her to have whatever she wanted. Her mother's inheritance, which had been invested to provide her with a tiny monthly allowance, was looked on as pin money; she wasn't expected to use it to clothe herself. 'We could have let some of the staff go...' She paused, as the full horror of her circumstances was borne home to her. 'Now, I imagine, they must all go.'

'I'm afraid so.'

'Even Daisy? She's been with me ever since I came out of the schoolroom.'

'I am very sorry,' he said.

'And this house?'

'It will have to be sold to pay his lordship's debts.'

'Oh. Then I shall have to repair to the country. We

haven't been there for two or three years, Papa never liked the Peterborough house, he said it was draughty and isolated from Society. And he still thought I would make a match if we stayed in town. . .'

'Miss Sanghurst,' he interrupted before she could be carried away by her plans. 'The Peterborough house was sold last year. His Lordship was hoping the money he realised on that would keep his dunners quiet for several months and pay for your tour but I am afraid he was over-optimistic.'

She looked up at him, her face betraying the horror and grief she had been feeling ever since her father had been discovered in the stables with his brains blown out. It was bad enough to have a father shoot himself, but suddenly to learn that the security you have always enjoyed was no more to be trusted than a puff of wind must be truly terrifying.

He had expected tears and wailing and a refusal to face the truth, but she had been surprisingly strong for one so slight, taking each blow on her pretty little chin and then sticking it out just that bit more. Her head was high and her back straight, but for how long? Surely she must break soon?

'Then I must find employment. I can teach, I love children, you know. Or be a lady's companion. Or perhaps I can be a clerk or a seamstress. . .' Each suggestion was more abhorrent than the last, but she must do something to earn a living and it was no good being top-lofty about it.

'There is one other thing I must mention,' he said, admiring her courage. 'His Lordship appointed a guardian for you.'

'A guardian?'

'Yes.' He smiled at her astonishment. 'Every young

lady, however mature she considers herself to be, needs someone to care for her and protect her if she should be so unlucky as to lose both her parents. Your father made this provision some time ago.'

'Who is he?' Ever since her father's death, she had accepted the fact that she was alone in the world, that she had no relatives, and must fend for herself, even though the full extent of it had only just been communicated to her by the lawyer—she was not only alone but almost penniless.

She had many friends, but none she could call close, so who could possibly have agreed to take her on? It would be a heavy responsibility, especially as she brought nothing with her. Instead of being the considerable heiress everyone believed her to be, she was a nobody, dependent on the charity of her sponsors and everyone would know it. The idea did not appeal to her at all.

'The Earl of Strathrowan.'

'I know no one of that name.'

'I believe he was a great friend of your father's when they served together in India. You were only a baby at the time, so you would not remember.'

'I certainly do not. Is he still out in India? Am I expected to go to him there?' Was there to be no end to the revelations being heaped upon her? She didn't think she could take many more without collapsing under the weight of them. Mourning a father she apparently did not know at all, was bad enough, but how much worse the humiliation of being foisted on a stranger and one that probably wouldn't want her anyway.

Oh, how she wished she were a man, then she could get on with her life. As a man she could find a gainful occupation and make her own way, but as a gentlewoman her hands were tied by convention. She was not expected to work for a living, she could not live alone, she could not even travel unescorted.

'I have discovered he is in Scotland,' Mr Benstead went on. 'He has an estate in the Loch Lomond region. He was a younger son and it was only on the death of his brother, the Viscount, that he became the heir. He succeeded soon after your father returned to England after inheriting his title.'

He might as well have said India, she thought, it was just as wild and inaccessible. 'Does he know that Papa...?' She gulped quickly and went on before she could lose her courage altogether. 'Does he know Papa is dead? And how he died?' The manner of her father's death was important too; it was a stigma she would have to carry with her.

'I have written to him and await his reply.' He shuffled the papers on the desk in front of him, drawing the painful interview to an end. 'There is nothing to be done until we hear from him.' He stood up and came round the desk to where she sat and put his hand on her shoulder. She had not moved since first sitting there, it was almost as if she dare not. 'I am deeply sorry to have brought you such distressing news.'

'Did you know how bad it was?' she asked, staring straight ahead. 'Before he died, I mean. Could you not have done something to stop him falling further into debt?'

He allowed himself a tiny smile. 'Your Papa was a very obstinate man, my dear, and if he would not listen to your mother when she was alive, how could I influence him? I tried. I warned him again and again that he was overreaching himself. It wasn't just gambling at the tables, he gambled on the markets, buying commodities and hoping to sell at vast profits. On each occasion he was confident he could recoup his losses. It never worked.'

'No.' She turned her face up to him at last and he noticed that the shock and misery he had seen there had been replaced by determination. There was a light in her luminous green eyes which could almost have been humour. 'If I ever marry,' she said. 'I shall ensure that my husband is not a gambler. I'll have it written into the marriage contract.' The humour spread to her lips in a fleeting smile. 'That is, if I am so fortunate as to find someone to marry me.'

'Of course you will, my dear,' he said. 'You are a handsome young lady, you know, and there must be dozens of young men eager to make your acquaintance.'

'In Scotland?' Now there was a definite twinkle in her eye and he breathed a sigh of relief. Her father had died by his own hand because he could not face up to life in poverty and he had wondered if she might be cast in the same mould, but evidently she was not. She was a fighter.

'We cannot tell what the Earl will decide to do,' he said. 'But as soon as I hear, I shall come and tell you.'

'Is there a Lady Strathrowan?'

'One must presume so.'

'And children? Sons and daughters, grandchildren, perhaps?'

'I have no way of knowing until I hear from him.'

'In the meantime?'

'You may live here until the sale is concluded, of

course, but please limit your expenses to the minimum. Do you wish me to inform the servants?'

'No, I'll do it. Is there enough to pay them?'

'No, not until the sale goes through and then. . .' He shrugged. 'There might be something we can give them but if the dunners get there first. . .'

'They must be paid,' she cried. 'It's bad enough losing a position without having to go without the wages owed to you. I shall pay them from my own money.'

'You will need every penny of that for yourself, Miss Sanghurst,' he said. 'And they will soon find other positions.'

'Nevertheless, I shall pay them,' she said firmly.

He sighed as he bowed and took his leave. She was as obstinate as her father had been. He only hoped that her tenacity would stand her in good stead in the future. She would need all her resources, of strength and determination, as well as money, if she were going to survive.

Helen did not rise, knowing that Coster was standing outside the door and would see the lawyer out. But Coster had to be told the news and so did all the other servants. Telling them was to be the first of many unpleasant tasks she was going to have to do and she supposed she had better get on with it.

She rose slowly and smoothed down the skirt of her mourning gown, reflecting that if she had only known how bad things were she would not have spent so much on it. Then, lifting her chin, she moved over to the door and opened it. The footman was shutting the outer door. 'Coster, will you ask everyone to come here, please. I have something to tell you all.'

'Poor little devil,' he murmured as he made his way

to the back regions of the house to convey her orders. All alone in the world and, if the rumours were true, not a feather to fly with. If the old devil hadn't shot himself Coster would have been tempted to do it for him, except that it wouldn't have helped Miss Helen. Nor would it have put bread in his own mouth, not to mention the mouths of all the other servants. He could guess what was coming next. They were all going to be out on their ears.

He was proved right before another ten minutes had passed. The house was being sold and Miss Sanghurst was going to live with her guardian. It was the first any of them had heard of a guardian but they were glad for her sake; she needed someone to look after her. They were very fond of her; not one of them would have hesitated to serve her on half-wages if she had asked it of them, but she didn't.

It was strange how she hadn't shed a tear until Daisy had asked if she could stay on for little more than her keep and then she had run from the room and they could hear her flying up the stairs. The door of her room banged shut and there was nothing any of them dare to do but return to their duties, knowing that the following day, there would be none to do.

Helen threw herself across her bed and sobbed as if she were trying to cry the Thames dry. She had loved her father dearly, but how could he do this to her? How could he turn his back on her when she needed him so much? How could he have had so little concern for her future as to gamble away every penny and everything they owned and then refuse to face up to what he had done? Why had she never suspected there was something wrong? The questions went round and round in her brain but she had no answers.

His answer had been to end his own life and leave her to a stranger, just as if she were a mongrel dog needing a good home. She hesitated to call his behaviour dishonourable, but she could find no other word for it. He must have known the disgrace would reflect on her, the daughter he professed to love. The tabbies would have a field day and she would be ostracised. It had already begun, for the Dowager Lady Carruther had cut her dead in the lending library two days before and Mrs Courtney had stopped her daughter, whom Helen considered a friend, from speaking to her in the park. Unable to condemn her father, she detested the unknown guardian instead.

She sat up at last and mopped her tears with a face cloth, then rinsed her burning cheeks in cold water from the pitcher on the wash-stand. Crying never achieved anything, except to make her look ugly. She sat at her dressing table and peered into the looking-glass above it. Her eyelids were puffed and red from weeping, and there were two high spots of pink on her cheeks, but otherwise she looked drained of all colour. Her hair, usually so neat, was falling down from its pins.

Was this the picture she was going to present to the Earl? A dishclout full of self-pity? Or someone strong enough to weather life's storms and take whatever was thrown at her right on the chin? She lifted her head and pulled a face at herself in the mirror. 'Now pull yourself together, Miss Helen Sanghurst,' she said. 'No one loves a watering pot, and sitting here feeling sorry for yourself will take you nowhere. Look on it as an adventure, an adventure into the unknown. Are you afraid? Of course you are not, you are your father's daughter. . .'

And then she began to cry again, but this time not for herself, but for the father she had lost. She had lost him long before that pistol went off; if the truth be known, she had lost him on the day her mother died. But only now could she grieve.

Her sobs subsided at last; she would not cry again. She washed her face, combed her hair and re-pinned it, then went downstairs to give orders for supper, the last orders she would ever give. Tomorrow all the servants except Daisy would leave, each clutching their wages and carrying their personal possessions; Daisy would remain until she herself left. Her maid was more than a servant, she was a friend, and Helen wished she could take her with her wherever she was going, but she had no intention of asking favours of her guardian.

Waiting was irksome, made worse by the fact that no one visited her except her father's creditors who, hearing the news, swooped on her to be first with their claims, and a few prying busy-bodies whose only motive was gathering titbits of gossip to pass on over the tea cups or behind their fans at the latest Society ball. It was easier to say she was not at home to callers.

By the same token, she could not go visiting and so her only recreation was walking in the park, which cost nothing, and sorting her father's books. He had a unique collection of military books and some fine maps; these were expected to fetch a good price. Not that she would see any of the money; Mr Benstead had told her that it was earmarked to pay debts.

The books, the silver and porcelain, the horses and the carriage, even his clothes were all going the same way. The furniture was expected to be sold along with the house; all Helen could call her own were her clothes and the little jewellery she had inherited from her mother. She wondered if some of it might have to be sacrificed.

'No, my dear, there is no call on you personally,' the lawyer assured her when he visited her a few days later. There was no real need to see her, he had no news to convey, but he realised she must be feeling very isolated in that huge house, with only the maid for company, and he wanted her to know she still had a friend, though there was little he could do to help her. 'Your private possessions, clothes, books, jewels are your own. If you choose to sell them, then that is your affair, nothing to do with your father's estate.'

'I have been thinking that it would be foolish to clutter myself up with clothes and jewels I am never likely to wear again,' she said. 'I must dress according to my status.'

'Your status has not altered, my dear,' he said gently. 'You are still the same person, a single young lady, properly brought up. That hasn't changed.'

He was just being kind to her, she knew that. How could she not change? She was going to have to learn to conserve her resources, to watch every penny, to be subservient to those who provided her bread and butter, to be grateful for every morsel. And how she was going to hate it! If she had accepted one of the young men who buzzed around her in her come-out year she might now be married and this whole sorry mess would not be happening, but she had made her choice and now she had to stop thinking of what might have been. 'Have you heard from the Earl?' she asked.

'Not yet. It is a long way to Scotland and back and the mail is not always reliable.'

'Supposing we never hear? Your letter might never reach him. He might have left and returned to India. He might have gone back to his regiment and be serving abroad. He might have died. He might not wish to be associated with me, after what has happened.'

'It is no good meeting trouble halfway, Miss Sanghurst,' he said. 'Let us wait and see, shall we?'

It was a month before he heard, and by that time the new owners of the house were anxious to move in. They pestered him every day, wanting to know when Miss Sanghurst would be vacating the premises. Now he would be able to tell them she would be leaving immediately. The Earl had agreed to take her in, though his letter, if you could call it that, had hardly been welcoming. 'Send her up', was all it said.

Benstead could not tell her that, it would break her heart all over again; he would simply say his lordship was pleased to comply with his old friend's request and hope she did not ask to see the missive. If he had been anything but a staid old bachelor, he would have taken her in himself rather than let her go where she wasn't welcome. But perhaps he was maligning the Earl; he might simply be a poor letter-writer or had delegated the task to a secretary who did not understand the need for tact. But that didn't account for the fact that he had not even sent the fare, let alone provided an escort, which she might have expected.

'How am I to get there?' she asked, when he told her. 'The carriage and horses have already gone. And

I couldn't have afforded to go post chaise even if they had not. I shall have to go by public coach.'

'The mail is by far the most comfortable,' he said. 'They limit the number of passengers, you know, and it's faster than the stage.'

'I am in no hurry, Mr Benstead,' she said, a faint smile on her lips. 'And comfort is not a consideration, but my purse is. I shall travel by stage.'

'Then I shall see if I can find a couple or a matronly lady to chaperone you. . .'

'Mr Benstead, at four-and-twenty I need no chaperone. The pampered daughter of Lord Sanghurst is no more. Hard though it may be, I have to learn to live in the world outside the narrow sphere I was raised in and be self-reliant.'

'You can have no idea of the risks.'

'Then I shall learn by my mistakes. Please do not give me a second thought, Mr Benstead.'

'It is my duty to see that all steps are taken to deliver you safely to your destination.'

'Like a parcel.' For the first time in weeks, she laughed. 'Mr Benstead, you have discharged your duty, more than was called for, considering the circumstances. I imagine you have not been able to pay yourself.'

He neither confirmed nor denied it, but smiled cheerfully; he did not want her to go, thinking he had misgivings. 'Then all I can do now is wish you a pleasant journey. Please write and inform me of your safe arrival.' Oh, how formal he sounded, but he had to remain dignified or he would give way to the urge to take her in his arms as one would a child, and reassure her that she had not been abandoned. He would watch over her somehow. He offered her his hand and she took it firmly.

The following day, he sent round her coach ticket as far as Glasgow, begging to be allowed to pay for it. It was very kind of him and would enable her to spend a little more on accommodation and board on the journey. Looking down at the slip of paper, she felt as if she held her fate in her hand, and she supposed it was true; her destiny was many miles away to the north. But now was no time to mope, now was the time to be positive. She enjoyed good health and, though she was small, she was strong; the journey itself held no terrors for her.

There was consolation in the thought that being so far from the capital, she would not hear the gossip being spread about her and her father and they would soon be forgotten. Besides, the tattle-mongers had more than enough to keep their tongues busy with the antics of the Prince of Wales who, on the death of his mad father, had now become king and was trying to divorce his wife.

Only four months before, Caroline had returned to the capital and demanded to be recognised as queen, and there were many who supported her. The conjecture about what would happen next was likely to go on and on. With such juicy tit-bits, who would be interested in a penniless nobody?

She went up to the attic and pulled out a trunk, bumping it down the stairs to her room, where she packed it, considering each item on the grounds of its necessity before including it, but a miniature portrait of her mother in a silver frame, two or three of her favourite books and writing materials went in along with her clothes.

She had sold all her jewellery with the exception of a diamond clip and her mother's betrothal ring. The brooch she would wear, while the ring in its velvet-lined box went into the very bottom of the trunk. Then she and Daisy manhandled it down the stairs to the hall, after which they ate a frugal, and largely silent, supper in the kitchen before going to bed.

The night seemed long and the old house creaked and groaned as if adding its own protests to the blow fate had dealt it. The wind rose too and a branch of a tree kept banging at her window, so that, even if her mind had not been full of the morrow, sleep would have been impossible.

She rose and sat at the window until the grey light of dawn lightened the roofs and chimney pots and the tops of the trees in the park began to show their branches. Almost overnight they had been stripped of their leaves and she realised that autumn was here and winter not far off. What was winter like in Scotland? Was it true they were often snowed in for weeks on end? Soon she might know.

She dressed in a neat black merino wool gown with a pointed waist and high neck which had a narrow white frill. It was buttoned at the front so that she would not need help with dressing; all her clothes had been chosen with that in mind. Under it she wore two layers of underwear, one flannel and one fine lawn, not only because she expected to be cold but because it had left more room in the trunk for other things. The bonnet she chose was of plain black straw and quite small.

She had never travelled in a public coach before,

but she imagined it might be a crush; wide brims and voluminous skirts would hardly endear her to her fellow passengers. Then, feeling decidedly dumpy, she went down to breakfast.

Daisy, who had found a new position with a large family, mostly girls, left immediately afterwards. It was an emotional parting and it took all Helen's resolve to stay dry-eyed, particularly as the maid was making no effort to stem her tears. 'You'll write, won't you, Miss Helen? I shan't rest easy until I know you've arrived safe and well and met your guardian. I pray he is kind to you.'

'Why should he not be kind to me?' she demanded, though the same thought had crossed her mind. 'My father would not have wanted me to live with someone who did not care for me.'

Daisy decided not to say what was in her mind regarding the late Lord Sanghurst. Instead she mopped up her tears and smiled. 'No, course not, Miss Helen, but you know what I mean.'

'Yes. Now off you go and don't worry about me. You mustn't be late on your first day.'

Helen spent the next two hours going round the all the rooms, making sure the dust sheets were in place on the furniture and the curtains were closed to stop the sun fading the carpets. She had lived in this house ever since her parents had returned from India when she was a baby. She had been brought up here knowing nothing of poverty or insecurity or evil, until a month ago when her whole life had been overset. Now it was up to her to make the best of it and not brood.

She went into her mother's boudoir, remembering how it always smelled so fragrant and how her mama's smile lit it, making it seem as though the sun shone even on the dullest day. As a small girl she would be taken onto her lap and would sink her head onto a bosom that was designed for comfort and listen to her telling stories. Story-time before bed was the best part of the day.

She remembered one about a poor little girl who was treated cruelly at the orphanage she was sent to when her mother died, but never gave up hope that one day she would find a loving home and live happily ever after. And she had, of course, when her long-lost uncle turned up. Would the Earl of Strathrowan be her happy ending?

She wondered what he was like to look at. She imagined he must be about the same age as her father if they had served together, but was he tall or short, fat or thin, handsome or plain? And did it matter what he looked like, so long as he genuinely welcomed her? And if he didn't? Then she would leave, her mind was set on that. She would find work and lodgings and be independent.

She heard the doorbell jangle and for a moment forgot she was the only person in the house to answer it, but when it rang a second time, she hurried downstairs to open the door. A hackney cab stood outside and its driver had his whip raised to bang on the door. 'Thought there weren't no one at 'ome,' he said. 'You ready?'

She had never been spoken to like that before, but she supposed he had taken her for a servant and she could hardly blame him. 'Yes,' she said. 'If you would be so good as to carry my trunk. I can manage the bag.'

She had left a warm cloak on a chair and now she picked it up and put it on, while he half-lifted, half-dragged the heavy trunk down the steps to the cab. 'What you got in 'ere?' he asked. 'The crown jewels?'

She smiled. 'No, only my clothes and one or two books.'

'Books, eh? What d'you want books for? Nothin' good ever come out o' books, tha's wot I allus says.'

Not wanting an argument, she did not reply, but locked the front door, put the key in her bag along with all the others belonging to the house, and waited until the trunk was safely strapped on to the back of the cab before climbing in and directing him to take her to Mr Benstead's office. She had to give him the keys but did not want to stop and talk to him; everything had been said that needed saying.

She had left very little time to get to the Blue Boar at Holborn where she would board the stage for the first part of her journey north. The lawyer was out on business and she left the keys with a clerk and returned to the cab. The past was behind her, all her tears had been shed and the future, whatever it held, was before her; it was up to her to grasp whatever opportunities were offered.

The Blue Boar was one of the busiest coaching inns in London. Stage coaches came and went all day, clattering into the yard and disgorging passengers and their baggage and taking on others going to all points of the compass. It was noisy with shouting and laughter, people saying farewell, others being greeted, horses neighing and chickens squawking.

The air was filled with smells, horse droppings, leather harness, cooking, sweat and perfume, all intermingled. Helen was almost overwhelmed as the cab drew up and the driver jumped down and deposited her and her luggage on the cobbles in front of the inn.

'Carry your bags, missie?'

She looked down to see a little urchin peering up at her with mischievous blue eyes, though his face was filthy and his feet bare. She smiled. 'I think the trunk will be a little too heavy for you, don't you?'

'I'm strong, miss.' He flexed his muscles, making her laugh. 'I can drag it along.'

'I think it would be better if you found me a porter. Would you do that, please?'

He made no move to comply but stood looking up at her and holding out his hand.

'I'm afraid he will not budge until you have put a coin in his palm,' a male voice said.

She swung round and found herself facing a broad blue jacket covered with gold braid and silver lace. Its wearer was so tall she had to tilt her head up to see his face. It was a handsome face, topped by short brown hair which curled over his ears beneath his shako. His clean-shaven chin was as firm as her own, but a great deal larger. But what set her against him was the twinkle of amusement in his brown eyes, as if she should have known the boy would not do as he was asked without being paid for it.

'Where I come from, children do as they are bid without inducement,' she said, noticing, without meaning to, that his wide epaulettes emphasised his broad shoulders, and the cut of his blue pantaloons, tucked into highly polished hessians, enhanced his slim hips and muscular thighs. It was the sort of figure the uniform was designed for.

'How fortunate for you,' he said, smiling openly and throwing the boy a coin which he caught deftly before dashing off towards another traveller; now the soldier had arrived, there was no point in hanging around.

'But I wouldn't class this lad as a child, I'll wager he has been earning a living in like manner for years, ever since he could walk and speak.'

'How dreadful!'

'Dreadful to earn his keep in honest toil, Miss. . .?'

'No,' she said, ignoring his obvious hint that she should tell him her name. 'I meant dreadful it should be necessary.'

'Yes, of course.' He stopped to look at her properly. She was in mourning, which didn't suit her somewhat pale colouring, but her features were good: an oval face, little turned-up nose, a firm mouth, pursed in perplexity, and large green eyes framed by dark lashes. She was obviously a well-nurtured young lady, too young to be travelling alone and he wondered how it had come about.

If she had run away from home, she must have been very resourceful to have crept out with that great trunk. Was she eloping? She was certainly pretty enough and, he imagined, guileless enough to be the target of some unscrupulous young blade and her mourning would preclude a wedding, even if the young man were acceptable. But if so, where was he? She was looking about her in bewilderment as if asking herself the same question. 'Don't worry, he'll turn up,' he said.

'Who?'

'The man. You are expecting to meet a man, are you not? I hesitate to call him a gentleman, since no gentleman worth his salt would allow a lady to struggle alone with a box like that.' He nodded at the trunk standing at her feet.

'It is none of your business.'

'No more it is,' he said cheerfully. 'I bid you good day.'

'Wait!' It was almost a cry of desperation.

He turned back to her, one eyebrow raised and a tiny smile lurking about his lips. 'I can be of service, after all?'

'I need a porter to take my trunk to the coach, but I cannot leave it here while I go and look for one.'

He smiled. 'Tell me, where do you wish your baggage to be taken?'

'I am booked on the coach to Glasgow.'

He had been right. She was off to Gretna Green. No wonder she looked scared to death. 'You can always go back home,' he said gently. 'I'm sure no one will blame you.'

'There is no going back and no question of blame.'

'You will be disappointed, I guarantee it.'

She looked up at him with startled green eyes; could he really see into her heart? 'What do you know about it? Who are you?'

'Captain Duncan Blair, at your service.' He swept her an exaggerated bow. 'I was simply pointing out that it is not too late to change your mind about this undertaking.'

'Oh, yes, it is, Captain, much too late.'

'Then let us find the coach.' He hoisted her trunk onto his shoulders as if it weighed nothing at all and strode into the throng of people. She had perforce to follow.

In no time at all he had located the Glasgow coach, which was emblazoned with the name The Flying Prince and its destination along with a great deal more information which made it look like a travelling billboard. He supervised the loading of the trunk, handed

her in and climbed in beside her, taking off his shako
and sitting with it in his lap.

'What are you doing?' she asked in alarm.

'Waiting patiently for the off,' he said. 'You are not
the only one setting off for Scotland today. I fancy
there will be six of us inside and many more on top. I
wish they'd get a move on, I am in the deuce of a
hurry.'

They were joined inside by an elderly man in a dark
suit, a farmer who, though obviously prosperous
enough to afford an inside seat, smelled of cattle and
spirits, and a woman of more than middle years, who
wore a great deal of face paint and had her hair done
up in a style that had been fashionable many years
before. The sixth seat remained empty.

Duncan concluded that the unknown lover had lost
his nerve, and he was curious to know what the young
lady would do. That she was a gentlewoman he did
not doubt; her whole demeanour proclaimed it, but
she was going to have a rude awakening before many
miles had passed, unless her lover was going to board
the coach when they changed horses.

He excused himself to lean across her and shout to
the guard, who was shepherding the outside passengers up the steps to the roof. 'How much longer are
we going to sit here? This coach is due to leave at
noon and it is already five minutes past by my watch.'

'Yes, but you see, sir,' the man answered equably.
'We don't go by your watch, we go when that there
clock points the hour.' He nodded his head towards
the clock above the door of the inn. 'And that lacks
two minutes to twelve.'

Duncan subsided into his seat. It was not the least

use being impatient; he would arrive when he arrived
and he prayed he would not be too late.

Almost immediately the guard called, 'All aboard!'
and the coachman appeared. He was dressed in a
brown boxcoat with several capes about his shoulders,
which flapped open to reveal a striped waistcoat and
small clothes which reached down to meet a pair of
jockey boots halfway up his calves. Helen watched as
he walked slowly all the way round the vehicle, check-
ing the wheels and axles, and then inspecting the
horses and their harness before moving to the off-side
and taking up the reins in his left hand. As the clock
moved to one minute to departure time he took up his
whip and climbed aboard. At exactly noon by the
clock, the inn staff stood back, and they were off.
Duncan smiled at the girl beside him because she was
looking decidedly shaky.

'How long does it take?' she asked. Being obliged
to him for carrying her trunk and overseeing it loaded
safely, she could hardly ignore him and besides, she
was no longer in Society and did not need a proper
introduction to speak to him. 'The journey to Scotland,
I mean.'

So the lovers were travelling separately. If *he* had
arranged to carry her off to Gretna Green, he would
have made sure he was with her every inch of the way.
Already he was beginning to dislike the unknown
suitor. 'It's usually twenty-four hours to Manchester,
non-stop. That's a good deal less than halfway. After
that, it depends on the state of the roads and the
weather.'

'Non-stop?' she queried, wondering why she had
never asked the question before. 'You mean without
going to bed?'

'Yes. We should arrive in Manchester at noon tomorrow, God willing.'

'Surely we must stop to sleep.'

'If you wish, you may stop at any one of a number of inns on the way and continue next day in another coach. It depends on how much haste you are in. Myself, I would rather doze as I go and arrive all the sooner.'

'And I certainly would not!' she said.

'Indeed? You surprise me, I would have wagered you were in haste to reach your destination.'

'You do not know my destination, sir, nor my state of mind,' she said sharply.

'No, I beg pardon,' he said, leaning back and shutting his eyes, effectively ending the conversation.

The farmer was already asleep and snoring and the elderly man was sitting in the corner attempting to read, though how he could do it in the swaying coach Helen could not fathom. The woman sitting opposite her fetched out a packet of food and began gnawing on a chicken leg. They were as motley a collection of individuals as you were ever likely to meet, she decided, and she had to admit to being glad the Captain was there.

She had an instinctive feeling he would protect her—she had recognised the insignia of Prince of Wales's Own Hussars on his shako—but his manner left a great deal to be desired. He spoke in riddles and didn't seem to mind how rude he was. Look at him now. He was dozing.

She did not know how he could sleep in that uncomfortable position, bolt upright with his head lolling because his stiff collar prevented him from dropping his chin on his chest, and with his long legs doubled under him. The passengers sitting opposite prevented him from stretching them out and he could not tuck them under the seat because that space was part of the rear boot.

But like that, he seemed more human, almost boyish, and she supposed he could not be much more than thirty, but there was a slight scar along his hairline and another on the back of his hand which was half covered by his sleeve, and she assumed he had been injured in the service of his country but, judging by the way he had carried her trunk, he was not too badly disabled.

He opened one brown-flecked eye and caught her looking at him and winked at her. Confused and embarrassed, she turned to look out of the window. Mr Benstead had said her status had not altered, but he had been wrong. Yesterday, she had been the pampered daughter of an aristocrat, today she was a nobody whom a common soldier could offend with impunity! She had told her lawyer she must learn to live in the world outside her ken, among people who knew nothing of Society except as a subject for gossip, to accept their ways as her own, but oh, how difficult it was going to be.

CHAPTER TWO

THEY were on a good road and, apart from slowing up for the guard to pay the toll, the horses rarely dropped below a canter. Islington, Holloway, Highgate and Finchley were left behind and then they were approaching Barnet. Helen knew all this because the guard had called out the names as they passed and now he was sounding his horn to warn the next staging post of their imminent arrival.

She was feeling cramped and slightly nauseous and she would be relieved to get out and stretch her legs. Two minutes later they drew into the yard of the Red Lion, where all was bustle as ostlers rushed forward with the new horses while the ones which had carried them thus far were taken from the traces to be rested.

'It takes forty-five seconds, no more,' the Captain said, seeing her hand on the door.

Before she could turn to reply, the guard let out a bellow of rage and dragged the little urchin who had accosted her in London from among the boxes and packages in the rear boot where he had been hiding. It was a miracle he had not been battered to death or thrown out and killed. 'Trying to get a free ride, were you?' he demanded, shaking the child until his teeth rattled. 'In my book that's a crime.'

'Lemme go!' the boy yelled. 'I ain't done nothin'.'

'No fear!' He cuffed him about the ears, rocking his head back on his shoulders.

Helen was out of her seat and down on the ground

before anyone realised what she was doing. 'Let him be!' she ordered, pulling at the man's arm to prevent further blows.

He turned in surprise. 'Go back to your seat, please, miss, this here's company business. Riding without a ticket 'as got to be punished.'

The child, feeling the grip which held him slacken, released himself and threw himself at Helen, burying his face in her skirts. 'I meant no 'arm, miss. Only I 'ave to get to me brother and I ain't got the fare.'

'Where does your brother live?' she asked, putting her arm protectively round him, ignoring the fact that he was filthy.

'Don't matter where he lives,' the guard said. 'Now, go back to your seat and leave me to deal with the little slip-gibbet.' He pulled the boy from her grasp. 'I ain't got time to hand you in, so think y'self lucky. Now get you gone.' With a final blow to the head, he pushed the child in the direction in which they had just come.

'You surely do not expect him to walk all the way back to London?' Helen demanded.

'It's all the same to me what he does, but if I see 'im anywhere near one of my coaches again, he'll be for it, I can tell you.'

'But he's all alone. . .'

She became aware that the Captain had left the coach and was standing beside her. 'Please return to your seat, ma'am. There is nothing you can do and you are holding up the coach.' He smiled. 'That's almost as bad a crime as travelling without a ticket.'

'Never mind the coach,' she said crossly. 'We can't abandon the poor child. He wants to go to his brother.' She turned from him and called out to the boy, who had taken half a dozen steps and then stopped when he heard her spirited defence of him. 'Where does your brother live?'

'St Albans, miss.'

'Then get in the coach. I shall pay your fare.'

'Oh, no, you don't,' the guard said, grabbing the child as he went to obey. 'Just 'cos this young lady is a soft touch, don't mean you can pull the wool over my eyes; you'd have everyone's pockets picked in the twinkling of an eye.'

'No, I would not. I ain't a thief.'

'For goodness sake, give him a ticket,' Duncan said, realising that the young lady was obstinate enough to stand arguing all day and too soft-hearted by far. 'We've wasted enough time as it is. I'll see he behaves himself.'

Helen gave him a look of gratitude, which was lost on him because he had already returned to his seat. She opened her purse and paid the requisite fare from London to St Albans, then she took the boy by the hand and followed, settling him between them.

'Thank you, Captain,' she said, as they set off once againt several minutes behind schedule.

'Don't thank me. And don't blame me, when he turns and bites the hand that feeds, because he will, you know.'

'Of course he won't. Will you?' She smiled down at the boy, but all he did was grin happily from one to the other. This was a much better way to travel than being flung about among the baggage in the boot.

'It's disgraceful!' the woman in the opposite seat exclaimed, endeavouring not to wrinkle her nose in case she cracked the paint on her face. 'The boy smells and I'll wager he is verminous. We shall all end up

infested. I cannot think what the coachman was thinking of to allow it.' She leaned forward and wagged her
finger at the Captain. 'As for you, sir, I should have
thought you could have prevented your wife. . .'

'Wife?' Helen repeated, colouring to the roots of
her hair. 'You are mistaken, ma'am, I am not the
Captain's wife. I am not even acquainted with the
gentleman.'

'Indeed?' She paused to look from one to the other,
then shrugged. 'Wife or no, he should have stopped
you bringing the brat on board.'

The Captain smiled. 'Ma'am, I doubt if anyone
could stop the young lady once she has made up her
mind to something, I certainly could not. And the
bratling is entitled to the ride, his fare has been paid.'

'He could have ridden outside,' the farmer put in.

'It isn't safe,' Helen said. 'And as for smells. . .' She
stopped, realising it would do no good at all to mention the fact that the pungent odour he was emitting
masked any smell from the boy. Quarrelling with her
fellow travellers would not endear her to them and
she felt isolated enough as it was. 'He might have
fallen off.'

'And good riddance too,' the farmer said.

'Oh, come now, sir,' Duncan put in. 'The boy is
hardly more than a babe, and if the young lady is
prepared to endure him, then we must acquiesce with
a good grace. He will not be with us for long, after
all.'

Helen smiled. 'Thank you, Captain.'

The boy grinned up at her. 'You're a real lady,
miss.'

'Huh!' The painted woman's expression said it all.

Helen found herself wanting to answer back, to say,

yes, she considered herself to be a lady, but then thought better of it. It smacked of pride and as she had vowed to put her old life behind her, there was nothing to be gained by boasting of it. She had not realised, before now, how much difference it made to how you were treated if people knew you came from the upper echelons of society. But she was learning fast. Instead, she turned to ask the boy his name.

'Ned Barker, miss.'

'And how old are you?'

'Ten.'

Helen was surprised; he was so small she had taken him for much younger.

'And what were you doing alone in London if your family live in St Albans?'

'It's only me brother in St Albans. Pa and Ma went to live in London when I was little. Pa were out of work—a soldier he were, back from the wars—and 'e thought he'd find something in London. It weren't so easy. 'E kep' sayin' one day his ship would come in, but it never did and when Ma die, he give up.'

'Oh, how sad. What happened then? After your mother died, I mean.'

'He took to the bottle, miss . And the dubbin' lay. . .'

'Dubbing lay?' she queried. 'I have never heard of that occupation.'

'It means breaking into houses,' the Captain put in with a smile. 'The boy's father is a thief.'

'Not any more, 'e ain't.' The boy grinned up at her. ' 'E got snabbled.'

'Arrested,' the Captain interpreted for Helen.

'Oh, dear,' she said, addressing the boy. 'And that left you all alone? Is that why you were working at the Blue Boar?'

'Yes, miss. But it ain't no great shakes as a livin', so I had a mind to go to me brother. 'E's married and settled in St Albans. 'E'll 'ave me.'

'I'm sure he will,' she said. The boy's situation was so like her own, even though it was on a different level, she could feel only compassion for him. That his father was a felon was neither here nor there. Felon or gambler, what difference did it make to the end result?

There was silence in the coach for perhaps a minute, but the boy had evidently not heard the maxim that children should be seen and not heard. He prattled on. 'Them's a good set of wheelers,' he said, nodding in the general direction of the horses.

'Are they?' The only knowledge Helen had of horseflesh was what she had learned from her riding instructor and that was little enough.

'Good strong hindquarters,' the boy went on. 'The leaders ain't bad neither, though one of 'em is pulling to the left.'

'How clever of you to notice,' she said, conscious that the Captain was hard put to stifle his amusement.

The boy switched his attention to the countryside outside the coach, pointing out cows, pigs, sheep, finding something to say about each, asking questions which Helen did her best to answer though she was not very knowledgeable about things agricultural.

'It's a bull,' the farmer said with a grin after the boy had referred to one animal as a 'queer cow'.

Helen felt herself go very red but said nothing.

'I ain't seen one afore,' the boy went on, undaunted. 'Cows in the park in plenty, but not them.'

'Well, they can be dangerous,' Helen said.

'Is that so?' And then, pointing, 'What's that?'

Helen decided she would be wiser not to answer for fear of contradiction. 'A plough, boy,' the farmer put in. 'Don't you know anything?'

'I'll wager he knows the quickest way from Covent Garden to Putney Steps,' the Captain put in. 'The departure times of all the coaches, which hotels throw out the best scraps; the best places to scavenge in the river mud and where to sell the proceeds. I'll wager, too, that he knows when every house in London is likely to have its knocker off.' He smiled at boy. 'When the owners are away, there are rich pickings. Your father taught you that, didn't he?'

The boy grinned. 'You're a sharp cove, but I ain't ever been nabbled.'

'Too slippery,' Duncan said with a laugh.

Helen had only a vague idea what they were talking about but decided it was a subject best not pursued. She opened the small bag she had brought to carry things she would need for the journey and took out a package of food Daisy had prepared before she left, some bread and butter, a slice or two of ham, a few chicken legs, a couple of apples. It was meant to save her having to buy anything until they stopped for the night. 'Are you hungry, Ned?'

'Starvin',' he said, which was nothing less than the truth.

She offered him the package and watched as he wolfed the lot.

The Captain was regarding her with a light in his eye which might have been mockery, but could equally have been empathy, and she found herself blushing. It was almost as if he knew all about her, knew she was pretending to be someone she was not. 'Oh, dear,' he said, indicating the few crumbs left on the paper on the boy's knees. 'Now you will have to go hungry, Miss. . .?'

Again there was that hint that she should reveal her name. 'It is of no consequence,' she said. 'I ate a good breakfast before I left.'

'And where would that have been?'

'Sir,' she said, stiffening. 'I do not think it is any concern of yours.'

'I beg your pardon, I was simply making conversation.'

'Not very subtle conversation, either,' said a voice from the corner. Helen was startled because the man, who appeared to be engrossed in his reading, had taken no part in the conversation at all. 'But then, what can one expect from a soldier, one of Prinny's Hussars or not. You do not seem to comprehend that not every female will fall into your arms, just because you favour her with a smile.'

'You would have me glower at everyone and never open my mouth?' Duncan queried. He had wondered about the girl, simply because she was so full of contradictions. At times she appeared lost and vulnerable, almost fearful, at others she gave the impression she could take on the world and win.

What had made her like that? Why had she championed the boy, paid his fare, given him all her food, in the face of all opposition, not least his own? Did she like being contrary and having everyone about her up in arms? Or was she simply unaware of the effect she was creating. She was tiny, but no one could ignore her.

'Oh, please, do not fall out over it,' Helen pleaded.

'If you wish for conversation,' the dark man went

on, addressing Duncan. 'I will oblige. My name is Tinsley. I am an attorney at law.'

'Blair, Captain Duncan Blair,' Duncan said reaching across to offer his hand. 'Have you been involved in the trial?'

Everyone knew what he meant, even the child, though it was not technically a trial. The House of Lords were debating a Bill which, if passed, would condemn the King's wife as an adulteress and she would forfeit her rights as Queen and be divorced from the King. Every word said and every tiny piece of evidence—some of it was very salacious indeed—was talked about and mulled over by a populace who had no great feelings for either protagonist. It was in the best traditions of a London farce.

'Only in a very minor capacity.'

'The poor woman.' This from the painted lady. 'The King has always hated her.'

'And has never taken the slightest pains to hide it,' Helen put in. 'I have. . .' She had been going to say she had met the Regent at her come-out, but stopped herself; the woman she was supposed to be would never have moved in Royal circles. 'I have heard he is as dissolute a rake as anyone would wish to meet. If I were married to him, I should certainly not wish to live with him, not even to be Queen. Why she did not stay living quietly in Italy, I cannot imagine.'

'Quietly!' Duncan exclaimed. 'She is incapable of doing anything quietly. She flaunts herself and her. . .' He paused, realising there were ladies present, and corrected himself. '. . .chamberlain all over Europe and then expects to come back as soon as the old King dies and be acclaimed Queen.'

'I can see where your sympathies lie,' the lawyer

said with a smile. 'But then, if I am not mistaken, the uniform you wear is that of the Prince of Wales's Own Hussars.'

'It is, sir.'

'How long have you been serving His Majesty?'

'I joined as an ensign in 1808 when I was eighteen.'

'Then you have seen some service?'

'I had the honour to serve under Wellington— Wellesley as he was then—throughout the Peninsula Campaign, and again at Waterloo when I was one of His Lordship's aides.'

'I believe that battle took a heavy toll of His Lordship's staff.'

'Indeed, it did. I was fortunate to have only minor wounds which soon healed.'

'You know Old Hooknose?' Ned asked, suddenly impressed.

'Yes.' Duncan smiled down at him. 'He eats little boys for breakfast.'

The boy laughed. 'You're gammoning me.'

'You did not consider resigning your commission at the end of hostilities?' the lawyer asked.

'No.' It was a question he had been asked before and unable to explain, he gave his usual answer. 'It seemed to me that there was still work I could do. I entered Paris with the triumphant army and when Wellington arrived there as Ambassador, I was appointed one of his aides. I have lately been in Vienna, working in a minor capacity for the Congress.'

'A notable career, captain.'

'Thank you.'

'I have heard that nothing can touch Vienna for social gaiety,' the painted lady put in. 'You must find yourself mingling frequently with the *haute monde*.'

'There are a great many balls and receptions, plays and operas, which it has been my duty to attend, ma'am, but I have no great love of pretentiousness. I am a simple man.'

'You are unmarried?' she queried, arching her brows and fluttering her lashes in a way which made Helen smile.

'Yes.' He gave no indication of having noticed the coyness.

'I thought so.' The lawyer smiled. 'You have not yet been gentled by a woman's touch. Too blunt by far. If you want something, you demand it. You must learn to tread more softly.'

'Sir, I do not need instruction from you on how to behave. And I have not always found women gentling. In fact, the reverse. They are masters of harshness and many have a rapier wit.'

'You must have been very unfortunate, Captain,' Helen said. 'We are not all unfeeling.'

He was saved from answering by the sound of the guard's horn, warning the next stage of their arrival, and two minutes later they drew up at at an inn where the horses were taken from their traces and substituted with fresh ones. A little over a minute later they were off again, with Ned giving his opinion of the new cattle. 'Ain't a patch on the other lot,' he said. 'Tame as mice. I could drive 'em m'self.' Which comment set them all laughing as they continued along a good road through open country and then down the hill into St Albans. When they drew up at the Woolpack, Helen was relieved to find they would be allowed to leave the coach for a short while. Even though Ned was small, she had never felt so cramped in her life.

'There will be an hour's stop on account of a repair

to one of the traces,' the guard called as they descended. 'Plenty of time for a good meal for those going on. We leave again at four o'clock.'

Helen, trying to find her land legs, stood with her hand on the boy's shoulder, and looked about her. St Albans seemed to be a bustling little town with several inns strung down the length of its long main street.

'Where does your brother live?' she asked him.

'Off Dagnall Lane, miss.'

'Do you know where it is?'

'No.'

'Oh, dear.' She turned to the Captain, who had just got down beside them. 'Do you know where Dagnall Lane is, Captain?'

'No, but I imagine the ostler does.' He called the man over. 'Can you direct this young shaver to Dagnall Lane?'

'It's that way.' The man pointed. 'On the other side of the market place.'

'Come on,' she said to Ned. 'I'll see you safely home.'

'Are you mad?' Duncan said. 'You can't do that.'

'Why not?' she demanded, angry at his rudeness. 'I brought him this far. I feel responsible for his safe arrival.'

'You will get lost, and how do you know the brother will be there? How do you know there is a brother at all?'

'Of course there is. Ned said so, didn't he?'

'Are you always so trusting?'

'I have no reason not to be.' She turned to the boy. 'Come, Ned, we are wasting time and I must be back in time to board the coach.'

'No.' Duncan reached out and held her arm. 'You'll be set upon, robbed, worse. . .'

'Fustian!' She shrugged his hand off and turned to the ostler. 'I shall be back within the hour. Tell the coachman to expect me.' And with that she took Ned's hand and led him in the direction the ostler had pointed.

They had not taken many steps before she became aware that the Captain was walking half a step behind them. She ignored him for several minutes, thinking he was on some errand of his own, but when he turned whenever she did and crossed the road when she did, she was forced to the conclusion he was following her. 'Captain, I do not know what you think you are doing, but I wish you would not dog my heels.'

'Then I shall have to walk beside you,' he said, taking his place beside her and matching his pace to hers.

'Where are you going?'

'To Dagnall Lane, where else?

'I do not need an escort.'

'You may not think so, but I assure you that you do.'

'You will miss your dinner.'

'And so will you.'

She stopped on the edge of the market place. It was packed with people buying and selling every conceivable commodity: chickens, goats, butter, cheese, vegetables, fruit, cooking pots, garden rakes, bonnets and yards of cloth. They were all pushing and shoving and shouting. A blind fiddler and a one-legged man with a penny whistle added to the din.

She took a deep breath and plunged into the throng, grabbing Ned's hand all the tighter, though whether it was to make sure he followed or to give herself courage she did not know. A moment later she felt the Captain's hand under her elbow and felt reassured, though she would not, for a moment, have admitted it.

He led her through the crowd, ignoring the importuning of the traders and beggars, until they emerged into a quiet street on the other side. 'Now which way?' he asked.

'I don't know. We had better enquire again.'

Having asked a passer-by, they set off again and soon found themselves in a maze of narrow streets, each more dismal than the last. Helen was glad that the Captain was with her. It took several more stops for directions before they stopped at the door of a dingy little house and knocked at the door. 'Let us hope your brother is at home, Ned,' Duncan said. 'I have no wish to track him down all over town if he is not.'

The door opened and a man in his middle twenties stood facing them. He was dressed only in breeches; the top half of him was completely bare except for a mat of hair which covered his chest and disappeared into his navel. Helen gave a gasp of shock.

'I'll deal with this,' Duncan told her. 'Wait for me at the end of the street. And do not speak to any strangers.' Without waiting for her to reply, he pushed Ned ahead of him into the house and the door was shut.

Helen, shaken to the core, did as she was told, knowing that she had been very foolish to insist on coming. And to think that she had been prepared to come alone! What would she have done, faced with that half-naked man, if the Captain had not been there? And she was lost; they had taken so many turns that she did not think she could find her way back to the inn alone. Her journey had hardly begun and already she had proved her inadequacy.

She was never more thankful to see the Captain striding towards her a few minutes later and they walked in silence back to the Wheatsheaf. Here she was in for another shock, because the coach was on the point of leaving without them and the guard was at that very moment taking her trunk from the boot.

She ran forward to remonstrate. 'Please put it back, I am here now and ready to go.'

'So are we. You don't seem to understand, miss, that coaches have schedules. People expect them to be on time. You made us late leaving Barnet and now you think you can hold us up again. Who do you think you are? Giving orders like a nob. . .' There was more in like vein until the Captain pressed a guinea into his hand and he agreed to return the trunk to the boot, even though it meant re-arranging everything, just when he had it loaded to his satisfaction.

Helen could do nothing but thank the Captain once again, before going to board the coach. He stopped her with a hand on her arm. 'A minute, ma'am.'

She turned to him in surprise. 'We have no time, we must get in or I shall be in trouble again.'

He smiled. 'No, a guinea will buy us another minute or two and I must speak to you privately.'

'Captain, I have thanked you for your escort and your intervention, what else is there to say?'

'I have something for you. If you do not let me give it to you privately, then I shall be obliged to conduct the business in the coach. I am sure you will not want that.' When she hesitated, he added, 'Come, we will

sit over there where we can be seen by everyone. You
should know by now you have nothing to fear from
me.'

Reluctantly she allowed herself to be escorted to a
bench outside the window of the inn, where they sat
down. 'Captain, I do not like mysteries...' she began.

He smiled, carefully removed his shako and tipped
it upside down in her lap. She found herself looking
down at a lady's purse, a watch and a diamond clip.
Instinctively she put her hand to her throat where the
brooch had been fastened, but she knew already it was
not there and that the one glinting in her lap was hers.
And so were the watch and the purse. Almost every
penny she possessed was in that purse, which had been
attached to the waist of her dress on a drawstring. She
had thought it safe, hidden as it was under her mantle.
'They are mine!'

'Yes.'

'Did you take them?'

'Now why should I do that?'

'To teach me a lesson?'

'I had no need to do that, Miss... Look here, what
is your name?'

After a moment's hesitation, she said, 'Sadler. I am
Miss Sadler.' Her father had been a well-known figure
and the Captain would have heard of him and the
shameful manner of his death, even if he did not know
him personally, and she did not relish having her real
situation made public. Daisy's surname would do her
very well.

'Miss Sadler,' he said slowly, savouring the name on
his tongue but not daring to ask her Christian name. 'I
guessed the boy would try something of the sort, so
before I left him with his brother, who was not exactly

overjoyed to see him, I might add, I pretended to help him off with his coat. Ragged though it appeared it had a very strong inside pocket. I relieved him of these items and glad he was to hand them over and not be taken to the magistrate.'

'It seems, Captain, that I am once again in your debt. I can only offer my grateful thanks.'

He smiled. 'You know, it was very foolish of you to keep all your money in one place and one so accessible too. I should hide it away, if I were you.'

'How do you know it's all the money I have?' she demanded, finding herself on the defensive and taking refuge in anger, which was not at all like her and she could not understand it. 'I have ample funds in my trunk. This is simply my travelling money.'

'And speaking of travelling, I cannot understand what you are doing travelling unaccompanied in the first place. Run away, have you?'

'That is not your business, Captain. Now, I think we should rejoin the coach. And please do not concern yourself about me.' She stood up and began to walk towards the coach, her chin jutting.

He followed. 'Do you think I am the kind of man who can sit back and watch a silly chit get herself into a pickle and not be concerned? There are many on the road who would not be so scrupulous; they would rob you blind. Do you not know the risks?'

'Risks or not, I have no alternative, Captain.'

He was about to ask her why because her shoulders had drooped a little and her voice had softened, but the guard was calling impatiently for them to take their seats or be left behind, and he did not say it. On reflection he was glad; she might have assumed he cared what happened to her and he certainly did not want her to think that. Women were the very devil! He climbed up beside her and they were off again, rattling through the main street and out again onto the open road.

The farmer and the painted woman had completed their journeys and now they were travelling with a nondescript-looking man of perhaps thirty who had a hacking cough, and a young mother and her baby. The baby evidently did not like the swaying of the coach and cried incessantly.

Helen sat gazing from the window, hardly aware of anything except the presence of the Captain sitting beside her and the fact that only her skirts and his pale blue pantaloons separated their thighs. Apart from her father, she had never been that close to a man before and his proximity was having a strange effect on her. Her limbs and face burned as if she had been standing too close to a fire and it was difficult to stop her hands plucking at her cloak in a kind of desperate attempt to put distance, if only inches, between them.

There was no room to do so, she knew, and to draw attention to the fact would only embarrass her, not him. She had had enough of embarrassment. He had saved her from her own foolishness and but for him she would now be penniless, but instead of being well disposed towards him, she found herself resenting the obligation he had put her under.

She had had no idea, when she started out, how difficult it was going to be to maintain her privacy, to keep up the pretence of being an ordinary young lady of limited means, used to looking after herself. Everyone, strangers until that day, seemed to expect introductions and confidences, particularly the

Captain. Could he have some inkling of the truth? She decided he could not possibly know who she was and she was being over-sensitive.

Pride comes before a fall, she scolded herself, and she had no cause to be proud. Having delivered her lecture to herself, she relaxed a little, telling herself that at least, sitting next to the Captain and not opposite him, she was not obliged to meet his eye. She smiled at the young mother who sat in the opposite corner and asked the child's name.

Duncan heard her speak and the baby's mother answer, but he could not have said what they were talking about. He was immersed in speculation of his own about the girl at his side. Why should she be so reluctant to divulge her name? And why did she have no choice but to travel alone? Had she left home in disgrace? Whom was she mourning? She was quiet, a little sad, but she did not act like someone in the throes of unbearable grief.

Perhaps he had been right all along and she was meeting her lover and going on to Gretna. But where was the object of her desire? Was he going to join the coach at some distant stage? Or was he already on it? He looked round. The lawyer had resumed his reading and the unexceptional newcomer hardly fitted the description of a lovelorn suitor. But what was that description? He knew from personal experience there was no accounting for women's tastes. Perhaps it was the man with the cough after all and their attempts at polite conversation were simply a cover.

'Would you prefer the window open?' he heard her ask the man. 'The fresh air. . .'

'No, don't do that,' the mother said. 'The baby will catch a chill.'

'Please do not trouble yourself on my account, ma'am,' the man said, surfacing from the depths of his handkerchief. 'I am perfectly used to my affliction.'

I am not, Duncan thought; the cough was almost as irritating as the child's continuous crying. Why couldn't the mother shut it up?

'Do you think your baby will be more comfortable if you face the way we are going?' Helen asked. 'We could change places.'

'No,' the Captain said, a little too sharply. 'It would be unwise to try and change places in a moving coach. You will make it unstable; we might even go off the road.'

'Oh, I am sorry,' Helen said, chalking up one more reason for disliking the Captain, not because he was wrong but because he was right; the coachman was trying to make up for lost time and was galloping the horses to the next stage. 'Then perhaps I can nurse little Emily for a while.' She held out her arms. 'Come, it will give you a rest.'

The baby was handed over and Helen settled herself against the squabs, gently rocking the child, whose sobs soon faded into hiccoughs and a minute later stopped altogether and she slept, much to everyone's relief.

'Thank you,' the mother whispered, smiling at her slumbering child, while addressing Helen. 'You seem to have the right touch.'

'Yes, I love children.'

'You have children of your own?'

'Goodness, no. I am unmarried.'

'Oh, I am sorry, I thought. . .' She looked in confusion from Helen to the Captain. 'How far are you travelling?'

'To Scotland.'

Duncan had noticed the mistake and was amused by it, though he knew Miss Sadler would not be. She was too top-lofty by far, considering she was probably a governess or a nursery nurse, judging by the competent way she had soothed the child. But she did not behave like a servant at all and in his view was more used to giving orders than receiving them—her manner was a mixture of imperiousness and gentle concern for others.

It was often the case that young women servants learned uppish manners from their employers. But was that true of Miss Sadler? He was more than ever convinced there was something havey-cavey going on and it intrigued him.

The coach rattled through Redbourn and Dunstable, where it stopped for a change of horses and where the man with the cough left them, saying his destination was Cambridge. Then they were off again with only five inside passengers now, but it did not seem to make any difference; Helen felt the Captain was as close as he had been before.

They ran straight through Hockliffe and, six miles further on, stopped at the Swan at Little Brickhill. It was a busy little place where several coaching routes converged and the yard was full of horses and people, and at least two carriages being changed.

The mother stepped down as soon as they stopped and reached up to take her sleeping baby from Helen. 'Thank you, Miss Sadler. My parents live nearby and my father is meeting me. I wish you a safe journey.'

Helen was sorry to see her go and, as it was nearly supper time, wondered if this might be a good place to break her journey. She left the coach, knowing that the Captain was watching her, though he made no move to leave himself, and made her way into the inn. She had never stayed at an inn before, not even with her parents. After returning from India they rarely went far from their London home; it was as if they had had their fill of travelling.

Until her mother's death they always spent some time each year at their country seat in Huntingdonshire, but that could be reached in a day. On the other hand, the prospect of travelling all night in that swaying, jolting coach was more than she could stomach and stiffened her resolve. 'Is it possible to stay here tonight?' she asked the man who was washing down the tables in the tiny parlour. 'I require a private room.'

He looked her up and down. There was no mistaking the tone; she was Quality and travelling alone too. He decided he didn't want to have any dealings with someone so unconventional. 'No private rooms, miss.' He grinned. 'Shared, if you like. . .'

'No, thank you.' Aware of his amusement, she turned and went out.

The guard was looking for her. 'Come along, miss, we can't have you holding up proceedings again, can we? Up you go.' And suiting action to words, he put both hands under her bottom and hoisted her into the coach beside the grinning Captain. She was furious but before she could protest, they were on their way again.

She settled herself in her seat to find herself facing a young fop in a buff greatcoat with enormous brass buttons. It was very long and came down over his calf half-boots, which were almost hidden by the length of his cossacks. He wore a green and white striped waistcoat and a tall crowned hat with a buckle on the band from which swept a long feather. Every time they were jolted, the feather touched the roof and threatened to take his hat off. The other two seats were taken up by a couple of middle years who were both exceedingly plump.

'Late again,' the woman said. 'Stages are supposed to work to time but they never do.'

'It is only five minutes late, my love,' her husband said. 'We shall soon make it up.'

'I'm sorry,' Helen said, realising she was being blamed for the delay. 'I had hoped to stay here overnight, but there are no private rooms.'

'There will be rooms at Northampton,' the lawyer said. 'It is the usual stopping place for passengers on this coach.'

'I hope we won't be late,' the young man said. 'I shall have to hire a carriage to take me on to my home and at that time of night. . .' He stopped and smiled at Helen. 'You are not going to be met at Northampton, are you?'

'No.'

'Pity. I could have begged a ride.'

'Are you not expected?' Duncan asked, unaccountably glad that the lovely Miss Sadler would not be sharing a vehicle with this young popinjay if he were getting off at Northampton.

'No.' He grinned ruefully. 'My father does not know I am returning home. I am at Cambridge, you know.'

'Is that so?' Duncan said. 'Then I'll wager you have been rusticated.'

'Only a prank, sir, only a prank. Went out on the town, got a little foxed, climbed back into the wrong window. Out for the rest of the term.'

'Irresponsible coxcomb,' the woman put in. 'Is that how you squander the opportunities you are given?'

'Ma'am, it was not my idea to go to university,' he told her. 'Papa insisted. I am not a bookish person at all. . .'

'Evidently not,' she said, pursing her lips.

The young man was about to protest again but thought better of it and stared out of the window, but it was already dark and there was nothing to see. Nothing to see inside the carriage either and they all fell silent. Helen leaned back and shut her eyes. She had hardly begun her journey but already she was wishing it were over. Although it was cold outside, the air inside the coach was very stuffy and she was hot and cramped and all she longed for was a comfortable bed.

Captain Duncan Blair, sitting beside her, mile after mile, was reluctant to let go of his theory that she was going to Gretna to marry and was unaccountably relieved to find that neither the man with the bad cough nor the young student were the object of her affections. What she needed, he decided, was a real man to curb her impulsiveness, a mature man of the world like himself. The thought brought him up short.

He was the last person, the very last person, to say whom she should or should not choose for a husband. What did he know about women? He had avoided having anything to do with them for years, except in a very superficial way, though he supposed that he would soon have to give way to his father's constant demand that he should find a nice young lady with a decent dowry and settle down into marriage and fatherhood. But he was not ready to do that yet.

They passed a house whose upstairs lights shone out

across the carriageway and he took advantage of the meagre illumination to look down at the girl at his side. She had closed her eyes and he wondered if she might have gone to sleep, but they were soon in the dark again and he couldn't be sure. He sat very still so as not to disturb her.

Several minutes later he became aware of a weight on his arm and realised she had dropped asleep with her head lolling against him. Slowly he eased his arm out and put it round her shoulders. With a contented sigh, she snuggled her head into his chest. He smiled, savouring the slight scent of her hair beneath his nostrils, content to let her sleep, even though he soon had pins and needles in his arm; it was a small price to pay.

It was late in the evening when they reached the Angel at Northampton, sixty-six miles from London, where not only the horses, but the coachman and guard were due to be changed. Helen stirred as they drove into the inn yard and came to a stop. She sat up sleepily and pulled her bonnet straight and then gave a gasp of horror when she realised she had fallen asleep and the Captain had his arm around her. She almost fell over her own feet in her anxiety to get down from the coach and escape from him.

The other passengers followed her and she lost sight of him, to her intense relief. He had declared his intention of riding on through the night, and she would be well rid of him. Officer or no, he was no gentleman if he could take advantage of her while she slept.

She started towards the door of the inn and then realised that the coachman and guard were standing between the coach and the inn door, touching their hat brims and bidding their passengers a safe journey. Taking her cue from her fellow travellers, Helen handed the coachman a shilling and a sixpence and the guard a shilling, thinking as she did so, that being coachmen must be a highly remunerative calling if they received a like amount from every traveller every day.

'Thank you, miss,' the guard said. 'The coach leaves again in an hour.'

'Oh, but I think I shall stay here tonight and go on in the morning.'

'But you are booked through.'

'Yes, I know.'

'And now I suppose you are going to ask me for a refund on your ticket.'

'Is that possible?'

Her expression had suddenly lightened with hope and he found himself smiling. Poor little thing, having to go all that way alone and her so innocent. He found himself returning her smile. 'Yes, miss, at my discretion.' He delved into a leather bag he carried over his shoulder and counted seven pounds into her hand. 'There you are, miss, but if you are going to stop overnight again, I suggest you buy your tickets in stages, though it will cost you more in the long run.'

'Thank you.'

'Good luck to you, miss.' And then with a twinkle in his eye, 'Don't let the Captain bully you, miss. You stand up for yourself.'

It was too much. She fled to the door of the inn and then stopped. What would she do if the only rooms available were shared ones, stay or go? But the prospect of continuing in the coach for another minute knowing what had happened and what might happen again if she could not keep her eyes open, was abhorrent. She took a deep breath and stepped inside.

CHAPTER THREE

THE inn was already very crowded and the waiters were hurrying about with loaded trays, so that it was some minutes before Helen could attract the attention of one of them and ask for a room for the night, stipulating it must be a private room. Having at last been told that one would be prepared for her, she ordered onion soup, bread and apple pie to be brought to her and then looked round for a seat. She realised at once that finding somewhere to sit should have been her first step and ordering a bed and food next; there didn't seem vacant chair in the whole establishment.

'There's a table in the corner, miss,' one of the waiters said, passing her with a tray loaded with roast beef and game pie, potatoes and pickles. 'Over there.' He jerked his head in the direction of a small table and two chairs almost concealed behind a potted palm. She thanked him and hurried to sit down before anyone else could claim it.

She felt quite strange, as if she were still in the coach; the floor seemed to be moving and her chair swaying. It was as if she had just stepped on shore after a long sea voyage and it was several minutes before her head stopped feeling giddy and her stomach settled and by that time her food had been put in front of her. 'What would you like to drink, miss?' the waiter asked.

'A glass of ratafia, please.'

'Don't have such refinements as that, miss. There's wine.'

'Wine will do very well,' a familiar voice said. 'The best you have and a carafe of water.'

Helen could not bring herself to look up into his face, though she resented his interference. As if she could not take wine without water! Did he think she was a child? Perhaps he would go away if she pretended she had not noticed he was there. But it was difficult not to notice him, he was so big he towered over her.

'Miss Sadler,' he said. 'I took the liberty of having your trunk taken to your room. You seemed to have forgotten it.'

How could he seem so calm where her heart was thumping with embarrassment? But she could hardly ignore him. 'Thank you, Captain. I was in haste to secure a room for the night. I had not forgotten it.' Liar, she accused herself; the need to escape from him had driven all other thoughts from her head.

'May I share your table?' he asked.

She looked up at him then, to find him regarding her with his head on one side as if unsure of her reaction to the request, though he showed no sign of leaving if it should prove unfavourable. 'Why, Captain, I thought you were determined on travelling on through the night.'

'I still need sustenance, Miss Sadler. The coach does not leave for an hour.'

'Oh.'

'So may I sit down? I fear there are no other seats and if you refuse me, you may find yourself sharing with some less savoury character.'

She was about to retort that she could think of no

one less savoury but then remembered the farmer and the student and Ned's half-naked brother, and fell silent. He was preferable to all of those. And if she were truly honest with herself, she had felt safe and comforted in his arms, and that was not a feeling she had enjoyed of late. She managed a tight little smile. 'Please be seated, Captain, or I shall get a crick in the neck looking up at you.'

He flicked up the skirt of his uniform jacket and sat down. A waiter appeared immediately, making Helen resentful that she, an unaccompanied woman, had had to wait so long for service. 'A capon,' he ordered. 'Some turbot, potatoes, a dish of vegetables and a slice of your excellent game pie.' Then to Helen, pointing at her bowl of soup. 'Is that all you are going to eat?'

'Yes, I am not hungry.'

'You have eaten nothing all day.'

'I expect it is the rocking of the coach; it has made me feel a little unsteady and quite taken my appetite.'

The Captain's food arrived, filling her nostrils with its succulent smell. He served himself and smiled at her. His tanned, almost weather-beaten, face creased attractively when he smiled, she noted, and the scar on his forehead almost disappeared. 'Come, let me tempt you to a morsel. There is more here than I can eat.'

'No, thank you,' she said stiffly.

'You are angry with me.' He poured wine for himself and one for her, pushing it towards her.

'Not at all.' She bent to her soup spoon.

'Yes, you are. Tell me why.'

'Captain, I am unaccustomed to being called a liar, or to being treated with such familiarity, even by people I know well, and we have not even been introduced.'

He laughed. 'There is no call to be top-lofty with me, you know. I can give as good as I get in that department, so why not be easy with me. Not half an hour ago. . .'

'Just because I was so foolish as to fall asleep, does not give you the right to take liberties,' she said, glad the light was not good enough for him to see the colour she knew was spreading from her cheeks right down her neck. She took a gulp of wine in an effort to cool herself.

'Good God! Who do you think I am? Bluebeard?'

'No, of course not.'

'I am glad to hear it. I am not so in want of female company I have to wait until a young lady is unconscious before forcing myself upon her. You were the one who fell asleep and if I had not supported you, you would have toppled over face first into the lap of that young dandy. He might have taken far more advantage than I.'

The picture his words created brought a tiny smile to her lips in spite of her determination to retain her hauteur.

So, she had a sense of humour and could laugh at herself; that was good. 'You should smile more often, Miss Sadler.'

'I have had little to smile about lately, Captain.'

'Do you wish to talk about it?'

'No.' She drank a little more wine and was surprised to find her glass was empty. He refilled it.

'Then what shall we talk of? What interests you? The doings of our fat monarch and his outrageous wife?'

'Not particularly. They are as distant from real life as the man on the moon.'

'You are right, that farce is hardly the stuff of intelligent conversation.'

She smiled then; a genuine smile which lit her piquant face and made her eyes sparkle. 'You do not subscribe to the maxim that young ladies should not converse intelligently, then?'

'Most of those I have met in Society would be hard put to even pretend to having a mind. Empty-headed little flirts.'

'Oh, dear, you do have a poor opinion of the fair sex.'

'I said "most", not all, Miss Sadler. I'll allow there are exceptions.'

'You would like me to prove myself one of the exceptions?'

'Are you?'

'I am not empty-headed, Captain, but I am not so vain as to claim a superior intelligence. I have been fortunate enough to enjoy a good education. . .'

'Good enough to teach?'

'What makes you say that?' She answered his question with another.

'I noticed how you handled that little urchin. There was nothing lily-livered about it.' He smiled suddenly. 'But did you really not know the difference between a cow and a bull?'

She laughed. 'Of course I did, but I did not want to offend the others in the coach if he quizzed me about it.'

'What subjects interest you most, Miss Sadler? Languages, poetry, antiquities. . .?'

'All of those. I read a little Greek and Latin, and I
have enough French to converse. . .'

'Gaelic?'

'No. Why do you ask?'

'I collect you saying you were going to Scotland and
it is the native tongue of the Scots.'

She did not rise to the bait, but turned the question
on him. 'Is it yours, Captain?'

'My father's, Miss Sadler, but being so much from
home, I am afraid I have acquired no more than a few
phrases.'

'I assume you have spent a considerable time with
your regiment?'

'Yes.'

'I imagine it is not all flags flying and bands playing.
There must be times when you wish yourself anywhere
but where you are. War cannot be a pleasant experience, whether you are victor or vanquished. The sight
of all those poor men coming home after Waterloo
was heart-rending. I found it difficult to join in the
general rejoicing.'

Was that what the mourning was for, a soldier lover
who had not returned? But she was too young for
that; he did not think she could be more than eighteen
now and would have been a mere child at the time.
'Did you know someone who was there?'

'Several young men of my acquaintance served on
that battlefield, no one in particular,' she answered
evasively. 'Please, tell me something of it.'

She had managed, with consummate skill, to turn
the conversation away from herself towards him. So
be it; if she did not want to tell him about herself, he
would enjoy her company for an hour, bid her farewell
and never see her again.

He smiled and talked about the dispositions of the opposing forces and which regiments had distinguished themselves. She ate some of his food, when he pressed her, and drank some more wine and finally relaxed. He was good company and very knowledgeable on a great many subjects, so that she became absorbed by what he was saying and did not notice the other passengers leaving the room to rejoin the coach.

He told her of the triumphant march into Paris and how Napoleon had tried to get onto a British ship and expected the Regent to give him sanctuary. He described Vienna and told her about the arguments and counter-arguments at the Vienna Convention which had been going on for years as the allies carved Europe up between them. He told her about the social life, every bit as hectic as that in Paris, and of the Grand Tour, now re-established for all young men before they settled down.

She answered him now and again and put forward some ideas of her own, but mostly she listened; it was all very easy and very pleasant, and she did not want to break it up and go to bed, though she was feeling very sleepy again and could hardly keep her eyes open.

He did not think she was the sort of girl to swoon at the mention of blood, but he was careful not to frighten her with gory details and was, therefore, very surprised when she suddenly said she felt very hot and would have fallen from her seat if he had not had the presence of mind to catch her.

He sat with her half-lying across his knee and looked about him. The dining room had emptied and there was no one to be seen but a waiter sweeping the floor. He called to him. 'Fetch mine host's wife, if you please.'

'That's more than I dare do, sir. She's long abed and asleep and she won't want to be disturbed on account of she has to be up betimes.'

'A chambermaid, then.'

'Now, sir, how can I go waking chambermaids?'

Duncan looked down at the girl in his arms. Her face was flushed and her bosom heaved gently, but she showed no sign of regaining her senses. He tried shaking her a little, calling her name, but all that happened was that her head wobbled, her bonnet fell off and she muttered something unintelligible. He cursed himself for a fool. She had eaten hardly anything all day and she was very tired; the unaccustomed swaying of the coach had made her giddy and the little wine she had drunk had done the rest. Why had he not noticed?

It was a long time since he had enjoyed a woman's company so much; talking to her and watching her animated face as she spoke to him had filled his mind. He had only been half aware that the coach had gone on without him and completely oblivious to the fact that she was not well. Tomorrow she would hate him. Tonight though, she needed putting to bed.

He knew which room was hers because he had had her trunk taken up to it. He scooped her up in his arms, surprised that she weighed so little, and carried her up to her room, pushing the door open with his foot and depositing her on the bed. Then he lit a candle which stood on a cupboard by the door and stood looking down at her. He could not leave her like that.

He put the candle on a table, sat on the edge of the bed and shook her gently. 'Miss Sadler, wake up, you

foolish child, wake up.' When she did not respond, he
pulled off her mantle and set about undoing the
buttons which fastened her gown up to the chin, but
when he had done that, he discovered the layers of
underwear. No wonder she had fainted! The sooner
she was rid of them and able to breathe freely, the
sooner she would recover.

She gave a huge sigh of relief and then giggled as
he pulled off the dress and untied the thick petticoat
beneath it. 'Oh, Daisy, you are tickling me. . .'

He took off the thick outer layer of underwear and
untied her corset and discovered that she was not the
dumpy young girl he had thought, but a woman, slight
to be sure, but perfectly formed. She certainly did not
need the corset.

His own words suddenly echoed in his mind: 'I am
not so in want of female company I have to wait until
a young lady is unconscious before forcing myself
upon her.' He stifled a harsh laugh. It was his fault; he
should have been watching out for her instead of
allowing himself to be carried away with his own
rhetoric. He could not leave her; tomorrow night, if he
were not there, someone less honourable might be
taking liberties, as she had put it.

The thought of anyone else doing what he was doing
made him go hot and cold with anxiety on her behalf.
She needed looking after and he cursed the unknown
man, whoever he was, who had brought her to this.
That it had been a man he was sure. Leaving her in
her shift and stockings, he covered her with the quilt,
dropped a kiss on her forehead and crept from the
room, closing the door softly behind him. Then he
went in search of a bed.

* * *

Helen woke with a start, wondering where she was. Her head ached abominably and her stomach was churning. She remembered boarding a coach, remembered her fellow passengers and a boy, a dirty little urchin who had stolen her money. It had been retrieved by Captain Blair and she had shown scant gratitude. They had come a long way after that, so where was she now?

Racking her brain, which did nothing to improve her headache, she recalled coming into an inn and sitting over a meal with the Captain. They had talked a lot and she had found him an agreeable companion, but after that her memory was a blank. She sat up and groaned as her head started to spin. She had taken rather more wine than she was used to and the Captain, who could know nothing of those extra undergarments, would undoubtedly think she had been foxed.

How had she got to her room? She must have come upstairs and half undressed before collapsing on the bed. But someone had been with her, she remembered soothing words and gentle hands. The Captain must have fetched the innkeeper's wife or one of the chambermaids to help her. Why was she forever in his debt? Why did she seem determined to prove she could not manage to travel a few miles on her own? He would be gone now and she was glad of that; she refused to admit that she had been grateful for his help.

A month ago, she would hardly have noticed him. She smiled suddenly; no, that was not true, you could not help noticing him, he stood out head and shoulders above everyone else and not only physically; he had a way of commanding attention, a way of concentrating on you as if he were truly interested in what you were saying. It was cultivated, no doubt, along with his skill as a soldier and his extensive general knowledge.

It was probably how he had managed to catch the eye of the Duke of Wellington, so one small, lonely young lady had little defence. But he had been right on one thing; there were sure to be others on the road who would not be so scrupulous and she would do well to be on her guard.

She could hear sounds outside her window; voices and horses neighing and the jingle of harness. She left her bed and padded to the window to draw back the curtains. Dawn was just breaking and there was a coach in the yard which had just driven in. Its passengers were tumbling out, half-asleep, to come into the inn for breakfast. If that was the coach to Manchester, she did not have much time.

Hurriedly she washed in cold water from the ewer, dressed in a pelisse-robe in black bombazine, packed her dusty round dress of the day before and the extra petticoats in her trunk, and went downstairs, carrying her small portmanteau. She met a chambermaid on the way, who bobbed and bade her good morning. Helen smiled, wanting to convey her thanks for whatever had been done for her without actually saying it. 'Would you be kind enough to ask someone to take my trunk to the coach?' she asked, handing her a sixpence.

'Yes, ma'am.' The girl grinned at the unexpectedly large gratuity. 'I'll have Jake do it straight away.'

Helen continued down to the dining room where the smell of breakfast cooking was making her feel decidedly ill, but she needed something to drink, preferably hot, strong coffee, before she could face another day of being jolted about in a coach.

She was surprised to see the Captain sitting over breakfast at a table near the fire. He was dressed in a military-style frockcoat over a kerseymere waistcoat in brown and buff stripes, cut in the Hussar style, and buff nankin pantaloons, so that even in civilian clothes, he still looked every inch the soldier. His dark hair was damp and clung about his neck and ears in tight little curls. He rose, smiling. 'Good morning, Miss Sadler. You are in good time for breakfast.' He half expected her to cut him for taking even more liberties but, to his surprise, she sat down opposite him.

'Good morning, Captain. No breakfast, thank you. Just coffee.'

He called a waiter and the hot drink was soon in front of her. She gulped it greedily and began to feel a little better. 'I am surprised to see you this morning, Captain,' she said, before he could make any reference to the previous evening. 'I collect you saying you were in haste to reach your destination and were going to travel through the night.'

He suddenly realised she did not remember him carrying her to her room and must be thinking she had found her way there by herself. He breathed a sigh of relief. 'I found the company so convivial, I could not tear myself away,' he said, deciding it would be unwise to say what was in his mind, that she was so helpless he could not abandon her. It would have invited a sharp rebuke and an assertion that she did not need looking after. 'And this is a passably comfortable inn.'

'Convivial,' she repeated. 'Are you inferring I had taken too much wine? Because if you are, let me tell you it was nothing of the sort. I was simply unwell.

The rocking of the coach, you know, and the heat in the dining room. . .'

'Please forgive me,' he said. 'I am afraid I have been too long a soldier and do not always choose my words with care. In truth, I found the heat in the dining-room somewhat overpowering myself, especially after the cold outside.'

'I do believe I heard the guard calling up the passengers for the coach,' she put in quickly, unwilling to continue the conversation.

He stood up, picked up his cloak-bag and her portmanteau and waited to escort her. She paid for her bed and board and followed him. Whatever she thought of his behaviour, she was obliged to him. She was feeling far from well and in any case, he was only treating her like the working woman he believed her to be and she had to be thankful that he was gentleman enough to accept her explanation.

As soon as she had purchased her ticket, he handed her in to her seat, checked that her trunk had been loaded safely and took his place beside her. They were joined by an elderly lady in a huge poke bonnet worn over her day cap, a parson in black robes and a low-crowned round hat, and a young couple, obviously in love, with eyes for no one but each other.

Judging by his dress, the young man considered himself something of a dandy; his pantaloons and coat were tightly fitting, his waistcoat colourful and his pale blue cravat extravagantly tied. His wife wore a high-waisted gown of barège with a pleated bodice and a great deal of decoration around the hem, over which she wore a fur-lined pelisse in blue velvet.

Helen could not see the outside passengers but they seemed a noisy group, laughing and calling to each other as they climbed aboard. She could hear the guard calling them to order as he took his own place in the seat above the back boot. A minute later the coachman, having completed his inspection, climbed aboard and they were off.

Helen was glad that her fellow passengers were disinclined to talk; she did not feel like conversation and she was all too aware of the Captain beside her. It was funny how much she remembered of his conversation of the evening before. He had been an agreeable raconteur and she had learned much she had not known about how wars were fought and the magnitude of the task of supplying an army of thousands with horses, weapons, food and clothing.

He had talked of Portugal with affection and of Wellington with admiration and loyalty. Helen had met the great man once, in 1814, in the brief spell of peace when he had come to London to be feted. Had she told the Captain that? What had she told him? She risked a peep at him from beneath the brim of her bonnet.

He was sitting staring into space as if his thoughts were far away, on some battlefield perhaps. Or was he thinking of what was at the end of his journey? He had said he was unmarried, but that did not mean there was not a young lady waiting for him. Where? Where was he going? Did she hope he would leave soon or did she want him to stay until they arrived in Glasgow?

Of one thing she was certain, she did not want him to meet whoever was sent to fetch her because then he would know she had lied, pretending she was something she was not. She surprised herself with how much his good opinion mattered to her.

* * *

Duncan had not slept well. Given the option of sharing a room with two or three other men or finding a warm corner of the stables, he had chosen the stables, waking at dawn with his hair and clothes full of straw and an unmistakable odour of horses about him. He had stripped to his waist and stood under the pump in the yard, allowing the cold water to refresh him and then taken a new suit of clothes from his cloak-bag, rolling up the uniform and stuffing it in the bag in its place.

He missed his personal servant, particularly when it came to shaving, but the man had family in London and he had could hardly drag him all the way to Scotland, especially when he had no idea how long he would be at home. If things were very bad, he might have to resign his commission. He had been a soldier for twelve of his thirty years, so perhaps it was time he settled down. But settling down meant marriage, at least in his father's eyes, and since Arabella, he had not trusted himself even to think about it.

He risked a sideways look at the young lady beside him. She was uncommonly beautiful and her figure, now that she had obviously discarded the extra petticoats, was curvaceous without being plump. He found himself picturing her in lighter colours, pale blues and greens instead of that unrelieved black, and decided that whatever she wore she would be lovely. Neither was she afraid to have an opinion of her own, nor of expressing it articulately.

He had long ago decided she was not eloping; such a forceful person as she was, would not need to resort to clandestine methods to get her own way. Was she affianced to some Scottish gentleman and going to her wedding? The thought made him catch his breath and his heart beat faster, as if it mattered to him whether she were engaged to be married or no, which it did not, he told himself.

She wore no ring and she would surely have told him last night if she had a fiancé. She was probably a nursery nurse or a governess, going to take up a post north of the border. On the other hand, her manner was not subservient, so perhaps she was really a lady, daughter of an aristocrat, royalty perhaps, travelling incognito. But even then she would have had at least one servant somewhere in the background watching over her. Miss Sadler, if that was truly her name, was definitely alone.

Servants often aped the imperious mannerisms of their mistresses, so perhaps that was it; she was a lady's maid. Whom was she mourning? Was she going to Scotland for a funeral? How had she managed to get him to talk about himself without volunteering anything of any import about herself? Almost all he had learned about her, she had divulged to their travelling companions, not to him. Was there a reason for that? Why, however hard he tried, could he not stop thinking about her?

'The countryside is beautiful at this time of the year, don't you think so, Miss Sadler?' he ventured into the silence after they had stopped at Harborough for a change of horses.

It was a moment before she realised he was addressing her, but then she smiled. 'Oh, yes, the changing colours of the trees are quite glorious, but each of the seasons has its own appeal, do you not think? I find that in October, I am in favour of autumn, but in March nothing suits me so well as spring when everything we thought dead is growing anew.'

'A good philosophy, ma'am,' the parson put in. 'One

should be content with what God gives us at the time and not be forever wishing it were otherwise.'

'I wish our outside passengers were otherwise,' the old lady put in. 'I do believe they are all drunk. There is one above my head who is banging his heels on the roof. I fear he will put his foot through before long.'

The outside passengers had been growing more noisy the further they travelled and now there was such a drumming on the roof, they began to think the old lady might be right. Duncan got up and put his head out of the door to shout up to them. 'Can you not be a little less boisterous; you are alarming the ladies.'

One of them grabbed the guard's tin horn and blew a blast down towards Duncan, then turned to one of the other young men, whom Duncan could not see. 'Go on, Bertie, I'll act guard if you drive.' And again he gave a toot on the horn, this time directed at the sky. 'Ten guineas says you can't take us to the next post.'

'You're on.'

There was more banging and scraping on the roof and a great deal more shouting of encouragement to the unseen Bertie. Duncan's remonstrances and demands that the coach should be stopped and the young men put off were ignored. A minute later they knew the reins were in inexperienced hands, for the coach began to lurch from side to side.

Duncan returned to his seat. 'I am afraid the coachman has allowed one of those thatchgallows to have the ribbons.'

'What! We shall all be killed!' the old lady said. 'You must stop him at once.'

'Ma'am, I can do nothing unless we come to a halt, or at least slow down enough for me to get down.'

They showed no sign of doing so and in truth began to go even faster, so that the inside passengers were thrown from side to side. Helen, her earlier uneasy stomach forgotten in this new sensation, found herself hanging onto the door strap and praying the young man would realise how reckless he was being and let the coachman have the reins back.

The parson was apparently doing the same thing; his eyes were shut tight and his lips were moving in prayer; the young couple were clinging to each other in terror and the old lady was screaming. Helen reached across and touched her arm. 'Ma'am, pray calm yourself. The coachman, irresponsible as he is, will not allow us to be overturned. We shall slow down directly.'

If anything they went faster and Helen, peering from the off-side door, saw another coach ahead of them, going at a steady pace. Unless they drew up very quickly, she did not see how they could avoid running into the back of it. She shut her eyes and tensed herself for a crash. She opened them when she heard the young lady in the opposite corner cry out and found herself looking right into the other coach as they hurtled along side by side.

'They're racing us,' the young man said. 'We'll never get by.'

Duncan leaned across Helen and shouted to the second coachman. 'Pull up, man. Let us past.'

But the man either did not hear or did not want to hear. They proceeded neck and neck for several hundred yards and then pulled slowly ahead. Helen let out her breath in a long sigh of relief, although they did not slow down. She suspected that the horses were out of control and she could hear their coachman yelling at the man with the reins to relinquish them, but he seemed to be frozen with fear and unable to do anything.

'Watch out!' Duncan yelled as they rounded a bend and he caught sight of a fat, milk-laden cow plodding up the middle of the road towards them. The coachman at last grabbed the ribbons and hauled on them for all he was worth. The horses veered to the left, but the coach, slow to change direction, ploughed into the cow, wobbled terrifyingly and then embedded itself in a pile of stones on the grass verge. The lead horses, unable to pull the coach through the stones, came to a shuddering stop, rearing up and neighing in fright. The outside passengers screamed and the old lady fainted in Helen's arms.

Duncan clambered out, followed by the parson and the young couple, and then Helen, supporting the old lady. There was blood everywhere, which set the young lady into hysterics. Her husband took her off behind the coach to try and calm her. The old lady, fully recovered, left Helen to find out if her baggage was safe.

Only Helen, of the inside passengers, was prepared to help the casualties and it soon became apparent that most of the blood belonged to the poor dead cow. The coachman, who had a broken arm, was cursing the young driver, who had been shot straight over the heads of the horses and had landed in the middle of a thorn bush. His language rivalled that of the coachman, which seemed to indicate he was not all that grievously injured.

Most of the other outside passengers had been

thrown from their seats and although they had sustained cuts and bruises, none seemed badly hurt. They
had become suddenly sober and shame-faced. It was
the guard who gave most cause for concern. He was
lying some way off and had been knocked
unconscious.

'I'll see to them,' Helen told Duncan. 'You look to
the horses.

'Are you sure?'

'Of course I am sure.'

He left her to go and look at the animals and she
went behind a tree to pull off her petticoat and tear it
into strips. She had hardly returned to the scene when
the second coach came round the bend and drew to a
stop.

'You cow-handed numbskull!' the second coachman
yelled at the first. 'You near had us off the road. Call
yourself a coachie, why, you're nothing but a buffle-
headed, cork-brained souse-crown!'

'And if you had anything in the attic at all,' the first
responded, 'you'd have known there was a green
amateur on the ribbons and pulled up instead of trying
to race us.'

'More fool you, Martin Gathercole, for allowing a
greenhorn to take over.'

There were more acrimonious exchanges, in which
the uninjured passengers joined, apportioning blame
as they saw fit, while Helen quietly got on with her
self-appointed task. Let them argue it out. There was
clearly blame on both sides but as long as they did not
come to blows and cause more injuries, she was indifferent to the outcome. It was more important that the
injured were cared for.

There was little she could do for the guard except

make him comfortable with her mantle as a pillow and bathe his face in cold water from the ditch into which they would certainly have tumbled if the pile of road-mending stones had not stopped them. He had a large bump on the back of his head and would need a doctor as soon as one could be fetched. Leaving him, she went to the young driver, who had scrambled out of the bush and was wandering around in a daze, holding his hand to his face. There was blood running through his fingers onto his cravat and down his expensive satin waistcoat.

'Sit down,' she commanded. 'Let me look at you.'

He sat on the bank and allowed her to pull his hand away from his face. 'It's a nasty cut,' she said, dabbing at it with a strip from her petticoat. 'And there's a bruise on your cheek which will certainly spoil your looks for a few days. Whatever did you think you were about? You could have killed us all.'

'It was only a prank,' he said. 'Everyone fancies being a coachie, don't they? It is often done. But the cattle wouldn't answer the whip, mean creatures, wanted to go their own way.'

'Perhaps their way was best.' She smiled suddenly. 'After all, they have probably been cantering up and down this road several times a week for two or three years while you. . .'

'I'm considered a good hand with the ribbons.'

'Driving a phaeton or a curricle with one or two horses at most, I have no doubt, but a four-in-hand is a different matter altogether. I am surprised you allowed yourself to be persuaded.'

'It was a wager, ma'am, couldn't ignore a wager, now could I?'

'Wager! It seems to me that gambling is all young

men think of.' Reminded of her father, she added,
'And men old enough to know better too. Could you
not have thought of the consequences? We could all
have been killed. As it is, the guard has a cracked
head and the coachman a broken arm, not to mention
the upset to the passengers.'

'I'm sorry, ma'am. I was a little bosky.'

'That is not an excuse either. Now, hold that over
the cut, while I look after the coachman.'

Martin Gathercole was still being harangued by his
opposite number, holding his injured arm in the good
one and obviously in great pain. 'Either help or go,'
he yelled back at him. 'I ain't got time to listen to you
gabbling on like a fishwife.' And with that he turned
and walked round to the front of the coach where the
Captain was soothing the horses.

The left leader had taken the brunt of the impact
into the stones and was still shuddering. Duncan was
speaking gently as if to a child who had fallen and
grazed a knee. 'There, my lovely, you've had a fright,
haven't you? But all is well. Rest easy. Be calm. There,
there.' The horse stood still, blowing a little, but its
eyes still reflected its unease. A sudden movement, a
loud noise, would set it off again.

Duncan moved to the off-side leader and spoke in
the same calm voice. As soon as both leaders were
quiet, the heavier wheelers stood still, patiently waiting for whatever orders were given. 'I reckon they'll
settle once we are on our way again,' Duncan said.
'It's the coach I'm not too sure about. One of the
wheels looks buckled and the nearside door has come
off its hinges. It's impossible to tell if it is safe to drive
until we get it out of the stones.'

'Then we'd best do that.' Martin turned and yelled

at the other coachman. 'Are you going to sit there all day? Or are you going to use those great fat shoulders of yours to do some good?' Feeling a hand on his good arm, he turned to find Helen at his elbow.

'Leave the others to see to it, Mr Gathercole,' she said. 'You need that arm looking after.'

'Go on,' Duncan said to him. 'I'll see to this.'

Reluctantly he followed Helen to sit on the bank a little way from the amateur driver who sat nursing his head. 'I never met such a crank-brained jack-at-warts,' he said, nodding in the young man's direction. 'And a liar to boot. He told me he could drive, said he'd done it any number of times before on the Brighton run.'

'More fool you for believing him,' Helen said crisply. 'You should have had more thought for your passengers. If the Company found out you would lose your job, isn't that so?'

'You'd tell?'

'Not me, but the other driver might. He was angry enough.' She glanced over to where all the uninjured passengers and the coachman and guard from the second coach were putting their shoulders to the wheels of the stranded vehicle while Duncan, standing at the front of the horses, urged them to pull.

'Not he.' He gave a laugh but it changed to a grunt of pain as Helen bound his arm to his chest. 'All wind, that's what he is. Done for the benefit of his passengers. He's a good mate.'

And it did seem to be true, for the man was huge and strong and was not sparing himself in his efforts to free the coach. Slowly, inch by inch, it was dragged from the stones and stood once more on the hard surface of the road. The passengers gathered round it, wondering if they dare trust themselves to it again. The young couple stood with their arms about each other, the old lady was threatening to sue the Company, though what injury she had sustained they could not see. The parson was looking at the bent wheel and muttering.

'I reckon it will go, driven slowly,' Martin said. 'We'll have to stop at the next inn and have it repaired.'

'That's all very well,' the parson said. 'But who's going to drive it, a one-armed coachman or a befuddled guard who doesn't seem to know which way is up?'

'I'll drive,' Duncan said.

'Give me strength, more amateurs!' exclaimed the old lady. 'I'm not getting back in that thing, not for the world.'

'Then you'd best ride on with us, ma'am, we've got two spare seats,' the second coachman said. 'We'll take one of the others too.'

'Then it had better be that young scapegrace, Bertie Billingsworth,' Martin said. 'For I have seen and heard enough of him for one day.'

The old lady's luggage was transferred and the two passengers climbed aboard; the coachman manoeuvred the vehicle round the first one and they were gone, disappearing round the bend in the road.

'Now, let's help the guard inside,' Duncan said. 'And you, young shaver.' He pointed to a young lad who had been knocked out when he was thrown from the roof and was still looking very dazed. 'You too, Mr Gathercole, if the Reverend does not mind sitting outside for a few miles.' No one seemed in the least surprised that he was directing operations and none objected.

'Not at all.' The parson clambered up on the roof

beside some of the other outside passengers who had resumed their places, sobered by what had happened.

'Not on your life!' the coachman said. 'I've never ridden inside my own coach afore and I'm not starting now. I'd die of shame.'

'Yes, you are. You are in no fit state to ride on the box. And we are wasting time.' Duncan turned to the young husband. 'If you would not mind giving up your place, Mr. . .?'

'Smith. Tom Smith,' the young man said. 'Of course. . .'

'No!' shrieked his wife. 'No! You must not leave me! You really must not.' She burst into noisy sobs.

'Dearest, it is only for a few miles.' He tried to soothe her, but she would not be pacified.

'I wish I had never come with you. If I had known it was going to be like this, nothing would have induced me to undertake the journey. I want my mama.'

'And how are we to produce your mama, ma'am?' Duncan queried, all but losing patience with her. 'You have your husband, is that not enough? He will be sitting directly above your head.'

'He's not my. . .' She stopped suddenly and looked round at the company all agog. 'Oh.'

'Let him stay with her,' Helen put in quickly before the young lady could make any more revelations. 'I'll ride on top.'

Duncan turned to her. 'Don't be foolish. Ladies do not ride outside.'

'This one does. Come now, you were the one complaining we were wasting time. I shall be quite comfortable.'

'Then you sit on the box beside me. At least I can make sure you do not fall off.'

And so it was arranged, not without much grumbling from the coachman, but as he was in a great deal of pain, he allowed himself to be helped into the coach beside the young couple. The door was tied with a piece of rope, Duncan retrieved Helen's mantle and helped her to climb aboard, guiding her left foot onto the wheel-hub, her right onto the roller-bolt, then left onto a step and the right on the foot-board. She hitched along the seat and he picked up the reins and sprang lightly up beside her.

'Everyone ready?' he called, wrapping the mantle round Helen's shoulders and the coachman's rug about her knees.

'Aye,' came a chorus from behind him.

'Then here we go.' To Helen, he said. 'Hold onto me, if you feel unsafe.'

Slowly they drew away from the scene, over two hours behind schedule.

CHAPTER FOUR

'I AM surprised he did not put up a greater fight,' Helen said, as they proceeded at a walk.

'Who?'

'Mr Gathercole. After all, we had all but been overturned by an amateur and he was scathing in his remarks about them, and yet he allowed you to take over. . .'

Duncan chuckled. 'There are amateurs and amateurs, Miss Sadler. I am well known to the coaching world as a safe pair of hands.'

'You mean you have done what that young ninny did?'

'Run a coach and four off the road? No, Miss Sadler, I have never done that, but I have shared the box with with some of the best coachmen on the road and they have asked me if I were wearing my driving gloves.'

'A hint that they are open to a bribe, I suppose.'

He laughed. 'Yes, but I do believe no one inside the coach has ever been the wiser.'

'Why do you do it?' She watched his brown hands on the reins; he seemed only to need the slightest pressure of one finger, a turn of the wrist or a little flick of the whip and the horses moved unerringly down the road, somehow managing to avoid the worst of the potholes, though they could not help but go through one or two and then Helen had to hang on tight.

'Why? Oh, for the challenge, the exhilaration of

guiding a team of excitable horses down a narrow country lane in a poor light, managing a top-heavy vehicle in a gale, ploughing through snowdrifts, fording swollen streams, turning the whole equipage on a sixpence, bringing everyone safely to the next stage. There is more to driving a four-in-hand than sitting on the box with the ribbons in your hand, Miss Sadler.'

'I am sure there is, so please enlighten me.'

He looked sideways at her, wondering if she were teasing, but she looked perfectly serious. 'First of all, you must know what each horse is doing the whole time. You must be aware if a leader is pulling to one side or if he is too eager, and be able to check him without upsetting the others. And if a wheeler is not pulling his weight, to give a touch of the whip which only he responds to.

'You must decide whether to hold the horses back going downhill or let them have their head, whether to stop and have the shoes put on the back wheels or whether the wheelers can hold the coach without them. You must judge to a whisker how much rein to give on a bend in order to get the wheelers to follow the leaders in a smooth arc without turning too soon. Wheelers sometimes have a habit of taking the commands of the rein to the leader in front and turn too soon if they are not held in check. You have to point your leaders and shoot your wheelers.'

She smiled. 'Whatever does that mean?'

'Well, if the bend is a right-hand one, the leaders have to be pointed into the turn, neither too soon nor too late, the nearside wheeler has to be held back slightly and the off-side wheeler urged on, so as to keep the pole between the leaders. For a left-hand bend it is the opposite. Watch me on this next bend, it

needs only the slightest touch. Put your hands over
mine, if you wish.'

She watched his hands, tanned, sure, capable hands,
but resisted the temptation to do as he suggested,
afraid of the intimacy.

'Go on. Feel how it is done. I shall not mind.'

She reached out and put a gloved hand over each of
his, but she sensed nothing of his driving, only a
quivering sensation passing along her arms and right
down into the pit of her stomach. Hastily she returned
her hands to her lap.

'You must be able to tell the speed you are doing,
even in the dark,' he went on, apparently unaware of
her reaction. 'Seven or eight miles an hour is safe,
though there are times when this is exceeded, going
downhill, for instance, or on a good stretch of road
when it is possible to make up for time lost elsewhere.'

'How did you learn to do it?'

'From one of the best coachmen on the road.' He
laughed suddenly. 'He used to say, "Horses are like
women. Never let them know they are being driven;
don't pull and haul and stick your elbows out. Don't
get flurried, let every horse be at work and handle
their mouths gently, then you might even drive four
young ladies without ever rustling their feathers or
their tempers."'

She smiled at the image he was creating; was he as
good at handling young ladies as he was horses? 'I can
understand that, but surely it is wrong for inexperienced pranksters to attempt it. And the coachmen
should never allow it.'

'No more they should, but some are indulgent and
see it as a way of adding to their income.'

'To put lives at risk for money seems to me to be nothing short of criminal.'

'You intend to report the matter?'

'No, but I fancy the old lady will. She was threatening to sue. Mr Gathercole will lose his job if she does, won't he?'

'Perhaps, but perhaps the Company will do no more than issue a reprimand and fine him.'

'Which he will pay from whatever the young scapegrace gave him and his gratuities. It seems to me they do very well from those, considering they have wages as well.'

'Do you begrudge paying a little extra for your comfort, Miss Sadler?'

'No, but I shall not tip this one.'

He laughed. 'No, I did not think you would. I heard you ringing a peal over him, and that poor sapskull who drove us into the stones. Just like a schoolma'am. Indeed, that is what I think you must be.'

'Then you would be wrong.'

'Oh?' He turned briefly to look down at her. 'What are you then?'

'Nothing. Nobody. I wish you would not give it another thought.'

'You are certainly not a nobody,' he said softly. 'But I think you must like to keep people guessing. Perhaps you are a princess. Yes, a princess, travelling alone and incognito for a dare.'

She laughed suddenly. 'How clever of you to guess.'

He fell silent at what was obviously a put-down, and concentrated on driving. They turned onto a broader, straighter road and he risked a trot. He hated secrets. Ever since Arabella had deceived him, he had found it difficult to trust any woman. And this one was more infuriating than most, managing to parry every enquiry, every light-hearted conjecture, so that he was eaten with curiosity.

But wasn't that what she wanted, for his interest to be aroused, for him to be charmed by her? No one could be so ingenuous and yet so compellingly feline. A kitten, a kitten with claws, that's what she was. Spirited and headstrong, she would be a handful for any man, but a handful a man could rejoice in.

He turned to look at her, sitting beside him, drinking in the air as if it were wine. Wine. She had been funny when tipsy, funny and lovely, and in her shift utterly desirable. It had taken all his resolve to leave her, even for a few hours' sleep. And now she was sitting beside him, not in a stuffy coach but on the narrow wooden seat of the box, in full view of the outside passengers, but private just the same, in a world of their own.

Helen sat upright, enjoying the feel of the cool air on her face, the steady rhythm of the horses' hooves hitting the road, the creak of the carriage. She was so high up, she could see over the hedgerows for miles, could see across the fields where the grazing cows looked up without interest as they passed and the workers in the fields waved them on.

This was good hunting country and away on the horizon, she saw a band of huntsmen galloping after a fox; she glimpsed its red back and tail disappearing into a copse and found herself wishing it would escape. And there a kestrel swooped and then rose with a small creature in its beak. A boat glided down a strip of grey water, its sails filled.

Her nausea was forgotten; she felt alive for the first time for weeks, alive and enchanted by all she saw.

Was that what he meant when he talked about the exhilaration of driving a coach and four?

It was strange how everyone had taken it for granted the Captain would take charge of everything, would sort out the muddle, find a way of getting them going again, would tell the coachman what to do. Being an officer, he had been used to commanding soldiers, but today he had shown he could order civilians too. He had a presence about him which invited trust. She knew she could trust him.

She smiled to herself. It was incredible that, two days before, she had never ridden in a public coach, let alone sat on the box of one. Less than a month before she would not have dreamed of speaking to a man to whom she had not been properly introduced and she would certainly not have dined with him alone. Her reputation would have been in shreds and there could have been only one possible outcome; the man would have been in honour obliged to marry her.

She wondered if the Captain would have succumbed to that kind of pressure and decided he would not. Not that she would ever have allowed herself to be compromised in that way. So what was different now?

Everything, she told herself. She was no longer a member of the *haute monde*, no longer a potential catch for any young blade who fancied his chances, no longer financially independent. She was poor, so poor she had to count every penny she spent, so poor she could not afford a maid. Was it any wonder he took her for a working-class girl, a teacher, a governess, someone to tease with jests about being a princess?

But would his manner be any different if he knew the truth? She would hate it if he began to behave like some of the fops she had known in London, dressed exquisitely, cravat just so, waistcoat dangling with fobs, hair cut and curled in the latest fashion, boots polished until you could see your face in them, pretentious coxcombs looking for heiresses to marry.

It was one of the reasons she had not enjoyed her come-out year, though she would never have upset her parents by saying so, particularly her mother, who had set great store by the proper behaviour. What would she think if she could see her daughter now, thigh to thigh with a man on the box of a stagecoach? The thought made her smile.

He turned towards her briefly and noticed the slight twitch of her lips. 'A penny for your thoughts, princess.'

She was tempted to tell him what she had been thinking, knowing it would make him smile too, but then remembered she was not supposed to be one of the idle rich. 'I fear they are not worth a penny, Captain.'

'Let me judge their worth. Come, tell me what was making you smile.'

'I was remembering the look on that young driver's face when he found himself sitting in a thorn bush,' she invented. 'He was using the most shocking language and most of it to do with his clothes being spoiled. And that when everyone else was in fear of their lives.'

'I do not recall you laughing at the time. I distinctly heard you roasting him.'

'He deserved it.'

'So he did, but I am glad I was not the object of your displeasure. I should be quaking in my shoes.'

'I cannot imagine anything frightening you,' she said. 'Certainly not a helpless woman.'

'Women are never helpless,' he said, as they approached the outskirts of a village and he slowed the horses to a walk. 'They have weapons more terrifying than anything man could invent.'

Before she could reply he drew the coach into the yard of an inn with a creaking sign which proclaimed it to be the Jolly Brewers. 'I think we had best stop here. The wheel must be repaired and our injured people looked after.'

Helen was the curious one now. His comment about women had sounded bitter, so what had made him like that? Had he been badly let down? If so, where and when? He had been very young when he joined his regiment, could it have been someone he met during the war? Portuguese? Spanish? French even, one of the enemy? Or more recently, someone in Paris or Vienna, both places reputedly full of intrigue and romance?

But she could not question him, not only because he would give her a decided put-down for her impertinence, just as she had done to him, but because there was so much activity around them as the outside passengers climbed down from the roof and the young couple emerged from the interior.

A bent old man with wispy ginger hair and a stubbly beard emerged from the inn and hurried towards them. 'I've been expecting you,' he said. 'The coach ahead warned me. I have sent for a doctor. Bring the injured men in. I have a room for them.'

Helen watched as the guard was carried from the coach. He looked very pale and she was afraid the movement of the coach, for all the Captain's care, had not helped his injuries. She turned to help the coachman but he shrugged her off. 'I ain't in need of help, miss, it's my arm that's broke, not my legs. As for travelling inside, give me the box any day.'

'Yes, I am sure,' she said soothingly. 'The Captain did his best not to jolt you too much.'

'Oh, I ain't complaining about the Captain's driving, miss. I know he is a nonpareil of the highest, one of us, you might say. It was lucky he was with us. There ain't many I'd trust with my cattle.'

She looked up to see if the Captain had heard this remark but he was busy talking to the ostler about the horses, which were being unharnessed. 'They will settle given rest and a good long drink,' he was saying. 'The coach needs a wheel repaired; it was lucky it carried us this far.' He helped the ostler lead the horses to the stables and Helen followed the other passengers into the inn.

They discovered the old lady and young Bertie Billingsworth ensconced by the parlour fire, having already had a good meal. They were not talking and Helen sensed that the old lady had spent most of the time castigating the young man and he, resentful, was sulking. As soon as the old lady set eyes on the coachman, she began all over again to grumble and threaten to sue. 'Shaken to bits, I was,' she said. 'I could have had a seizure, I could have died. . .'

Helen bit back the retort she had on her tongue and said, 'Indeed, ma'am, we could all have died. Fortunately no one did, though the guard is injured and must be looked after.'

'That means more delay. I can see it will be Christmas before we arrive.'

'Oh, no!' Young Mrs Smith, who had come into the parlour hanging onto her husband's arm, sat down suddenly on the nearest chair. 'We cannot stay here. Tom, tell them we must proceed at once.'

'But, my love, how can I? The coach has to be repaired and we have no driver or guard.'

She grabbed his hand. 'But we must go on. We must hurry. Find another conveyance. Do something. Surely you do not want us to be overtaken?'

'Of course not, but. . .'

Duncan came into the room at that point. 'I am told the wheel can be given a temporary repair, which will be good enough to take us on to Leicester, where they will be able to fit a new wheel and mend the door. It should be done by late afternoon.' He turned to the landlord. 'If you can provide the ladies with a room in which to rest and refresh themselves. . .'

'I haven't any free rooms,' the man said. 'They must make do with this.'

The room they were in was intended for people coming in to eat while their horses were changed, or while waiting for a connection, and had nothing but a wooden settle against the wall, several hard chairs set about small tables and an armchair by the fire, now occupied by the elderly lady. It was not conducive to comfort and it was certainly not suitable for a lady to change her clothes, which Helen wished to do.

She was very conscious of her ripped petticoat, dangling about her knees under the bombazine of her dress.

'I need to change my clothes,' she told the innkeeper. 'And the young lady is very upset. I think she should lie down for an hour or two.'

'I'm sorry, ma'am, but the bedrooms are all in use and you can't have the best parlour on account of the doctor is in there examining your guard.'

Duncan drew the man to one side, whispered a few words and handed him something which chinked. When he turned back to the ladies, the innkeeper was smiling. 'You can use our bedroom, ladies. My wife will go and prepare it. Please be seated and have some refreshment while you wait.'

Ten minutes later the innkeeper's wife arrived to conduct them upstairs. The old lady declined to accompany them. 'Soft, that's what young chits are nowadays,' she said. 'Always wanting to rest and change their clothes. Why, in my young day, we thought nothing of travelling the full twenty-four hours in the same garments and been fresh as a daisy at the end of it.'

The young lady giggled suddenly, even though a minute before she had been weeping. 'Fresh!' she whispered to Helen. 'I'll wager her fellow passengers kept their distance.'

'If she is right, they would all have been as bad as one another,' Helen murmured, as they left the old lady to her grumbling and climbed the stairs behind the innkeeper's wife to a bedroom at the back of the house.

There had been frantic efforts to tidy it, the quilt had been hastily thrown across the bed and there was still dust on the dressing table where a white garment poked from one of the drawers, but the water in the ewer was fresh and there was soap and clean towels laid on the washstand. Helen's trunk and the young lady's portmanteau stood in the middle of the worn carpet.

'Thank heaven,' Helen said, undoing the hooks and eyes that went down the front of her pelisse robe from neck to hem and revealing the torn petticoat. 'I felt everyone could see my legs.'

The young lady sat on the edge of the bed, watching her, doing nothing to help herself. 'You are very capable, but then I suppose you must be used to looking after yourself.'

'One can become accustomed to anything if one tries hard enough,' Helen said evasively, delving into her trunk for a fresh petticoat.

'I don't think I could. I hate this. I hate the dust, the dirt, not having anyone to help me, not having anything except that old portmanteau. I didn't know what to pack in it. I've never packed in my life before. I've never even undressed myself. . .' She stopped suddenly and her eyes filled with tears. 'Oh, it is so dreadful. And if Tom leaves me. . .'

Helen looked at her in surprise. 'Why should he do that?'

'I made him angry. He said I made him look small in front of the Captain and the others. He admires the Captain, you see. I believe he would like to have travelled on the box with him and I would not let him.'

'He would not leave you for anything so trifling. He seems devoted to you.'

'I wish I could be sure. I am not at all certain I should have undertaken this journey at all. What will everyone say? I had thought I could carry it off, but I can't, I know everyone is staring and talking about us.'

'I collect you saying Mr Smith is not your husband?'

'Did I?' She answered vaguely. 'That just proves I cannot carry it off.'

'An elopement?'

'Yes. You see, everyone has guessed.'

'It doesn't matter what people think they know. It's what you feel about Mr Smith that matters.'

She laughed shakily. 'His name isn't Smith, it's Thurborn. Tom Thurborn. He is from Canada. And my name is Dorothy Carstairs.'

Helen had wondered about the young man's accent. 'Mr Thurborn is a long way from home.'

'That's just what Papa said. He forbade me to see him or speak to him. He said he didn't know anything about his family or background. He said he would not have me affianced to some ne'er-do-well with no money and no prospects who would carry me off to the other side of the world, where I was bound to be miserable.'

Helen could quite see Mr Carstairs's point of view. 'How did you meet Tom?'

'At a ball at the American Embassy in London at the beginning of the season. Papa is a diplomat, you see, and it is my come-out year. Oh, it was such a glittering occasion, with the whole of London Society there. My card was full almost from the first. As soon as I saw Tom, I fell in love with him. He is so handsome, don't you think?'

'Indeed, yes,' Helen said, though the young man was a parrot compared to the Captain's eagle. 'Do go on. I shall respect your confidence.'

'Oh, you don't know the relief of being able to talk to someone who understands. You do understand, don't you?'

'I think so.'

'We danced twice and went into supper together, which made Papa cross because he had almost promised Lord Danminster I should go into supper with him. I think he had already spoken to Papa about offering. I meant to refuse him, even if Tom had not come along. He is thirty if he is a day and fat, too.'

'How old are you, Miss Carstairs?'

'Oh, do call me Dorothy. We are hardly strangers, after all we've been through today. I am seventeen. When I told Papa I could not love a man so old, he said I had been reading too many novels and love had nothing to do with it. Do you not think love between husband and wife is very important, Miss Carstairs.'

'Please call me Helen. Yes, but then I would be considered a little eccentric for saying so.'

'I knew you would understand! Tom and I fell in love from the very first. We both said afterwards we became aware of it at the same moment, halfway through supper. I found myself feeling hot and breathless and he took me onto the terrace because it was cooler. We were not alone, there were any number of other people out there and Tom behaved perfectly properly.

'We talked a great deal, I cannot remember what about, but afterwards he crossed one of the names off my card and waltzed with me. I did not think anyone had noticed, but Papa was furious, he said I had no idea what I was about and Mama agreed with him, though she was nothing like as angry. They forbade me to see Tom again, but I managed to meet him at a friend's house.

'He was angry with Papa for denying us our happiness. He asked him for an interview. I don't know what they said to each other, but Tom left without speaking to me and I was locked in my room for a week afterwards. I was only let out when I promised to be good and obedient.'

'I imagine you were nothing of the sort,' Helen said dryly.

'I had to do something, didn't I? I sent Tom a letter, asking him to meet me in the garden after everyone had gone to bed. Papa saw us from the window and came down in his dressing-gown with a sporting gun. You can't know how frightened I was and thankful he did not use it. Tom bolted over the garden wall. The very next day Papa sent me to our country house in Norfolk. I thought I would never see Tom again and wept all the way.'

'Tom followed you?'

'Yes. He watched the house until he saw my maid, Jenny, coming out and gave her a letter for me.' She sighed. 'It was a beautiful letter, saying how much he loved me, how he could not live without me and if Papa and Mama could not see that, then he would carry me away to be married in secret.'

'So, you decided to elope to Gretna Green?'

'Yes. Tom hired a chaise and waited for me in the lane behind the house. It was still dark when we set off. We had to leave the chaise in Northampton to be picked up by its owner and caught the stage. I thought it would be a wonderful romantic adventure, but everything keeps going wrong. I never imagined coach travel would be like this, crammed into a jolting wooden box with all manner of other people, vulgar people too some of them, and being jostled against them, with hardly room to breathe. People asking questions when it is perfectly obvious you do not wish to talk. And when the coach ran off the road. . .' She shuddered. 'I thought I was going to die for my wickedness, I truly did.'

'We were all very alarmed,' Helen said.

'Tom called me a faint-hearted pudding,' she said. 'He has never been angry with me before. I begin to wonder if he truly loves me at all.'

'We all say things we do not mean when we are under stress,' Helen said. 'I am sure he did not mean to hurt you.'

'I miss Mama and Jenny. I want to go home.' She looked round the ill-furnished room with distaste. 'I half wish Papa would catch up with us.'

'Do you think he will come after you?'

'Yes, but he will be very angry. I do not know which is worse, his anger or Tom's. And if Tom decides he has had enough of me, I will be quite ruined. And I shall have to stay here forever and ever.' And again her eyes filled with tears.

Helen bit off the comment that Dorothy should have thought of that before setting out, and instead offered to help her off with her dress so that she could wash.

'I wish I could remain as calm as you do,' the girl said, as she stepped out of her dress and stood in her petticoat and chemise. 'Nothing seems to upset you. Look how you tended the wounded. I could not have done that, the blood made me feel sick.'

'Most of it belonged to the cow. And truly, I did nothing exceptional. Shall I find you another gown?' She opened Dorothy's portmanteau and pulled out a flimsy lace nightgown, a pair of satin shoes, two petticoats and a round gown of pink gauze with a satin slip in deep rose. It had a very full skirt, caught up with little garlands of silk roses, but it had been rolled up and stuffed into her bag without thought and was so creased as to be unwearable, even if it had been suitable for travelling. 'Is this all you've got?'

'Yes. I told you I had never packed before.'

'Then I will brush this one.' She picked up the worn gown from the floor. 'Have a wash, you will feel better.'

Given something specific to do, Dorothy complied. 'Have you been a lady's maid?' she asked, as she towelled herself.

'Me?' Helen asked, startled. 'Good heavens, no. What gave you that idea?'

'You seem to know exactly what to do.'

'Do I?' she repeated. 'It is only common sense, you know. Think what you would do if you were at home and then do it. Now you would sit and brush your hair, would you not?'

'Jenny would.'

'Yes, of course.' Dorothy was homesick, it did not need a soothsayer to tell that, and thinking of home and what her life used to be like made Helen homesick too. She envied Dorothy having parents who cared for her, who would be worried by her disappearance, who would, she was sure, forgive her and welcome her back into the family fold. For Helen there was no going back, only an uncertain future. She smiled, unwilling to let Dorothy see her misery. 'But if you want me to do it, then you must wait until I have washed and dressed myself.'

'I'm sorry I am so helpless.'

'It is not your fault. But if you are to survive, you must learn to be a little more self-reliant. Is Tom able to provide you with a maid?'

'No, not yet. Later, when we are settled.'

Helen wondered what Tom had told her about his prospects, if anything at all. 'Why don't you both wait for your papa to catch up with you? I am sure he will

understand and forgive you. If you want to marry Tom
after that, I doubt he will put obstacles in your path,
knowing how determined on it you are.'

'Do you think so? Do you really think so?' She
sounded so eager to accept the idea that Helen prayed
she was right.

'Yes.' She helped Dorothy back into her dress and
did the buttons up at the back, glad that she herself
had had the foresight to make sure her dresses were
easy to get into and out of. 'Now you rest on the bed.
I am going downstairs.'

'You will not leave me?'

'No, but do you mind if I tell Captain Blair what
you have told me? I am sure he can be relied upon to
be discreet and he may have some advice to offer.'

'No, but do make him promise not to repeat it.'

Why she had suggested the Captain, Helen did not
know, except that she had come to rely on him. She
wanted confirmation that she had been right to suggest
the young couple should wait for Mr Carstairs and beg
his forgiveness.

She found him in the parlour alone. He was sitting
on the settle under the window and staring out onto
the cobbled yard, deep in thought. 'Captain?'

He started up at the sound of her voice, as if he had
been in another place, another time, listening to voices
she could not hear, seeing people she would never
know. 'Oh, Miss Sadler, I beg your pardon, I was in a
brown study.'

'Fretting at the delay, Captain?'

'Yes, among other things. Did you wish to speak to
me?'

'Yes. I have just come from Miss. . .' She stopped.
'The young lady who has been travelling with us.'

He smiled. 'She has pitched herself into a bumble-bath, hasn't she?'

'Yes. She and the young man, Tom Thurborn she tells me his name is, are eloping.'

'That much was obvious from the first.'

'Oh, do you think so? I did not notice anything amiss until the accident when she admitted he was not her husband. She is in a very excited state and I am quite concerned for her. She is beginning to regret her foolhardiness. I came to ask your advice.'

'My advice, Miss Sadler? What can it possibly have to do with me? Or you, either. They got themselves into this mess and must get themselves out of it.'

'But she is very confused and quite helpless without her maid. I have advised her to wait until her father comes and to beg his forgiveness.'

'Is that what you would do, Miss Sadler? In her shoes, I mean.'

'I do not know. If she really does love the young man. . .'

'*If.* That is the question. It seems to me, she does not know her own mind.'

'I am sure she must do. No young lady would contemplate such an enormous step and risk everything she values, if she were not truly in love. . .'

'Love what is love, but "an abject intercourse between tyrants and slaves"?'

'Oliver Goldsmith,' she said, green eyes twinkling. 'I am familiar with the quotation, but is a bitter comment on life. Surely you are not so cynical?'

'It is what I have come to expect.'

'Then you have been very unfortunate.'

'And you have not? Love has treated you kindly?'

'It has not been unkind. But we are not speaking of

me, but of Tom and Dorothy. It must be truly dreadful when parents refuse to consent to a match when two people are in love. No wonder they eloped.'

'Would you elope, Miss Sadler?' His dark eyes seemed to be burning into hers, trying to make her reveal her innermost secrets, and she knew she would need all her strength to resist. But it had become a kind of deadly serious game between them; him probing, her parrying, asking, refuting, finding out things about each other and scoring points for how difficult or how easy it had been, losing them when the fantasies were exploded.

What made it worse was that there were no rules about telling the truth. Who would be the winner, the one who discovered the most or the one who revealed nothing, the liar or the truth teller?

'Does it take so long to decide?' His voice came to her through her reverie.

'To decide?'

'Whether you, being in love, would ever consider eloping?'

'That is irrelevant.'

He laughed. 'Oh? But do you know, that's what I thought you were doing when I first saw you at the Blue Boar, when you said you wanted the Glasgow coach. I wondered where your lover was.'

'You forget, sir, that there would be no question of my having to elope. I am of no consequence at all, an ordinary young woman, who has to earn her living and who is certainly old enough to make up her own mind on the subject of marriage.'

'How old are you? Nineteen, twenty?'

'Sir, you are very wanting in conduct to ask me that. And we are talking about Tom and Dorothy, not me.'

'I crave pardon,' he said, but there was a twinkle in his eye. 'I can ask a working girl her age, but not a princess. I should have remembered.'

'I am not a princess and it is unkind of you to mock me.'

'Oh but you are. No one but a princess could be so top-lofty.'

'I am not accustomed to. . .' She stopped suddenly. That was exactly what he meant; she was giving herself away all the time. She wished she were a princess then she might pass the whole thing of as a prank—the reason for her journey, her poverty, her obligation to him. She tried again. 'I am not used to dealing with men like you, helpful one minute, hateful the next. It is almost as if you were two men, not one.'

She had done it again; she had turned the conversation right round so that they were talking about him and not her. Two men indeed! But was she right? 'You have brought it on yourself by being so secretive.'

'Why should I satisfy your curiosity? That is all it is, idle curiosity. If you had been a woman, I would have set you down as a gabble-grinder with nothing in your head but gossip.'

'But I am not a woman,' he said, refusing to be offended, though that was what she had intended. 'I am a mere man, with a man's instincts to look after those who are weak and vulnerable.'

'I am neither weak nor vulnerable.'

'I stand corrected.' He laughed aloud, throwing back his dark head so that the long line of his throat showed against the pale lemon of his cravat. He had a mole beneath his chin, she noticed, and felt a sudden urge to reach out and touch it. Then, seriously, 'But you think Miss Carstairs is?'

'Yes.'

'What do you want me to do about it?'

'Talk to Mr Thurborn, find out his intentions. . .'

'I fancy the young lady's papa has already done that and found the answers unsatisfactory.'

'Yes, but you could point out how this escapade is affecting Dorothy, see if a solution can be found.'

'Where is the young man?'

'I saw him in the yard five minutes ago.'

'Very well.' He sighed heavily and stood up. 'Wait here for me. We will talk some more.'

Why had he said that? he asked himself as he strolled out to the yard in search of Tom Thurborn. What did it matter to him whether she was a princess or a servant and why was he so determined to find out? Was it simply curiosity? He had told her to wait for him, though there was nowhere she could go. Would he wait for her if she asked him to? He knew the answer without thinking. He would wait forever, he could never leave her. Princess or pauper, it did not matter.

He shook himself as he crossed the yard to where the young man stood kicking at stones with dusty hessians, watching the ostlers. He was being ridiculous. She was nothing to him, simply a young woman on a coach, amusing herself baiting him. And he was fool enough to fall for it.

Tom looked up at his approach. 'Hallo, Captain. This is a deuced inconvenient business, ain't it?'

'Yes. I fancy more for you than for me. I am told you are expecting to be pursued.'

'How do you know that?'

'Miss Carstairs confided in Miss Sadler, who told me.'

'It is none of your affair, sir.'

'I couldn't agree more,' he said, smiling. 'Unfortunately, Miss Sadler has made it her affair and that means I cannot avoid becoming involved.'

'I cannot think why Dorrie should even mention it.'

'Are you blind? Have you not been aware of Miss Carstairs' distress?'

'Of course, I have. It is the accident, the delay, you know what women are.'

'No, I don't think I do. Do you?'

'Oh, you know what I mean. Dorrie will be as right as ninepence when we are on our way again.'

'You are determined to go through with it, then?'

'Good God, Captain, you surely do not think I would abandon her?'

'She apparently thinks you would.'

'Why? I have never given her the slightest reason to doubt me. I would not. She is everything to me.'

'And yet you took her from her parents and put her through an ordeal which would have strained the stoutest heart. . .'

'Miss Sadler manages very well.'

Duncan smiled. 'Yes, not all young ladies are as practical and self-reliant as Miss Sadler. You cannot measure Miss Carstairs against that young woman. The cases are very different.'

'No, but what else could I do? Her father would have none of me, though I am not the penniless cur he believes me to be. I come from good stock, farmers who left England half a century ago and made good in Canada. Out there, we are in the top one hundred, not quite what it is in England, but well enough. In any case, I have an inheritance in this country, a small estate in Berkshire, I have no intention of uprooting my darling, if she does not wish it.'

'At this moment I believe she wishes she was safe back home.'

'No, I do not believe that.'

'Could she go home if she wanted to? Would there be any reason why she should not go back unmarried?'

'What?' He looked puzzled. 'Oh, you mean. . . No, Captain, I would not harm a hair of her head and I'd kill anyone who tried. She is still the innocent.'

'Then take her back. Speak to her father again, perhaps he will relent.'

'I doubt that.'

'Then enrol the help of the mother. Women understand these affairs of the heart better than men. Let Mrs Carstairs be your advocate.'

'If that is what Dorrie wants, but I must hear it from her own lips.'

'I'll send Miss Carstairs out to you.'

Duncan returned to the inn, leaving Tom to dwell on what he had said, though whether he would take it to heart, he was unsure. Miss Sadler was sitting where he had left her, a slight, downcast figure in unrelieved black, but not dull, by no means dull. She was like a beacon in the wilderness, lighting a path to. . .

He stopped. Where? Where was she going and why? She was frowning a little as if trying to solve a puzzle, and her lips were pursed. Very kissable lips. For one brief moment he allowed himself to imagine what it would be like to kiss her. Behind him he heard the door open and Miss Carstairs came into the room.

Helen looked up and saw them both, the man, dark

and brooding with a half-smile on his lips, the girl, all flounces and eagerness.

'I could not stay on that bed a moment longer,' Dorothy said, sitting down beside Helen. 'I should not have poured the whole story out to you like that, complaining about everything. It is not your fault. It was only the upset of nearly being overturned in the coach and seeing all that blood which made me behave foolishly and caused my doubts about what we were doing. I have no doubts at all. I want to marry Tom as soon as I can. If you can put up with the inconvenience for the one you love, then so can I.'

Duncan drew in his breath audibly making them both turn to look at him. So there was someone. Miss Sadler had confided in the chit that she was going to meet a lover. He should have known. Oh, what a fool he had been!

'Excuse me, ladies,' he said. 'I have arrangements to make for my onward journey.' And with that he turned on his heel and strode from the room, intending to hire a riding horse, or walk on to the next village and see if there was another coach going on, any-where, away from the girl in black with the huge luminous eyes who had made him want to protect her, who frustrated him beyond endurance.

'I must find Tom,' Dorothy said into the heavily laden atmosphere. Helen and the Captain had quarrelled, judging by the thunderous looks he had given them when he stormed out. She hoped it had not been over her and Tom. 'Have you seen him?'

'The Captain was talking to him outside.'

'Will you help me look for him? Oh, I do hope he has not disappeared.'

'Of course he hasn't disappeared,' Helen said, more sharply than she intended. The Captain had been upset about something or why had he left so abruptly, as if he were washing his hands of the whole affair? She knew he had not wanted to be dragged into it, but he had gone off to speak to Mr Thurborn quite happily. What could they have said to each other to have brought about such a change?

And what was that Dorothy had said? 'If you can put up with the inconvenience for the one you love'? Where had she got that idea? But that would not have caused the Captain to take himself off. After all, he had thought she was eloping and that only strengthened his surmise. Why did she wish Dorothy had never said it? Why did it matter so much?

She stood up and followed Dorothy out to the yard where they searched high and low. There was no sign of either man. 'I saw the young one walking down the lane that way,' one of the ostlers said, when Dorothy spoke to him.

'Was he alone?' Helen asked.

'Yes. Gone for a stroll until the coach is ready, I'll be bound.'

But Dorothy did not believe that. She began to wail that Tom had left her and Helen was obliged to put aside her own concerns to comfort her. 'Come back inside, he may be there.' She put her arm about the girl's shoulders and drew her indoors, wondering what she would do if the young man did not turn up. She could not leave her and neither could she afford the expense of extra nights' lodgings waiting for Mr Carstairs to turn up. He might not come or he might miss them.

And now the Captain had gone too, bored with

their game and exasperated by the eloping couple and who could blame him? But without him to guide her, she knew she would be lost, whatever she had told him to the contrary. Two days she had known him, only two days, and yet she already knew that life without him would be bleak indeed.

CHAPTER FIVE

TOM was nowhere to be found inside the inn either and Dorothy became inconsolable, crying loudly enough to have everyone in the building running to see what was wrong. 'Whatever shall I do? Whatever shall I do?'

'Stop weeping all over Miss Sadler, for a start,' Duncan said, pushing his way past the innkeeper, the innkeeper's wife, the old lady and assorted passengers, to her side.

Helen, her arms round Dorothy, looked up to see his tall figure standing over them and breathed a huge sigh of relief and pleasure. He stood looking down at them with a quirky smile; so, she was pleased to see him back, her expressive eyes gave her away. 'Now, tell me, what the matter is this time,' he demanded, doing his best to sound severe.

Dorothy was incoherent and it was left to Helen to explain what had happened. 'I do not know what you said to him,' she said. 'But you seem to have driven him away instead of making him face up to his responsibilities.'

'I did no such thing.' He had got no further than the stable door in his quest for a riding horse, deciding he could not leave her, however much she infuriated him, however many loves she had waiting for her at the end of her journey. At the rate she attracted problems, other people's as well as her own, she would never reach journey's end.

He was torn between his need to get home as soon as possible and wanting to stay and do what he could for her. It was an inclination so strong that to deny it was to deny his inbred sense of chivalry. But there was more to it than that; she held him like a magnet and he could not tear himself away. Yet, if he did not do so, where would it lead? To more heartache, more humiliation? He was gambling with his hard-won peace of mind.

And now, for his pains, he was saddled with not one but two helpless females and his own homecoming was destined to be delayed still further. 'If the foolish muckworm hasn't the ginger to face up to what he has done, it is none of my doing.'

'You are not to speak of Tom like that,' Dorothy cried. 'I love him. He is a good kind man. . .'

'Then where is this good kind man?'

'I do not know.' She dabbed at her eyes with a lace handkerchief. 'But it is all my f-fault. I am not usually such a w-watering pot but I could not h-help it and he was so angry with me. . .'

'You do not seriously think he has abandoned you because you cried?'

'Y-yes. N-no. Oh, I don't know.'

'Merciful heaven, save me from weeping women. It is bad enough having to watch over one helpless female. . .'

'Captain, are you by any chance referring to me?' Helen put in, wishing she had not so readily shown her pleasure at seeing him again. His reference to facing up to what you had done reminded her of her father; the Captain would undoubtedly condemn him out of hand. 'I am not helpless and I do not need watching over. If you have assumed the mantle of my protector, then it was entirely unnecessary. And you are being cruel to Miss Carstairs who is too upset to defend herself.'

'She doesn't need to defend herself when she can get other people to do it for her.'

'And why should I not speak up for her?'

'Because you have enough to do looking after yourself. I never met such a one for getting into scrapes.' The only way he could control the feelings which threatened to run away with him was to keep his sympathy well in check; any sign of weakness and he would be lost.

'And you, sir, are so hard and unfeeling you cannot recognise true distress when it is right under your nose. I fancy you have been too long a soldier. We are not one of your men, to be bullied into submission. I do not know why you came back, if you have nothing helpful to offer. You could have been halfway to wherever you are going by now.'

Oh, why had she said that? Now he would leave and this time he would not come back. Why did she say one thing when she meant another? She wanted him to stay. So why was she behaving so waspishly? It was no longer a game, it was a clash of minds and hearts, a fierce battle and her only defence was in attack and that made matters worse.

'So I could. Is that what you wish?'

She could not truthfully say yes and her pride would not allow her to say no. 'You must please yourself.'

They were so absorbed in their exchange, they had almost forgotten the cause of it, when Dorothy cried out. 'There he is!' and dashed from the room, along the corridor and out into the yard, where Tom had returned and was speaking to one of the ostlers.

The watchers from the window saw her fling herself into his arms, saw him comforting her, talking gently to her, taking both her hands in his and kissing them one by one.

'Oh, what it is to be in love,' Duncan said wryly. 'I think I would sooner have indigestion.'

'Now, Captain, you know you do not mean that,' Helen said, thankful that she could relinquish responsibility for Dorothy to Tom.

'I am not in the habit of saying things I do not mean.'

'Then you are cynical beyond belief.'

'Perhaps I have reason to be.' His dark eyes reflected a remembered pain, but she would not allow herself to feel sympathy.

'If you have suffered at someone else's hands, it is hardly civil of you to belittle other people's feelings,' she said, wishing she understood her own. 'I, for one, am pleased for Miss Carstairs and wish her happy and if you cannot do the same, then you should not have come back. You should have left us to manage.'

'I am not so easy to shake off, Miss Sadler,' he said. 'Nor such a scapegrace as to leave any young lady to her fate, however much she might deserve it.' If he had said it with a smile instead of something approaching a scowl, she might have felt better.

A few minutes later the young couple returned indoors hand in hand to where Duncan and Helen waited. 'It's all right,' Dorothy said. 'He hadn't left me. He just wanted to go away and think about what to do.'

'A trifle late in the day, don't you think?' Duncan murmured. 'The thinking should have been done long ago.'

Tom ignored the jibe. 'We have decided to go on to Derby.'

'I have an aunt there,' Dorothy explained. 'We will go to her and send word to Papa that we are there, then he will come and fetch me. Aunt Sophia will help us to persuade him to let us marry.'

'Recruit the distaff side to your cause, how very clever,' Duncan said, laughing.

Tom coloured but made no comment.

'Oh, I am so happy,' Dorothy said. 'I really shan't mind riding in the coach knowing it is not for long. Papa is sure to bring the carriage.'

'That is a splendid idea,' Helen said. 'Derby is not so very far away.'

'In miles, perhaps not,' Duncan said. 'In time, it is another matter. The coach is not yet repaired and we shall be kicking our heels here for several hours more. We will be lucky to reach Leicester tonight, let alone Derby.'

'Then I, for one, shall go for a walk,' Helen said. 'I need a little exercise.'

'Alone, princess?' queried Duncan, raising one well-shaped brow, making the scar on his forehead stand out.

'Dorothy and Mr Thurborn will come too, won't you?' she appealed to the other girl.

'Of course, but surely the Captain. . .?'

'That goes without saying,' Duncan said, with a lopsided grin. 'I don't think I dare let Miss Sadler out of my sight.'

'I should think not, either,' Dorothy said, taking Tom's arm. 'Come, Helen. Captain Blair.'

Duncan chuckled and held out his arm to Helen. 'Come, princess, let us play chaperone to young love.'

There was nothing she could do but lay her fingers on his arm and accompany him from the inn and even that small physical contact was giving her shivers.

'I believe there is a very pleasant park nearby,' Tom said, as they walked. 'I glimpsed it while I was out earlier.'

'Wistow Hall,' Duncan said. 'During the Civil War, its owner, Sir Richard Halford, was host to Charles I before the Battle of Naseby. I believe it belongs to Sir Henry Halford now.'

'Isn't he one of the Royal physicians?' Helen asked, and could have bitten off her tongue. She had made up her mind not to mention anything which could connect her with London Society, even if any well-read young lady could have known about it.

'Yes. He treated the late King and I believe the present one. Wellington and Pitt too.'

'Do you think he is at home?' The last thing she wanted was to meet anyone who might have known her father.

'It is doubtful.' Detecting the slight concern in her voice he turned to look down at her, but all he could see was the brim of her black bonnet, a wisp of curl and a pert little nose. 'Are you afraid of meeting him?'

'No, why should I be?' She laughed a little unsteadily. 'But I should hate to be accused of trespass.'

'Then we will avoid the gentleman's residence.' He pointed to a lane to the left, running through a spinney. 'This looks a pleasant little byway. Shall we take it and see where it leads?'

It led, they discovered, to a tiny village with a quaint little church and a handsome manor house. Having admired both, they resumed their walk, turning south along the bank of a river.

'How peaceful it all is,' Helen said. 'It is difficult to imagine it was the scene of a great battle.'

'The battle was a little to the south,' Duncan said. 'But I can imagine the countryside would have been filled with troops, horses and pikemen, supply wagons and hospital carts being marshalled to their positions, trampling down the crops, taking over farmhouses and buildings.'

'It must have been dreadful for those who lived in their path, whichever side they favoured,' Helen said.

'War is always terrible,' he went on. 'But civil war especially so, neighbour fighting neighbour, brother against brother, son opposing father. I am glad I did not live in those times.'

'Would you have opposed your father?'

'One opposes my father at one's peril,' he said, somewhat caustically.

'Oh.' He was evidently speaking from experience and she wondered just what he had done to displease his father. Had he formed an unsuitable attachment or refused to obey him in some other way? Had he been banished? Was that why he had been so long a soldier? She would have liked to ask him, but knew he would not welcome her questions any more than she wished for his.

'I fought for King and country, Miss Sadler, not in a Civil War,' he said. 'Being a second son, it was expected of me.'

'How hard it is always to do what is expected of one,' she said softly.

'Yes.' He did not elaborate, leaving her feeling unsatisfied.

'Oh, look!' Dorothy cried, pointing. 'The hunt is out.'

They stood and watched as a band of noisy horse-man hallooed after a pack of hounds in full pursuit of a fox, thoughtlessly flattening a carefully ploughed field and tearing down hedges as they jumped them. Helen, watching them, realised that the damage they were doing was minute compared to what an army would cause, but it was bad enough. 'Tomorrow, some poor labourer will have to plough the field again and mend the hedges,' she said.

'He will not mind that,' Duncan said. 'It is work, after all, and he will be paid.'

'I suppose so, but I abhor wanton destruction, either of crops or animals.'

'Very commendable, but have you ever hunted, Miss Sadler?'

She paused, casting her mind back to happier times, to visits to their country home near Peterborough, before everything had gone so badly wrong. She had hunted with Papa then. She was considered a good horsewoman and had enjoyed the exhilaration but had always been relieved when the fox escaped, but she could not tell him that. A schoolma'am, which is what he thought her to be, would certainly not have hunted. Unwilling to face the cross-examination if she told the truth, she took refuge, once again, in lying. 'No.'

'Then you can know nothing of the excitement of the chase.'

'No, but I have eyes to see.'

'What you see, is not what you feel. To feel some-thing, you must experience it.'

'Is that so?' Had he ever experienced the confusion she was feeling now? She doubted it; he seemed so self-possessed, so iron-hard, and yet she detected a softness he tried hard to disguise.

'Do you ride, Miss Sadler?' he asked, changing the subject abruptly. 'I imagine you must have taken a gentle hack in the park.'

'That pastime is for ladies,' she said, evasively. He was still playing their game of cat and mouse, still probing, and she knew he would counter any reply with more questions. To stave them off, she must divert him. 'I prefer walking, there is time to see so much more. I used often to walk in Hyde Park.'

'I wonder you found the time,' he murmured. 'Being a working girl.'

'I thought Miss Sadler must be a lady's maid,' Dorothy put in. 'But she tells me I was mistaken.'

'Of course you were mistaken,' Duncan retorted. 'Can you not tell she is a princess in disguise?'

'No!' She looked from him to Helen, both of whom were unsmiling, and then laughed. 'You are gammoning me.'

'Of course he is,' Helen said. 'He has a very strange sense of humour.'

'Then if you must earn a living, how do you do it?' It was Dorothy's turn to ask questions and these were not so easy to parry. She could hardly snub her.

'I was a companion to an elderly lady, a widow to a wealthy nabob who had made his fortune in India.' Worse and worse! Not content with being evasive, she was being inventive; until now she would never have believed it possible.

'India?' queried Duncan, his interest aroused. 'Who was she? I have been in India, I might be acquainted with the lady.'

Helen felt the colour flooding her face; being a liar needed more wits and guile than she possessed. 'I do not think so, she was not much in Society,' she said lamely.

'What happened? Did you lose your position?'

'No, she died.' Oh, where was it all going to end? She was falling deeper and deeper into the mire.

If that was the reason for the mourning, Duncan thought it a little excessive unless the old lady were related. 'My condolences, Miss Sadler.'

'It must be dreadful being a companion,' Dorothy said before Helen could find a suitable reply. 'I should hate it, being at the beck and call of an old lady's every whim. "Fetch my wrap." "Read to me." "Make me a drink." No time to yourself at all. . .'

'But Miss Sadler has just said she did have time to walk in the park,' Duncan said pointedly.

'Carrying the old lady's parasol, I'll wager,' Tom put in. 'Going at a snail's pace.'

'She was very good to me,' Helen said, deciding she may as well be hung for a sheep as a lamb. 'She allowed me two half-days off a week when I could please myself what I did.'

'Goodness me, two half-days!' Dorothy exclaimed. 'How fortunate you were. I know someone who is companion to a friend of my mother's, who has no free time at all. She is a poor little thing with no spirit at all.'

'I should think that spirit is the last trait you would need for that occupation,' Duncan said, smiling at Helen. Of all things, she was undoubtedly spirited. 'Would you not agree, Miss Sadler?'

'Not necessarily. If people behave like mice, then they cannot complain if they are treated like mice.'

'But if your bed and board are dependent on doing as you are told. . .'

'Captain, have you never heard of compromise?'

'Naturally I have. One must tread the tightrope, is that not so, Miss Sadler?'

The barb went home and she lapsed into silence. How much had he guessed? Did he know she was lying through her teeth and did not even know why? She supposed it must be her pride driving her. Unhappy and disappointed in her father, penniless, having to pretend to be inferior to Dorothy Carstairs, travelling alone to heaven knew where, she had been forced to call on her pride to sustain her. It was all she had left. Pride. And according to her old nanny, that came before a fall.

How much further could she fall? Were there greater depths? She straightened her back and strode on, so that the others were obliged to quicken their pace, until they came within sight of the inn.

'You have ample time to have a meal before you go,' the innkeeper said, coming from the back regions as they entered the parlour. 'The coach is not yet ready and my wife is the best cook in the county. You will fare better here than in Leicester. It will be late by the time you arrive and all that's left will be scraps.'

Duncan had a fair idea that the old man had told the wheelwright not to hurry over the repair and at any other time he would have roasted him for it and insisted on haste, but this afternoon had been more enjoyable than he had expected it to be and a good meal in the quiet surroundings of this out of the way inn would round it off nicely. He was becoming philosophical about the constant delays; it was fate and it was never a sensible policy to kick against fate. He smiled. 'What do you recommend?'

'The partridge pie is very fine and so is the stew.

Finest scotch beef went into that, Captain. There's oysters too and a roast capon. Syllabub and apple pie to sweeten the taste buds and wine to wash it all down.'

'All of it,' Tom said heartily. 'I am hungry as a hunter.'

Having succeeded in persuading them to stay, the innkeeper set about proving his claim that the cooking was the best in the county, which he did to everyone's satisfaction. It grew dark while they ate and their host lit the lamps, but they hardly noticed, being absorbed in cheerful conversation. Not until they had all declared they could not eat another thing, did he tell them the coach was ready in the yard with the horses, now nicely rested, back in the traces.

Duncan insisted on paying the bill, then left them to oversee the stowing of their luggage and speak to the coachman who, with his broken arm still strapped to his chest, was busy inspecting every inch of the equipage.

'How is the guard?' Duncan asked him.

'Staying here. The doctor said it would be unwise to move him tonight. I'll call for him on the return journey.'

'And you?'

'Middling fair.'

'But not yet able to drive, I'll wager. I'll take us on to Leicester, if you like.'

'I was hoping you might offer, Captain, but I'm not travelling inside again, not nohow. And you'd best wear my spare coat; it'll be cold on the box.' He dragged a heavy buff benjamin out from under the box and handed it to Duncan. 'You may as well look like a coachman.'

Ten minutes later, everyone was back in their seats and Tom, who had purloined the horn from the long basket attached to the side of the guard's seat, blew a tantivy into the night and Duncan, muffled from neck to heels in the big coat, set the horses in motion.

Helen half wished she were still on the box, but then decided it could not be so pleasant in the dark with nothing to see of the countryside and unknown obstacles lurking in the shadows. The glimmer of the lamps on each side of the coach illuminated little more than the backs of the wheelers. Driving an unknown team must be ten times more hazardous at night and she did not envy the Captain.

But then he seemed able to deal with any and every situation that occurred with unerring self-confidence, from petty thieves and amateur whipsters to eloping couples and driving a coach and four, not to mention giving orders to ostlers and innkeepers and making one and all jump to obey. He had been a thoughtful and agreeable travelling companion, when he was not grumbling at her for some misdemeanour or other. He had made an unbearable journey bearable, almost a pleasure.

If he were to leave her, as he almost had at the last inn, she would feel bereft, as if her last ally had deserted her, which was absurd. They were strangers on a journey, thrown together by circumstance, never to meet again. And it was just as well, she told herself, she had lied to prevent him discovering who she really was. It had started as self-preservation, an unwilling-ness to divulge the reason for her journey, to admit that she was ashamed of her father and afraid of the future, but the future had to be faced.

The journey would eventually come to an end. If

Captain Blair was still with her when she reached Glasgow, he would see, perhaps speak to, whoever had been sent by her guardian to meet her and that would mean her deception would be uncovered. She had to make sure they parted before then.

Telling herself it was of no consequence made not the slightest difference; it was as if she had known him all her life, right from the beginning in India, a time she could not remember at all. But that was foolish. He had said his home was in Scotland, not India, though he had admitted he had been there. Why had she been so foolish as to tell that Banbury tale of the nabob's widow?

'There's a nasty bend ahead with a high bank which won't take feather-edging, so don't point the leaders too soon,' Martin Gathercole advised Duncan. 'And you've a couple of steep hills too, so watch what you're at. Don't let them drop to a walk going up or you will lose the horse's draught and when you get to the brow, don't stop to put the chain on; without the guard to do it, it would be asking for trouble. I've known many a coach and four gallop off down a hill without its driver.'

'I can imagine it,' Duncan said, smiling. 'But I shall take your advice and stay on the box.'

'I can get down and put the shoe on if we have to,' Martin went on. 'But I reckon they'll hold well enough and the tackle is good, I checked it particularly before we left. We should make the outskirts of Leicester in about fifty minutes, though we might have to put the drag on going down the last hill.'

Duncan grinned to himself in the darkness, taking the advice in the spirit in which it was given, though he did not need instruction. He had not been boasting to Miss Sadler about his prowess and his eyes were younger than the coachman's; he could see the dark shadow of the trees on the bend. He negotiated it to perfection, eliciting a 'Good turn, Captain,' from the coachman.

Helen, her name was, he had heard Miss Carstairs call her that. Helen, wife of Menelaus. Wasn't she reputed to be the most beautiful woman in the world? She had run away with Paris and caused the ten-year siege of Troy which ended in the destruction of the city. But this Helen would not behave so shamefully, he was sure of that. He chuckled to himself in the darkness, which made his companion turn and look at him in surprise. 'Captain?'

'Nothing. I was pleased with the compliment.'

'And very forward it was of me to utter it.'

'Not at all.'

Helen. How did he know that she would not behave shamefully? He was a fair judge of character when it came to his own sex; he could tell when a trooper could be trusted, by looking in his eyes. He could tell a trickster at the card table simply by his hands. There had been men in his own command he would not have given an inch to, and others among the enemy he would have trusted with his life. But nothing in his experience had led him to believe himself a fair judge of the ladies, whatever their station.

Dorothy Carstairs, for instance. She was a spoiled empty-headed chit, selfishly taking it for granted that everyone would fall in with her wishes, taking and never giving, assuming Miss Sadler would wait upon her. His aversion to the young lady was not based on

anything except her behaviour when confronted with
a situation she had never met before.

Was that how you should judge everyone, by taking
them out of their normal environment and putting
them to the test? In that case, Miss Helen Sadler had
passed with flying colours, because he was convinced
she was not what she said she was. Every incident on
the journey, her behaviour towards the different people they had met on the way, scraps of information
she had let drop into the conversation, had revealed
just a little more of her character, of Helen Sadler, the
woman, a woman of spirit and compassion, culture
and education, but as to how those traits were
acquired, her family and upbringing, not a thing.

He was convinced it was deliberate, but why the
deception? What was she hiding? Shame, dishonesty,
scandal? Such a situation was not new to him. He had
suffered at Arabella's hands. Years ago it had been,
when he was green and trusted everyone, before he
learned that beautiful young ladies could not be relied
on.

He had been home once or twice since then, to visit
his father and brother, Andrew, but he had never
stayed very long and had never strayed onto the
neighbouring estate where he might come across
James, his one-time friend, now Lord Macgowan, or
his lady wife. Such an encounter would be painful and
embarrassing to them both. But now his father had
been taken ill and, according to Andrew, was asking
for him. He had been given leave to come home, but
oh, how slow the journey was proving to be!

He had ridden horseback from Vienna to Calais and
that had been bad enough, then the packet from
France had been delayed by adverse winds and a

terrible storm, which had everyone but the hardiest of sailors sick in their bunks. His horse, which had carried him faithfully for years, had broken free in its terror and been so badly injured he had been obliged to shoot it. He had taken the mail from Dover to London but missed the ongoing mail on which he intended to continue and been obliged to take the slower stage. Ever since then it had been one thing after another.

If he had gone on with the coach instead of staying the night at Northampton, he would have been at least twelve hours ahead, but that would have meant forgoing that delightful meal with Miss Sadler and carrying her up to her bed. He did not regret that for one moment. For the first time for years he had forgotten his avowed antipathy to the female of the species and enjoyed her company; she had been intelligent, funny, naïve. He smiled to himself in the darkness. Fancy wearing all those clothes! Did she imagine they were travelling to the Arctic?

But she had also been clever enough to parry every attempt to find out where she was going and why, and was not in the least over-awed by him. But why should she be? She did not know who he was other than his name and he had no intention of revealing his antecedents and spoiling the rapport they had built up, soldier and lady's companion, nobodies enjoying each other's company for a day or two, even if it was all a sham.

But supposing she did know who he was, supposing it was all a game to her? Many a man had been ensnared by a woman's apparent helplessness; they were not helpless at all, but artful, as he knew to his cost. What had set him thinking along these lines?

Deceit and dishonesty, that was it, and whether Miss Sadler was capable of either.

For the first time since Arabella's betrayal, he was unsure of his judgement. All the evidence told him he was being a fool, that the more he became entangled the more difficult it would be to extricate himself. On the other hand, his curiosity had been aroused; he would not be satisfied until he knew all there was to know about Miss Helen Sadler. But it was more than that, it was the girl herself.

She was as unlike Arabella as it was possible to be. Arabella was fair-haired and blue-eyed, with a rounded figure which he had to admit might become even rounder as she grew older. It was a fashionable figure and she had been a fashionable young lady, dressed in the latest mode, her conversation tempered by the instruction she received from her mama. It was not her fault she could not stand up to the pressure of her parents, he told himself in those early days of his disappointment, but she should have told him, not waited until he came home and found out for himself.

Miss Helen Sadler, on the other hand, was tiny and dark with huge green eyes which looked straight at you, a girl with a mind of her own and who was not afraid of expressing it. What she lacked in stature she made up for in fire; he could not imagine her allowing herself to be coerced into a marriage she did not care for.

'There's no call to go at a snail's pace, you know.' A voice at his elbow broke in on his reverie. 'You'll have the cattle asleep as they walk.'

'Sorry,' he said, flicking the reins alongside the leaders and setting them going at a trot. 'I was thinking.'

'The only thinking you should be doing, Captain, begging your pardon, is what you are about. Once over the next crossroads, you can spring 'em to the top of the next hill. Then you'll be able to see the lights of the town ahead of you.'

Duncan smiled and shouted over his shoulder to his passengers. 'Leicester coming up.'

His answer was a toot on the guard's horn from Tom.

Ten minutes later they drew up at the staging post and everyone tumbled out. Duncan, standing by the coach in true coachman fashion, tipped his hat to each of the passengers and wished them a safe onward journey, not in the least disturbed when he was given a coachman's gratuities, even from the old lady, who was by now so tired that she did not recognise him. Tom, in the spirit of the jest, handed over half a crown, saying, 'Thank you, my good man, a very pleasant ride. I congratulate you.'

'And you?' Duncan asked Helen, speaking softly, his brown eyes looking down into her uptilted face, making her insides quiver. 'Was it a pleasant ride for you?' For a brief moment they held each other's gaze.

'Yes, thank you,' she said then, averting her eyes, delved into her reticule. 'I suppose I had better tip you too, or I shall be labelled a pinchcommons.'

'Oh, indeed you must.' The moment of intimacy was gone like a dandelion seed on the wind.

She gave him a handful of loose change, which he took and sorted out in his palm. 'This will do nicely,' he said selecting a farthing and returning the rest to her. Then he turned and tipped all but the farthing into the coachman's good hand. 'Give this to your guard when you see him next.'

'I will, Captain.' He touched his low-crowned beaver. 'I wish you both a pleasant journey.'

Duncan pealed off the huge coat and handed it back to its owner before offering Helen his arm. She put her hand on it and they walked into the inn behind Tom and Dorothy. The old lady had completed her journey, the parson was making a local connection and the outside passengers were either retiring to their beds or joining another coach which was getting ready to leave.

'Tom and I are going to stay here for the night,' Dorothy said, as they joined them. 'If we go on to Derby now, we shall arrive in the early hours and we cannot wake my aunt up then; it would give her a seizure. Besides, we shall both be tired and not in a fit state to explain ourselves. I want to be fresh when I come face to face with her.'

'That's very wise of you,' Helen said.

'You and the Captain must be in haste to continue your journey,' Tom said. 'So please don't let us delay you. We will manage very well.'

'I could not possibly leave you now,' Helen said. 'I am determined on keeping you company until we reach Derby.'

'You think Miss Carstairs is in need of a chaperone?' Duncan queried, sighing heavily.

'Yes, don't you? It will help her when it comes to telling the story to her aunt if she is able to say she was not alone with Mr Thurborn.'

'So you intend to stay yet another night? Three days on a journey intended to take twenty-four hours. At the rate we are going we shall have to buy the coaching schedules for the whole of Britain.'

'We, Captain Blair? There is no call for you to stay.'

'Goodness, you surely have not quarrelled,' Dorothy said, looking from one to the other.

'No, of course not, but what has that to do with it? What the Captain does is his own affair. We are not travelling together.'

'You're not? But I thought. . .' She stopped in embarrassment.

Duncan laughed. 'Oh, my dear Miss Carstairs, please do not be discomfited. It is perfectly simple. Miss Sadler is determined to look after you, whether you will or no, and I am determined to look after her, even though she maintains she is perfectly able to manage alone. We will, all four, stay here for the rest of the night and journey on together tomorrow morning. I will endeavour to procure rooms.' And with that he sketched a small bow and left them to seek out the innkeeper.

Dorothy smiled conspiratorially at Helen. 'Your secret is safe with us, is it not, Tom?'

'What?' He was busy watching how Captain Blair handled the innkeeper, intending to learn by his example. 'Oh, yes, of course, perfectly safe.'

'My secret?' echoed Helen. How did they know? Had she some time in the past, met Miss Carstairs and forgotten it? But Miss Carstairs had said she thought Helen was a lady's maid; why had she said that if she knew the truth? Was she testing her, trying to find out just how far she would go to deceive?

'Yes. We will not say a word.'

Before Helen could try to explain, Duncan rejoined them. 'There is a room available for the ladies on the first landing,' Duncan said. 'I am afraid you will have to share, I hope you do not mind.'

'Not at all,' Dorothy said.

'I have asked for your baggage to be sent up.'

'Thank you, Captain,' Helen said coolly. 'If you do not mind, I think I will retire. It has been a very long day.'

If she had hoped to be allowed to go to bed and straight to sleep, she was mistaken. Dorothy needed help undressing and she was determined to talk, notwithstanding that Helen was being very quiet.

'Oh, I am so sorry if I put you out of countenance with the Captain,' Dorothy said over her shoulder as Helen stood to undo the buttons on her gown. 'I would not for the world have put you to the blush, but I did not think it was meant to be such a secret.'

'What was?' She was weary beyond imagining, not only from the journey, but from watching every word, playing her little game with Captain Blair and looking after Dorothy, who seemed to have recovered completely from her distress and was now bright and cheerful and anxious to exchange confidences.

'Your elopement. I did not think it mattered mentioning it, considering we are all on the same errand.'

'My elopement?' So the secret Dorothy thought she had uncovered had nothing to do with her identity, after all. But to imagine she was running away to marry was ludicrous. 'My elopement! It is Tom and you who are eloping, not me. . .'

'But you and the Captain. . .'

'Good Heavens! I am quite sure Captain Blair did not tell you that.'

'No, but it is obvious.'

'Not to me it isn't. I do not know the gentleman.'

'Oh, come, Helen, be blowed to that for a Banbury tale. You and he already behave like an old married pair, arguing all the time. . .'

'That is because we do not agree and I am not so pudding-hearted as to let him have it all his own way.'

'That's exactly what I mean.' She stepped out of her gown and rummaged in her luggage for her nightgown. 'I'll say this for you, you are carrying it off with a great deal more aplomb than Tom and me.'

'Once and for all,' Helen said sharply, leaving the girl to tug a brush through her own hair, pulling at the tangles and hurting herself. 'I am not eloping with Captain Blair. He does not even like me. In truth, he does not like women at all; he as good as told me so.'

'Fustian! Anyone with half an eye can see he is in love.'

'Not with me.' She got into bed beside Dorothy. 'Now, if you do not mind, I want to go to sleep.'

But she could not sleep. She was wide awake long after Dorothy's heavy breathing told her that her bedmate was out to the world. Whatever had given Dorothy the idea that Captain Blair was in love with her? He had been chivalrous, to be sure, but that meant nothing more that he had been well brought up to care for the weaker sex and he obviously looked on her as weak and helpless and needing protection.

The trouble was, she did need him. Without him she would have been robbed by everyone with whom she came into contact: coachmen, ostlers, innkeepers, urchins with honest blue eyes. You couldn't call that love, could you? Not only had they met just two days before, but she also knew very little more about him than she had at the beginning and that only what he chose to reveal.

But it was equally true she had not been very open either. She had led him to believe she was a lady's companion, which was not, she decided, the sort of person a captain in the Prince of Wales's Own Hussars would consider as a wife, especially as he had said he was a second son. That usually meant he had come from a titled family. But would such a man be travelling on a public coach without a servant? Had he invented it? But wasn't that exactly what she was doing, pretending to be someone she was not? She really ought to put an end to the pretence, tell him the truth, apologise. But if they were both playing the same game, why apologise, why be the first to admit defeat? Oh, why couldn't he have ridden on into the night, out of her life?

CHAPTER SIX

'MISS SADLER, Miss Sadler, do wake up.'

Helen opened her eyes to see Dorothy sitting on the bed half-dressed. 'Oh, dear, have I overslept?'

'A coach has come in the yard and I heard someone shout it was the Independent for Manchester. That's the one we want, isn't it?'

'I believe so.' Helen scrambled out of bed and hurried to wash and dress. 'We must make haste if we are to have breakfast before we leave.'

They went downstairs to find Tom and the Captain already at the table with food enough for four in front of them, though Tom had evidently only just arrived and was grumbling about his accommodation. 'I had to share a room with half a dozen others all of whom snored in a different key,' he was saying. 'I hardly shut my eyes all night. If it had not been for Miss Sadler, Dorothy and I could have booked a room to ourselves. . .'

'Mr Thurborn!' Helen exclaimed, realising he had not noticed them arrive. 'I do hope I have misunderstood your meaning.'

He looked up and had the grace to look ashamed. 'We would not have shared a bed, I promise you.'

'As the opportunity did not arise, there is no point in wasting conjecture on it,' Duncan said.

'I'll wager you managed a room to yourself,' Tom went on, addressing Duncan. 'You seem to be able to command the best without putting yourself out at all.'

'On the contrary, I chose the stables. Horses do not snore and they are infinitely preferable to sharing with assorted other livestock.'

Helen shuddered, wondering about the bed she and Dorothy had shared, but the sheets had been newly laundered and the blankets clean. She suspected the Captain had made sure of that when ordering the room to be made ready. 'And were you able to sleep?'

'As a soldier I have learned to sleep anywhere whenever I can. Do not give it another thought. Please have some breakfast, we must leave soon.'

The girls had hardly begun to eat when a guard came in and announced that the Independent was about to leave. 'All aboard as is coming aboard,' he called. Reluctantly they prepared to abandon their breakfast and follow the other passengers outside.

'Sit down,' Duncan said. 'Finish your breakfast.' Then, to Helen's amazement, he looked about him to make sure no one was watching, gathered up the cutlery on an adjoining table which was littered with the remains of a half eaten breakfast, and put it into the empty teapot.

The innkeeper, following in the wake of his departing guests, began to clear the tables and suddenly missing the cutlery, set up a hue and cry. 'I've been robbed! Someone has gone off with the silver.' Then to one of the waiters, 'Stop the coach! Stop everyone! No one leaves until I have my belongings back. It's bad enough people walking off without paying, but to take the knives and forks. . . How is a body to make an honest living? You, sir.' He pointed to a burly countryman in a huge topcoat. 'What have you got in your pockets?'

'A kerchief and a purse,' the man said, turning to

go, but his way was blocked by the waiter, who required him to turn out his pockets.

'Eat up,' Duncan told the girls, who were so interested in what was happening they were forgetting to eat. 'The coachman will not let him hold us for long.' Suiting action to words, he calmly resumed his own breakfast, while the furore went on all around them, with the innkeeper accusing and the passengers angrily maintaining their innocence. 'Time to put an end to it,' Duncan said at last, picking up the teapot and shaking it, making a great play of finding something inside it. 'Landlord, is this what you are looking for?' he asked, producing the missing cutlery.

The innkeeper dashed over to him and grabbed the knives and forks, while everyone in the room was convulsed with laughter. 'Someone hid them,' he said, glaring at Duncan. 'Some people never grow up, do they?'

'And some are too quick to accuse,' Duncan said, though how he kept his face straight Helen had no idea. 'Now, if you would be so good as to stand aside, we have a coach waiting for us. Come, Miss Sadler, Miss Carstairs, it is time to go.'

Helen's eyes were so filled with tears of laughter she could hardly see where she was going and they began the next stage of their journey in high good spirits. As there were only the four of them travelling inside, they were far less cramped.

Miss Sadler, so beautiful in repose, was equally attractive when animated, Duncan mused, as they took their seats. She ought to laugh more often. He would make it his business to make her laugh. She should not be grieving for an old lady who doubtless treated her with disdain.

'Mr Gathercole told me some extraordinary tales about his life as a coachman,' he said, deciding to amuse her with a few anecdotes and see if he could make her green eyes sparkle again.

'If the incidents we have met with are any measure, I imagine his life is never dull,' Helen said. 'But he brings his troubles on himself if he allows widgeons to take over the ribbons.'

'Oh, I am inclined to forgive him,' Dorothy put in. 'It brought us together, did it not? Instead of sitting here stiff and silent, we are the best of friends. I would be happy were it not for the thought of confronting Aunt Sophia. I wish. . . No, I could not ask it of you.'

'We are both in haste to reach Scotland,' Duncan said quickly, before Helen could offer to accompany the young lady to her aunt's. 'There has already been too much delay.'

'Yes, of course. I understand how impatient you must be.'

'Captain, you were speaking of Mr Gathercole,' Helen put in quickly to prevent Dorothy explaining how she thought Captain Blair was eloping with her; the young lady evidently preferred to believe her own theory than the truth she had been told. 'Do tell us some of his tales.'

'He told me that a coach was left unattended outside an inn while the coachman and guard went in to lubricate their throats, but the horses apparently knew the importance of keeping to schedule better than their crew. They set off without them at a smart trot. The only outside passenger was a fishwife, who waved her arms at everyone they passed, pointing to the empty box but to no avail, no one could stop them. Thankfully she had the sense not to scream and upset the horses. The inside passengers assumed the coachman was in his usual place on the box and were completely unconcerned.'

'How far did they go?' Helen asked.

'Seven miles. Apparently they negotiated all the hazards on their route, including oncoming traffic, a bridge and a tollgate before coming to a halt outside the next stage dead on time.'

'I do believe you are gammoning us,' Dorothy said. 'The horses must have known there was no one on the box.'

'If they did, they thought nothing of it,' he said. 'When horses cover the same ground day after day, they learn the way blindfold. Some are quite blind, you know, especially those on night runs, where sight is of little significance. There was a one-eyed coachman who boasted that he and his four horses had only one eye between them.'

Helen smiled. 'Ah, but it was the coachman who had the eye.'

'Yes, but horses can be as unpredictable as people, you know. There is another story of a horse dealer who was offered a horse for ten pounds, a price which made him immediately suspicious because it looked as though the animal was worth five and thirty pounds at least. He was promised it was sound in wind and limb and would never kick and so, in spite of his misgivings, he decided to buy it. It was only when the beast was put into harness he discovered he would not budge and nothing would make him do so. Even setting light to straw beneath him did no more than make him jump and throw himself to the ground.'

'I assume your friend turned his whip on the vendor,' Tom said.

'No, for he had been given no warranty. He took the horse down to the canal and persuaded a barge-man to hitch him up with his two horses, but the animal was as recalcitrant as ever. He bucked and reared and threw himself down on his haunches, but the other two simply plodded forward as they had always done, taking no notice of him at all. He tried his tantrums again, but all that happened was that he rolled right off the towpath and into the river. After his wetting he decided to surrender and became a model of a good coach horse.'

'I do believe you are every bit as bad as the coach-men with their Canterbury tales,' Helen said. 'I have heard they like to embroider their stories when they have a gullible audience.'

'Why not, if it helps to enliven a dull journey? It is for the listener to decide whether to believe them or not.'

'Do tell us more, Captain,' Dorothy begged.

'Mr Gathercole is the master, not I,' Duncan said. 'But he did tell me a tale last night about a gentleman who boarded a night coach and wiled away the hours talking to a fur-coated gentleman beside him, only to discover, when dawn came, that his travelling com-panion was a performing bear.'

'Now I know you are teasing us,' Helen said, though she was laughing. 'He must surely have wondered why his fellow passenger never offered a comment of his own.'

'Some people like the sound of their own voices,' he said, pleased that he had succeeded in making her smile again.

'I heard of a coach being attacked by a lioness,' Tom put in, not to be outdone.

'Fustian!' Dorothy said. 'There are no lions in England.'

'Yes, there are! It had escaped from a circus. And there's another tale of two ladies who joined a coach where the only other inside passenger was another lady, but she had unfortunately died on the road an hour or so before. Rather than walk, they shared the coach with the stiffening corpse all the way from Chelmsford to Norwich.'

'Ugh!' Dorothy said. 'I do not wish to hear another word on the subject.'

'Neither do I,' Helen said, as they stopped for a change of horses. 'I have had enough adventures these past two days to last me a lifetime.'

'Then I hope the remainder of your journey is uneventful,' Dorothy said.

'From here to Manchester is plain sailing,' Duncan said. 'After that, who knows? We could have tempests and floods, roads washed away, bridges down.'

'Captain Blair,' Helen said. 'Are you determined on frightening me?'

'I doubt that is possible. Such a staunch and valiant traveller I never met before. I am simply saying we must not be complacent; delay could be serious.'

'I recollect you are in haste,' she said. 'You may rest assured I am entirely in agreement with that.'

'I should think so too,' Dorothy said, almost wistfully. 'I almost wish we were coming too. I am not at all sure of my aunt's reception.'

'I am persuaded she will be perfectly content when you tell her everything,' Helen said. 'How could she be otherwise when she realises how much you love each other?' She heard Duncan give what sounded like a grunt of derision but chose to ignore it. 'And your papa too, when he realises how determined you are. That is the secret, being determined.'

'And you are an authority on the subject?' Duncan interposed. 'You can tell how a father is going to behave over his daughter's disobedience without even meeting him? You know how he will react to determination which he will view as nothing but wilfulness?'

'Oh, you think he will be dreadfully angry, don't you?' Dorothy countered, tears welling in her eyes again. 'Why did you tell Tom to face up to Papa if you believe that?'

He controlled his exasperation with an effort; after all, she was little more than a spoiled child. In some ways she reminded him of Arabella and that was perhaps why he had so little patience with her. He softened his tone. 'Not at all, I was simply pointing out to Miss Sadler she can have no knowledge of how your father will react and she should not pretend she has.'

'And you, sir, are so cynical, it is a wonder you have survived at all,' Helen said. 'You must allow people to have hope. . .'

'Even misplaced hope?'

His quirky smile belied the harshness of his words. His apparent arrogance was at odds with the hurt she could see in his eyes. Helen felt as if she wanted to hit him for his stupidity and hold him to her breast to heal his wounds at one and the same time. Not for the first time she wondered whether there was a woman in his past who had caused the contradictions in his character. Perhaps she was still there, still plaguing him. It was extraordinary how annoyed that thought made her. 'Why not?' she countered. 'Wasn't hope the only thing left in Pandora's box after all the evils of the world had flown out to plague us?'

He smiled and his eyes softened. '*Touché*, Miss Sadler. You must forgive an old grouch who has seen too much of the evil and too little of the good.'

Two minutes later they heard the guard's horn and in another minute drew up at an inn in Derby where the horses were due to be changed and where Tom and Dorothy got down, a little despondent at parting from their new friends and anxious about the future.

'Have no fear,' Helen said, smiling. 'Whatever faces you, it cannot be any worse than what is ahead of me if half the Captain's Banbury tales are true.'

Dorothy laughed, putting a hand up to where Helen's rested on the door. 'In that case, perhaps I am glad I am going no further, but I shall miss you dreadfully. Do write when you are settled, won't you?'

'Yes, of course.'

She moved aside to allow two new inside passengers to board and then stood beside Tom, waving until they were out of sight. Helen turned in her seat and leaned back against the squabs, sorry to part from the young couple. They had acted as a buffer between her and the Captain and now she was bound to be thrown more in his company than ever. And if he started quizzing her again, she would give herself away.

There were ony two other inside passengers, an army sergeant with a curly moustache and a thin little man who looked as though he had not eaten in several days, both of whom were dirty, unshaven and malodorous. They ought to be travelling outside, she mused, but then if they were, she and Captain Blair would be alone in the coach and the thought of that sent her heart racing and the colour flaring in her cheeks.

'I never met such poor beasts,' the sergeant said, nodding towards the horses. Stretching across the little man, he put his head out and shouted up at the coachman, 'Spring 'em, driver. Let's see what they can do.'

Helen felt, rather than saw, the Captain stiffen, but fortunately the driver paid not the least attention and continued at the regulation canter wherever it was possible to do so, but the terrain, though beautiful with gorse-covered moorland and craggy outcrops of rock, did not lend itself to a steady pace. They found themselves dashing down the hills in order to give themselves a good start up the next, with the sergeant shouting encouragement and the little man sitting in the corner with his chin on his chest in brooding silence. He did not seem to be aware of his surroundings but he must have been carefully watching for an opportunity because at one spot when they were reduced to a crawl by the steepness of the gradient, he opened the door and would have flung himself out if the sergeant had not grabbed his coat tail and hauled him back inside, beating him about the head with his fists. 'Oh, no you don't, you little runt,' he said.

'Really, sir, there is no call to attack the poor man like that,' Helen protested, shrugging off the Captain's restraining hand on her arm. 'What has he done to deserve such violent treatment?'

'No one escapes Sergeant Hollocks and lives to tell the tale.' He gave him one or two more blows for good measure and then turned to Duncan. 'Be so good as to hold on to him, sir, while I tie him up. Seems he can't be trusted to behave himself. Promised me he wouldn't cut and run and I was fool enough to take his word.'

The Captain leaned forward and grasped the man's shoulders while the sergeant fetched a rope from his belt and tied the man's hands together and secured them to the door handle. 'That should fix him.'

'What has he done?' Helen asked, feeling sorry for the poor man whose lip and nose were pouring with blood. 'You can't sit there and let him bleed.'

'Beg pardon, ma'am, you ain't about to swoon, are you?' the sergeant asked. 'Look the other way, you'll soon come about.'

'Of course I am not going to faint. I am concerned about your companion.'

'Companion! I would rather have a snake for company.'

'Here, wipe his face,' Duncan said, pulling his cravat from his neck and handing it to the sergeant.

The man complied, none to gently, after which he offered the neckcloth back to its owner. Duncan shook his head, whereupon the blood-soaked muslin was pocketed.

'What do you suppose he has done?' Helen whispered to Duncan, disinclined to risk speaking to the sergeant again.

'He's a deserter,' the sergeant said, before Duncan could venture an answer. 'A runaway, a lily-livered coward, what's disgraced the King's uniform. I'm taking him back to the regiment.'

'Where is that?'

'We're barracked near Manchester.'

'Is that where he deserted?'

'No, sir, he left the field of battle, "deserting in the face of the enemy" it's called.'

'I know what it's called,' Duncan said. 'Which battle?'

'Beg pardon, sir, am I to assume you are a military gentleman?'

'Yes. Captain Blair of the Prince of Wales's Own Hussars. I am presently on leave.'

'Then you, sir, will know the battle. He ran from the field at Waterloo.'

'But goodness, that was over five years ago,' Helen said. 'Surely. . .'

'The army never gives up on deserters, ma'am.'

'What will happen to him?'

'He will be tried and hanged.'

'Hanged! Oh, no, that's too barbaric.'

'You think he should be shot? That's only for officers, not for the likes of this thatchgallows.'

'No, I did not mean that. I do not see why he should die at all. I expect he was afraid and who can blame him for that?'

'Deserting in the middle of a battle is the worst crime a soldier can commit, ma'am. Isn't that so, Captain?'

'Yes.'

'But surely you do not hound a man for five years. . .'

'Please do not argue, my dear,' Duncan said. 'You really do not understand.'

'I understand cruelty and injustice.' She turned to the little man who had been looking from one to the other, saying nothing on his own behalf. 'Tell me what happened.'

'My dear, I really do not think you want to know about it,' Duncan said.

'Of course I do, or I would not have asked,' she

said, wondering why he had twice called her 'my dear'. She had never given him any indication she would allow such familiarity. She looked across at the sergeant who was grinning as if he were enjoying a secret joke.

'Go on.' He nudged his captive. 'You may tell the Captain's wife your sorry tale, I shan't stop you.'

Helen opened her mouth to deny she was related in any way to the Captain, but stopped when he gripped her arm so tightly she winced. She looked round at him and saw him shake his head imperceptibly. So, he had deliberately given that impression and perhaps he was right. She was a lone female among three soldiers and the Captain was definitely the lesser of two evils, the third being trussed up like a chicken for the oven.

'You do not have to, if you do not wish to talk about it,' she said to the trooper. 'If it is too painful. . .'

'I don't mind tellin' you, ma'am, no one else will listen. I've been a soldier all my life, since I was little more than a nipper and I've been in many a battle, but Waterloo, that was different. I never met the like. Hour after hour of artillery barrage and then the charges. Give old Boney his due, he knew how to direct a battle, ain't that so, Captain?'

'Yes, it was very bad. Wellington had it right when he said it was a close-run thing. We were never so near defeat.'

'As far as I could tell, we were done for,' the soldier went on. 'Everyone round me fell. God knows how I survived. I found myself alone with a whole troop of Boney's cavalry advancing on me. It was fight and be killed or captured or run for me life.'

'And so the little coward ran,' the sergeant put in.

'It weren't like that. I left the sector intending to

join others still fighting but I lost me way. I wandered about the battlefield for hours, but all I could see were dead and dying. I found a road. It was full of people, mostly wounded but there were hundreds of others fleeing on foot or on horseback, whole regiments of them, all going in one direction, so I went too. No one took any notice of me. We ended up in Brussels. I hadn't meant to desert, not then. I walked about the city looking for mates or officers, anyone who could tell me what to do, but there weren't no one. The wounded were being evacuated by barges, so I tied a bandage round me 'ead and joined them and no one stopped me. We went to Antwerp and got on a hospital ship. When we got to London, I slipped off without being stopped and walked all the way home.'

'My goodness, I do not think that was cowardly at all,' Helen said. 'But how were you caught now, so long afterwards?'

'I told my wife I'd been discharged but I couldn't find work and she was forever nagging me, telling me she'd be better off if I was still in the army and I begun to wish that m'self.'

'So you decided to give yourself up?'

'What, and be hanged! I ain't that dicked in the nob. It was just my bad luck the sergeant came from the same town. He was on leave and recognised me. So, here I am.'

'I cannot think you will be punished after such a long time,' Helen said. 'And your story cannot be exceptional. . .'

'What has that to do with the matter?' the sergeant said. 'He knew what he was letting himself in for as soon as he got on that barge in Brussels.'

'Captain. . .' She turned to Duncan for support but

all he said was, 'Let it be, my dear. We are nearing the next stage. Would you like me to fetch you anything, a drink or something to eat?'

'No, thank you.'

They drew up at an inn, the exhausted horses were taken from the traces to be rested and new animals brought forward. Duncan and the sergeant took the opportunity to get down and stretch their legs, leaving Helen facing the prisoner.

'Ma'am, it is terrible uncomfortable sitting like this. I've got cramps and me nose itches. I beg of you to untie me.'

'I cannot do that. What will the sergeant say?'

'He won't dare say anything, you being the Captain's wife. Come on, ma'am, I promise not to run for it and you may tie me up again afterwards.' He grinned suddenly. ''Less, of course, you was to scratch me nose for me.'

The idea of doing that made her shudder. She looked out of the window. The Captain and the sergeant were deep in conversation with the guard, each with a pint pot in their hands. Quickly she moved over to sit beside him and untied his bonds. 'There, hurry up and do what you have to so I can tie you up again. They will be back soon.'

'Sorry, ma'am,' he said, pushing open the door and jumping down. She watched in horror as he disappeared behind a coach house and then reappeared on the road, dashing across it into a copse of trees on the other side. She opened her mouth to shout, then decided to give him a fighting chance and shut it again. But the sergeant, and probably the Captain too, would be furious that she had done nothing to alert them. She got down and walked over to them. 'I have changed my mind about that drink,' she said. 'I should like a glass of water.'

'Very well, but we must be quick.' The Captain took her arm to conduct her into the inn, leaving the guard and the sergeant to continue their conversation and finish their ale. 'I assume you found the man's company distasteful. We should not have left you with him.'

'He is bound up, what harm can he do? I simply did not feel like listening to him any more.'

'No, but you did ask for it.'

'So I did.'

He called to the innkeeper who fetched a glass of water, which she drank quickly. 'I suppose we had better return to the coach.'

'Yes. At least they are only going as far as Manchester. . .' He stopped when he heard the sergeant shout. 'Something has happened.' Leaving her to make her own way, he raced back to the coach.

Helen walked more slowly, knowing the cause. When she arrived, she found the sergeant, his face red with fury, insisting that Captain Blair go with him to help fetch the prisoner back. 'You too,' he shouted at the guard and then pointing up at the coachman. 'Wait here, he can't be far away.'

'I've got a schedule to keep, I can't dally around waiting on your pleasure, sir,' the coachman said. 'And I need my guard. You may come or not, as you please.' To Helen he said. 'Madam, be so good as to take your seat.'

Helen found herself wishing she had not been so foolish. Now she would have to go on without the Captain and the thought of all that had happened and might yet happen filled her with alarm. She did not want to be carried away without him. She put a hand on his arm. 'Please. . .'

'I cannot refuse to help,' he said. 'Go on. Wait in Manchester for me. . .'

'Wait?' she echoed in surprise.

'Yes, wait. You will not have to complete your journey alone.'

'Come on, Captain, we are wasting time, and there is no need for your wife to worry,' the sergeant said, before Helen could find a reply. 'The coach is going nowhere without us.'

'If you do not board this instant, it most certainly is,' the coachman said.

'No, for I have the power to hold you until I have caught the man and we can all resume our journey. I am on the King's business and the King's business takes precedence over everything, ain't that so, Captain?'

Duncan was not at all sure the sergeant was correct, but the thought of the lovely Miss Sadler continuing without him and possibly finding herself in more scrapes decided him. He looked up at the coachman, whip and reins in hand. 'I am afraid the sergeant is right, coachman. He can demand assistance and we must accede or find ourselves in trouble with the law.'

Helen heaved a huge sigh of relief as the coachman put down his whip and looped the reins over the back of his seat. 'Hold 'em,' he said to the ostler who stood at the leaders' heads. 'I might as well do my bit to hasten our departure.' With that he clambered down and followed the Captain, the guard and the sergeant into the copse, to the accompaniment of cheers from the outside passengers.

'They've come out onto the field further down,' one

of them shouted after a few minutes. 'No sign of the quarry though.'

'There he is!' One of the others grabbed his arm and pointed.

'Oh yes, I see. Tally ho!' he cried. 'Tally ho!'

'What's happening?' the ostler called up to the outside passengers on behalf of all the people on ground level who could not see above the hedges.

'The hounds are in full pursuit. The cunning fox is dodging them, doubling back into the wood.'

'Now the gentleman is heading him off. He's surrounded.'

'Oh, he's nabbled.' The other man's voice dropped in disappointment. 'I thought he'd give 'em a better run for their money.'

Two minutes later pursuers and pursued returned to the coach, the coachman climbed on the box and took up the reins again, the guard took his place on the back seat and pulled his horn from its basket beside him, Duncan helped Helen into her seat and the sergeant, having tied the deserter more securely than before, got in behind him.

'How did he get hisself undone?' the sergeant demanded as they drew away. 'I reckon he must have been 'elped.' He glared at Helen. 'Anyone aiding and abetting a deserter is breaking the law and could go to prison for a very long time.'

'Sergeant,' Duncan said. 'You forget yourself. Mrs Blair is not to be accused in that impertinent fashion. The man is back in custody, that is all that need concern you.'

'Beggin' your pardon, Captain, but there weren't no way he could ha' got away by hisself.'

'Then look elsewhere for your conspirator. My wife

was with me in the inn at the time, as you yourself know.'

Helen shot him a look of gratitude but his face looked thunderous and she knew he had no illusions about her complicity and was decidedly angry. If she were really his wife, she would be due for a scolding as soon as they were alone. In truth, she did not think the fact that she was not his wife would make the slightest difference to him.

'It weren't the lady's fault, if you didn't tie them knots tight enough,' the soldier said. 'I slipped out o' them m'self and much good did it do me.'

The sergeant gave him a murderous look, but said nothing. The Captain was duty bound to defend his wife, but he knew the truth and so did everyone else. She had shown an uncommon interest in the prisoner, felt sorry for him, that was obvious, so it stood to reason she would help him if she could. If she hadn't been married to the Captain, he'd have roped her in as well.

He sighed and gazed out of the window, wishing they could move a little faster. Why, he had made more miles an hour on the back of a gun carriage in the mountains of Spain. You couldn't call these little bumps mountains, nor even hills, and a coachload of people wasn't any heavier than a gun on its limber. And now it was beginning to rain. What a way to finish his leave! But there might be a reward for bringing a deserter, a few shillings to wet his whistle. He could look forward to that.

Helen, seeing the rain and hearing it beating on the side of the coach, was reminded of the Captain's stories. Perhaps he had not been teasing, in which case she was very glad he was sitting beside her even if he was silent as the grave. His hands were folded and his head was sunk on his chest, a position made easier by the absence of his cravat, but she did not think he was asleep. She had come to think of him as a man who never slept.

Her supposition was born out when he turned his head slightly and she saw his brown eyes regarding her with a faint hint of mockery. She did not know which was worse, his mockery or his anger, or why his good opinion mattered so much to her. But it did and she was dismal over it.

Another two changes of horses, when the sergeant sat and glared at his prisoner, defying him to move so much as a whisker and they arrived at the Bridgewater Arms in Manchester, just as it was getting dusk. Helen, descending ahead of the Captain, found the coachman and guard at their usual place, touching their hat brims to the passengers and apologising for their late arrival. 'We leave you here,' the coachman was saying. 'But no doubt you will make up for lost time on the next stage.'

Helen handed over her usual gratuity with a smile, unwilling to let anyone know that she found the constant tipping onerous. Buying one's ticket was only the beginning of the expenses of travelling; bed and board took a vast amount, and drinks at the shorter stops and the endless tipping were taking their toll of her purse.

The Captain had offered to pay for her on several occasions but the only time she had allowed it was when they had dined with Tom and Dorothy. She was determined not to be under any more obligation to him than she could possibly help, but the further they went the more she depended on him to smooth her path, to alleviate the discomfort of travel, to amuse and enlighten and pull her out of the bumblebaths she was constantly falling into.

She had realised that coach travel might be cramped and cold, that sometimes her fellow travellers would not be congenial, but never had she imagined it would be so packed with incident. She had had one adventure after another and, if it had not been for the Captain's presence, she did not know how she would have managed.

The sergeant disappeared into the darkness with his prisoner while the outside passengers, wet and shivering, were escorted to the bar parlour, where they were assured there was a good fire, leaving Helen and Duncan to make their way into the dining-room. 'I'll see about your room,' he said curtly and disappeared.

So, there were to be no more cosy dinners, no more rapport. She smiled wryly, being his so-called wife was far less agreeable than being a stranger. She was suddenly struck by the thought that he might want to prolong their fictitious relationship; she had given no indication she did not like it. Was he even now arranging a room for a married couple?

She hurried to the door, intending to search out the landlord and make her own arrangements and bumped straight into the Captain at the door. She found herself held firmly in his arms, her head on his broad chest, with her bonnet hanging from its ribbons down her back. She could feel his heartbeat right against her ear, fast and erratic, as if he were gripped by fear or agitation of some kind, though he gave no outward appearance of being anything but calm. 'Princess,' he murmured, making no move to release her. 'Where were you off to in such haste?'

'To see to my trunk.' Her voice was muffled against his kerseymere frockcoat. 'I forgot it again. I didn't want the coach to carry it off.'

She moved her head slightly and found herself looking up at his throat. She saw him swallow hard before he chuckled. 'No, that would have been one more disaster to contend with and I am becoming tired of them. Your baggage is safely in your room.'

'Thank you.' She tilted her head up to see into his face and wished she had not. His soft voice belied his looks; she could tell by the twitching of the muscles in his cheeks and the fierce expression in his brown eyes that he was still angry. Then why were his arms still around her, his thighs pressed against her skirt, making her shiver with something she refused to recognise as desire? 'Are you going to let me go?'

'Let you go?' He sounded puzzled. 'Go where?'

'To my room.'

He released her at once. 'Of course. I have ordered a tray to be taken up. I shall find convivial company in the tap room. There is a game of cards I have a mind to join.'

'Oh, you are going to gamble.'

'Is there any reason why I should not?'

'What you do is no concern of mine,' she said crisply. 'If you choose to lose your money at the gaming tables, that is your affair.'

'Indeed it is.'

'Please excuse me.' And with that she rushed away from him up the stairs. At the top she stopped. Which was her room?

'Number seventeen,' he called after her.

Without answering, she made her way along the corridor until she found the room with her trunk standing in the middle of the floor. She went in and shut the door behind her with a bang, then sat on the edge of the bed, her hands in her lap, staring at the closed door.

It meant nothing to her that he was going to spend the night gambling. It was not her money he was playing with, not her inheritance slipping through his fingers. Would it have made any difference if it were? Would he still take the risk, just as her father had done, just as countless other irresponsible men did to their families every night of the week? Oh, how disappointed she was in him!

It just went to show how foolish it was to make judgements about people you had met only three days before. You could not possibly know what a man was really like in so short a time, and you should never make up your mind that this was a man with whom you would be content to spend the rest of your life. She brought herself up short. What, in God's name, was she thinking about? The rest of her life? They were strangers brought together by unusual circumstances, no more than that. The journey would come to an end and they would say good-bye without any regrets.

No regrets? Oh, there would be regrets in plenty. She had lied to him; their whole conversation had been one enormous hum, a contest of strength with no thought for the outcome. Just when they were getting on so much better, just when they had established a rapport, shaky though it was, she had to go and spoil it all by untying that man and making him angry. He would dislike her all the more if he ever found out the truth. She could not bear that.

She had not fallen in love with him, that was too

outrageous an idea even to contemplate, but she was hurt by his changes in mood, the sudden desire to seek other company, the curt way he had said he was immune to a woman's wiles. As if she had set out to trap him! Oh, he was above everything conceited and she had best put him from her mind, eat her supper and go to bed.

In spite of that conclusion, she could not eat the food on the tray though it looked and smelled delicious. Neither did she do anything to prepare for bed. He might knock on the door before retiring himself, just to say goodnight, and she would sleep all the better if they were not at odds with each other.

She fetched a book from her trunk and settled down to read. But she could not concentrate on the printed page; her whole being was tense, listening to the sounds coming from the room below her where the men were playing cards. There were long silences, followed by gusts of laughter and then murmured conversation and the chink of coins.

The book dropped from her lap, as she sat straining her ears for signs the game was finishing, for cries of goodnight, footsteps coming up the stairs, the gentle knock at the door. She would not let him in, of course, but just to hear him say goodnight was all she wanted. She was so very, very tired.

She heard the clock strike one and then two. Had he even arranged for a room for himself? Was he going to roll into the straw of the stable as dawn lightened the sky? Would he lose? What would that mean to him? Ruin, just as Papa had been ruined? Oh, why did she let it trouble her so much? She stirred herself and stood up to undo her dress. It was nothing to do with her what he did with his life or his money and she was being foolish worrying about him. She finished her toilette and climbed into bed, too weary to think about it any more.

Duncan had intended to play cards, had even had his hand on the door of the taproom, when he thought better of it. He would not have his mind on the game and he would be bound to lose. He was not enough of a gambler to risk that. He went out into the town for a walk. The rain had eased a little but the wind was cold and it was wet underfoot. He was glad of his greatcoat and the good leather hessians he wore. But the air cleared his head. Not that it helped him to come to any conclusions about Miss Helen Sadler.

It had been the height of folly to allow himself to become involved with her, but what else could he have done? He could not have turned his back on her. Their lives seemed to have become intertwined, at least for the duration of the journey, but after that? He did not even know her final destination; all she had said was that it was Scotland and then she had been speaking to their travelling companions, not to him. Almost everything he had discovered about her, he had learned through a third party, as if talking directly to him demeaned her in some way. Was she afraid of him? He did not think that for a minute.

She was a consummate liar, of that he was certain. Her manner was at odds with her supposed station in life and her clothes, though black, were exquisitely cut in the most expensive materials, not what you would expect a lady's companion to wear mourning her employer. She was so spirited and headstrong he wondered why she had not come to a bad end long before. But her apparent innocence was her greatest strength, making people protective of her, as he was. But she wasn't the one needing protection, he was.

She had managed, in the space of three days, to aid a pickpocket, assist in an elopement, set free a deserter and upset the whole schedule of a notable coaching company and, in the process, charm everyone with whom she came into contact, himself included. He had said he was immune but that was far from the truth; he had become ensnared and he would have no peace while she continued to wreak havoc all around, particularly with his heart.

Slowly he made his way back to the inn and up the stairs to his room. Outside her door he paused, then smiled and crept away. Tomorrow was another day.

CHAPTER SEVEN

HELEN dreamed she was sitting at a card table opposite Captain Blair. His features were clear enough though the other two players were hazy; she thought one of them was her father. There was a pile of money and jewels heaped up in the middle of the table. She looked down at her hand. King, knave, ten of hearts. Who had the queen? Dare she risk all on it being the Captain? Could she stand up and walk away? Which was the greatest gamble? She felt a sense of panic, of not being able to breathe, of someone shaking her.

'Miss, the Captain said I was to wake you at five. The coach is due to leave at six.'

Helen opened her eyes, to find herself looking into the face of a chambermaid, only inches from her own. 'The Captain said he thought you would like breakfast in your room, so I've brought it up.' She indicated a tray on the table beside the bed, lit by a lamp she had just placed beside it. 'There's bread and butter and ham and eggs. And a pot of coffee.'

'Thank you.' Helen struggled to sit up. Supper in her room and now breakfast; she felt like a naughty schoolgirl being punished for some misdemeanour, too mischievous to be allowed to eat in the dining-room. Not since she was fourteen had such a punishment been dealt out to her and she could not remember now what she had done to deserve it.

'He said to help you dress and make sure you

weren't late,' the girl went on. 'Very particular, the Captain is.'

'Too particular,' Helen said, throwing back the covers. 'You need not stay, I can manage.' She found her reticule and handed the girl a coin. 'Please ask someone to come in fifteen minutes to take my trunk and bag down.'

'Yes, miss.' The girl bobbed and left, grinning.

As soon as the maid had gone, Helen scrambled from the bed, washed in the hot water which had been brought along with the breakfast and then searched in her trunk for a warm dress. The further north they went, the colder it was likely to become, and she did not want the Captain to misinterpret her shivering.

She pulled out a merino round gown with a fan-shaped silk insert in the bodice front. It had leg o' mutton sleeves and white fur trimming around the hem. With her mantle and ankle boots, she would be warm enough. Having packed her trunk again and fastened the lid, she picked up the tray and carried it down to the dining room.

Captain Blair was sitting at one of the tables, calmly enjoying his breakfast and reading a newspaper, with no sign of the raucous night he had passed in the taproom. He looked wide awake and his clothing was as pristine as it was possible to make it under the circumstances. Although he wore the same coat, he had changed his shirt and put on a brand new cravat. She carried the tray over to where he sat and set it on the table. 'Captain, if I wish to have my meals in solitary splendour then I will request it myself.'

'Good morning, Miss Sadler,' he said, looking up at her angry little face. 'You must have slept well, you are as sharp as ever, I see.'

'I slept tolerably, sir.'

'I am glad to hear it,' he said, deliberately returning his attention to his newspaper.

She sat down opposite him and made a pretence of enjoying the food, though by now the ham and eggs and the coffee had gone cold. 'There is something of import in the paper?'

He put it down. 'Not unless you count the collapse of that idiotic trial.'

'The Queen has been found guilty?'

'No, that farce has degenerated into slapstick. Liverpool moved that the Bill do pass this day six months, which is a parliamentary term for abandoning it.'

'Does that mean she is still Queen and the King has to acknowledge her?'

'In theory, yes, but in practice...' He shrugged. 'It is impossible to make a man love someone he holds in aversion and I doubt he will live with her again. But it does make the succession a problem. While Caroline is Queen, the King will never have another legitimate offspring. It might not have been so bad had Princess Charlotte or her child survived...'

'All that fuss, all those months of accusation, stirring up the most disgusting evidence,' she said. 'All that hate and invective, and nothing has changed. I feel for them both, I truly do. I could never enter into an arranged marriage.'

'Sometimes, there is no choice, *noblesse oblige* and all that.' He smiled suddenly. 'But you are a princess. Is that your problem, a marriage you do not relish?'

'No, certainly not,' she said, deciding not to persist in telling him she was not a princess. He didn't really believe it anyway; it was all a game to him. 'I shall marry whom I please. There is no one to gainsay me.'

'And the poor man who has the misfortune to fall in love with you?' he ventured. 'What of him?'

'There is no such person.'

'No?' he queried softly. 'I'll wager otherwise.'

'Then you would lose your money.'

'Oh, I do not think so.'

'My goodness, how confident you are. But isn't that what gambling is all about, betting on something you can have no knowledge of?'

'There is skill as well as luck involved, Miss Sadler. It comes down to using the information you have to make rational judgements.'

'I collect you were going to play cards last night,' she said. 'Did you win?'

'I almost always win,' he answered evasively, wondering why he did not tell her he had been nowhere near the card table.

'And that attitude is the height of folly. Sooner or later, everyone loses, even you.'

'And you are an authority on the subject of risk, I presume.'

'No, but I abhor gambling. It is the worst of vices.'

'The worst?' He raised one eyebrow at her, a tiny smile playing about his lips. 'I should think pretence and deceit are equally abhorrent. At least, they are to me.'

'Oh.' She looked down at her plate to hide her confusion and shame. He knew she had lied! But he didn't know why. Should she tell him? Should she confess and hope that he would understand and forgive? He did not seem to be in a forgiving mood, judging by his coolness since the episode with the deserter. She allowed the opportunity to pass.

'Do you never gamble, Miss Sadler?' he went on.

'No.'

'Then, pray, what are you doing now? Life is a gamble, Miss Sadler, and yours more than most, and I'll gamble on that too.' He leaned forward the better to look into her eyes and was surprised to see tears glistening on her lashes. He had touched a raw spot and wished he had not teased her. He reached out to her hand but thought better of it and picked up the coffee pot instead.

'You are still angry with me,' she said.

'I would not be so uncivil.'

'Oh, yes, you would. If I am cause for annoyance, why did you stay? You could have gone on.'

'And left you to fall into more scrapes. First it was the young shaver who stole from you and then you must help Dorothy and Tom and yesterday was worst of all. We could both have been in the most serious trouble. You did untie that man, didn't you?'

'I felt sorry for him. And he promised me he would let me tie him up again after he had scratched his nose.'

He suppressed a smile. 'And you believed him!'

'He seemed so honest.'

'Honest? I doubt a single word of what he said was true and even if it were, I hold no brief for him. You can have no idea what it is like to be in the middle of a battle and have to depend for your life on the man either side of you doing his duty and staying firm. Breaking ranks can have disastrous consequences. Courage does not come into it.'

'But have you never been afraid?'

'Often, and any soldier who tells you differently is a liar, but I have never turned my back on my companions.'

'No, I cannot imagine you would, but all men are not so steely.'

'That is not the point, Miss Sadler. The point is that the man was under arrest, being taken back to a court martial, which is not a matter to be treated lightly. What you did was criminal and I would have been the one to be blamed if he had got away.'

'But you were not the one who set him free,' she cried.

'I said you were my wife. I would be held responsible for your actions.'

'But you did not have to let them think that, did you? You could have denied it. We are strangers sharing a coach, that is all.'

'Yes, that is all,' he repeated. 'Strangers on a coach, ships that pass in the night. But when one of those ships looks set to founder, then the other must come to her aid, it is the unwritten law of the sea. Now, eat up, you have twenty minutes before the coach leaves, I would advise you to waste no more time.'

'You do not mean to hide the cutlery again, then?' she queried with a smile, trying to lighten the atmosphere.

'Not today. Those tricks are for schoolgirls. There is none here.'

She put down her cutlery and stood up. 'Excuse me, I have to pay my bill and I believe I heard the coach arrive.'

He rose, inclined his head in a sketchy bow and watched her leave, then he returned to his breakfast and his newspaper, chuckling at the salacious evidence brought by the Queen's accusers. He did not doubt for a minute she was an adulteress, but she knew how to use publicity to her advantage. She was wildly popular wherever she went and even people who had never seen her in their lives, swore her innocence. The poor King had not stood a chance.

Miss Sadler was right, arranged marriages were full of pitfalls. On the other hand, an arranged marriage eliminated the greater hazard of falling in love. He had escaped both, not quite unscathed, but as near as made no matter and he meant to keep that way.

'Anyone for Carlisle?' a voice boomed from the doorway. He looked up to see a guard, muffled in a greatcoat with at least six capes and with a wide brimmed hat pulled firmly down on his brow, indicating the weather outside was no better. 'The Rob Roy is about to depart.'

Duncan rose hurriedly. Where was Miss Sadler? They could not go without her. He strode outside to find she was already in her seat, along with a florid gentleman in a yellow waistcoat, checked trousers and a huge neckcloth; a thin faced man with a wart on the end of his nose; a woman in widow's weeds and a young boy of about twelve who was obviously the woman's son. They were back to the discomfort of six inside passengers. He took his place beside Helen, the grooms stood back from the horses and they were off once more.

The girl beside him was silent, brooding about what he had said no doubt, but then she had asked for it, always sparring with him, causing mayhem. But now the fire had gone from her eyes and she looked tiny and vulnerable. He had not noticed her lack of stature before because of her apparent self-confidence, but now he wanted to take her in his arms, tell her everything would be all right, he would always protect her; she need not look so worried.

'Hartley,' the man in the yellow waistcoat said, leaning forward and offering Duncan his hand. 'I am in cotton, import the stuff from the Americas. Visiting the mills hereabouts.'

'Captain Duncan Blair, Prince of Wales's Own Hussars,' Duncan said, shaking the man's hand. 'I am going home on leave.'

'Where are you bound, Captain?' the widow asked.

'Scotland, ma'am.'

'Oh, then we shall be travelling together until Lancaster.' She leaned forward and smiled at Helen in friendly fashion. 'My name is Mrs Goodman.'

'And mine is Helen Sadler.' What else could she say? Lies were becoming second nature to her now.

'Oh, then you are not. . .' She stopped, looking from Helen to Duncan. 'I am sorry, I thought. . .'

'Unfortunately not,' Duncan said with a smile.

'Oh, I beg your pardon.' This to Helen. 'I would not for the world. . .'

'Oh, please, think no more of it,' Helen said. 'Unhappily I am obliged to travel alone and I am glad to have congenial company.'

Mrs Goodman poked her son in the ribs. 'Say how do you do to Miss Sadlert, Robert.'

He obeyed with a mumble.

'I am very pleased to meet you, Robert,' Helen said.

'You have also recently suffered a bereavement?' Mrs Goodman went on, indicating Helen's black clothes.

'Yes. My father. He died two months ago.'

'Your father?' Duncan queried. 'But I thought. . .'

She turned to him and smiled. 'What was that you said about using the information you have to make rational judgements, Captain?'

'*Touché*, Miss Sadler. But I wish you had told me.'

'Would it have made any difference?'

'Of course it would. May I offer my condolences now?'

'Thank you.'

'And are you also going to Scotland?' Mrs Goodman asked her.

'Yes, I am going to Killearn.'

Killearn! How many more surprises was she going to spring on him? Killearn was his home town. He found himself mentally listing everyone he knew, wondering who might need a companion or a governess, but he could think of no one. It was probably another of her fabrications; perhaps she did know who he was, after all and was baiting him. One day, perhaps, she would surprise him with the truth.

'I have just buried my husband,' Mrs Goodman volunteered. 'I had the boy home for the funeral. I am taking him back to school now.'

'Oh, I am dreadfully sorry.'

'He weren't my father,' the boy said, almost defiantly.

'Father or stepfather, what's the difference?' his mother snapped. 'He brought you up, provided for us.' She smiled at Helen. 'I've buried three husbands now. Robert's father was the first, when I was very young indeed, no more than a child bride.'

'Oh, how dreadful for you,' Helen said, then added hastily, 'losing your husbands like that.'

'Careless, you mean,' Duncan whispered in her ear.

'Yes, indeed.' Mrs Goodman had thankfully not

heard the comment. 'But they left me well provided for.'

Helen heard Duncan mutter, 'And now she'll be looking for a fourth,' and smothered a smile with some difficulty.

'My husband, the last one, died of wounds received last year at Peterloo. You have heard of that, Miss Sadler?'

'Indeed, yes. My condolences, ma'am. Such a dreadful thing to have happened. It was intended as a peaceful demonstration, wasn't it, a meeting to air the grievances of the handloom weavers? I believe they have been very distressed by all the new machinery coming into use.'

Duncan groaned inwardly. This could be contentious, especially with a cotton importer in the coach with them, but Helen never seemed to sense danger. She jumped straight in with both feet and was surprised when she found herself in deep water. And the meeting had ostensibly been about Parliamentary reform, a platform for Orator Hunt.

'That's no reason to start a riot,' Mr Hartley said. 'Workers have to move with the times, it is the only way. Shouting the odds and demanding rights they do not have, is no way to go on.'

'My husband was not one of the rioters, you understand,' Mrs Goodman put in quickly. 'He was simply doing his duty as a militiaman.'

'Oh, I see, one of the law enforcers,' Duncan said with a note of irony in his voice which was not lost on Helen. The militia had been even more enthusiastic at putting down the insurgents than the army itself and there were those who firmly believed the whole episode had been created by *agents provocateurs*. Mr

Goodman, perhaps, or people like Mr Hartley, with an axe to grind?

'Yes,' Mrs Goodman agreed. 'The militia were ordered to charge the mob. There were thousands of them, carrying banners and sticks and suchlike and chanting insults against the troops who were sent to calm them.'

'You were there?' Helen queried. 'You saw the massacre?'

'I was not on the spot, but it could be heard from miles away. If I had been there, I might have prevented Francis being hurt. He was run through with his own sword, taken from him by one of the mob.'

'Oh, I am so sorry,' Helen murmured, realising her mistake. 'I did not mean to distress you.'

'A year he lived afterwards, a year and two months, lying there in his bed, staring at the ceiling, unable to move except the fingers of one hand, unable to speak properly. I nursed him night and day, but he never knew I was there. To me he died that day in August last year, not two weeks ago. It was only the burial of him that was delayed. And no one brought to book over it. They won't be now, of course, he took too long in the dying.'

Helen could hardly say she was sorry again, but what else was there to say? This coachride, besides being a journey into the unknown, was a journey of discovery; so many different people, so many harrowing stories, so much to learn. She was beginning to realise how easy her life had been up to now. She should be thankful for what she had had, the happy childhood, the loving parents, not spend her time blaming her father for deserting her, or being afraid of the future.

'You think I am callous, don't you?' Mrs Goodman went on. 'That I should be weeping behind my veil?'

'I imagine you did all your weeping twelve months ago,' Helen said.

'I did that. It was fortunate Robert was at school most of the time and knew little of it. He is a good boy and very clever, like his father. He was an engineer, you know.'

She went on in like manner for mile after mile, with an occasional comment from Helen and Mr Hartley, while the thin man with the wart on his nose sat in the corner with a small case on his lap and uttered not a word, and Duncan smiled wryly.

Killearn. But where in Killearn? Did it matter? He could hardly go calling on his friends and acquaintances simply for the pleasure of seeing one of their employees, and his father and brother would think he had run mad. Arabella! If memory served him, James and Arabella had a child just the age to begin a little tuition at home. If she were going there...

He stopped his thoughts running back to his hurt. He had been no more than a naïve youth and Arabella had been a childish dream. But when you are very young you do not have the wisdom to see such things in proper perspective; every emotion, high or low, every joy, every hurt is doubly felt, remembered with embarrassment.

But he had put it behind him, made himself get on with a life that was full and interesting, except that he never *quite* trusted himself to fall in love again. He had almost forgotten that early hurt until he met Miss Helen Sadler. But why should meeting her bring it all back? She did not look like Arabella, did not sound like her, certainly did not behave like her.

He glanced out of the window as they slowed over a particularly bad patch of road, so full of ruts they were bounced and bumped about like potatoes in a sack and all conversation ceased while they held on to their seats. Thankfully the rain had ceased, but the potholes were full of water and it was difficult for the coachman to see which holes, being the deepest, were best avoided.

It was no surprise to Duncan when a sudden lurch sent them all sprawling in a heap on top of Mr Hartley and the thin little man in the corner seat. Duncan, who had managed to save himself from joining them, grabbed Helen round the waist and hung onto her until the rocking of the coach stopped and they came to rest.

'God's teeth!' This from Mr Hartley as he scrambled off the little man. 'Are you hurt?'

'No, I do not think so, though my hat is broken.'

Duncan opened the door on the offside and helped Helen to alight. To Robert he said, 'Come on, young shaver, out you come and let me help your mother.' Robert emerged, followed by Mrs Goodman, complaining that she thought her last hour had come, then Mr Hartley and finally the little man and his battered hat. The coachman, the guard and the solitary outside passenger had all descended unhurt and were standing on the nearside verge looking at the back wheel, which was smashed beyond repair.

'Oh, not again!' Helen exclaimed, as she joined them. 'How many more disasters are we to suffer?'

'It's not a disaster,' Duncan said. 'No one is hurt, not even the horses. It is simply a setback.'

'And one I would rather do without,' the coachman said. 'We'll never make Carlisle tonight now.'

'Can it be repaired?' Mrs Goodman asked.

'I've got tools for minor repairs,' the guard said. 'But this ain't minor, not nohow. This is major. A new wheel, no less.' He bent down and examined the underside of the carriage. 'And an axle-tree.'

'And where are we to find those?'

'In Preston. There will be a coachbuilder and wheelwright there.'

'But that is miles away,' Mr Hartley said. 'I have important business to transact, I cannot waste my time, sitting in a broken-down coach counting the hairs in my beard. Something must be done and done at once.'

'Of course something must be done,' the coachman said somewhat irritably. 'And the first thing is to get the vehicle off the road. If we leave it where it is, someone is bound to run into it and then it won't be an axle-tree we'll be needing, but a whole new carriage. And I could do with help, not hindrance.'

The guard and all the passengers, except Helen and Mrs Goodman, heaved at the coach while the coachman, standing at their heads, urged the horses to pull, until it was half-hauled, half-manhandled to the verge and allowed to drop lopsidedly onto its broken axle. 'They might have a spare coach at the next staging post,' the coachman said, unharnessing one of the leaders. 'I'll ride on and see what I can find.' Then to the guard, 'Charlie, you look after our passengers and keep your eye on their belongings. And walk the horses. I'll be back as soon as I can.'

There was nothing for it but to wait and try to keep warm until help arrived. The little man elected to settle down in the lea of the coach with his battered hat on his head and his chin in the turned-up collar of his coat, while the guard released the horses from the traces and began to walk them up and down the road. Robert ran back the way they had come and climbed onto a knoll which gave him a good view of any approaching traffic which might take some of them on.

His mother paced up and down, avoiding the water-filled potholes, accompanied by the outside passenger and Mr Hartley, who found in her a willing listener. Helen, pulling her cloak closely round her, walked up the road a little way, to see what was beyond the group of trees which surrounded them. Duncan, unwilling to let her out of his sight, accompanied her, matching his stride to hers.

The bitterly cold wind whirled her bonnet off and would have taken it away if it had not been securely tied under her chin. It hung down her back on its ribbons and she left it there. Her raven-black hair escaped from its pins and tendrils of it drifted across her face. Her eyes were bright and her cheeks glowing. He had never seen anyone so beautiful, so full of life.

He walked beside her, watching her, watching the way she tipped her head back and lifted her face to the sky, the way she put up a gloved hand to push the hair back, the sudden smile and just as sudden frown, dainty feet picking her way over the rough ground. Everything she did was a delight. And yet, in the back of his mind were doubts, doubts about her, doubts about his own feelings. She had lied, of that he was sure, but what he did not know was why. What was her secret? And did it matter?

'I am truly sorry,' she said, breaking in on his thoughts.

'Sorry, Miss Sadler?'

'Yes. You seem to have appointed yourself my escort and though I did not ask for it, I have been grateful for your kindness. I am sorry I was such a crosspatch this morning, ringing a peal over you because of a game of cards. It was very impertinent of me.'

'It is of no consequence. Think no more of it.'

'But for me you would have been safe home by now.'

'Perhaps,' he said, as they left the trees behind and emerged on a slight hill. The road, empty of traffic except for a farm cart in the distance, wound through moorland dotted with sheep and disappeared below the hill towards a distant hamlet; there was no sign of the returning coachman. 'But just think of the adventures we have had. I would not have missed them for worlds.'

'It is unkind of you to tease me.'

'I am sorry,' he said contritely. 'But you make it so easy.'

She ignored his comment and marched on. He really was insufferable. Why she had bothered to apologise she did not know. The wind was biting through her clothes and she could not stop herself shivering. 'How long do you think the coachman will be?'

'Not long, I hope.' They turned to go back. 'Let's go this way, it is more sheltered.' He took her arm and guided her off the road between the trees where a narrow path wound its way parallel to the highway. It was not quite so windy there, though they could hear it soughing in the tops of the branches. They walked side by side without speaking, their feet scuffling the fallen leaves.

She could not understand him; the two sides to his nature were so at odds. He was a perfect escort, except for the fact that he was obviously acting against his will. He wanted to be riding on and rid of her, and yet he stayed glued to her side. He had spoken of duty, was that how he saw it? But why? Strangers on a coach, they had agreed on that. He had no duty towards her and she had no obligation to be grateful. It would be the same with the Earl of Strathrowan when she arrived in Killearn. When she arrived. *If* she arrived.

Busy with her thoughts, she failed to see the tree root sticking up in her path and stumbled over it. She put out her hands to save herself but she was not allowed to fall; the Captain caught her in his arms almost before she knew it had happened. He stood there, his arms about her, feeling her body shaking, like a tiny bird trapped in a net. 'Helen.' His voice was hoarse.

Hearing him say her name, she tipped her face up to his. The brittle look had gone from his eyes and the hard line of his jaw had softened; it was as if she saw him through a haze. For the first time she glimpsed the man beneath the shell. He bent his head and put his lips to hers, softly at first, then more urgently.

Somewhere in the depths of her being something stirred, something new and exciting which filled her whole body with a tingling sensation which spread from her arms down to her stomach and thighs. It was both exhilarating and weakening, so that she could hardly support herself. She pressed herself closer, allowing the kiss to deepen, opening her mouth to his, tasting the essence of the man, clinging to him with her hands about his neck. The wind took their hair and intertwined it about their faces, her cloak blew across his thighs, making them a single being, alone among the leafless trees.

How long she would have allowed it to go on, she would never know because a voice, loud and insistent, brought her suddenly to her senses. 'Captain! Miss Sadler! Where are you?'

She sprang away, scarlet with embarrassment. He did not move. She turned and ran, darting out of his sight among the trees, towards the sound of Robert's voice.

Duncan stood and watched her go, cursing himself. Just as he thought he was making headway, he had spoiled it all with that impulsive kiss. He would have to behave more circumspectly than that if he wanted to win her in the end. He pulled himself up short, wondering exactly what he meant by that. Did he mean to enjoy her charms as one would a mistress or make her his wife? He could not believe he had had either thought in his head.

Lady's maid or governess, she was hardly the sort of wife of whom his family would approve and she was far too young to make a satisfactory mistress. Had she known what she was doing to him? Was she the little innocent or a woman who knew exactly what she was about? 'Damnation!' he muttered, following more slowly.

Helen stopped her headlong flight. She could not dash into the company like a frightened rabbit; they would know instantly that something had occurred. How could she have been so wanton as to allow it to happen? She had trusted him and where had that trust led her? Down into the depths.

How could she have been so wrong about a man? She had thought he was dependable and kind, when all the time he was a philanderer and gambler. He had taken her for a simpleton the moment he she had asked for his help at the Blue Boar in London and ever since then had been playing with her as a cat plays with a mouse, waiting for his chance to catch her unawares. And, oh, how he had succeeded!

'Miss Sadler.' Robert appeared through the trees. 'Mama sent me to find you. The coachman has returned. Did you not hear him?'

'No.' She managed a smile, settling her bonnet back on her head and pushing her hair up under it. 'I expect the wind drowned the sound of the horse's hooves.'

'Where is Captain Blair?'

'Captain Blair?' She swallowed hard. 'I have not seen him for some time.'

'I'll go and look for him, if you like.'

'Yes, do. The sooner we are away, the sooner I shall be pleased.' And if Captain Blair had managed to get himself lost and they left without him, she would be even more pleased. How was she going to endure the rest of the journey, sitting beside him, pretending nothing had happened, she did not know. Robert darted off, calling the Captain's name and she made her way slowly back to the coach, trying desperately to compose herself and behave naturally.

Beside the broken-down coach stood another, which hardly looked in better shape except that it had four wheels. It was very small and its paintwork was scuffed and old leather curtains hung in the windows instead of glass. There was no rail on the roof for the outside passengers. Two old horses stood in the traces. The guard was busy transferring their luggage, some of which had to be strapped onto the roof. Helen stood and stared at it.

'It's all I could find,' the coachman said apologetically. 'But it will carry us to the next village.'

The little man rose from behind the broken coach and climbed inside without speaking, settling himself in the corner as if he had changed coaches at a normal stopping place. Mr Hartley, who had struck up a rapid rapport with Mrs Goodman, took her arm. 'Come, my dear, let me help you up.'

'Where is Robert?' she asked, looking about her.

'He has gone to look for Captain Blair,' Helen said, surprised that her voice sounded perfectly normal. 'They will be here directly.'

Almost before she had finished speaking, Duncan and Robert appeared and Mrs Goodman climbed in, followed by Helen. It was cramped and there was no room for anyone else. Momentarily she wondered if the Captain might be left behind, which would have served him right, but quickly realised that was unlikely. She sat there, staring straight ahead, wishing they could be on their way and this dreadful journey over and done with.

The whole thing was a nightmare, it must be. Soon she would wake to find herself in London, safe in her own bed with Daisy hovering over her with hot water, and the sun shining in the window and her father downstairs sitting over his breakfast without a care in the world. And later she would go shopping and buy a new gown, something light and frivolous, not this dreary black. Black was for mourning.

She pinched herself hard and knew it was no dream; she really was sitting in a battered old coach surrounded by strange people, not least a man who thought it was perfectly permissible to grab hold of her and kiss her without so much as a by-your-leave.

'Ah, there you are, Captain,' the coachman said. 'Will you ride one of the spare horses?'

'It will be a pleasure.' Duncan said, looking at Helen, who was busy rolling up the leather blind to let some light into the coach. A little smile played about his lips. The ghost of Arabella had been well and truly laid to rest, Miss Helen Sadler had seen to that. She noticed the smile and turned her head away. He was laughing at her, laughing at her naïvety, at the easy way he had conquered her. It increased her fury, not only with him, but with herself for her weakness.

'If you would ride the leader, Captain, Charlie can ride one of the wheelers and lead the other.' The coachman's voice seemed loud in her ears, interrupting her jumbled thinking.

'Yes, of course,' Duncan said, taking the bridle of one of the horses, while the guard mounted another and took up the reins of the third.

'You sit on the box beside me, young shaver,' the coachman said to Robert, much to the boy's delight, and then to the solitary outside passenger. 'If you sit close behind and hang onto the back of the box, you'll be right as ninepence.'

It was soon arranged to everyone's satisfaction and they set off at a shambling gait which suited the two old horses, who were more used to pulling farm carts than coaches. At least, Helen thought, she did not have to sit beside Captain Blair.

It was getting dusk as they drew into a yard where chickens flew up squawking at their approach and where a solitary coach lamp hung at the door. An old man hurried out towards them, a huge grin on his face. It was evident as soon as the passengers alighted that here was not a coaching inn. 'What have you brought us to, coachman?' Mrs Goodman demanded. 'This is nothing but a hedge tavern. Can we not go on to something a little more agreeable?'

'Sorry, ma'am, but this is where the coach and horses belong and they have to be returned.'

'So what are we to do?' Mrs Goodman looked from Mr Hartley to the Captain. 'We surely cannot all stay here. It looks a dreadful place.'

'It's better than the roadside, ma'am,' Duncan said. 'And I am sure we shall be made welcome.' They would be welcome, there was no doubt. How often did a coachload of people arrive on this particular doorstep with no alternative but to accept its hospitality? He strode over to the door, ducking his head under its low lintel. There was only one parlour, low-ceilinged and dingy, the smell of stale tobacco smoke clinging to the air.

He went through a door at the other end and found himself in a kitchen, where a fat woman was stationed over a stove stirring something in a pan and a scrawny girl stood at a table cutting up a cabbage. They looked up when his large frame filled the doorway.

'We need food,' he said, laying two sovereigns on the table beside the cabbage. 'The best you can manage. And a bedroom for two ladies.'

'The food you can have,' the fat woman said. 'But we don't have no beds. This ain't an inn.'

'That is evident,' he said. 'But you must have one room with a bed in it.' He put down two more coins which chinked beside the first.

'Only my own, if that's what you had in mind.'

'That will do but clean sheets and blankets, mind you.'

It took the couple and their daughter all of two hours to produce a meal which turned out to be surprisingly good. All the passengers, even the man who travelled outside which was unheard of, dined together around one large table with the tavernkeeper and his wife, a situation which pleased Helen. There was no intimacy with Captain Blair and she could allow the conversation to drift around her without feeling she had to take part.

From now on she would hold her tongue, and no matter how many more untoward incidents occurred, she would stay out of them. Perhaps Captain Blair would then realise he had made a very grave mistake; she was not the sort of woman to fall into his arms at the drop of a hat. But she had, oh, she had, and God forgive her, she had enjoyed it, had wanted it to continue, had felt her insides turn to quivering jelly. There must be something very dissolute in her make-up for that to happen and she must be very wary of it.

Perhaps, when they reached Preston, which was the next town of any size, he would decide he had had enough of her company and ride on. The thought of that filled her with dread. What was the matter with her? Did she want him to stay or to go?

If only there was someone she could confide in, but there was only Mrs Goodman, and somehow Helen did not think she would receive very good advice from that quarter. The lady in question was doing her obvious best to captivate Mr Hartley who seemed not to mind at all, laughing at her jokes and agreeing with everything she said, calling her 'my dear' and beaming at Robert, who had seen it all before and simply scowled back at him. Helen was reminded of the Captain's comment that the good lady would be looking for husband number four and found herself smiling in spite of her anger with him. Unless she missed her guess, number four was already hooked.

Helen and a reluctant Mrs Goodman were the first to break up the party and were shown up to the room under the rafters where the landlord and his fat wife usually slept. Helen was doubtful about the sheets, but their hostess assured her they were freshly laundered, and accepting her word, she undressed and crawled into bed beside Mrs Goodman, hoping fervently that that good lady would draw breath long enough to fall asleep. She need not have worried; without the gentlemen to entertain, she was not in the least interested in conversation and was soon snoring. Helen turned her back on her and stopped her ears and in a little while, exhausted from all that had happened, she fell asleep herself.

A wheelwright arrived next morning in a flat-bottomed cart containing spare wheels, a couple of axle-trees, a hub or two and the tools of his trade. He was taken out to the abandoned coach by the coachman and the guard, riding two of their original horses and leading the other two, long before the passengers woke for their breakfasts. All except Duncan.

While the other three men passengers and Robert had curled up under blankets on the hard floor of the parlour, if such a dismal room could be given that grandiose name, and the landlord and his wife tried to share a settle in the kitchen, he had chosen to sleep in the hayloft above the horses, who being more than usually crowded themselves, snorted and snuffled the whole night long. As soon as dawn crept between the cracks in the wooden slats of the building, he rose and went for a walk to clear his head.

He prayed his father had recovered from his illness, or if not, that it was not as serious as everyone had at first thought. Duncan loved his father, just as he loved his brother and his nephew and niece, but he could no more have left Helen to go to them than take wings and fly. Mind you, he told himself wryly, he wished he could fly, wished he could take Helen Sadler by the hand and whisk her into the sky.

He looked up at the lowering clouds; there was bad weather on the way or he missed his guess and the sooner they left the better. He heard the drum of hooves and the clatter of wheels and returned to the yard to find their old coach, with a spanking new yellow-painted wheel, being loaded with their luggage and the little old tavernkeeper dashing about trying to be helpful but in reality getting in the way of the coachman and guard who were, once again, their professional selves. He joined the other passengers and climbed aboard.

Helen, sitting once again thigh to thigh with Duncan, was acutely aware of his presence beside her. It seemed as though he had been sitting there, her uninvited escort, since the beginning of time instead of just four days. Why didn't he go on? He could long ago have changed to the mail or acquired a horse to ride; either would have been quicker and he had said more than once he was in a hurry.

She felt as if she were doomed to be riding in a coach, mile after mile, stage after stage, flitting from one incident to another, to eternity. It was difficult to think about how it had come about, to remember the lovely old house where she had lived in such comfort, difficult to recall the face of her beloved mother or the father who had decided to end it all.

Nor had she ever seen the place where she was going: could not picture the man she was going to meet, her guardian. It was as if she had no past and no future, flotsam buffeted by life's storms. No wonder she had clung to the lifeline thrown out by Captain Blair. They were strangers at the outset and they were still strangers. She knew nothing whatever about him, except that when he had kissed her she had been able to offer no defence at all and even thinking about it made her burn with shame.

She had an itch in the middle of her back and would dearly have loved to put her hand behind her and given it a good scratch but she could not move without disturbing the man beside her. She tried not to fidget, knowing as the itch moved from one place to another, that she had probably picked up a flea or two and, in spite of herself, smiled. There was a first time for everything, for kisses and for flea bites.

Duncan saw the smile and wondered what had prompted it; only a moment before she had looked on the verge of tears. He knew he had caused her distress and hated himself for it, but he also knew that a public apology would make matters worse. Until he could speak to her alone, he would do better to pretend there was nothing wrong and that was made easier by Robert, who was determined to quiz him, asking if he had ever met Napoleon or the Duke of Wellington and was the King as fat as everyone said he was? Had His Majesty really led a charge at Waterloo?

Duncan humoured him, answering his questions, telling him that if His Majesty imagined he was leading a charge, then who was he to say differently, but he wondered how he had managed to mount the horse because he hadn't been able to do that for years. And not even a King could be in two places at once.

'But you were there, sir?'

'Indeed I was, along with a few thousand others.'

And so it went on until, at last, they arrived in Lancaster where Mrs Goodman and her son were whisked away in Mr Hartley's carriage, which had been sent to meet him. Helen said goodbye and watched them go, with a tired heart. Travelling was like that, bone-shakingly tiring, a time for making new acquaintances whom you never saw again after the journey ended, a time for conversation and for reflection, but not a good time for making decisions; it was too transitory, too unreal. Everything seemed unreal, even the tall shape of Captain Blair with his firm jaw and laughing brown eyes, as he escorted her into the inn as if nothing at all had happened.

CHAPTER EIGHT

THERE was time only for a hasty meal and none at all for conversation and Helen was glad of that; the last thing she wanted was to talk to Captain Blair. He, sensing her mood, made sure she was comfortably seated and some food ordered and then excused himself. She had no idea where he had gone and told herself she did not want to know. An hour later she returned to the coach, to find the wart-nosed man already in his seat, hugging his case on his lap as if he had never moved. His hat with the broken crown was still on his head.

Captain Blair was talking to the coachman at the head of the horses. He seemed to have an easy rapport with everyone, Helen noted, high or low, it seemed to make no difference.

Seeing her, he came over and handed her in without speaking and sat down beside her. She hitched herself as far away from him as she could and stared out of the window so that she did not have to look at him, because looking at him would remind her of that kiss and how it had affected her. The sooner she put it from her mind, the sooner her peace of mind would be restored.

The outside passengers climbed aboard, the coachman did his ritual inspection and they were off again at a canter, trying to make up for lost time. But there seemed to be little hope of that; the further north they went, the worse the weather became with high winds and driving rain and they were soon reduced to a walk. Helen began to wonder how much of the Captain's teasing had been been true and how much invented. She could see nothing from the window, but a curtain of water. The travellers on the roof, she realised, must be suffering dreadfully.

'Captain, could we not ask the coachman to stop and invite some of the outside passengers to come inside?' Her concern for them overcame her reluctance to address the man beside her. 'They must be wet and frozen up there.' Then to the little man. 'You would not object, sir, would you?'

'I doubt the coachman will want to pull up on this incline,' he said, which was as near as he dare go to refusing altogether. 'He will never get the horses going again.'

'Then we could ask him to stop when we get to the top. I think it is shameful for us to sit here in the dry with seats to spare when they are being soaked.'

'It is what they paid for,' he said. 'To ride outside and risk the elements. They may not wish to spend the extra.'

'Goodness, sir, I am not asking you to give up your seat, simply to ask others in out of the wet. Where is your humanity?'

Duncan groaned inwardly. She was at it again, trying to rule other people, imposing her will and not taking kindly to being denied. He could not deny her. There was nothing wrong with her humanity; she had demonstrated it enough in the last four days.

'It is a question of common practice,' the man said. 'Outside passengers are outside passengers and those who choose to travel inside do so because they do not

wish to consort with their inferiors and they pay for
the privilege.'

'I never heard anything so top-lofty.'

'And you, if I may say so, miss, are rag-mannered
and impertinent.'

Duncan who had been enjoying the exchange,
decided it had gone far enough. 'Sir, Miss Sadler asked
out of the goodness of her kind heart, if we might
share the coach with others less fortunate. I think it is
very considerate of her and I, for one, am happy to
comply.'

'But I am not.'

'You, sir, are outnumbered.' And with that he put
his head out of the window and shouted into the teeth
of the gale. 'Coachman, would you be so kind as to
stop a moment?'

The coachman, thinking one of his inside passengers
had been taken ill, pulled the horses up so quickly,
they reared and then shuddered to a halt. 'What's
amiss?'

Duncan opened the door and jumped down.
'Nothing is amiss. Miss Sadler would like to invite two
or three of your outside passengers in out of the wet.
You have no objection, have you?'

'None.' He grinned, though the rain was dripping
off his hat brim and his shoulder cape was soaked.
'You can take pity on me too, if you like.'

Duncan smiled back at him and looked up at the
passengers huddled on the roof. 'You, you and you,'
he said, pointing to a wizened old man in a brown coat
and a felt hat tied on with string, a little old lady
wrapped in a black cloak and a lad of about fourteen
in nothing more than trousers and short jacket who
was shivering so violently he was shaking the vehicle.

'You can ride inside if you've a mind to. Nothing extra to pay.' He turned to the coachman. 'That's right, isn't it, Mr Grinley?'

'It's all the same to me.'

In no time at all the three selected passengers were seated inside, loud in their thanks to the kind gentleman.

'Don't thank me,' he said, as they moved off again. 'Thank the lady.'

'Then I do so with all my heart,' the old man said. 'My wife is fair frozen.'

'Poor dear,' Helen said, removing her mantle. 'Here, you have this, it's warm and dry. I don't need it, truly I don't.' She slipped the old woman's cloak from her shoulders and wrapped the mantle round her, then took the tiny wrinkled hands in her own and rubbed them gently. 'You'll soon be warm again. Such dreadful weather to have to travel in.'

'Yes, and like to get worse,' the man said, rubbing his own gnarled hands up and down his thighs to try and restore some feeling to them. 'It was fair enough, though cold, when we set out yesterday to visit my brother and go to the Preston horse fair, but today its seems that winter has come early. I shouldn't be surprised if it snowed afore the week is out.'

'Poppycock!' exclaimed the man with the wart on his nose. 'It is only a bit of rain.'

'Then I suggest you go and sit on the roof and try it,' Helen snapped, and returned to her task of reviving the old lady.

Duncan, watching her at work, was filled with an aching longing to have her hold his hands like that and look at him with the compassion she was showing the old lady. But to him she was coolly impersonal and it was all his own fault. How to put it right he did not know.

On the hilly roads they needed to change horses more frequently and that was not always easily accomplished; the smooth, practised changeovers of the coaching inns of the south were no more and everything was chaotic, made worse by the weather. Even getting down from the coach and going into an inn for refreshment meant dashing through a downpour. And without her mantle, Helen was cold to the bone by the time they reached Kendal and was glad when she learned the coach was going no further that night.

'It is too dangerous to travel over Shap Fell in the dark,' the guard told them. 'Specially in this weather. We'll set off again as soon as it's light.'

Duncan, afraid that Helen might catch a chill, did what he had done all along, saw to her trunk, arranged for a room for her and ordered a bath and hot water to be taken up to it, though he knew he must draw the line at settling her bill. It was not that he could not afford it, nor that he did not want to pay but simply because she would fly up in the boughs if he suggested it; she had done so on a previous occasion and that was before he had been foolish enough to insult her with that kiss.

'Captain,' she said, summoning all her dignity. 'I am perfectly capable of ordering such things for myself. I wish you would go away.'

'Do you?' he asked softly.

She could not bring herself to look him in the eye. 'Yes.'

'Then I will not burden you with my presence.' He delved into his bag and produced a small jar, handing it to her with a smile. 'Use this after your bath, you may find it efficacious.'

She took it, looking down at it with a puzzled little frown until she realised it contained ointment, guaranteed to kill fleas and soothe their bites, so it said on the label. She was astonished that he had even noticed her discomfort when she had made every effort to hide it and even more surprised that he had diagnosed the trouble. She felt like dashing the jar to the floor and castigating him for his impertinence but the sensible, practical side of her told her it would be foolish. 'Thank you, Captain.'

She turned and climbed the stairs, leaving him to join a crowd of men in the taproom. Let him play cards if he wanted to, what had it to do with her? She was well rid of him.

The room she had been given was large and beautifully furnished, unmarred by a single speck of dust, with pristine linen on the bed, a bath on the rug before a glowing fire filled almost to the brim with steaming water, soap and fluffy towels on the rail by the wash stand. The chambermaid was moving about, making sure everything was just as it should be.

'The gentleman said I was to stay and help you undress, miss,' she said.

If the girl had not mentioned the Captain, Helen would have been grateful for the offer, as it was, she decided he took too much upon himself. 'It was kind of him to think of it,' she said. 'But I can manage very well, thank you.' She found a coin for the girl. 'I should like a tray brought up in half an hour, some soup, I think, and a little chicken and vegetables, whatever you have to hand. And hot chocolate.'

'Very good, miss.' The girl bobbed and went out,

shutting the door carefully behind her. Helen stood and looked about her. It was almost like home, with Daisy in attendance and everything done exactly as she liked it. Would those days ever come again? She sighed and began slowly undressing.

The bath was hot and scented and she sat and soaped herself, examining the bites which had caused so much irritation. She must have caught the fleas at that run-down old tavern, though they could equally well have come from any one of her fellow passengers. It was one of the hazards of travelling by public coach.

Another was meeting people like Captain Blair, handsome, thoughtful, kind and completely unscrupulous. She had never had to deal with men like him before and had no idea how to handle him. He simply refused to be handled. Every put-down was met with a smile which set her quivering as if she hadn't a bone in her body, every attempt at haughty disdain, which was the normal way for a young lady to let it be known a gentleman's attentions were not welcome, was simply ignored. He persisted in helping her, almost as if he had been paid to do so, which, of course, was nonsense.

It would not have been so bad if she had really been as capable and independent as she pretended to be, or even if she had not begun the whole thing by telling a lie. To him she was Miss Sadler, lady's companion, and Miss Sadler she had to remain. To admit to anything else now would just be inviting more mockery. Young ladies who pretended to be what they were not, simply did not deserve to be treated as ladies.

He would never have dared to kiss Miss Sanghurst like that and he would never have had the presumption to offer Miss Sanghurst flea ointment. She smiled suddenly. Miss Sanghurst had every right to be offended, but Miss Sadler had not and Miss Sadler had liked being held so securely in his arms and being kissed. Not that she would ever admit it to him.

She climbed out of the bath and towelled herself dry, before smearing herself with the ointment. She had just taken her nightdress from her small portmanteau and slipped into it when a second maid arrived with her meal on a tray. She found her reticule among the discarded clothes on the bed and fished inside for a sixpence. The girl pocketed it, then dragged the bath out onto the landing, where Helen could hear her shouting down the stairs for someone to help her with it.

Helen guessed the room was the best the inn had to offer and she was sure she had been given it on the Captain's orders, but she wished sometimes, he would not be so careful of her; the best was also the most expensive. She sat on the bed, noticing how soft the mattress was, and tipped out her reticule. The little cascade of coins and paper money was pitifully small, just enough to pay for her night's lodging and a meal later the next day.

She had brought what she thought was sufficient for her needs on the journey, arranging for her next month's allowance to be paid into a bank in Killearn, still many miles, even days, ahead of her. Never before had she been obliged to count her money so carefully and she had not realised how fast it was disappearing.

Her generosity towards the little urchin, whose fare had cost her five shillings; her stubborn insistence on stopping every night, her own fares and tips to the chambermaids and the men who carried her trunk, besides those to the coachmen and guards, had taken every bit of eight pounds on top of the seven pounds' refund she had been given in Northampton.

Everyone who had provided even the smallest service had expected to be paid, and though on several occasions the Captain had offered to stand buff for her, she had refused and must continue to do so. She could not stop him looking after her baggage and giving orders on her behalf—after all, it had made a big difference to her comfort—but the last thing she wanted was to be even more beholden to him. Mr Benstead had written to her guardian asking him to arrange to have her met and she prayed he would fetch her quickly or she would end up penniless.

She went down to the dining-room next morning in good time to enjoy a leisurely breakfast, intending that it would be the last meal she had until they stopped that evening. And then she would travel on through the night to Glasgow. Wondering what her uninvited escort would do about it made her smile. Would he forgo the pleasures of food, bed and the card table to remain glued to her side, or decide to leave her to her own devices? For all she knew, he might already have done so. Perhaps another coachman had not been so faint-hearted about going over the fell in the dark and taken the Captain on. The thought that she might now be completely alone filled her with a kind of panic. There had already been so many hazards and so many pitfalls to catch the unwary, who was to say there would not be more? Uninvited or not, she needed him.

When she saw him at the breakfast table, tucking into ham and eggs, she heaved a huge sigh of relief. Her pride would not let her show it, nor would she deign to sit with him. She moved towards a table on the other side of the room, although she had to pass him on the way.

'Good morning, Miss Sadler.' He greeted her cheerfully, as if he had done nothing wrong at all.

'Good morning.' Her voice was clipped.

He grabbed her hand as she went to pass him. 'Where are you going?'

'To have my breakfast. Over there.'

'Oh, so I am still banished, is that it? I am not to be allowed the pleasure of your company?'

She tried to pull herself from his grasp, but he would not release her. 'Captain Blair, will you please let go of my arm?'

'Yes, if you promise to forgive me for my dreadful lapse and have breakfast with me.'

'I do not see why I should.'

'And I do not see why you should not. I am penitent, as you see.' She saw nothing of the sort but she had ceased to struggle from his grip. 'We have come a long way together and there is still a long way to go and being at odds with each other will not help to pass the time pleasantly.'

He smiled. 'I promise to behave. I will not kiss you again unless you wish it. Come, share my breakfast. There is too much for me and it would be a shame to waste it.'

Pure economics decided her, or at least that is what she told herself it was, as she relented and sat opposite him.

'Good,' he said. 'We have twenty minutes before the coach leaves. Mr Grinley tells me he is not going to risk Shap Fell. Someone arrived during the night with news of a landslide blocking the road, so he has decided to go the longer route through Windermere and Grasmere to Penrith. With luck we should reach Carlisle by nightfall.'

'Carlisle, is that all? I had hoped we might get as far as Glasgow.'

'You are becoming impatient to arrive?'

'Naturally, I am. And I collect you were in haste when we left London. Has that changed?'

'No, but we can only go at the pace conditions allow.'

'And the further we go, the worse they become. I am surprised you did not think of hiring a horse and riding.'

'Oh, I did think of it, but I decided against it.'

'You must be regretting that decision.'

'Not at all,' he said cheerfully. 'I would have missed so much.'

She smiled, choosing to misunderstand him. 'Yes, I had no idea the journey would be so full of incident.'

'More than usually so,' he said with a hint of amusement in his voice. 'But then you must admit that you have been the instigator of most of it.'

'I do not remember ordering the rain, nor a broken wheel, nor. . .' She stopped. She *had* held the coach up while she argued about the boy; she *had* insisted on staying with Tom and Dorothy; she *had* released the deserter. Rain and broken wheels were nothing to that. 'I promise from now on, not to do a single thing to hold us up,' she said.

'Then I suggest you finish your breakfast and pay your reckoning, because I heard the horses being put in the traces and the guard directing the stowage of the baggage.'

She did as he suggested, paid her fare as far as

Carlisle and a few minutes later took her place in the coach, only to discover that she and Captain Blair were the only inside passengers.

'Where are the others?' she asked, looking round in something close to panic.

'Perhaps they did not want to be taken out of their way,' he said. 'Or they thought the road would be cleared soon and they would beat us to it.'

'Do you think they will?'

'No. By all accounts the fall was a big one.'

'Is there no way round it?'

'Not on that stretch of road, it is hazardous at the best of times. No, Mr Grinley is in the right of it.'

Miles and miles to go with no company but the Captain and if he were to try to kiss her again. . . She did not know if she dare go on, but if she stayed and waited for another coach, it would mean more delay and that meant more expense. She was in a cleft stick.

Before she could come to a decision the coachman and driver took their places and, with a toot on the horn, they moved off. Now she would have to sit beside him for hours in silence or try to make polite conversation when all the time they must both be thinking about that kiss. What a simpleton she had been to allow it to happen, but it had felt so right at the time she had not given a thought to the consequences.

But perhaps he would not be thinking of it, perhaps he kissed young women at every available opportunity and forgot it afterwards as of no consequence. Her best plan was to pretend it had never happened.

'There is one advantage of coming this way,' he said, as they headed for Windermere. 'We shall see a little of the Lakes. I think they are one of the most beautiful parts of England, almost to be compared with Scotland for scenery.'

'You know the area?'

'I had an aunt who lived in Grasmere. My brother and I stayed with her occasionally when we were children. She died while I was abroad.' He paused. 'Have you been here before, Miss Sadler?'

'Not I am afraid I have not. I have never travelled further north than Peterborough.'

'The Fens. Very flat round there, I understand.' No wonder she had seemed so bewildered, so ingenuous; it was a new experience for her. It made him admire her all the more for her courage.

'Yes, very different from all these hills, but it has its own charm. You can see for miles and it only seems a stone's throw, and the skies are huge, riven with clouds tinged with pink and mauve. There are a great many waterways too; almost everything is conducted by water.' She laughed suddenly. 'Much easier and smoother than being shaken about in a coach on some of these roads.'

'You do not like hilly country?'

'Oh, yes, in a different way. The light and shade on the grey rocks and the green of the fells as the clouds move across the sun makes it seem they are forever changing. In the Fens the sky is the focal point, here it is the hills.'

'And the Lakes,' he said. 'We shall see Windermere soon.'

She realised suddenly that she was completely at ease with him; her earlier stiffness had gone, as if, having accepted the inevitable, she might as well enjoy it. And because there was plenty of room in the coach, he was not pressed so close to her. She did not have to think about his thigh against her, his elbow nudging her side, nor worry that she might accidentally move and find herself in his arms. No, better not to think of that at all. She took refuge in talking, chattering like a magpie about nothing at all.

The northernmost tip of Windermere was glimpsed as they stopped at Ambleside for a change of horses; now that the rain had stopped the sun was shining on its rippling water and showing the myriads of boats in sharp relief. On the opposite side she could see what looked like a castle and a wood. A little to the right the heather-covered hills rose, purple and grey, dotted with the white of sheep. 'Oh, it is beautiful!' she exclaimed, leaning forward in her seat to see the better.

'Yes, when the sun is shining,' he said laconically. 'It has a reputation for being wet, you know.'

She laughed. 'Oh, I know it looked very different yesterday when it was raining, but isn't that the beauty of England? The weather and the seasons change everything. It is impossible to be bored by it.'

'You do not mind the rain?'

'No, for I know the sun will shine again.'

'What a wonderful philosophy for life,' he said, smiling at her. She enhanced whatever setting she was in. Just now she was making the weak sun stronger, dull colours bright, simply by being there.

'Is it?' she asked, surprised that she could have said anything so profound. But it was true, wasn't it? If her life was going through a rainy patch, then perhaps she could look forward to the sun in days to come. Sitting here beside him, enclosed in the little world of a stagecoach, enjoying the scenery, talking amiably, she had almost managed to forget how she came to be here and where she was going.

'Tell me about Scotland,' she said. 'Is it like this?'

'Scotland,' he mused. 'I suppose it is, but more so. The lochs are like the lakes, but deeper, and the fells are nothing to the mountains of the Highlands. Sometimes the snow never leaves the top of them, you know. And there is a grandeur, a wildness, which is impossible to describe. You have to feel it.'

'Perhaps that feeling is only for those who are born and bred there, not for those who come to it late in life,' she said a little wistfully.

'Not necessarily. You will love it, I am sure.' He hoped that would turn out to be true, that she would be happy with her new employers in spite of their off-hand treatment of her. They should have arranged for her to be escorted; it was almost as if they did not care if she reached them or not. Surely, if it were James, he would have had more thought for her? 'I believe I heard you say you were going to Killearn?'

'Yes. Do you know it?'

'Very well. Where in Killearn do you go?'

She was tempted to tell him everything, to explain about her father and the money and the unknown guardian, but then, realising her insecurity, he might take it as a signal he could behave badly again, and she wanted to keep everything on the same pleasant, impersonal level. But most of all she did not want to confess that she had lied; he had said he hated pretence and deception, more than she hated gambling, and though she longed to confide in him, she could not do it. 'I do not know exactly, I am being met in Glasgow.'

'But you do know the name of your employer?'

Now, she was in a fix. If he knew Killearn as he said he did, then he would also know of the Earl of Strathrowan. 'Yes, I know his name.'

'Let me guess. Is it Macgowan?'

'How did you come to that conclusion?'

'Lord and Lady Macgowan have a young son who is in need of instruction. I can think of no one else, not among anyone of rank, that is. Unless. . .' He paused suddenly. 'There are the Strathrowans. . .'

Her heart began to beat in her throat and she felt the colour suffusing her face. What had her mother always told her? Be sure your sins will find you out. How could she possibly have known at the outset that Captain Blair would be familiar with Killearn? How big was the place? Was it big enough to hide in? But then, she would not be included in any social gatherings the family might go to and a mere captain was hardly likely to attend them either.

'Who said I was going to anyone of rank, Captain? Surely such a family would have arranged a chaperone for me?'

'Yes, of course they would.'

'Then you have your answer, Captain.'

It was highly unsatisfactory, but she obviously did not want to tell him any more and he was beginning to wonder if she had any employment to go to at all. But then, why mention Killearn? It was not a great town; few people from south of the border had ever heard of it. She was either being forced to make the trip against her will or she was being very clever and he wished he knew which it was. And he was a complete noddicock for letting it bother him.

He decided to change the subject and began a discourse on the relative merits of Glasgow and Edinburgh and the difficulties of travelling to the very north where there were few roads and riding was the best way to get about and where, until recently, packhorses were still the accepted way of transporting goods.

'But we are progressing,' he said, as they stopped for one of the many changes of horses. 'Telford and McAdam are both Scotsmen. Telford, in particular, has built over a thousand miles of road, connecting all the sizeable towns, and bridged over a thousand rivers.' He smiled. 'Like the fen country, we have a great many waterways too, Miss Sadler.'

Relieved to be talking generalities again, she encouraged him to go on, soaking up the facts he told her, descriptions of people and places, the local customs, until they arrived at the Crown in Penrith where the horses were changed for the last eighteen miles to Carlisle.

The road ran over very rough country and she was shaken about like a rattle in a drum, musing ruefully that when the coach was full there was less room to be thrown about, though whether the close proximity of her fellow passengers and Captain Blair in particular was preferable she did not know. And to add to her discomfort, the sunshine of the morning had turned to rain again and her feet and fingers were frozen. She was glad when they sighted the walls and towers of Carlisle and a few minutes later turned into the yard of the Crown and Mitre and drew to a stop.

It was then she was dismayed to learn that this was a scheduled stopping place and the coach was going no further that night. 'No, miss,' the guard told her, as she gave him the usual tip, before going into the inn. 'The coach don't move no more until five in the morning. Me and Joe Grinley, we're off back to

Manchester, you'll have a new driver and guard tomorrow.'

Now she was really in trouble. For a foolish minute she thought of sleeping in the coach until it left again but she knew that would not be allowed. Besides, the Captain already had hold of her elbow and was guiding her indoors out of the rain, and issuing his usual orders. He had a way of making people take notice, of jumping to do his bidding at once and a that without a single complaint. She concluded he was not short of funds. But she was.

She sat through a meal she had no appetite for, wondering what would happen when the innkeeper discovered she had no money to pay for it, or for her room, which was even now being made ready for her. What did one do in such circumstances? Ask for time to pay? Pretend you had been robbed? Borrow? Captain Blair would lend her money if she asked him, but on one thing she was determined; she would not confide her dilemma to her unsolicited escort. Although it was still only six in the evening, she excused herself, saying she was very tired and was going to bed if they were to make an early start in the morning.

'Of course.' He rose. 'I will go and make sure your room is ready.'

She went and waited in the vestibule, so wrapped up in her problem, she was unaware of what was going on around her. She would have to offer her brooch as payment. But her brooch was worth a great deal more than a single night's bed and board and she needed money for Glasgow as well; she had no idea how long she would have to wait there, and without the benefit of Captain Blair's assistance.

She would have to sell the trinket. But where? She looked around a little wildly. Whom should she ask? Through an open door she caught sight of the coachman enjoying a pipe of tobacco with his guard. The room was full of smoke and there were no ladies present, but she felt she had no choice. She went to the door. 'Mr Grinley,' she called softly, not daring to enter the male sanctum. 'May I speak to you?'

He excused himself from his fellows and joined her. 'Yes, miss, what can I do for you?'

'Is there anywhere nearby where I can sell a piece of jewellery?'

'Jewellery?' he queried in surprise. 'Do you mean to say you are that low in the stirrups. . .'

'Not yet, but this journey has been fraught with delay, and I may yet have need of more funds before I reach its end.'

'Why not ask the Captain? I'll wager he'll stand buff.'

'No.' She spoke more sharply than she intended, making him smile. 'He need know nothing about it. If you do not know where I may dispose of some jewellery, then tell me who might. And do not say the Captain,' she added fiercely as he opened his mouth. 'I want you to promise you will say nothing of it to him.'

'If you say so, miss,' he agreed. 'There's a pawnshop about two streets away. It's not difficult to find. Come, I'll point the way.'

She accompanied him to the door and listened carefully to his instructions, then she returned to the vestibule to find Captain Blair had returned from his errand.

'Your room is at the top of the stairs and facing the

front,' he said. 'Your trunk and hot water have been taken up.'

'Thank you. I will bid you goodnight, then.'

'Goodnight, Miss Sadler. I have asked the chambermaid to call you in good time to have breakfast before the coach leaves.'

'That is very kind of you.'

'Think no more of it.' He paused, wondering why she looked so distracted. Her eyes were bright and her cheeks more than usually pink. Surely she did not think he was going to kiss her again? Much as he would have liked to, he would not risk it a second time. 'The talk is that the weather is set to become still colder and may even snow,' he said. 'You would be wise to wrap up as warmly as possible tomorrow. I believe extra undergarments are more efficacious than top clothes for maintaining warmth.'

She stared at him in shocked disbelief, unable to answer him. That he had been insolent enough to mention her underwear at all was more than enough, but she was suddenly confronted with a memory of her first night on the road. She had been wearing two layers of underwear and someone had helped her to bed; she remembered gentle hands and a soft voice. They had belonged to the Captain! Without a word, she turned from him and fled up the stairs to her room, banging the door behind her and flinging herself on the bed.

How could he? How could he humiliate her like that? She had forgiven him for that kiss, but how could she forgive him for that? She lay on the bed, shaking with mortification, imagining his hands on her clothes, undoing the tiny buttons, touching her flesh. She had been irredeemably compromised long before he had kissed her. How could she go on? But there was no way back. And she still had the hotel bill to pay the next morning.

Pulling herself together, she rose and went to the mirror to tidy her face and hair, replaced her bonnet, put her cloak about her shoulders and left the room, watching carefully for Captain Blair as she made her way down the stairs and out onto the street.

Joe Grinley, sucking thoughtfully on his pipe, was wondering how he could let Captain Blair know what Miss Sadler planned without breaking his promise to her, when he caught sight of her slight figure in its all-enveloping black cloak passing the window.

'Captain,' he said, addressing the man sitting morosely on the other side of the hearth with a quart of ale in front of him and his chin sunk on his chest. 'I do not know if you are interested, but that there little lady has just gone out into the street.'

Duncan, who had been brooding over his asinine stupidity, lifted startled eyes to the coachman. 'What did you say?'

'I said Miss Sadler has just gone out. I wonder where she is off to at this time o' night?'

The young man abandoned his ale and flew out of the door, 'like a bat out o' hell,' the coachman was heard to say.

Helen was just disappearing round the corner as Duncan emerged from the inn. He hurried after her. What was the silly chit up to now? he asked himself. Surely he had not driven her to do something silly, she was much more level-headed than that and was more inclined to ring a peal over him than take flight. He resisted the impulse to run after her and demand to know where she was going; such an action would put him into even deeper hot water. He walked slowly behind her, ready to dodge out of sight if she should look back, but she was intent on her errand and marched steadfastly forward.

He watched her enter a building over which hung the three balls of a pawnbroker. He crept closer, though he dare not enter. He stood and peered in through the grimy window and saw her hand something over to the man who sat on a stool at a high table. He could see the man's lips moving but could not make out what was said and then the man offered her money, some paper, some coin. She hesitated, then took it and turned to leave. Duncan hid round the side of the shop and watched her walk back the way she had come. So that was it! She had run out of blunt. Poor child; as if she did not have enough to contend with.

He went into the shop. The pawnbroker was still sitting on the stool with a magnifying glass in his hand, examining the piece of jewellery Helen had just sold him. 'How much do you want for that?' Duncan demanded, pointing to the brooch.

'This?' The man turned it over in his hand. 'Fine piece, this.'

'I am sure it is. How much?'

'Two hundred pounds.'

'Two hundred! Are you run mad?'

''Tis worth every penny.'

'Never mind how much it's worth, how much did you give the lady?'

'What's it to you how much I give her?'

'She is my wife.' He grabbed the man by his collar, almost pulling him off the stool. 'How much did you give her? I want the truth, or you'll rue the day you ever tried to gull me.'

'Twenty quineas.'

Duncan released the man and took a purse from his tail pocket. 'Here's the twenty and five more for your trouble. That's a fair profit, wouldn't you say?' He slammed the money on the table, making both it and its owner jump. 'The pin, if you please.'

Silently the man handed it over. Duncan put it into his purse and returned it to his pocket. 'I bid you good day, sir.'

It was not until he was safely in his room at the inn that he took the brooch out to examine it. He had had it in his hand before very briefly when he confiscated it from the little pickpocket but he had assumed it was paste. But pawnbrokers did not give twenty guineas for imitation jewellery, nor were they generous even for the real thing. A careful look at it soon established that the gems were real and the gold eighteen-carat. Two hundred pounds was perhaps its true value.

But how did a little nobody like Miss Sadler come to own such a piece? Was it hers to sell in the first place? If she had stolen it and was running from justice, why wear it so openly? And why wait until now to dispose of it? Unless she thought someone was after her. Was that the reason for her continually changing coaches; to foil her pursuers? But that was nonsense, a thief would be quiet as a mouse, try to blend in with her surroundings, not draw attention to herself. Miss Sadler had a knack of making herself noticed.

He smiled to himself. This latest fantasy of his was every bit as wide of the mark as his idea that she was a princess. As soon as the opportunity presented itself he would grill her, find out, once and for all, where she was going and why, and how she came to be in possession of such a valuable piece of jewellery. If she could offer him a satisfactory explanation, then he would return it to her. If not... He refused to dwell on the alternative.

With the money in her hand—far less than she thought the brooch had been worth—Helen hurried back to her room at the inn and went to bed. At least she could pay for her night's stay now and no one the wiser. Mr Grinley was off back to Manchester the next morning and in any case he had promised not to say anything.

She woke next morning to find the rain had turned to sleet and in spite of her undiminished fury with Captain Blair, she decided to take his advice and wear extra clothing. As soon as she was dressed she went downstairs to be told the coach was just leaving; there would be a stop for breakfast at Gretna Green. She hurried to join the other passengers in the yard, determined to behave with the dignity she should have maintained from the first; the cool politeness of a lady of quality. She would make it clear to him that such familiarity was not to be tolerated. The trouble was that it was all too late, much too late.

She was not given the opportunity to put her resolve into practice because the Captain was nowhere to be seen. Nor had he put in an appearance when it was time to leave. Telling herself that she would not mind if she never saw him again did no good at all; she found herself watching the inn door for his tall figure to appear, searching the people milling about the yard for a tanned face and curling brown hair, listening for that warm voice, even if it was teasing her. She did not want to go on without him.

The nearer she came to her destination, the more nervous and apprehensive she grew. She needed a friend to see her to the end, someone to turn to if things went badly wrong. For all his over-familiarity, for all his insolence, the Captain had been considerate and helpful and protective. And could she honestly say she had not encouraged his impertinence by allowing him to help her, even dictate to her? It had all started with that young urchin; she should have left well alone.

'All aboard!' the new guard called, as the coachman who was to take them the rest of the way took up the reins and climbed onto the box.

She took her seat, hardly noticing the other passengers, knowing only that she felt miserably alone and more afraid of the future than ever before.

It was exactly five o'clock and the coach had begun to move, when the door was flung open and Captain Blair climbed aboard. Helen was so relieved, she forgot she was supposed to be angry with him, and gave him a fleeting smile as she wished him good morning.

It began to snow in earnest as they toiled up hill and down dale, with the coachman urging the horses on, unwilling to risk being bogged down. None of the other passengers, three men and a woman, was inclined for conversation and apart from a greeting and trivial comments on the weather and the advisability of staying at home if you didn't have to travel, nothing of any importance was said.

Duncan, conscious of the brooch in his purse and

dwelling on what he might have to say to Helen when he was alone with her, said not a word, though when he would be given the opportunity to interrogate her he did not know. After his dreadful error of the night before, he doubted she would allow him anywhere near her. Why could he not have held his tongue, or at least chosen his words more carefully? It just proved he had been too long a soldier.

She had said she was being met in Glasgow and he might learn more if he saw who met her. But that did not ring true either because no one could possibly know when to expect her after all the delays.

He glanced at her as the coach stopped on the brow of a hill and the guard climbed down to put a drag on the rear wheel. She was staring straight ahead looking very depressed and he longed to comfort her, to tell her he did not care who she was or what she had done; he wanted only to see her smile, to laugh with her, to hold her. . . He stopped his errant thoughts; that was what had caused the trouble between them in the first place and telling himself she had asked for it, did not console him at all.

An hour later they crossed the border into Scotland and drew up at the Gretna Hotel. Helen stepped down before Duncan could emerge and help her and hurried into the inn ahead of him. After the poor supper she had had the night before, she was hungry and knowing she now had more than ample money to pay for her breakfast, she was determined to enjoy it. She crossed the threshold of the dining room and then stopped so suddenly that Duncan, immediately behind her, almost fell over her. She ignored his apology, because sitting at a table near the window, laughing at her obvious amazement, were Tom and Dorothy.

CHAPTER NINE

'WHAT are you doing here?' Helen asked, hurrying over to where they sat. 'What happened? I thought you were going to your aunt's.'

'We did but she wasn't at home,' Dorothy said, as Tom rose to greet her. 'Would you believe the house was all shut up? We were told she had gone to Bath, of all the things to do in the middle of winter. We were at a stand.'

'Sit down and we will tell you all about it,' Tom said, drawing out a chair for Helen. It was then that she realised Duncan was right behind her and was pulling up a fourth chair. There was nothing she could do but sit down beside him with a good grace. Now was not the time to tell them that she and the Captain had had a falling out.

'There was nowhere we could stay in Derby,' Dorothy went on. 'And even if Papa had thought of looking for us there, I did not want it to be like that, with us unmarried and no one to persuade him to allow it. I had been counting on Aunt Sophia.'

'There was nothing for it, but to revert to our original plan,' Tom put in.

'But how did you get here ahead of us?'

'We came post chaise.'

'Over Shap Fell?' Duncan queried. 'We heard there had been a landslip.'

'So there was. We came by way of Appleby and I can tell you the terrain was infernally rough. We were lucky to have a very light vehicle and good horses. Those we picked up at Kendal were top-of-the-trees prime cattle.'

'The best in the country, so I've heard,' Duncan said. 'They need to be with the work they have to do.'

'But how did you get here, if Shap Fell was closed?' Dorothy asked.

'Oh, we came by way of the Lakes,' Helen said. 'Windermere and Grasmere and Ullswater. It was beautiful country and I am glad we made the detour.' She paused. 'Does that mean you are married now?'

'Not yet, we only arrived a few moments before you. You cannot imagine how delighted I was when I saw you getting down from the coach. Now we can have a proper ceremony and you can be witnesses. You will, won't you? Both of you? You have no idea how much it will mean to me, to have friends to see us married instead of strangers. Do say yes.'

'Of course we will,' Helen said without even bothering to consult Captain Blair. Let him refuse if he dare!

Duncan smiled and said nothing, knowing it would make no difference if he did. He had to stay; he had not yet spoken to her about the brooch.

'The truth is, I am not sure how we go about it,' Tom said. Then, to Duncan, 'I believe we have to find the blacksmith.'

Duncan laughed. 'Blacksmith, landlord or toll-keeper, it is all the same. All you have to do is declare, before witnesses, your willingness to marry, no banns, no licence, no parson.'

'And that is legal?'

'Yes, as legal as being married in church.'

'It doesn't seem right to me,' Helen murmured. 'Not

without a priest. After all, you are making a sacred vow and it should be done before God.'

'Oh, please do not put obstacles in our way,' Dorothy cried. 'I shall die of shame if we cannot be married at once.'

'Why not see the parson?' Duncan said. 'I am sure a proper ceremony can be arranged.'

Dorothy clapped her hands with delight. 'There! You see how much we need you.'

The men went off to make the arrangements and Helen accompanied Dorothy up to a private room Tom had bespoken for her to help her dress. That was the reason for the pink gauze gown with the rose satin slip and the rosebuds, Helen decided, as Dorothy took it from her portmanteau and shook it out.

'It's very creased,' Helen said. 'Shall I ask a chambermaid to press it? We could have hot water and towels brought up too. After all that travelling, I, for one, feel very grubby.'

An hour and a half later all four stood in the little church as the parson, still rubbing sleep from his eyes, began the marriage service.

Helen found the words of the service very moving and the shy responses of the young couple made her yearn for the kind of love they had for each other. But who would love her now, penniless, unchaperoned, thoroughly compromised by the Captain's behaviour? A tiny bit foxed she had been that first night, too tired and unwell to know what she was doing. If Captain Blair had been a true gentleman, he would not have taken advantage of her.

No, she scolded herself, she could not entirely blame him; she had wanted to be accepted as one of the lower orders, had lied to achieve it, and she had no cause for complaint when she was all too successful. Right from the first she and Captain Blair had behaved with the easy familiarity of old friends, something which would have taken months to achieve in her former life, if they had ever met at all.

She could not understand it. Did losing all your money make you a different person? Was she no longer the properly brought up daughter of a peer simply because she was almost penniless? She risked a glance at the man at her side. He was looking very serious, his brown eyes fixed on Tom and Dorothy, but he was the most handsome man she had ever met.

One searching look from those remarkable eyes and she found herself shaking, one touch and she melted like wax running down a candle. And the thought of parting from him filled her with panic. It was simply no good trying to be angry with him, she loved him. The discovery was too much for her; the tears started to roll slowly down her cold cheeks and she could do nothing to stop them.

Duncan, hearing the faint indrawing of her breath, turned to look at her and was surprised to see her tears. The disdainful, the haughty, the cool Miss Sadler was weeping, and she was no longer disdainful or haughty or even cool, though her cheeks were pinched with cold. Something had touched a soft spot to make her cry and he longed to comfort her. He half lifted a hand towards her but thought better of it and dropped it back to his side.

'I now declare you man and wife.' The parson's words broke in on his thoughts. Man and wife. Duncan Blair and Helen Sadler. Could it, would it work? But he did not know if that was her real name. Did it matter? And she was not a gentlewoman, not of the aristocracy, not someone of whom his father would approve. Did that matter either? She was probably a liar, might even be a thief. Was that important to him? No, he told himself, the only thing that mattered was that he loved her.

Why he loved her, he could not say, except that his whole mind was concentrated on her, on everything she did and said, every nuance of her speech, every fleeting expression which crossed her piquant face. His body ached to hold her in his arms, to rouse her from her underlying sadness to ecstasy, to make her happy. He knew he was a fool but he could not help it.

'Oh, I am so happy for you!' Helen brushed the tears from her cheeks with the back of her gloved hand and moved forward to embrace Dorothy. 'May you have all the happiness in the world.'

'Not all,' said Duncan wryly. 'We need some of it.'

'Yes,' Dorothy said, beaming round at everyone. 'I wish you both happy too.'

Duncan felt tempted to ask Helen to become his wife there and then, but she had deliberately turned from him to offer her congratulations to Tom and he knew she would not accept him in her present mood.

'Come back to the hotel,' Tom said. 'We have a wedding breakfast laid out in a private parlour, just for the four of us.'

'Oh, but we would be intruding,' Helen demurred. If she spent any more time with Duncan, pretending in front of Tom and Dorothy that there was nothing wrong, she would give herself away. 'I am sure you want to be by yourselves.'

'No, no, we have plenty of time for that, all our lives,' Dorothy said, making Duncan smile. Having obtained her heart's desire, the chit was frightened of what came next. He did not think Helen would be afraid, her response to his kiss had told him that. There was fire beneath that cool exterior, fire and depths he had as yet no knowledge of. But she could cry too. . . Why had she been crying? He must know.

He grinned at Tom. 'You stopped us having breakfast if you recall. Miss Sadler and I have eaten nothing since supper last night and I, for one, am extremely hungry.'

Helen silently followed as Tom and Dorothy led the way back to the hotel. The coach had gone on to Glasgow without them and there was nothing to do before another one came along with spare seats, and she, too, was hungry. But if Captain Blair thought he could come up sweet once more, he had better think again.

They were halfway through the meal and drinking a toast to the newly weds when a commotion outside heralded the arrival of an unscheduled carriage. Helen became dimly aware of the ostlers calling out and horses neighing and a voice, loud and insistent. 'Where are they?' A moment later the door was flung open and a tall man with greying hair stood on the threshold. His top hat and well-cut frockcoat were covered in mud splashed from horses' hooves and the ends of his muslin cravat, once pristine and carefully tied, were drooping.

Dorothy, who had her back to the door, heard it crash back and turned to look. 'Papa!'

'I'll give you Papa,' he said, striding forward and stopping in front of the quartet. 'What do you think you are about, child? Your poor Mama is distraught and I have had to leave important negotiations to come chasing after you. I pray God it is not too late.

You will never take if this escapade gets out, you know that don't you? No one will have you. And as for this scapegrace...' He pointed at Tom. 'I've a mind to thrash you within an inch of your life. Now, get out of my daughter's life. We will concoct some tale. Dorothy has been staying with her Aunt Sophia, that will do.'

'Aunt Sophia is from home,' Dorothy said, as if that were the most important point to pick up in the whole tirade. 'We went there.'

'You went to see your aunt?' He stared at her in surprise. 'Why do that?'

'To wait for you. We thought Aunt Sophia would help us to persuade you.'

'I never heard such a fribble. My sister would no more condone this than I would.'

'Then I am glad she was not at home. Tom and I are man and wife now. There is nothing you can do about it.'

All the fight seemed to go out of him. He sank into a vacant chair at an adjoining table and stared at her for a long time. She reached out and took Tom's hand. 'It was done properly by the parson, with witnesses.'

'When?'

'An hour ago.'

'Then you have not...' He stopped. 'The marriage has not been...'

'Consummated?' queried Tom, guessing what was in his mind. 'No, sir, it has not. But that doesn't make it any less of a marriage. Unless Dorothy wants it, there will be no annulment.'

'Certainly not!' Dorothy said, finding a new courage now that she had the ring on her finger. 'Tom, how could you think I would want that?'

'Then married we are and married we remain, to the end of our days.'

She smiled at her father. 'Papa, please accept it. There is no way you can undo it and I do so want you to be happy for me.'

Mr Carstairs looked at Duncan and Helen. 'And am I to assume, sir, that you were party to this? You helped take my child from me.'

'Mrs Thurborn is not a child,' Duncan said, making Dorothy giggle at the sound of her new name and almost proving Mr Carstairs' point. If Arabella had not been faint-hearted when he suggested it all those years ago, they would have been married in like manner. It took real conviction to go through with a runaway marriage and Arabella, in spite of her protestations, had not been sure enough of her love to defy her father. For the first time he was glad of that. Now, he realised, fate had had something else in mind for him.

'The Captain and Helen were our chaperones and witnesses,' Tom put in.

'Captain?'

'Captain Duncan Blair of the Prince of Wales's Own Hussars, at your service, sir,' Duncan said, inclining his head.

'And this?' He turned towards Helen.

'Mrs Blair,' Duncan said before Helen could reply herself. 'My lady wife.'

Helen drew her breath in sharply. How dare he! How dare he be so presumptuous! 'Mr Carstairs. . .' she began.

'Tom wanted to do everything aboveboard,' Duncan went on. 'He told us of his plans right from the first and as my wife and I were already making arrangements to come to Scotland, we agreed to chaperone the young couple.'

'It seems a bit smoky to me,' Mr Carstairs said, not altogether convinced. 'Where does Sophia come into it?'

Duncan shrugged and looked at Tom; he had done his best and now it was up to the young man.

'Dorothy wanted someone from her family at her side,' Tom said. 'We thought that if Miss Carstairs could persuade you to see things our way, there would be no necessity to come all the way to Scotland. As she was not there. . .' He smiled at the older man. 'We had no choice. Captain and Mrs Blair could not delay their journey and they would not leave us unchaperoned. You do see how it came about. . .'

'Oh, what's done is done, I suppose,' Mr Carstairs said, making Dorothy fly across and put her arms round him.

'Oh, Papa, I knew you would come round.'

He disentangled himself from her. 'But I still have words to say to that young man. In private, I think. After that, I shall be hungry as a hunter.' He looked at the food left on the table. 'I'll have some of the capon and that game pie.' He rose and Tom followed him to the other side of the room, where they were deep in conversation for several minutes.

'Captain Blair, I must thank you for what you did for us,' Dorothy said. 'I am sure that telling Papa we had a married couple to chaperone us all the way made all the difference.' She giggled suddenly. 'What a good fibber you are, Captain Blair. I do not know how you kept a straight face. And you, too, Helen.'

'Oh, Miss Sadler is a master when it comes to

hummery,' Duncan said laconically, looking not at
Dorothy but at Helen as he spoke.

Helen had no answer to that, but it reinforced her
conviction that he suspected her of telling untruths.
Could he possibly know her real name? Oh, how she
wished she had never started the deception! Scott's
verse came to her mind: 'Oh, what a tangled web we
weave, When first we practise to deceive.' She, who
had always been honest as the day, had woven a web
of deceit which was going to enmesh her totally unless
she could rid herself of the ubiquitous Captain before
they reached Glasgow. It was enough to make her
dear mother turn in her grave.

Mr Carstairs and Tom shook hands and returned to
the rest of the party. 'Food,' Mr Carstairs said. 'Then
back to Derby. Sophia will be back by now. She will
have to be a conspirator whether she wills it or not.'
He sat down and helped himself to food while the
others, who had already eaten their fill, sat and
watched.

'The weather is not good, sir,' Duncan said. 'I advise
you not to delay your return.'

'No, you are right.' Reluctantly he put down his
knife and fork and stood up. 'Come, Tom. Come,
Dorothy. My carriage is outside. I ordered the horses
before I came in.'

Duncan and Helen followed them out to the yard
where a roomy private carriage with good springs and
padded seats stood with a pair of top-class horses
already in the traces. A liveried driver sat on the box,
reins and whip in his hands. Helen embraced Dorothy.
'I wish you happy, my dear, and all the luck in the
world.'

'And you,' Dorothy said, then added in a whisper,

'don't let him get away, whatever you do. You were made for each other.' Then she skipped away and got into the coach, while the men shook hands. Helen stood beside Duncan and watched them go, her smile stiff on her face. As soon as they were lost to view she turned from him without speaking and made her way back into the inn.

'Miss Sadler.' He hurried after her. 'We must talk.'

'I have nothing to say to you.'

'No? But I have something to say to you.' He put a hand on her arm. 'At least hear me out.'

She shrugged him off. 'Why should I? You have behaved abominably and you know it.'

'By introducing you as my wife? If I had not done so, what do you think Mr Carstairs would have said? What would he have done? An unmarried couple as escort would hardly be considered suitable chaperones. And your reputation. . .'

She did not need him to tell her that her reputation had been thoroughly compromised and wondered what the Earl of Strathrowan might say if he learned about it. 'It is in shreds already because of you, Captain Blair,' she said. 'I did not ask for your escort or your protection. I should have been better off without it.'

'If you truly believe that you are deceiving yourself as well as me,' he said, taking her elbow and guiding her firmly back to the private parlour where the innkeeper was clearing away the remains of their meal. 'Leave us,' he commanded, then to Helen, as the man disappeared, 'Sit down.'

He was so much taller than she was and she hated having to crane her neck to look up at him; it gave him the advantage. She sat down suddenly, as if her knees would no longer support her, but she managed to sound cool. 'I am seated, Captain Blair, but I tell you now, I am not accustomed to being treated with such arrogance. I'll allow that telling Mr Carstairs I was your wife was perhaps for the best, and it was not that I objected to, and you know it.'

He drew a chair up and sat facing her. 'You are complaining that I kissed you?'

'Yes. And that first night in Northampton. . .'

'What about it? I did no more than I would have done for any drinking companion who was a little cut over the head, I carried you to bed and loosened your clothing, no more, though I admit I should not have alluded to it afterwards and for that I apologise.'

'Drinking companion!' She sprang to her feet, anger making her green eyes glitter like emeralds and her cheeks scarlet. 'Is that how you think of me?'

He laughed; she was even more beautiful when angry. 'No, I do not usually kiss drinking companions.'

'No, but I expect you kiss ladies at every opportunity.'

'Now that is something which I confess has been puzzling me.'

'What has?' she asked, taken by surprise.

'Whether you are a lady or no. A lady would never travel alone and even a lady's companion would have an escort. I cannot imagine any responsible employer expecting you to make the journey unaccompanied. . .'

'No doubt he has his reasons.'

'He? Not she?'

'Both,' she said quickly.

He noticed the slip. 'You know,' he said gently, 'you are either a great simpleton or a great deceiver and to be honest I do not really care for either.'

'Then why insist on staying with me?'

He smiled ruefully. 'That, too, is something that has been baffling me. It might be plain curiosity, but I think it is more than that. I do not wish to see you in a bumblebath, you are too beautiful to languish in gaol. . .'

'Gaol?' She was startled.

He took the brooch from his purse and laid it on the table among the dirty plates with their congealing food, where it winked incongruously up at them. 'Is this yours?'

She gasped. 'Where did you get it?'

'I bought it from the man you sold it to.'

'Why? How did you know I had sold it?'

'I followed you to the shop. Now, are you going to tell me where you got it?'

'It was mine to sell if I wished. I have had it ever since my seventeenth birthday. My papa gave it to me.' Tears stood in her eyes, making him hate himself. 'I did not want to sell it, but I needed the money. I thought I had enough to last me until we reached Glasgow, but what with one thing and another. . .'

'You could not pay for your board and lodgings?'

'No.'

He sank on his haunches beside her chair and covered her hands with his own. 'Oh, my dear, I am so sorry. But why did you not tell me of your difficulties? I could have paid your bills, given you money. You did not need to sell your most precious possession.'

'It is not my most precious possession. I still have my mother's betrothal ring but if there is no one to meet me in Glasgow, then that will have to go too.'

'No, it will not.' He put the brooch in her hand and

gently closed her fingers over it. 'Take it back, my dear, with my compliments.'

She gave a cracked laugh. 'And what will I have to pay for it? Another kiss? Perhaps something more?' She put the pin back on the table. 'No, Captain Blair, the price is too high.'

He smiled. 'You have not heard it yet.'

She sighed. 'No doubt you are going to tell me.'

'Do you think you will be happy with your new family? What is it you are going to be, a governess or a companion?'

'I truly don't know until I get there. It was all arranged for me.'

'Good God!' He could not suppress his astonishment and his admiration for her courage. That she was now telling the truth, he did not doubt. 'I think you are too young to be a governess or a companion. . .'

She was about to give him another set-down but decided against it. 'I am four-and-twenty.' She smiled ruefully. 'Not quite at my last prayers, but very close to it.'

'Nonsense!' he said, concealing his surprise. He had taken her for nineteen or twenty at the most. 'Why is someone as beautiful as you are still single?'

'Because that is what I choose to be, Captain.'

'Then you are not going to Scotland to be married?' he queried. 'There is no impatient bridegroom waiting for you?'

'Of course not.'

'What manner of man might he be, the man to capture your hand?' he went on. 'No doubt he would need to have a title and a fortune, so that you would never have to sell any of your possessions again.'

'Wealth would not be a consideration,' she said,

wondering where his questions were leading. 'I may be poor, but I am not mercenary. To me love and fidelity are the foremost requisites on both sides. They are more important than riches and definitely more important than a man's consequence in Society. I could not marry a man who did not love me and whom I did not love. My papa and mama adored each other. Papa was inconsolable when Mama died. It changed him. He was never the same afterwards.' Her voice had taken on a wistful note which was mixed with a kind of brittleness.

'And now you are quite alone?'

'Yes, but not as helpless as you would like to believe, Captain.'

'Oh, I do not think you are helpless, Miss Sadler. What will you do if word gets out about this little misadventure?'

'Misadventure! Is that what you call it? But why should anything be said about it?'

'Dorothy or Tom have only to drop a hint when they return to London. . .'

'Captain, we are a long way from London and I cannot think that any of my one-time friends or acquaintances have the least interest in my doings. I need consider only my own conscience and that is clear.'

'All the same. . .' He paused, taking her hand again. 'We could be married. Here. Today.'

She looked up at him and was nearly undone. If he had asked her in any other circumstances, if she had a dowry, if her father had not been a suicide, if he had said he loved her, she might have said yes. She would have said yes because she loved him.

As it was she stiffened her back and looked back at

him with unblinking green eyes. 'Captain, have you run mad? We are complete strangers. You know nothing about me and I know nothing of you.' He opened his mouth to say something, but she stood up and went on. 'And that is how it will stay. Now, I am going to see if there is another coach to Glasgow today. The sooner we reach there, the sooner you may give up your self-appointed task of looking after me.'

'Oh, but I know a great deal about you,' he murmured to her departing back. 'You have shown me yourself with everyone we have met, everybody you have spoken to, fellow travellers, coachmen, innkeepers. You have demonstrated a huge concern for your fellow human beings and sympathy for their sufferings. You have shown a generous spirit and great courage, pride and humility in equal measure, a wide knowledge and wider intelligence, and a refusal to be beaten which is little short of obstinacy, traits far away and above what is necessary for a little schoolma'am or a lady's companion, though they could be the attributes of a loving wife.'

Love. She would not marry where that was lacking. But he had enough for both of them and he should have told her so instead of making it sound like a cold-blooded contract to get her out of a hobble. Sighing, he followed her and discovered there was a coach about to leave for Glasgow and little Miss Sadler was issuing orders about the stowing of her luggage. He smiled and went to her aid. Once that was done, he handed her in and took his place beside her in silence.

The coach was full both inside and out and everyone was talking about the prospects of severe weather and expressing their hope that they would reach their destinations before the roads became impassable, telling each other tales of blizzards and people getting lost and houses being covered, of horses floundering and coaches getting stuck fast, each story more improbable than the last.

But Helen hardly heard them. Captain Blair had made her immune to tall stories and she was more concerned with what lay in wait at the end of her journey. Now the Captain had put the idea in her head that no good employer would allow a young lady to travel alone, she could not shift it. The Earl was not her employer but her guardian; surely that should have made him more caring, not less? Had he been reluctant to take responsibility for her and hoped she would not attempt the journey at all?

She might, after all, have been better off accepting Captain Blair's offer. But what did she know of him, apart from the fact that he was a soldier and a second son? She did not think he was without funds and she knew he could be kind and generous, that on many issues they agreed, that he could be a staunch ally and probably a fearsome enemy. He could be domineering too, and he was a card-player, but she knew nothing of his family, nor of his home. Did he live at home or in the saddle on some campaign or other? If she married him, would she be a camp follower? She shivered suddenly.

'You are cold?' His soft voice right against her ear startled her.

'No.'

'But you shivered.'

'Thoughts, Captain Blair, only thoughts.'

'A penny for them.'

'They are worthless, sir, still quite worthless.' She turned away from him and looked out of the window.

The steady rain had turned to sleet, melting as it touched the road, but it was enough to make visibility poor and they slowed to a walk.

'I think not.' His voice was insistent. 'I'll wager you were thinking about the future, about what lies ahead of you, and wondering which is worse, a position you don't know about with a family you have never met, or being a soldier's wife. Am I correct?'

He was right, dreadfully right but she would never admit it. 'No. You would lose your bet, Captain, and serve you right too. And you know how much I loathe gambling.'

'That was not gambling, it was a certainty, and saying "I'll wager" is merely a figure of speech.'

'I know that, but you do play cards, you admitted it, and you said you always win.'

'Surely a game of cards to pass the time and a small bet on the outcome to enliven the interest, does not make me an out and out villain?'

'No. But it is a beginning, the start of the dreadful slide downhill to penury. . .'

'You have perhaps some experience of that? Is that why. . .?'

'No, it is not,' she snapped.

'Then why this aversion?'

'I could not marry a gambler and that is all there is to it.'

He laughed suddenly. 'No wonder you have never married if your requirements are so particular. I enjoy a hand of cards but I am not what you call a gambling man and I would not mind if I never had another wager, but I'll be blowed if I'd allow a woman to dictate to me on the matter.'

'Then it is just as well I refused you, isn't it?'

'It is indeed,' he said, with a grim smile. Which was not at all what he had meant to say.

They remained silent throughout the remainder of the journey, though there were a thousand questions she wanted to ask him, a thousand thoughts buzzing in her head, none of them coherent. Her fear of the perils of the road was nothing compared with her apprehension at what lay ahead of her.

They stopped frequently for a change of horses, sometimes being allowed down to take some refreshment, sometimes having food and drink brought out for them to consume on the way. No one wanted to be delayed a second longer than was necessary and they all gazed at the sky, gloomily expecting the worst or optimistically forecasting a change for the better, depending on their temperaments.

They passed through Sanquar at a brisk trot, then on to the Elvanfoot Inn and up across the moors to Douglas Dale, where they stopped at what the coachman proudly told them was the biggest and busiest hostelry in Scotland. Here the horses were changed and they were allowed half an hour for a meal. Then on again to Knowknock and Hamilton where the horses were changed for the last time and, with the smell of home in their nostrils, made a final burst of speed through wooded countryside and clattered into a town which could only be Glasgow itself.

It was late at night, but the place was still busy, with lights showing in many of the shops and people on the cobbled streets, some wrapped up well against the bitter weather, others poorly clad and shivering. For once, Helen was too absorbed in her own concerns to worry about them.

The guard gave a blast on his horn as they turned

into Gallowgate and two minutes later they pulled up in the yard of the Old Saracen's Head.

'Here we are, safe and sound,' Helen heard someone say and they all tumbled out, one after the other, clapping their hands to their sides and stamping their feet while their baggage was taken down, and then hurrying into the inn for warmth, food and possibly a bed.

Helen, conscious that the Captain was still with her, hurried in ahead of him, anxious to make enquiries about being met before he could overhear.

'Someone from the Earl,' the innkeeper repeated when she cornered him in the back parlour. 'No, there's been no one.'

'Are you sure? It might have been any time in the last three days.'

'Nay, I'd know if there had, lass, the Earl is well known to us and we'd have been told if he was expecting anyone. Besides, he's been ill, not entertaining visitors, you see.'

'Ill? How ill?' This was something she had not considered.

'Bad, I think, but he pulled through, though he's no been out since.'

'But he is expecting me. Is there a coach to Killearn?'

'Not this side of Saturday, miss, and only if the weather improves.'

'I shall have to stay here then and hope someone comes for me. Have you a room? A single room?'

'I think I can find ye one, miss, but are ye sure ye've not made a mistake? It is the Earl who's expecting ye?'

'Yes. And please, could you show me up to my room at once? I am very cold and tired.'

'Yes, miss. If someone were to come from the Earl, who shall I say is waiting? Not that I think they will, there'll be nothin' moving' on the roads taenight.'

'Miss Sanghurst. Miss Helen Sanghurst. My trunk is in the hall; it is engraved with the letters H and S intertwined. Would you have it brought up?'

'Of course, miss. Follow me.'

He led her through a door on the far side of the room, so that when Duncan came in two minutes later she was nowhere to be seen. And neither was the innkeeper, who knew Captain Duncan Blair very well indeed and would have wondered why she was looking for a messenger from the Earl when his son had come in on the same coach.

Having discovered from one of the servants that the young lady had retired to her room, Duncan ordered a room for himself and went to bed. There was nothing to be done until the morning. Now he was almost home he began to wonder what might be in store for him. He prayed he would find his father well and in good spirits. After India, the damp climate of Scotland got into his bones, he said, and the mists which gathered on the hills filled him with aches and pains. Perhaps it had been no more than a chill and he would find him hale and hearty.

Duncan was up, dressed and out before dawn. The snow and sleet had stopped but the wind was whipping up slate-grey clouds from the north and he knew there was more to come. The sooner they were on their way the better; he had no intention of waiting until Saturday for a coach. They had come so far and he was not going to be baulked at the last hurdle. Miss Sadler wanted to go to Killearn and to Killearn they would both go.

He wrapped his cloak around him and pulled his hat firmly on his head as he set off into the centre of the town, where he knew there was a coachbuilder. An hour later he returned to the Old Saracen's Head with a stout box-like carriage pulled by two small but sturdy ponies, one of which was ridden by a postboy, who was not a boy at all, but an ancient Highlander, as tough as they came.

Leaving the equipage in the care of an ostler, he strode into the inn just as Helen came down the stairs, muffled in a cloak and with her bonnet tied on with a scarf. Seeing him she hesitated with her hand on the rail and then lifted her chin and came down the last few steps. 'Good morning, Captain Blair.'

'Ma'am.' He made a perfunctory leg. 'Have you had breakfast?'

'Yes, in my room.'

'Good, we have no time to waste.' He stepped forward to take her elbow. 'Come along.'

She pulled herself away just as the innkeeper came through from the back regions of the house. He looked up at them and smiled. 'So you found each other then?'

'Yes,' they answered in unison, each thinking that the other had been making enquiries.

'Ye'll be leaving at once, then?'

'Yes, at once,' Duncan said. 'Please have the lady's trunk brought down and put in the chaise in the yard.'

'Verra good, Captain.'

'And make up a hamper of food and a bottle of wine.'

'Aye, sir, and shall I be fetchin' a hot brick for the lady's feet?'

'Good idea. Yes, please.'

The man disappeared and Helen turned on Duncan. 'Just what are you about, Captain?'

'We are going the rest of the way by chaise.'

'The rest of the way?'

'To Killearn. That is where you want to go, is it not?'

'Yes, but. . .'

'No buts. Unless you want to be stuck in a strange town for the rest of the winter?'

'No, I do not, but I am told there is a coach on Saturday.'

'Three days away. I, for one, am not prepared to wait that long.'

'And I would rather do that than spend another minute in your company.' Oh, why was she snapping at him? The reason she did not want his company had nothing to do with his behaviour, not if she were honest with herself. It was all to do with being Helen Sanghurst, not Helen Sadler, and the shame she felt.

'And what if it snows so hard nothing can move? You could be here for weeks.'

She craned her neck to look past him into the street as someone opened the door. 'It has stopped snowing.'

'That is just the lull before the storm. Ask anyone. Ask that waiter over there.' He saw her hesitation and his voice softened. 'Please let bygones be bygones, Miss Sadler. I would not, for the world, have upset you. I apologise most humbly and I promise you that I will deliver you safely to wherever you have to go and nothing more.' He smiled crookedly and encompassed the inn with his hand. 'Better the devil you know. . .'

She could not risk being stuck; even if she sold her pin again and her mother's ring, she would not be paid their true worth and whatever they fetched would not last long. And a busy inn with all kinds of people coming and going, and where several virile men were employed who would not see her as a gentlewoman, was not a pleasing prospect. He was right; she would be better to trust herself to the devil she knew.

'Very well,' she said.

In no time at all, she was tucked into the corner of the coach all wrapped round with rugs and a hot brick at her feet. The Captain climbed in beside her and the ancient postboy mounted the nearside horse and they were away.

Out of the town they went at a steady trot, then along the north bank of the Clyde where Helen could see the spars and rigging of a myriad of ships lying at anchor there. A short rest at Dumbarton, more for the benefit of the ponies than the humans, then on again northwards in blinding snow, so that there was nothing to see of the distant mountains and even trees and cottages a few yards from the track were blurred.

'Can the old man see the road?' Helen asked.

'He knows it blindfold.'

'He might just as well be blindfold,' Helen said. 'I never realised that Scotland could be so bleak.'

'Anywhere would be bleak in a blizzard,' he said. 'You should see it in summer when the mountains are clothed in green and purple and the burns are tumbling crystal clear over the rocks; with deep, deep lochs reflecting the clouds, heather and coltsfoot and dog daisies carpeting the slopes and the yellow of

gorse stark against a sky, blue as forget-me-nots.
Sheep are scattered over the hillsides, grouse and
woodcock nest in the grass and the rivers are full of
fish. If anywhere on earth is heaven it is here, in
summer.'

'You must love it very much.'

'I do.'

'How could you bear to leave it to go into the
army?'

'I had little choice. I was sent by my papa.'

'Why?'

'Oh, he had his reasons.'

'Tell me.'

He grinned, half shame-faced. 'I fell in love.'

'You?' She resisted the impulse to laugh.

'It was what you might call puppy love,' he said,
smiling a little at himself. 'It was considered unsuitable
and I was sent away to get over it.'

'And did you?'

'Yes,' he said and meant it. 'I recovered.'

'But you never married?'

'I never found anyone else to engage my heart.
There was a war on too, you remember.'

'And now are you going home for good?'

'I might be. It depends. I heard my father was ill.'

'And you were hurrying to his side! Oh, dear, all
those delays and most of them caused by me. Oh, why
did you stay with me, you could have gone on?'

'No, I could not. Something told me I had to look
after you, an inner voice, my conscience, if you like. . .'

'Your conscience?'

'Conscience or heart, I am not sure which.'

They had been going slower and slower while they

talked and now had come to a stop. He put his head out of the window. 'Hamish, what's amiss?'

It was no more than a short step for the man to get off the pony because the poor beast was up to its belly in snow. The rider struggled in driving snow to the door of the coach. 'I've lost the road, Captain. And the poor brutes is all but done for.'

'How far are we from home?'

'Six or seven miles, mebbe a wee bit more.'

'We could try and walk,' Helen said.

'Or ride.' Duncan stroked his chin. 'Hamish on one and you and I on the other.'

'Ye'd never mek it,' Hamish said bluntly. 'The pony'll niver carry the both of ye and the lass will freeze. Ye ride and I'll walk.' He floundered back to the ponies, only to find one of them had caught its foot in a hidden pothole and was so lame, it could not be ridden and indeed could not be expected to pull the carriage any further.

'How long d'you think it will take you to fetch help?'

'I canna say, Captain. There's auld Bailey's place nearby, if I c'n find it.'

'Then take the good pony. We will wait here.'

He was out of sight in a few yards. Helen was very afraid for him. How could he possibly find his way when there was nothing to see but a few trees and white and more white?

'If the snow eases, he'll be able to see the mountains,' Duncan said, returning to sit beside her. 'He knows their shapes and the shapes of all the rocks, and every twist and turn of every burn. He'll find his way.' But he was less confident than he sounded.

The waiting stretched from minutes to hours and

there seemed no let-up in the snow. Everywhere was blanketed and as silent as the grave. Helen's feet and fingers soon became so numb that she could not feel them, and when Duncan fetched out the food and wine and encouraged her to eat she shook so much that could hardly put the food to her mouth and spilt the drink.

'This is what comes of giving that old lady your cloak,' he said. 'As if we did not have enough to contend with, you have caught a chill.'

'She needed it more than I did. I am not ill, just sleepy, so very, very sleepy. . .'

'No!' he commanded, shaking her. 'You must not go to sleep. Whatever happens, you must stay awake.'

'Sleep,' she mumbled. 'Let me sleep.'

'No! Talk to me. Say whatever comes into your head.'

'How long will we be stuck here, do you think?' Her voice was hardly more than a sigh and he had to bend his head to hear her.

'I do not know.'

'Shall we die here, do you think? Will they find us frozen in each other's arms?' Her lips flickered into a tiny smile. 'Oh, that will give the tabbies something to talk about, won't it?' Her voice faded to almost nothing and her head lolled. 'On top of everything else. . .'

He had a small flask of brandy and put it to her lips. 'Miss Sadler—Helen, my darling, stay awake—please.'

'Not Sadler,' she murmured, choking on the fiery liquid. 'Sanghurst. Helen Sanghurst.'

Sanghurst! Where had he heard that name? 'It doesn't matter,' he said, enfolding her in his arms, rocking her. 'Nothing matters now except keeping you awake.'

'If you only knew the truth. . .'

'It is not important.'

'Yes, it is. I lied.'

'About being a companion?'

'Yes.'

'And about where you are going?'

'No, that is true. Going to Killearn. Going to the Earl of Strathrowan. Papa made him my guardian. . .' She could not keep her eyes open and her voice was becoming fainter and fainter. She was no longer cold, could feel nothing, except an urgent desire for sleep.

Strathrowan! His own father was her guardian! That was why he felt instinctively he had to look after her; she was Lord Sanghurst's daughter and he had met her before, long ago in India when he was hardly out of petticoats and she was a baby.

'Helen, wake up!' He shook her almost savagely and then crushed her to him. 'Helen, you must not go to sleep, you must not. I love you. I need you. We will be married. . .'

But she was slumbering and did not hear him.

CHAPTER TEN

DUNCAN lay down beside Helen along the seat, wrapping the rugs round them both, holding her close, trying to warm her with his own body, talking and shaking her alternately, making her groan and protest, but he could not let her slip away. He told her of his home at Strathrowan, of his brother and sister-in-law and his nephew and niece. He told her she would be made welcome and everyone would love her.

He talked about India, knowing she would not remember it. He did not recall much himself, except the journey home, though it had not been home to him then; he had never been to Scotland. His father had not expected to inherit, being a second son, and had gone out to the sub-continent to make his fortune. In that he had succeeded, marrying the daughter of a nabob and siring two sons, before his wife had died giving birth to a still-born daughter.

Duncan had been ten and his brother fifteen when their father learned that his father and brother were both dead and he had become the Earl of Strathrowan. Home they had come to Scotland, home to the mountains and glens of Killearn, which Duncan had come to love and still loved even after the affair with Arabella had sent him far from it.

He barely remembered Lord Sanghurst, who had left India two or three years before they did, but he had heard of him since. He had been a well-known figure, something in government, a consort of the

Prince Regent, though when George became King, he had fallen from favour. He had been a rake and an inveterate gambler, who would bet on raindrops on the window pane if he happened to be confined indoors because of inclement weather.

Duncan's father, who had once called him friend, had long since ceased to stand buff for him, saying that Sanghurst's gambling had killed his wife and would ruin his daughter if he were not stopped and while people continued to allow him to owe them money, he would never change. When he was in favour at Court, he had been allowed endless credit, but after his fall from grace the dunners closed in on him. In the end he had taken the coward's way out and shot himself. It had been the talk of the *ton*, even in Vienna. Poor, dear Helen, no wonder she hated gambling.

'We will be married,' he repeated again and again, though whether she heard or understood what he said, he did not know. 'I promise never to gamble, never even to mention the word "wager" if it upsets you so. I am a second son, but I have a good annuity from my maternal grandmother, besides my captain's pay. I can do better. I'll join the Diplomatic Corps. They say I am a good negotiator...' On and on he went, hardly drawing breath, trying to make her answer, to say something, anything, just to let him know she was conscious. But she had not spoken for some time now and he was afraid...

Helen could hear a voice, quiet, urgent, ragged-edged, but she could not understand the words; she knew only that as long as the voice was there, she was safe from harm. Then through the mist which surrounded her brain and refused to let her think, she heard other sounds, dogs barking, a horse neighing, more voices. Momentarily she knew that whatever had been keeping her warm was gone and icy air fanned her face, then she was being carried.

She moaned a little and heard the voice again, clear as day. 'Thank God, she's alive.' And then she was lying in something which was carrying her over the snow and the warmth and the soft voice were with her again and she sighed in contentment and slept and this time no one tried to shake her into wakefulness.

When she woke she was in a bed. It had all been a dream, a nightmare of epic proportions. Soon Daisy would come with hot water and chocolate to drink. She would lay out her clothes, chattering about the day, whether it was fine or wet and whether she would need stout boots or light shoes if she was going out walking. She turned her head towards the light. The curtains were drawn back and sunshine filled the room.

But the curtains were unfamiliar and the room was different. It was huge, with a large four-poster bed in which she was almost lost, a big wardrobe and several smaller chests and a long mirror. There was a thick blue and pink carpet on the floor and a fire burning in the grate. She moved again and a face came into focus, a finely-drawn face, surrounded by curls of golden hair. 'Who are you? Where am I?'

The vision smiled. 'I am Viscountess Blair, my dear. Margaret to you. And you are safe at home.'

'Blair?' Her heart began to thump uncontrollably. It had not been a dream, it had been real. Captain Blair had brought her here. But why? 'Viscountess?' she queried. 'You are Captain Blair's wife?'

Lady Blair laughed lightly. 'No, I am his sister-in-law. He is unmarried, did he not tell you?'

'Oh, yes, I remember now.' The Captain had asked her to marry him and she had refused him, but that was before she had confessed. She had confessed, hadn't she? That wasn't part of her dream? 'He looked after me and saved my life.'

'Yes, I believe he did. Old Hamish McFaddern came to us through the blizzard and guided my husband, that's the Viscount, and some of the servants with a pony and sled back to where he had left you. You were only half a dozen miles away. If the snow had held back for an hour or so longer, you would have been safe home long before. Duncan blames himself, of course, and he has been very anxious about you.'

'I am deeply indebted to him.'

'We are all truly sorry. You should not have had to face that journey alone but. . .'

'How long have I been lying here?'

'Three weeks.'

'As long as that?' she asked, surprised that three weeks of her life should have disappeared without trace. 'When do you think I might get up?'

'As soon as you feel strong enough. There is no hurry.'

'But I have to go.' She lifted herself on her elbow.

'Go? Go where?'

'To Killearn. To the Earl of Strathrowan, he is expecting me.'

'But that is exactly where you are. Did Duncan not tell you?'

'I am at Killearn?' It was unbelievable. What had the Captain told her? 'I heard a voice, but I was so sleepy, I am not at all sure what was said. Oh, I am so confused.'

'It is little wonder, my dear, but it is simple enough. The Earl of Strathrowan is my father-in-law and Duncan's father. We sent for Duncan to come home because the Earl was ill and we thought it was high time he left off his wandering. When Papa-in-law heard from Mr Benstead about you, he wrote to Duncan at his London club, knowing he was on his way, and asked him to look out for you and bring you to us. . .'

'He knew who I was all along?' No wonder he said he hated pretence. He had given her the opportunity to tell the truth and she had let it go. How could she have been so stupid?

'No,' Margaret said. 'That was the strange thing about it. He was so anxious to come home, he did not go to his club and he never received the letter. It was all a most extraordinary coincidence that he should meet you as he did.'

'And I delayed him with my foolishness. The Earl. . .'

Margaret smiled. 'Fortunately, Papa-in-law made a full recovery, though he has to be careful not to exert himself.'

This was almost too much to digest at once and Helen fell back on the pillow, trying to understand what it all meant. Was this truly her home now? It seemed her fears about not being welcome had been groundless. But had that changed anything? She was still a pauper, still the deceiver. 'Is Captain Blair still here?'

'Of course.'

'Will he be returning to Europe now that he knows the Earl is well?'

'I do not know. We would like him to stay here, of course, but the decision will be his. It is time he put the past behind him.'

'The past? There was some trouble?'

'He did not tell you about it?'

'No, though he did say something about falling in love and being sent away to get over it. He called it puppy love.'

Margaret smiled. 'He *was* very young, but that is not to say he did not feel very deeply about it. And what made it worse was that Arabella married his boyhood friend and became Lady Macgowan. Papa-in-law blamed himself. He said he was wrong to have sent him away, he should have let the affair run its course, instead of which I believe Duncan brooded over it and that fastened his attachment even more.'

'Why did his lordship object?'

'He thought the match was unsuitable. Second son or no, Duncan was expected to marry someone from a good family with a worthwhile dowry. Second sons cannot entirely rule out the possibility of inheriting—after all, the Earl himself was a second son—and they must take that into consideration when choosing a wife. Arabella Novello's father had come over from Italy before the war; nothing much was known of him, except that he had made a great deal of money in commerce. The irony of it was that the Macgowans were not so particular; their estate was facing ruin and Mr Novello's money brought it to rights. Arabella is now Lady Macgowan.'

'The poor man,' Helen murmured. So that was why he had seemed a little bitter. Indigestion indeed!

'Yes, but after all that, James is dead. He died just over a year ago in a fall in the mountains.'

'Oh. Do you think. . .?' Helen could not bring herself to ask and yet she needed desperately to know. 'Will they. . .?'

Margaret smiled and stood up. 'Who knows? As soon as Arabella heard he was home, she came over by sled to see him. She has been three times already.' She leaned over and straightened the coverlet. 'I should not be prattling on about it, you know. Please don't tell Duncan I spoke of it, he is still very sensitive on the subject.'

'No, I won't.'

'Good. Now I am going to tell Papa you are well on the way to recovery. Tomorrow you will be able to dress and come downstairs. Flora shall look after you. She is young, but my own maid has trained her and I think she will do you very well.'

She left and Helen lay back among the pillows, still unable to believe she had arrived. That it was also the home of Captain Blair was almost incredible. All those lies, her false name, her occupation, the story of the nabob's widow, must all be telling against her now. Unless Captain Blair had said nothing of it. He had certainly not told his sister-in-law of his proposal to her or she would not have mentioned Lady Macgowan.

Surely, if he had meant it, he would have said something to his family, he would not have let them assume he would take up his old love again. And the lady in question was obviously intent on renewing the courtship. And this time it seemed the Earl would not stand in their way. What had she told him in her half-conscious state? She hadn't admitted to being in love with him, had she? Oh, why must she fall in love for the first time in her life with someone whose affections were engaged elsewhere?

She looked up as she heard a soft knock on the door and before she could call out, Duncan had put his head round it, grinning cheerfully. 'May I come in?'

She tried to ignore the pounding of her heart and smiled at him. 'Of course.'

He strode into the room, even more handsome than she remembered him. He wore a well-fitting frockcoat in deep blue superfine, pantaloon trousers in soft doeskin strapped under his foot inside soft kid pumps. His yellow and blue striped kerseymere waistcoat framed a neckcloth of starched muslin. He sat on the side of the bed and took her hand in his, his expression one of gentle concern. 'How are you?'

'Better, thank you.' She tried to smile, but though her lips responded her eyes remained bleak. 'I must thank you for saving my life and to ask your forgiveness for deceiving you about who I was.'

'Why did you?'

'Pride, I suppose. I did not want anyone to know that Lord Sanghurst's daughter was penniless and I did not think Lord Strathrowan truly wanted the encumbrance of a ward he had not seen since she was a baby and, if I had to earn my living, then the sooner I became used to the idea the better. I thought travelling incognito would give me a good idea of what that might be like.'

'And you had no notion of who I was?'

'No.'

'Would it had made any difference if you had? Would you have behaved any differently?'

'No, I do not think so.'

He smiled. 'I am glad about that. It is Miss Helen Sadler I came to appreciate for her humanity, to admire for her courage. . .'

She drew her breath in sharply; she could not let him go on, it was twisting the knife in the wound. 'Miss Sadler does not exist, Captain.'

'"What's in a name? A rose by any other name would smell as sweet."'

'Quoting Shakespeare at me does not change anything, Captain Blair. I am still an imposter, a deceiver.'

'You are too hard on yourself. And I am not entirely blameless. Can you forgive me for my lapses from good manners?'

She smiled, remembering that embrace in the woods when she had realised how wonderful it was to be kissed by him; she could hardly reproach him for it. 'Yes, please forget it, I have.'

'Have you?' he queried softly, his warm brown eyes searching hers. 'Have you also forgotten I asked you to marry me?'

'You asked Miss Sadler. And Miss Sadler refused.'

'You have just said she does not exist. What about Miss Sanghurst? Would she refuse?'

He was testing her, trying to find out if she expected him to repeat his offer. He would be in a hubble if she did. 'Yes. Miss Helen Sanghurst and the son of the Earl of Strathrowan are strangers to each other.'

'I am persuaded you do not mean that, not after all we've been through.'

'That is precisely the point. We were two people thrown together on a coach journey, a journey which took seven days, that is all. . .'

'But packed with incident.'

She smiled wryly, though she felt more like crying. Somehow or other she had to harden her heart, at least until she found out more about Arabella. If what Margaret said was true, then there was no future for her with Captain Duncan Blair. 'That is just it. If there had not been so many misadventures, if we had never met Tom and Dorothy, if we had never witnessed their wedding, if we had not been stuck in the snow, you would not have given me a second thought. . .'

'Fustian!'

'You think you have compromised me, that it was acceptable to carry Miss Sadler to her bed, to take her unawares and kiss her, but not Miss Sanghurst, the daughter of your father's friend. Now you feel you must do the honourable. . .'

'Bunkum! Did you not hear a word I said to you when we were alone together in the snow?'

She had heard only a distant, soothing voice, the words had been lost on her, but she could hardly ask him to repeat them now. 'Said *in extremis*, Captain. I am persuaded you have already regretted your rash proposal. If you are worried that I will hold you to your offer, please be easy. I understand, truly I do.'

'It's more than I do.'

She could not explain, not without betraying Margaret's confidence. 'Captain, I am still very tired. . .'

He released her hand and rose at once. 'I beg pardon. I had not meant to tire you.' His words were clipped. 'I will leave you to rest.' With that he bowed and left the room, closing the door with a firm click.

She was as prickly as a hedgehog, he could tell it from the stiff way she smiled at him and the way she held her chin, as if holding her head up was all that mattered. He cursed her father for his unfeeling selfishness, for leaving her so vulnerable. Her pride was all she had to fight with and he wished with all his heart she would realise that she did not need to fight him, that he understood because he loved her. But he also respected her and because of that, he would try to be patient.

The following day Flora came to help Helen to dress ready to go downstairs. All her clothes were mourning black and there was little to choose between them, but she picked out a warm merino wool, relieving the drabness of the colour with a white shawl of fine silk. Looking in the mirror, she realised she had lost weight and her eyes were overbright in a very pale face. 'You could do with a little carmine on your cheeks, miss,' the maid said, standing behind her, hairbrush in hand. 'And if you wear your hair down, with little curls about your face, so, it will make it look fuller.' She teased out a curl or two as she spoke.

Helen smiled at the girl in the glass. 'It will make me look like a schoolgirl.'

'And where's the harm in that? They will be falling over themselves to take care of you.'

Her toilette complete, Helen stood up and slipped her feet into black satin slippers. 'What now?'

'I'm to take you to the library, miss. His lordship is waiting for you.'

Helen took a deep breath and followed the girl down a beautiful carved oak staircase, lined on one side with portraits, to a vestibule whose vaulted ceiling reached the whole height of the building. Several doors opened from it, no doubt leading to the rest of the house. The maid conducted her to one, knocked and ushered her in.

The man who stood by the hearth was an older version of Duncan. He had the same firm features and his hair curled in much the same way about his ears, although it was greying about the temples. Though very thin, he was tall and upright, impeccably dressed for country living in a check cloth jacket, breeches and topboots. He greeted her warmly and invited her to be seated. She perched herself on the edge of the sofa, her back straight and her hands in her lap. He sat down beside her and took her hand. 'You are recovered from your ordeal?'

'Yes, thank you, my lord.'

'Good. I am only sorry it happened. You should not have been obliged to make your own way here. I can only say I was not in plump currant or I would not have been so foolish as to rely on a letter reaching my son. I hope you will forgive me.'

'It is of no consequence,' she said. 'After all, it is many years since you and my father last saw each other and you could not be expected to be overjoyed at finding yourself guardian to an impoverished nobody.'

'My dear child, you must not think of yourself like that. You are most welcome. This is your home now and you must look on us as your family. Think of Andrew and Duncan as your brothers. They already regard you as the dear sister they never had.'

So, the Captain had not told his father of his proposal and that proved he had never seriously meant it. She had been right to refuse him.

'I shall make you a decent allowance, so that you can buy any little frippery that takes your fancy,' the Earl went on, before she could find anything to say on the subject of brothers. 'When the roads are free of snow, you will be able to go to Glasgow or Edinburgh, the shops there are as good as those in London, you will see.'

'But, my lord, I have an allowance sufficient for my needs. . .'

'That! Your lawyer has written to me of that. It will hardly purchase one new bonnet a year.' He smiled and patted the small hand which lay in his own. 'I cannot have my friends saying I treat my ward worse than my own children, can I? It is selfish of me to want my neighbours to think well of me, but there it is.'

'Thank you, my lord,' she said, not in the least deceived but loving him for his thoughtfulness, a thoughtfulness Duncan had inherited. He had demonstrated it on the journey from London when he did not even know who she was. But that was all it was, solicitude for her helplessness, even his unconsidered proposal was only an extension of that. At the time he had not known that Lady Macgowan was free.

'Now, you must make the acquaintance of the rest of the family. Duncan has gone out, I am afraid, but the others are gathered in the morning room to meet you.'

The Viscount, when they were introduced, was equally attentive towards her and Margaret was already like a sister to her, making her feel at home, chattering about fashions and what Helen could wear when she came out of black gloves, telling her how she ran the household. The house was not a house at all, but a real castle, with thick stone walls, turrets and winding stairs.

The two children, Robert, who was eight and Caroline, a very pretty six-year-old, were curious about her, but had obviously been told not to pester her, for they were as polite as two boisterous children could possibly be. In no time Helen had become part of the family and was happier than she had been for years, except for the lingering desire for Duncan which she could not suppress however hard she tried. It was made worse when she saw Arabella Macgowan for the first time.

Christmas had come and gone, and it was the last day of 1820. There was to be a joyous celebration to herald in the new year; Hogmanay, the Scots called it. Everyone from miles around arrived by sled drawn by sturdy little Highland ponies, to dine and play parlour games. Helen, halfway down the stairs, saw Lady Macgowan arrive and knew at once who she was and any hope that Duncan's love for her might have cooled over the years, vanished.

She was beautiful. She was much taller than Helen, with a curvaceous figure which was almost voluptuous. She had even features, blue eyes and a rich red mouth, which spread into a smile as she she caught sight of Duncan, resplendent in his blue uniform, standing to receive the guests. Neither was she in mourning as Helen was. Her cloak was taken from her and she was revealed in a gown of azure gauze over a deep blue satin slip. It had puffed sleeves and a very low neckline which revealed the curve of her breasts, between which nestled a diamond and silver pendant. She held out both lace-gloved hands to Duncan, who moved forward to greet her, taking her hands in both his own and appraising her from her crown of golden hair, dressed á la Grecque and threaded with deep blue ribbon, down to her dainty feet in matching satin slippers. They murmured a few words to each other which Helen was too far away to hear, but whatever was said, they smiled at each other before Arabella turned towards a servant who was carrying a small boy. Duncan took the child and, laughing, threw him into the air, making him giggle and grab his hair with pudgy fists.

'Ouch!' Duncan removed the hand and set the boy down. 'Run and find Robert, Jimmy. He is in the small parlour playing with his toy soldiers.'

The child ran off, obviously very familiar with the layout of the castle, and Duncan offered his arm to escort the lady into the large salon to join the other guests.

The intimate scene made Helen want to fly back to her room, to stay there until everyone had gone home, but her pride came to her rescue and she continued down the stairs to be met at the bottom by the Earl, his handsome figure enhanced by the Blair kilt, complete with the sash fastened over his shoulder with a huge silver brooch. The full sleeves of his white shirt ended in a fall of lace over his hands. He offered her his arm. 'Come, Helen, do not look so nervous. We are going to enjoy ourselves.'

He led her into the large reception room where a piper was playing, and introduced her to a great many people, including Lady Macgowan, who smiled and asked her how she did, while appraising her from head to foot and making her feel even smaller than she really was. The Earl moved on, taking Helen with him. She smiled and chatted inconsequentially to everyone she met, trying not to let her hurt show.

Andrew went out just before midnight carrying a lump of coal in order to return and knock at the great iron-studded front door as the clock struck the hour.

They sang 'Auld Lang Syne' and everyone kissed everyone else. Duncan, she noticed, stood looking at Lady Macgowan just a little too long before he kissed her and whispered something which made her laugh, before moving away to join the rest of the company in a Highland reel, his feet and arms working rhythmically to the sound of the bagpipes played by a ghillie in Highland dress.

Helen, not knowing the intricate steps, sat and watched, marvelling at the energy of the dancers. At the end of it, to encouragement from everyone, Andrew and Duncan took two swords down from their place on the wall and laid them crossed on the floor and as the bagpipes began another tune, they danced over them, placing their feet so exactly that they were only inches from the blades but never touched them. 'Better than drawing them in anger, don't you agree?' said a voice at Helen's elbow.

She turned to find Lady Macgowan at her side. 'Yes, indeed.'

'They grew up together, Andrew, Duncan and my husband. James and Duncan fell out over me, you know. There was a sword fight. That's how Duncan got that scar on the back of his hand. I'll wager you thought he had earned it in the war.'

'I didn't think about it at all.'

'No?' She laughed lightly. 'How strange. Perhaps you found other things to talk about on your journey to Scotland.'

There was more to the lady's conversation than appeared on the surface and it set Helen's hackles rising. 'The discourse was very general among all the passengers,' she said coolly. 'And there were other incidents. . .'

'Yes, quite. I have been told of those, but I would not wish you to be under any misapprehension. Duncan was sent away because he loved me. His father was too top-lofty to consider an heiress outside his own narrow circle. After he went, I was forced into marriage with James. Now James is dead, the boot is on the other foot. I have the title and a great deal of money. The Earl will no longer stand in our way.'

'Then may I wish you happy.' Helen forced a stiff smile.

'Thank you. I am so glad we had this little talk.'

Helen wanted to escape, to run away, anywhere where she could give vent to her misery alone, but the dance had ended and Duncan was bearing down on them, a broad smile on his handsome features. He stopped before them.

'Helen. I wish the new year will bring you everything you could hope for, your heart's desire.'

'Thank you, Captain Blair.'

'And will you not wish me the same?' The voice was soft, the voice she had heard in her frozen delirium, the voice of the siren.

'Yes, of course.' Oh, let her be strong, let her be resolute. 'I wish you happy, always.'

'Oh, Margaret is playing a waltz,' Arabella broke in before he could say any more. 'Come along, Duncan, you used to dance this very well. Show me you have not forgotten.' And with that she took his hand and dragged him into the centre of the room, where he put his arm about her waist and they began to move gracefully round the room, her blue skirt swishing about his pantaloon-clad thighs, her eyes lifted to his.

'Why did you do that?' he demanded.

'Do what, Duncan, dear?'

'Drag me away from Miss Sanghurst. Anyone would think you are jealous.'

'Jealous! Of that little black mouse! You were always the jealous one, as I recall.'

'That was a long time ago. We have both grown up since then.'

'But you have not forgotten me, have you? We can start again and this time your papa will not be so stubborn.'

'I am glad he was.'

'Why yes, as you say, we have both grown up, we are not so easily swayed by what other people expect of us. James is dead.'

'I know and I am very sorry.'

'Do not be, because I am not.'

'You can't mean that?'

'Yes, I do. I wish you had killed him when you took that sword to him. We would not have wasted all these years.'

'They were not wasted. And the only thing I regret is that I fell out with James.'

Although he continued to dance, a faraway look had come into his eyes, as if he had been transported in time and was young again, a lonely ten-year-old boy, wandering over the hills and moors of his new home. It was hardly surprising that he and James, who lived on the neighbouring estate and was the same age, should meet and become friends. They had grown up together, fished and hunted together, went off to school together, and later, when the opportunity arose, attended social gatherings together in Glasgow and Edinburgh, meeting young ladies of their own class, flirting a little and afterwards comparing notes.

But when, at eighteen, Duncan had fallen in love

with Arabella, James had been neglected in his pursuit of her, a pursuit which caused some amusement to the older generation who waited for it all to blow over. When it did not, the Earl had purchased Duncan a commission in the Prince of Wales's regiment and sent him away to get over it. Duncan had accepted that he was far too young to think of marriage and once he realised there was no help for it, he had not minded going. With James's connivance, he and Arabella had managed a few minutes of privacy in which to say goodbye. Their parting had been tearful on her part and grim on his, but she had reassured him with kisses and promises. 'They can lock me up in a tower for ever, I will marry no one but you,' she had said.

'Then I will scale that tower, inch by inch, to reach you,' he had replied, with all the confidence of an eighteen-year-old unused to letting obstacles get in the way of his heart's desire.

He might not have been so complacent if he had known that the war would drag on for years, years in which he had written to her at least once a week and hoarded up her replies to be read over and over again whenever the fighting died down and he had a few minutes to spare.

When the advance took them deeper and deeper into Spain and then over the mountains into France itself, the letters became less frequent, but that was hardly surprising, he had told himself, it would be a miracle if they managed to follow him at the pace of the advance and Wellington's diplomatic bags had more important things to carry than love letters. Not for a moment did he doubt Arabella's fidelity. If only he had questioned it, the final humiliation might have been easier to bear.

He had received a head wound in the last days of the fighting and found himself on a ship coming home, home to Arabella, waiting in her fantasy tower for her lover to return and claim her. But it was his fantasy, not hers.

She was already married to James, had been for three years, even while writing to him of her constancy, James his boyhood friend, James who knew exactly how he felt about her. Duncan had challenged him to a duel, but fortunately his father put a stop to it before any lasting damage could be done, but he had regretted it ever since. 'You, my dear Arabella, were not worth the loss of James's friendship and the last thing I want is to begin all over again.' He smiled as he spoke and no one, glancing at them from a distance, would have guessed that they were quarrelling.

Helen could not bear to look at them and turned away. She found a seat in a corner, half hidden behind a potted palm, but she was not there long before Andrew found her and asked her to dance. Her protests that, being in mourning, she ought not to, were brushed aside and she was whirled into the middle of the floor. He danced well, but how she wished it was Duncan and not Andrew who was holding her. She kept a fixed smile on her face, but her heart was breaking.

Any hope she might have had that Duncan had forgotten his first love, and would propose again, had faded to nothing. Oh, if only she had the wherewithal to be independent, she could go away, make a life for herself, become the lady's companion she had pretended to be. By the time the party broke up, just before dawn, she had made up her mind. She would not stay.

She watched the weather carefully in the ensuing days, waiting for a thaw, waiting for the roads to be opened, so that she could begin planning an escape. But they remained obstinately frozen and the longer she stayed, the more firmly she became entrenched in her life with the Strathrowans.

She loved the people, loved exploring the castle and finding delightful hidden nooks, watching the birds pecking in the snow for the scraps put out for them, turning her eyes to the mountains where, every now and again, she glimpsed a stag, standing on a crag, antlers outlined against the sky. She knew the men would go out stalking it, but refused to dwell on it. How could she walk away and leave all this? But she must. Sooner or later, Duncan would marry Arabella and she could not bear to be there when he brought his bride home.

It was the second week of February when she woke to the sound of water dripping off the eaves. She slipped from her bed and went to the window, pulling back the heavy curtains and looking out on the sight of a few blackened shrubs in the garden below her appearing above a layer of snow. The paths had already been cleared by the outdoor servants and she could see the nodding heads of snowdrops peeping through the ground near the terrace. For the first time she could see its shape, the steps from the lawn up to the higher level, the outlines of the borders. It was thawing fast and time to think about leaving.

But before she could make any plans at all, Margaret came to her room one morning before breakfast, to tell her a visitor had arrived in a hired chaise all the way from London to see her. 'He says his name is Benstead,' she said. 'Do you wish to receive him?'

'Benstead?' Helen repeated, then as realisation dawned, 'Goodness, he was Papa's lawyer. What can he want with me?'

'Come down and you will see. I'll send Flora to you. Hurry up, do. I am consumed with curiosity.'

Margaret was no more curious than she was, Helen thought, as the maid came in with hot water and towels and began to lay out her clothes, half-mourning now, a lilac satin over a white slip decorated with white ruching and silk violets. Half an hour later, she went downstairs to find the little lawyer in the ante-room, gazing out of the window at the dripping trees. He turned when he heard the rustle of silk behind him. 'Miss Sanghurst, your obedient.' He made a rheumaticky leg. 'I hope I find you well?'

'Very well, sir. But what has brought you here? The journey must have been quite dreadful.'

'The winter has not been too severe in England, Miss Sanghurst. I did not realise it had been so hard in Scotland until I crossed the border. I came post-haste as soon as I could.'

'Why? Is something wrong?'

'Wrong, my dear Miss Sanghurst? Oh, dear, no, quite the reverse. Your papa's cargo arrived safely in dock.'

'His cargo?' She was mystified.

'Yes, you remember him saying all would be well when his ship came in. Well, it has. It did. A fine cargo of spices and rich silks from the Orient, all highly sought after. I have been able to dispose of everything very profitably. Lord Sanghurst's debts are all paid and there is a surplus over expenditure which is yours. I came to appraise you of it and to await your instructions.'

He smiled slowly. She had come on a lot since he had last seen her; she had a new poise as if she had grown up from child to woman, which was a foolish thought because she had been a grown woman when she left. 'It will provide a good dowry, not top of the trees, you understand, but enough. . .'

It was a moment or two before the news could sink in, before she realised that it could make a great deal of difference to her life. 'It was very kind of you to come all this way to tell me of my good fortune,' she said, so solemnly he wondered if she was pleased by the news at all. 'Is the money entirely mine, to do with as I please?'

'Yes, subject to your guardian's agreement. According to your late father's will, his lordship has the last word on any decision you may make until you marry, or if you do not, until your thirtieth birthday.'

'Will the money buy an annuity?'

'Yes, but why do you need that?'

'I mean to leave here and live independently.'

'My goodness, Miss Sanghurst, you do surprise me. Have they not treated you kindly? I gained the impression from Lady Blair that you were thought of as one of the family.'

'So I am, no one could have been kinder, but that is half the trouble. They are too kind and I am too dependent. I would like to live quietly on my own with Daisy for a companion. Do you think she would come?'

'I am sure she would, but I do not understand why it is necessary.'

'My reasons are private, Mr Benstead. Do you think you could rent a cottage in the Lakes for me? Ambleside, perhaps.'

'Of course, but I must speak to the Earl first.' He looked at her, trying to divine her reasons from the expression on her face. She had smiled at him and expressed pleasure at seeing him, but she was not happy. He could not blame her surroundings, which were nothing short of luxurious; he could only surmise it was a man who had put the bleak look in her eyes; it was even worse than when he had told her about her father's gambling debts.

Who had put it there? Lady Blair had told him, in the few minutes conversation they had had, that Captain Blair had met with Miss Sanghurst on the journey and escorted her to Killearn in appalling weather conditions and she had been very ill as a result, though now fully recovered. If that young man was responsible for her unhappiness, then he must be brought to book over it. He had been offered hospitality for the night and he would contrive, in that time, to speak to Captain Blair as well as the Earl.

'Miss Sanghurst wishes to leave here?' queried Duncan when Mr Benstead begged a few words in private after everyone else had retired. They were sitting in the library enjoying a glass of brandy beside the dying fire. 'Are you sure you have not misunderstood?'

'Oh, I am sure. She asked me to find her a cottage in the Lakes and send for her maid to join her. She said she meant to live quietly alone.'

'Cork-brained ninny!'

'Really, sir, I see no call to insult me.'

'I do not insult you. I am cursing myself for a cow-handed clunch. Did she say why?'

'No. She said her reasons were private. I deduced from that that there was a man in the picture. . .'

'Yes.' He sighed. 'I had better tell you the whole, you may have good advice, for I have not been able to make her see reason.'

'Women are not renowned for their aptitude in deduction, Captain. They think with their hearts.'

'And Helen's heart? What is that telling her?'

'She feels she has to flee from a situation she cannot deal with. I am sure you understand.'

Duncan looked up in surprise. 'Did she tell you that?'

'Naturally she did not. I surmised it. I also surmised it had something to do with you.'

'I made a cake of myself, Mr Benstead.' He smiled crookedly and went on to tell the lawyer of all the incidents on the journey to Scotland. 'I have put myself utterly beyond her touch,' he finished. 'She is convinced I offered her marriage to salve my conscience and will not believe I want to marry her because I cannot contemplate life without her.'

'Is that all?'

'All? Is it not enough?'

'Perhaps she will come about. She cannot leave without the Earl's consent.'

'You do not know Miss Sanghurst very well if you think coercion will serve,' Duncan said gloomily.

'Captain Blair, are you a gambling man?'

Duncan looked across at him, taken aback by the question. Was it a trick? 'If you are alluding to Miss

Sanghurst's unhappy experience with the late Lord Sanghurst. . .'

'Not at all. I meant are you prepared to take a gamble on Miss Sanghurst admitting what her heart is telling her? I have a plan. It might work.'

'Then, for the love of God, let me hear it.'

CHAPTER ELEVEN

MR BENSTEAD left next day to execute Helen's orders and she settled down to wait for his return and the arrival of Daisy. She told herself that life in a cottage by Lake Windermere was exactly what she wanted, that in the peace and solitude there her heart would mend. Duncan had accepted that she was leaving, just as his father had done, expressing his regret and saying that, of course, she must do as she pleased. It had all been too easy, which just went to show what they really thought of her. Only Andrew and Margaret continued to try and persuade her to stay, but then they did not know the reason she could not.

She tried to fill her days so that she did not have time to think. She read a great deal, borrowing books from the his lordship's extensive library, walking on the lower slopes around the castle, getting her feet wet and smiling enigmatically when Margaret or Duncan scolded her. Sometimes Duncan accompanied her, striding beside her with a sporting gun under his arm which he never used, and his dog scampering about in the heather sniffing for rabbits.

'Will you miss all this?' he asked one day, using his arm to encompass the view. They were on the top of a knoll which overlooked the castle, standing in the shelter of its valley. In the distance was the gleam of a large expanse of water and further in the distance, the mountains, still snow-capped.

'Yes,' she admitted. 'It is lovely.' Then half-smiling,

so that he would not know what she really felt, 'But the Lakes are also beautiful.'

'Yes, I collect you saying that when we passed through.'

She wished she had not reminded him of that journey, especially that section when they had been at peace with each other, when the first faint glimmering of her love for him had made itself felt. Every time she looked at his firm profile, every time he spoke to her in that soft, sensuous voice, the voice which had kept her from dying, she felt herself crumble a little more. 'I shall miss the people too, everyone has been very good to me, the Earl and Margaret especially. She has been like a sister to me.'

He stifled the retort that she did not have to leave and instead commented that with her capacity for making friends, she would not long be alone. 'But you must be careful,' he added. 'You have a penchant for falling into a hobble.'

'Daisy will see that I don't.' She forced herself to laugh. 'At any rate, she will not scold me like you do. Or tell me what I ought or ought not to do.'

'How dull,' he said wryly. 'Do you mean to have no adventures at all?'

'None. I shall spend my time in good works, reading and walking over the fells.'

'But that is what you have been doing here. No one has prevented you.'

There was no answer to that and she remained silent for a time, watching the dog chasing after a stick he had thrown for it. It came running back, its tail wagging, dropping the stick at their feet. 'Good dog,' he said, bending to pat its head.

'I think I will buy a puppy for company,' she said.

'A puppy?'

'Why not?'

'Why not indeed.' He smiled, this time with genuine pleasure. 'But you do not need to buy one. One of the retriever bitches has had pups; Robbie, here, is the sire. Come, I will choose one for you.' And with that he turned and set off back to the castle, leading her down the winding track to the road and over the drawbridge to the stable block, followed by the faithful dog.

The kennels were at the far side of the yard. He opened the door and disappeared inside. A few moments later he emerged with a soft, sandy-coloured bundle. 'Here,' he said, putting the puppy into her arms. 'He's yours.'

She cuddled the puppy, rubbing her cold cheek along its soft fur. It responded by licking her ear, making her laugh. It was the first time he had really seen her laugh since she arrived, and it made his heart ache to hold her, to reassure her, but he held back, watching her. 'He's been weaned, though he hasn't a name yet. I think the handler calls him number three because he was the third of the litter.'

'Oh, how unfortunate for him to be called by a number. Are you sure you want to give him to me? Will the Earl mind?'

'Yes to the first and no to the second. Keep him. Let him remind you of me, when you are walking in the hills of Cumbria.'

'Thank you.' She turned and fled, dashing across the yard, in at one of the side doors, along the corridor and up the stairs to her room. She just managed to shut the door behind her before her tears overwhelmed her.

She sat for a long time on the bed, nursing the puppy, with tears streaming down her face onto his head. 'Oh, Pup,' she whispered. 'Why couldn't Papa's ship come in before he died? There would have been no suicide, no stigma, no dreadful gossip about his cowardice, and I would have had my dowry and Miss Sadler, the deceiver, need never have been invented. I would have been acceptable in Captain Blair's eyes. And the Earl's.' She chose to overlook the inescapable fact that if her father had not died and left her penniless she would never have been making the trip to Scotland at all, might never have met the Honourable Captain Duncan Blair, never been compromised by him, never kissed, never seen him dancing with Lady Macgowan. Her ladyship was the real problem, though strangely she had not been visiting since the New Year. Had they quarrelled? She refused to allow herself even that small hope.

The puppy was licking her face, doing a good job of mopping up her tears. 'You don't care who I am, do you, Pup? Names are unimportant.' She smiled down at him, a crooked rueful smile, weakened by crying. 'You do understand, don't you? I have only my pride.'

She put the puppy down on the bed, where it snuffled round and round to make itself comfortable before settling down to watch her with a baleful eye. She washed and changed for supper, taking great care with her appearance. The skin around her eyes was puffed and red, but a little discreet maquillage hid that. She dressed in a white crepe gown over a delicate lilac slip. A mauve velvet ribbon outlined the high waist and was also threaded through the hem and tied in a series of tiny bows with floating ends. The same ribbon was threaded through her dark hair.

Flora, who had come to help her, expressed herself satisfied. 'Beautiful, Miss Sanghurst, truly beautiful. Just wait until ye go tae London with the Viscount and Lady Blair in the summer, I ken ye will be a great success. Not that London has anything to beat Edinburgh,' she added. 'You should ask Mr Duncan tae take ye there.'

'Thank you, Flora, that will be all,' she said, rather more stiffly than she intended. There would be no summer in London with Margaret, no trip to the Scottish capital with Captain Blair. Nothing. She put her feet into mauve satin slippers and picked up her fan. 'Look after Pup for me, will you? I imagine he is hungry.' With that she took a deep breath to steady herself and went down to the drawing-room where everyone was gathering before supper.

'Helen, how charming you look,' Margaret said, ignoring the evidence of the tears. 'Isn't that so, Duncan?'

'Yes indeed,' he agreed. 'She will be quite wasted in Cumbria.'

'Then persuade her not to go.'

'She would not listen,' he said with a smile as he offered her his arm to take her into supper. 'Is that not so, princess?'

Helen laid her fingers on his arm and even that small touch nearly overset her again. Forcing her trembling limbs to obey her, she walked beside him into the dining room.

'Princess?' Margaret queried, as they took their places at the table. 'Why do you call Helen that?'

He laughed, a slightly mocking laugh. 'Because when I first met her, she would not tell me who she was or where she was going and when I suggested she was a princess in disguise, she asked me how I had guessed.'

'He did not really believe that, did he?' Margaret asked Helen.

'No, of course not. He was roasting me.'

'And he is still doing it. Duncan, I think it is very uncivil of you.'

'Oh, Miss Sadler does not mind, Miss Sadler is an altogether more agreeable person than Miss Sanghurst.'

'Duncan,' his father remonstrated with him. 'I think you should not tease Helen. She will think you have taken a dislike to her and wish her to be gone and that is not true. It is certainly not true on my part. I am her guardian and pleased to be her guardian until she marries. This is her home and she is more than welcome to stay.'

'And I second that,' Margaret put in, looking from Duncan to Helen and wondering what had passed between them on that long journey from London. What was going on now? They were both Friday-faced, refusing to look at each other. 'Helen is like a sister to me and I do not want to part with her. You should be persuading her to stay, not driving her away.'

'Oh, I am not driving her away, she is old enough to know her own mind,' he said. 'She has told me so often, and I would not, for the world, hold her against her will.'

Helen sprang to her feet, fresh tears flowing down her cheeks. 'Stop it! Please stop it.' Then to the Earl, 'Please excuse me.' She pushed back her chair and fled back to her room.

'I do not know what manners they teach in the army

these days,' Andrew said. 'But I never thought to see a brother of mine behave so abominably towards a lady.'

'Yes, Duncan,' his father said. 'Whatever game you are playing, you have taken it too far. I suggest you try and make amends.'

Duncan, seeing Helen run from the room in tears, knew his father was right and he had overplayed his hand. He excused himself and followed her up to her room, where he knocked on the door and called her name.

'Go away.' The voice was muffled.

'No. Helen, I am sorry.' He rattled the door but she had locked it. 'Please let me in. I must speak to you.'

'To deal out more of the same, I suppose. I have had enough of your mockery. Keep away from me.'

'I was not mocking you, rather myself for making such a mull of things. I am sorry if you thought I was. Please let me in.'

'No.'

In desperation he put his muscular shoulder to the door and burst it open. She was pulling clothes from the wardrobe and throwing them into her trunk.

'How dare you!' She turned to face him, though she could hardly see him for tears. 'Captain Blair, I insist you leave me.'

'No.' He forced himself to smile, though the sight of her nearly undid him. 'You are evidently going on a journey.'

'So, what if I am? You knew that anyway. I am simply bringing it forward.'

'Why?'

'I have my reasons.'

'Which you will not tell me.' His voice softened.

'Why can't you talk to me? Why can't you tell me what is wrong? Surely we are not still strangers?'

'Strangers?'

'Miss Helen Sanghurst and the son of the Earl of Strathrowan are strangers, that's what you said. It was your reason for refusing my offer of marriage, wasn't it? And if you insist on leaving, we shall never have the opportunity to remedy that.'

'Not strangers,' she said, so distressed she did not take in the significance of what he was saying. 'Brother and sister.'

He was astounded. 'Wherever did you get that idea?'

'That is how your father said I should think of you. He said you and Andrew considered me the sister you never had.'

'When did he say that?'

'When I first met him. You did not tell him you had asked me to marry you, did you? He would not have said that if you had. You knew he would not approve.'

'Why should he disapprove?'

'Because even second sons are expected to marry someone of consequence. They never know when they might inherit and if they never do, they need a good dowry.'

'I never heard anything so cork-brained. I am sure my father did not tell you that.'

'No, Margaret did, but it makes no difference because she also told me the Earl has set his heart on putting right the wrong he did you when he sent you away and. . .'

'He did me no wrong. On the contrary, he did me a favour and I have told him so. It gave me time. . .'

'What difference does that make? I am persuaded you are not one to change your mind with the wind.'

'Indeed, I am not.'

'Then I will not embarrass you by staying. I shall do very well in Cumbria.'

He sighed heavily. 'Very well, if you insist, but you will need an escort.'

'No, I am perfectly able. . .'

'You said that before and look what happened. Do you think I could let you go alone, knowing you would fall into a scrape before you had covered half a mile?'

'That is no longer your concern.'

'No? I think it is. I think it is very much my concern. If you do not allow me to accompany you, then I must follow on behind like the puppy I gave you.'

'Follow?'

'I cannot let you go. I shall continue to follow you and look after you until you recognise the fact that your life and mine are indivisible.'

She stopped with a petticoat in her hand and stared at him. 'But you can't. . .'

'Why ever not?'

'Lady Macgowan. . .'

'What has she to do with it?'

'Everything. Isn't that what we have been talking about? Goodness, you fought a duel with your best friend over her and it is obvious. . .'

'Not to me it is not. What has she been telling you?'

'It was not only her, Margaret did too. Now that Lord Macgowan is dead. . .'

'You thought we were going to take up where we left off?' He laughed suddenly and joyfully. 'Oh, my darling Helen, Arabella cannot hold a candle to you. She is a selfish, scheming woman who wants to keep her cake and eat it too. I am glad my father sent me away, very glad indeed. I am afraid I told her so, when she was here for Hogmanay.'

'You did?' She could hardly believe it.

'Yes.' He stepped forward and took her shoulders in his hands. 'Now I am asking you again. Will you marry me?'

'Why?'

'Why? For no reason, for every reason, because my life is empty without you, because I love you. How many more reasons do you want? The only way you will be rid of me, is if you tell me you do not care for me and never will.'

She simply stared at him with her mouth open.

'Go on,' he urged. 'Say it. Say, "Duncan Blair, I do not love you. I will never love you."'

She dropped the petticoat on the floor and silently stared at him.

'Are you going to speak?'

She shook her head.

He took her face into his hands, tipping it up so that he could look into her eyes. Tears glistened on her lashes and he hated himself for causing her unhappiness. 'I am sorry for the Turkish treatment, my love. I wanted you to change your mind about marrying me. I wanted you to see that we belong together and instead of that I nearly drove you away. Will you forgive me?'

She found her voice at last, but it was so weak he had to listen hard to hear it. 'If you had decided against Lady Macgowan, why didn't you ask me again after Mr Benstead had been instead of letting me think you would let me go?'

He smiled. 'And risk another put-down? I do not think, even then, you were ready to admit the truth.'

'And what is that?'

'That we love each other, that it is of no consequence at all who we are, princess or lady's maid, common soldier or aristocrat, it makes no difference.'

'And Papa? The manner of his death. . .'

'Good heavens, you did not think I considered that, did you?'

She nodded.

'I think your father was wiser than you have given him credit for,' he said slowly. 'He made my father your guardian because he knew that if you came to Scotland you would be sure to meet me and he hoped we would make a match of it. It was his last gamble.'

She knew he was only saying that to make her feel better about her father and she loved him all the more for it.

'It was mine too,' he said. 'I gambled on making you accept the truth and it nearly finished me.'

She laughed. 'It was no greater than the risk I took, especially as I did not know I was taking it. But are you sure. . .?'

His answer was to lower his mouth to hers in a kiss which went on for a very long time and drove all their doubts away.

'Helen.' It was Margaret's soft voice which made them draw apart.

'In here,' Duncan said, raising his head reluctantly, then, as his sister-in-law appeared beside the broken door, 'I have breached the defences. Miss Sanghurst has capitulated. You may congratulate me.'

'Oh, indeed I do.' She hurried to embrace them

both. 'I never thought to see you wed, Duncan, you have taken a prodigious time coming to it.'

'But I had to wait to meet my match, didn't I?' he said, smiling at Helen. Then, turning to his sister-in-law, 'And I intend to have words with you later. . .'

'Why, what have I done?'

'Duncan, please,' Helen said. 'Margaret did not know, did not understand. There is no need. . .'

He smiled. 'You are right, my darling. No recriminations. I am too happy. Let us go down and tell the others. We must celebrate.'

Which they did, to everyone's satisfaction.